# Adrift
## IN THE
# Sound

### A NOVEL
### By Kate Campbell

NutTree Media
Sacramento, California

NutTree Media

Sacramento California

ISBN: 0615570798

ISBN 13: 9780615570792

This is a work of fiction based solely on the author's imagination. Apart from well-known people, events and locales that factor into the narrative, all names, characters, places and incidents are fictitious.

Book design: CreateSpace

Cover photo: Vladimir Piskunov, Moscow Russia

Chapter graphic: Todd Jason Baker

Author photo: © Ching Lee

Library of Congress Cataloging-in-Publication Data

For
Mark Robert
&
Mark and Mike
Who know and believe

# DEBTS OWED & HONORED

WRITING THIS BOOK HAS BEEN A LONGER JOURNEY THAN EXPECTED, and I'm grateful for the friends who've gone the distance—Steve Adler, Nancy Barth, Cynthia Cory, Kari Fisher, Dave Kranz, Ching Lee, Elisa Noble, especially Margaret Rodriguez, who spent many hours helping me sort out the story and characters; and Anthony and Carol Rogers, who provided unwavering spiritual support. Artist and author Sara Sheldon and national affairs/crime reporter Christine Souza read numerous versions of the novel in draft.

Gratitude goes to the teachers and writers who've helped hone my creative writing skills, particularly Sands Hall, whose encouragement helped me start and then finish this book. The Community of Writers at Squaw Valley continues to provide ongoing inspiration and invaluable support. At Tomales Bay Writers Workshops, novelist Tayari Jones offered insightful guidance during the early stages of the writing, while Ray and Barbara March of the Modoc Writers Forum added confidence in my Western perspective and the value of stories that spring from the environment.

Thanks to Julia O'Connor, gifted teacher and former Sacramento Poet Laureate, for her help with lyrical prose style. Writer and teacher Adair Lara provided guidance for the novel's structure at a critical juncture. Frank and Maggie Allen of the Institute for Journalism and Natural Resources immersed me in environmental issues and introduced me to Pacific Coast tribal leaders who fed me salmon and took me on an expedition to the sacred rock at the center of the world.

Various libraries, online collections and museums were of research assistance, including the University of Washington online digital collections and Burke Museum of Natural History and

Culture, as well as the Washington State Library, and the Seattle City and *Seattle Times* archives. Thanks to bluesman Taj Mahal for permission to use lyrics from his 1969 album *Giant Step/De Ole Folks At Home*, which helped rhythmically inform the writing of this book.

And, thanks to friend, writing partner and fellow author Elizabeth Kern of HillHouse Books, who believed *Adrift in the Sound* should be shared with readers and pushed me to make it happen. Friend and novelist Thomas T. Thomas served as readers' advocate and provided superb editing that brought out the best in the story. Smart and talented, Sacramento's Old Soul Writer's Group, provided much needed moral support and laser-guided critique and copy proofing.

Finally, thanks to my family—my sons, Mark and Mike and granddaughter, Ada—my brothers Richard, Steven, and Robert, and sister Joyce, as well as my grownup niece and nephew, Krista and Justin. They've served as a tireless cheering section on the long road to creating this book.

Thanks to the love and support of all these people—and many more—this story is now humbly offered to you, the reader, to enjoy and make of it what you will.

Whatever befalls the earth
befalls the children of the earth.

CHIEF SEATTLE - SUQWAMISH & DUWAMISH

FROM AN 1854 PUBLIC SPEECH

# ONE

"SO...YOU'RE HERE." Einar Karlson spoke to her through the screen door on the back porch. "When did you get out?"

Lizette stood at the bottom of the backstairs and looked up at her father swaying behind the rusted mesh, saw his wariness and stiffened her own guard. She pulled a wad of damp envelopes from the metal box beside the steps. He put her mail there so she could pick it up whenever she liked, avoiding him if necessary. She sorted out the county disability checks and dropped them into her lumpy canvas bag then studied the postmark on a mildewed envelope— December 1972. "What's the date?" she asked, without looking up.

"Come in?" he suggested. "Have some tea?"

Lizette shrugged, continued sorting, mostly junk—art school ads and half-off sales from Christmas. She realized the holidays were over, that she'd missed them, but since her mother died, she hadn't felt like celebrating anyway.

"It's February 2," he said. "I presume you know it's 1973."

She climbed the steps, paused on the narrow porch. The screen door swung out and her father held it open while she hesitated. The wood felt spongy under her feet, softened from years of Seattle rain and a lifetime of entrances and exits.

He took the pipe out of his mouth, cupped the bowl protectively in his hand as she passed. She noticed gray rime on the pipe's stem, smelled the cherry tobacco on his blue plaid shirt. He smiled a pained welcome. *What am I afraid of?* she wondered as she moved past him into the kitchen. *He's old and weak.* A pang of sorrow popped up in her chest. At least her mother would never be old like him, she thought, and a ripple of comfort passed through her. She also knew she'd never hear her mother laugh again, not that it happened all that often in this nut house. She looked around the kitchen at the sad walls, at the old cuckoo clock, oddly out of place in a house filled with sculpture, paintings and historic Indian artifacts.

The kitchen felt warm, not from cooking, Lizette realized, but from more than twenty-five years of memories that heated the surfaces—the green Formica kitchen table and vinyl chair seats, the canisters and potholders. Recollections radiated from the cabinets and walls. Clicks and pings, sounds of her childhood, came from the house's furnace, the heat closing in on her. She watched her father's bony shoulders work as he ran water into the tea kettle, thought about how big he used to seem, how shriveled he looked now. His shirt hung from his clothes-hanger frame, its fullness overlapped under his cinched belt. He settled in the chair across from her, his presence too close, pressing on her diaphragm, making her pull for air.

She crossed her arms over her chest and recalled the rumble of his voice when she was a child, sitting on his lap and resting her head against him, hearing the stories, feeling his resonance. Always stories. He told tales of the first people. The Indians who lived here before the explorers came, about Chief Seattle and his people, about the animal spirits who ruled the world. She conjured the energy of the university students who'd gathered in her family's living room in the evenings, who'd talked earnestly about their theories and research, and she remembered how her father, the famous anthropologist, would listen to their ramblings, amused. They were finding out things he'd known and written about before many of them were born. Her mother would appear at those times like a spirit, offering plates of Swedish cookies, her blonde hair braided and coiled into a crown. Then she'd glide out the kitchen door to her art studio in the back garden.

Lizette remembered sitting cross-legged on the floor beside the couch. He'd bring little treasures out of his study—totems, the two-headed soul catcher that was carved from a bear femur, dance wands, rattles, skin drums with thunderbirds, and finally the chief's headdress with long ermine pelts attached. He'd always offer to let someone else try on the chief's headdress, never fitted the elaborate piece to his own head, held it out, acting like an acolyte with ancient sacraments.

Most of all Lizette had waited to see the mask of Watches Underwater. Even after centuries, the colors leapt from the carved cedar, Watcher's unflinching eyes eternally scanned the upper world for danger, vigilant and prepared to warn the creatures in the sea below of any threats. The mask's red puckered lips showed the legend perfectly, she thought, and pictured the beautiful woman floating on her back just below the water's surface, watching, supping air with those voluptuous lips, watching, and she ached now to put the mask on her own face, but knew her father wouldn't permit it. "It's not a toy," he'd said when she was small and tucked the artifact back into its box. She knew he'd deny her now so she let her desire fade. The tea kettle whistled. Her father went to the cupboard and pulled down two mugs.

"What kind of tea?" he asked.

"Uh...orange spice," Lizette said, looking at the blue and white plate above the sink with her name written around the rim: Elizabeth Lena Karlson—April 10, 1947. Her nursery totem. Her middle name, her mother's name, Lena, leapt at her from the Delft ceramic. The plate had hung there for more than a quarter century, she thought, an artifact from her birth displayed like it had been dug from an ancient midden, a Swedish custom that announced her presence to those who ventured into her parent's kitchen. She remembered that when she was small her father had called her "Little Liz," sometimes "Liz Bit," eventually transforming her name play-fully to Lizette. After that everyone called her Lizette—teachers, neighbors, playmates, and the clerk at the art supply store where her mother had worked and sometimes taught painting classes in the back room.

The store manager had framed some of Lizette's paintings and hung them behind the work table where the clerks made picture frames. A couple of them sold, and her mother took her for ice cream, told her she'd put the sale money in Lizette's college account at the bank, that she was going to the Pratt Art Institute in Chicago or the Sorbonne in Paris and she'd grow up to be a famous artist, if she studied and developed her own technique, if—her mother added in an acid tone—she'd stop copying others. Lizette had asked for a double scoop of pistachio and felt she'd somehow done something good and wrong at the same time. Her mother ordered plain vanilla and they sat on wire chairs at a small table, silent, licking their cones.

"Pfeffernüsse?"

She snatched herself back and watched her father reach for a blue tin on top of the refrigerator. He popped the lid and took out a handful of cookies, dropped them on a plate. Lizette picked up a cookie, pecked at the edge, set it down, scattered powdered sugar dust on the table.

"Where will you stay?" Einar said, sitting down and reaching a veiny hand toward her. Lizette did not reach back. She sensed he wanted to say something, but instead of speaking to her truthfully, she watched him shift away, felt his dodge. "Have you made plans?"

Lizette doubted his interest. "I'll be on Orcas Island, at Marian's," she said flatly. "She has the ranch now, since her father died."

She looked up and saw a stunned expression. He didn't know Hal Cutler had died, she thought, and realized how isolated he'd become in the years since her mother died, his life narrowed to an occasional faculty meeting, TV at night, maybe an ambitious graduate student between the sheets once in a great while.

"He's been gone over a year, I think. You know the cabin by the water, below the main house?" He nodded. "That's where I stay. Marian said it's mine as long as I want."

"That old shepherd's shack?" She heard the judgment in his voice, winced. He tried again. "Good spot. Not the best light, though. Kind of rough. No running water or electricity. But, I guess it's better than hanging around downtown."

"It'll do." She felt the disapproval in his voice, almost added that it was none of his business what she did, decided to avoid an argument, studied her ragged fingernails, switched tempo.

"Spring's coming and the sun will move higher," she said. "A lot of my things are stored out there, some canvases I've been working on and I can help out around the ranch."

"Will you see Poland and Abaya?"

She nodded and fluttered her fingers impatiently in her lap at the obvious question about the ranch's foreman and his wife. "I saw Raven downtown," she said. "Down by Skid Row."

"Who?"

"Their son. Raven...The youngest one. The one who used to hunt. He was in Vietnam." She didn't add that he'd joined the

American Indian Movement and was on his way to South Dakota to help the Lakota take over the town of Wounded Knee.

"I remember him," Einar said. "The trickster. A natural born hunter, that kid. Nearly broke Abaya's heart when he ran off and joined the Army. She tried not to let on, partly it was her own reaction, she'd already lost a couple of boys, but also it's part of the Lummi culture. To not grieve openly, I mean. It goes against tribal tradition." He said this last part offhandedly, as if he'd been half listening.

She checked the clock, saw the torture of sitting there with him had gone on twenty minutes. She marked the relentless tick-tock, tick-tock by keeping time with her foot. For a while Einar joined Lizette in staring out the window at the rain, sipped his tea.

Eventually, he said, "I wish I had time to get out there, walk on the island, fish. I always feel restored after being there. Poland's a good man. We used to do a lot of hunting together."

*He's telling me this like it's news and I'm a stranger*, she thought impatiently, wondering if he was losing it, going senile.

"He knows the land. Will you give everyone my regards?"

She wasn't sure she'd even mention him. He took the empty mugs to the sink and rinsed them, splashing water on the countertop, not bothering to wipe it up as her mother would have done.

"Why don't you go up to Orcas yourself?" she said on impulse, then regretted it, couldn't stop herself, added: "It's only a hundred miles from here. Give them your own regards. Don't you still have the land out on the point that you and Mom bought for when you retire?"

"Do you want some of your mother's art supplies?" he said, ignoring the question and turning from the sink with a pained expression. "You can have what you want from the studio. I can't stand going out there. It's like a dig where the village was wiped out by smallpox, everything broken in midstream, lost."

"Maybe a palette knife." She glanced around the kitchen, looking for something to take from there, a meaningful object worth carrying, saw nothing. Her father sat at the table again and she stood, looked down on him. "I've been mixing my own colors using roots and leaves and metal filings to make pigments, working encaustic with beeswax. I have a big canvas I'm painting and sculpting at the same time, layering it on. I have to get back to the ranch, see if the colors held."

The talk of paint and canvas reassured Einar, who'd spent his adult life talking with his wife about the mundane details of art—mixing paints, stretching canvas, choosing frames, making crates for shipping finished work to galleries and shows, packing canvases up when the shows ended.

"You're mother used to worry about that, too."

His wistful tone brought back the stories her mother told her about going to New York for art openings, about how much she loved the city, the excitement over her first big sale to an important upstate collector. That was a magical night, her mother had said, colored lights flashing over the sidewalk throngs, the cab ride to their hotel, holding hands, kissing her father in the backseat like people in a movie. This last bit had embarrassed her as a teenager, an age when she'd tried not to think about her parents as boyfriend and girlfriend. She'd never seen the affection at home.

Einar looked at his daughter, saw his wife in the shape of her jaw, in the expression around her eyes, the long blonde hair carelessly braided and draped over her shoulder, and then the resemblance flickered. Lizette emerged as herself, troubled and unpredictable, but he felt she'd be all right if she kept working. He'd grown used to her showing up at odd times and then she'd be gone for long periods. He knew she hung around downtown, that she lived on the city's streets. He suspected she did drugs.

"What happened this time?" Einar tried to keep his face blank, voice flat. "How long did they keep you?"

The heartbreak of her condition had scabbed over years ago. Now he accepted that she would live her life as she could, coming to see him when needed, a lost soul wandering aimlessly. He'd stopped giving her money or urging her to go upstairs to her bedroom to sleep. He stopped loving her unconditionally and guarded his heart. He only hoped she'd keep painting, for therapeutic reasons, if nothing else. He hated to think of her locked up in some mental hospital. She'd become like a savant, he thought, and felt ashamed, saw a beautiful gift going to waste.

"I got attacked by a dog under the freeway and freaked out, that's all," she said softly, sat down at the table again, checked the clock. No way could she tell him the truth.

"I was crashing there with friends," she lied. "Camping out for a few days. They kept me a while to stabilize, adjusted my medication."

*Which I don't take anyway*, she thought, but didn't say it because she didn't want to get into it with him. Instead, she said, "I want to see Watches Underwater."

Her father twisted in his chair, raked his thinning ash-colored hair, said he didn't recall where it was stored.

"You know where she is." She said it like an accusation and stared into the dining room, toward his study in the front of the house, pictured the closet where he kept his artifacts, saw in her mind the mask's red lips supping air, Watches Underwater skimming along beneath the water's surface.

He followed her glance, finally said, "Not now."

"How did you get it?" She studied his face, looked for flinching lies around his watery eyes.

"What do you mean?"

"It's not yours. You took it."

"I got it years ago. I've taken care of that mask and everything else all this time. I could've sold it, gotten a lot more than I paid. I know the history. And, I know dealers who'd buy it, but it has been safe here. What are you suggesting?"

"Everyone knows what you did. Raven told me. We've talked."

"What do you mean?" Her father pulled back from her, dismay creasing his face.

"I've seen all the stuff, Dad. Spirit drums, carvings, masks, breast plates. It belongs to the Lummi people." She scowled at him. "You took advantage and you know it. Raven calls it grave robbing, even if you try and say it's archeology."

She saw she'd hurt his feelings, and reached out to pat his boney arm, but he jerked away.

"Get out of my house." The sound came like a growl from a disturbed animal, warning her.

Lizette jumped up and checked the clock, grabbed her bag from under the table.

"I'll get a palette knife from the studio and go," she said defiantly to his bowed head. In a few minutes the clock would make its mechanical noise and she wanted to be gone before it sounded its mocking accusations. "I have to catch the afternoon ferry out to Orcas." She gathered her bag and bolted out the back door. "I'm late."

The cuckoo sounded as she fled across the grass to the studio that squatted under a low roof, weighed by encroaching vines and tree limbs. Two big windows stared into the tangled garden, watching the house through rain-streaked eyes. The air inside was stiff from lack of use. She pursed her lips to suck air like the woman of the mask, skimming under the water's murky surface, alert to trouble.

Tools lay scattered on the work bench, as if her mother would arrive soon and put them in order, prepare them for work. She picked up a worn palette knife, its blade nicked, the wooden handle spattered with paint. Turning it over, looking closely, she felt her mother's fingers in her hand. Dropping it into her canvas bag, she noticed a small, framed photograph in the corner of the workbench, behind a wadded rag. It was her, dressed in a white, gauzy robe with a crown of burning candles on her head.

*St. Lucia, the Light Queen*, she thought, and remembered the night the photo was taken, recalled the smell of warm candle wax, the hush of the Swedish Lutheran church when she entered and glided down the center aisle. Her parents sat in the front pew. The choir filled the darkened sanctuary with sound like bubbles that lifted into the ceiling timbers, popped against the jeweled surfaces of the stained glass windows, the music buoying her as she walked alone to the altar.

In that moment long ago, Lizette gave up the hard edges of her will and yielded to the sacred energy that ebbed and flowed around and through her. She surrendered her boundaries to the spirits, to the sounds. That night she had her first menstrual period and knew she'd grown up. From then on, when life pushed on the edges of her being, she exited from the pressure like music exhaled, submerging, releasing into the depths of her being, rising, always wary. Watching.

She dropped the photo into her bag and left by the side yard. She sensed him spying and looked up at the dining room window, caught a glimpse of his blue plaid shirt through the glass before he pulled back. She hurried down the narrow path beside the house and into the rain-slicked street, feeling like a grave robber.

# TWO

WAITING FOR THE BUS AT 45TH AND WALLINGFORD, she felt lost and confused, remembered when she'd felt the same way, that day at the market, before it happened, people handing her cash for quickly drawn portraits, while she sat surrounded by vegetable stalls and singing fish mongers. Thanksgiving shoppers had washed through Seattle's Pike Place Market, carrying armloads of russet and white chrysanthemums, orange pumpkins and yellow gourds, the air heavy with the smell of salt and roasted coffee beans.

A child. She remembered a toe-headed boy. He'd stuck out his hand to thank her for his picture. They shook. She could almost feel his plump hand, now, see the baby dimples over his knuckles. His parent's had read the handmade sign she'd taped on the metal beam above her stool and easel. They'd stopped and thrust the child onto the stool, paid her five dollars for the sketch when she was done, said she was a regular Picasso, loud, like they wanted the indifferent crowd to stop and marvel at their baby's image. Then they rolled the sketch and put it into their vegetable sack.

Loneliness washed through her as she thought about that day, about watching them disappear in the throng, vanish into the dusk.

She wanted her drawing back, but more than that she wanted the child, wanted to feel the plump rise of new flesh, and thought about her mother and the warm, yeasty smells of baking bread. That day in the market she felt like she did now standing on the sidewalk—waiting, alone, without a place to go, without a place to call home, a discarded puzzle piece. She shivered, pulled her jacket tighter, peered into the February rain, clamped her mind against the dark memory, submerged.

When a bus bound for downtown pulled up, she hopped on and changed her mind about the ferry to Orcas. She knew she'd never make it to the ferry landing at Anacortes before dark and right now she needed to stop this gnawing loneliness. She got off on Eastlake Avenue, headed up the hill to Sandy Shore's house on Franklin Street, next door to Rocket's place. The two run-down houses used to be home to Norwegian fishing families, but that was years ago. Now the houses served as a gathering place, a crash pad for junkies, losers and odd-ball sports fans.

Lizette had lost her bedroll and the drawings tucked inside when they picked her up in the alley that night and hauled her off in the ambulance. The attack was sometime in December, she thought, or was it January? No. *This is January*, she thought. *Isn't it?* She couldn't remember when it happened. After Thanksgiving, she thought. She still had her bag with sketch pads and paints and knew she could work, but not on Franklin Street. She could figure that problem out later, she thought.

Dazed and hungry, she climbed Sandy's front steps, waved to a couple of the guys carrying baseball gear into the house next door, noticed Rocket's two-toned Olds 88 parked in front, and let herself in the unlocked front door. She knew Sandy would be at work, topless dancing at Vixen's in Tacoma, and hoped she wouldn't throw her out when she got home. Lizette called out for her in the empty house, just in case, and felt the hollowness. She settled on the couch by the front window and spread an afghan over her legs, soothed herself with coos, and watched the rain come down.

Startled awake at the sound of a car door slamming, Lizette watched Sandy totter up the walk in spike heels, swinging a red garment bag in the dark. She dropped it in the front hall and flipped on the light. Lizette sat with folded hands, the blanket over her knees, and noticed Sandy's false eyelashes and rouged cheeks, the doll face she used when stripping.

"What the hell you doing here?" Sandy said, sniffing like she smelled bad meat. "Where've you been, anyhow? Marian asked about you a couple of weeks ago. I thought you were staying downtown."

"I was…before I got attacked," Lizette said, downplaying what'd happened. "I just got out of the hospital." She hung her head.

Sandy looked at Lizette huddled in her old afghan and snorted. "You can only stay the night, Liz. That's it! Sleep on the couch. You gotta stop sneaking in here. I'm not runnin' a rescue mission. Go home to your dad's or get your own damn place."

Sandy headed back out to her Volkswagen bug. "How about helping with Bella?" she called and Lizette followed her into the cold.

"She's getting heavy, hard to handle." Sandy yanked the car door open, leaned into the backseat, pulled the huge snake out of its travel box. "Shits like a horse!" She controlled its head and grunted as she lifted the snake's thick mid-section, shifted her hips so Lizette could squeeze in and hoist out the long tail.

In the days that followed, Lizette found ways to make herself useful to Sandy—doing the dishes, mopping, running to the co-op for raw milk and bulgar. Sandy let her slide. Lizette folded laundry in the basement now and watched Bella the Beautiful Boa, star of Sandy Shore's striptease act, expand and contract under a heat lamp in its glass cage.

Sandy came down and poked around, checked to see how much laundry soap was left in the box, told Lizette she'd quit her job, had decided to stop dancing. Lizette finished folding and watched Sandy drop a live rabbit into Bella's cage, then secure the hatch. Bella went after the prey, the rabbit squeaking, beating its hind legs against the glass as the big snake fit its slimy mouth over its furry head. Then the rabbit went still, only the dryer's rhythmic tumble stirred the air.

Pulling laundry from the dryer, Lizette said, timidly, "I get money from the county for disability. I can help pay rent."

"What disability?" Sandy scanned Lizette up and down. "You seem pretty healthy to me."

Some arrangements would have to be made on the rent, Sandy knew that and pictured the landlord's hairy back and discolored toenails, but she didn't see skinny-assed Lizette as the answer to her problems. She turned and studied the bulge in Bella's long body and patted her own tummy, smoothed the fabric of her flannel shirt over her abdomen. She studied the piles of Bella's expelled waste from past meals—clumps of fur and bones—deposited in the cage's shredded newspaper. She turned her scrutiny back to Lizette, who flinched at the disapproval she saw on Sandy's face. Climbing onto a wobbly step-stool, Sandy opened the cage's hatch and reached inside, scooped the waste piles into a paper bag with a rusted coal shovel, whacked the snake on the head when it nosed toward the tank's open top.

"You sick or what?" Sandy said, looking suspiciously over her shoulder at Lizette, who shrugged and kept folding laundry. "Why don't you just go home, make up with your old man, get a job, stop hanging out?" She bent over the rim of the cage, butt in the air. "The 60s are over and this ain't a crash pad," Sandy said, coming upright. "I've got a lot of shit to do here."

"My dad doesn't want me," Lizette whispered. "He told me to get out. No one wants me."

Sandy bent again and stirred the shredded newspaper with the little shovel, finally got down from the stool and dropped the paper bag with Bella's droppings on the floor, pushed it aside with her foot. "Save the sorry shit," Sandy said, turning squarely to Lizette. "I don't feel sorry for you. At least you have an old man and a place to go. That's more than me."

Lizette started to protest. Sandy put up a hand to stop her.

"My friend Jerry owns this whole block," Sandy said sweeping her arm around the basement. This house, the Dog House next door, and all the empty lots around here. It's not like he needs the money. I can work something out with him on the rent."

Lizette wandered to the crooked basement door and opened it, looked out at the gray morning. The vacant lots along Franklin Street were snarled with blackberry brambles, sagging sheds and weeds, a leaning post with a clothesline pulley still attached. People guessed Jerry was some kind of urban renewal scam artist with plans for a high-rise apartment building. She'd heard them talking on the TV. It was easy to see through the morning drizzle that Lyndon Johnson had lost the "War on Poverty" several years ago.

She looked over at the battered side of Rocket's house, wondered what the guys were doing, if they were getting ready to go out, if she could tag along. The way Sandy told it, she'd picked Rocket up at Vixen's on a slow night and they hit it off. He moved in next door after the old folks he'd been staying with in the Wallingford District, died and left him a grand piano, plus the money to move it and keep it tuned. He'd said it was some kind of Bosendorfer, more than 130 years old, which Sandy told her she doubted because it looked new. After the old couple died, the story went, relatives in Spokane sold the house and, when Rocket suggested renting a room from Sandy on Franklin Street and moving in with the piano, she told Lizette she'd blurted out "Hell no!" Sandy said he looked hurt at the time, but she said the piano monstrosity was like a boat anchor—once the thing dug in, she'd never get rid of it—or Rocket. Sandy said she didn't want to chance it.

When she'd checked on the empty house next door to her, and, after giving Jerry the landlord a good spanking with her hairbrush during a visit to their usual motel, Sandy said the rent he'd wanted was pretty cheap. She gave him an extra blow job and he didn't ask a lot of questions about the new tenant. He made it clear, however, he wasn't into repairs because the place needed to be torn down, said he was waiting for his project financing to come through and he'd put up some apartment units. Lizette remembered Sandy telling her Jerry gave her a bunch of bank deposit slips for his business account and warned her to pay the rent on time or else. A bargain Sandy told her she'd always kept.

Rocket, his piano, and the pack of softball bums who called themselves the Franklin Street Dogs, had lived side-by-side with Sandy ever since. Probably two or three years by now, Lizette figured, as she surveyed the decay from the doorway. She heard the Dogs rummaging around, recognized the sound of beer bottles breaking. She grabbed a stack of folded laundry and took it upstairs, bounded up the flight to the second floor, shoved the fresh towels into the linen closet, and slipped into the small bedroom where she slept on a saggy twin bed, shut the door.

# THREE

"HEY, MAN, WHAT'RE YOU DOIN'?" Rocket dropped his sea bag on the kitchen floor, startling Bomber, who leaned over the sink with the water running.

"Suckin' chicken bones. What's it look like?" Bomber wiped his lips on the sleeve of his Army jacket. "Somebody left meat."

Rocket opened the refrigerator and pulled out a carton. "Want some Chinese?" He shoved the brown-stained container at Bomber, who gave it a hungry look. "Went to the Lotus Garden last night. Me and Sandy. We had sweet-n-sour pork. Good shit, man. Brought back leftovers, broccoli beef."

"Far out." Bomber grabbed the carton, fished a fork out of the sink, wiped it on his pant leg. "Thanks. You shippin' out?" he asked, mouth full.

"What's it look like, dumb shit?"

Rocket turned the knob for the one stove burner that still worked, checked the clock on the spattered enamel backboard, marveled that it still worked, set the timer, dropped three eggs into a small pot of water and passed a hand over the electric burner to make sure it came on, set the pot down. "Lizette's over at Sandy's again."

Bomber had seen Lizette hanging around, braiding her blonde hair on the porch.

"Pretty good lookin' for a head case." He glanced out the window at the blank side of Sandy's house. "I thought Sandy got rid of her."

"She showed back up. Been here a few days now." Rocket sighed. "I feel sorry for her, man, I really do. She got attacked by a dog, about tore her arm off, and she ended up in the hospital. Tell her I'll pay her if the dishes are done when I get back from work. We're heading up to B.C., towing gravel barges out of Vancouver. Be back in a few days."

Rocket moved into the dining room, tapped a few perfectly pitched notes on the piano. "Middle C," he called out to Bomber, who was busy licking the edges of the Chinese carton in the kitchen. "Sounds pretty good, don't it?" The timer went off. He slid off the bench and moved around the piano, its glossy black top closed flat, and hurried to pull the pot off the heat, shook his hand from the hot handle, blew on his fingers.

Bomber looked sideways, smirked. "You're spendin' a lot of time with Sandy, ain't you?"

Rocket cracked an egg, yolk ran down his fingers and he licked them, turned on Bomber. "What?...You my mama?" Rocket's tone made Bomber step back.

Rocket finished cracking and spooning the runny eggs into a mug, slurped them, and went back to his piano, which gleamed in the light from the kitchen, defying the house's squalor. He admired its graceful lines, ivory keys set perfectly, like an orcas' smile, he thought.

"Sandy's a friend," Rocket said over his shoulder. "OK? We do a little business together. That's all."

Bomber offered a half-hearted "No sweat, man," to avoid an argument and rummaged in the refrigerator, dripped soy sauce from a half open packet on the floor. "I lost all my money at the bar last night," Bomber said, head in the refrigerator. "Must've dropped my roll when I was shootin' pool and somebody snagged it. Dickheads!"

Rocket half heard Bomber and thought about Fisher, was glad he hung around. He was the only one who could actually play the piano, probably the main reason he hung out with the Dogs, that and his love of weed. Rocket could find Middle C and play a few songs. Which was more than he could say for the Dogs. They barely knew how to play softball. He'd stopped complaining about them spreading out newspapers on the piano's top. He knew sometimes when he shipped out they'd set up a chess board on the piano's shiny top and cheat their asses off, changing the rules as they went along, playing until a fight broke out and somebody yelled: "Checkmate!" He'd put the piano top off limits for a while, but knew the Dogs crept their way back to the surface when he was gone. Checking the piano's condition now, he thought the finish was holding up pretty good.

*Assholes* he muttered to himself. He'd seen Fisher's sly smile when he played the "old dorfer." They both knew that nowhere else in the city was there a finer instrument. He hated to leave the piano now. It was the most valuable thing he owned, followed by his classic Oldsmobile Rocket 88.

Bomber watched Rocket pace the kitchen. He threw the empty food carton in the sink, stepped into his path. "How well do you know Lizette? I mean, what if she robs the place? We had this gook woman once in Nam. Cleaned our hooch . . ."

"Look," Rocket interrupted the well-worn story. "This place is a shit hole." He bent and picked up cotton balls under the chair, looked at the blood stains from somebody shooting up and tossed them toward the overflowing garbage bucket by the back door. He shouldered his sea bag.

"I know her. OK? Her old man's some kinda professor at the U. Caught her smoking a joint once, threw her out. Her mother offed herself. She was staying with Marian out on Orcas Island for a while. Now she's back." Rocket headed for the front door, turned and pulled a ten dollar bill from his pocket with his free hand, gave it to Bomber. He closed the door before Bomber could thank him.

Bomber rinsed his hands in the kitchen sink, the warm water feeling so good he rummaged around for a bar of soap. He scrubbed carefully and shut the faucet off hard to slow the perpetual drip. A knock at the front door interrupted his search for a towel. Before he could get to the door, a knock came again. *No one knocks*, he thought, shaking his wet hands. *Except the mailman and it's too early for that.* Opening the door, he found a man, slight and crisp, dressed in a dark business suit, white shirt, gold cuff links.

"Shit, man," Bomber got a whiff of English Leather cologne and stepped back, wiped an eye. "What's up?"

"Rocket here?"

"You just missed him." Bomber looked the guy up and down. "Who's asking?"

"I'm Jerry." The man shifted nervously. Bomber smelled fear under the cologne. "I'm the landlord. Here's my card. Tell him to call me when he gets back."

Bomber studied the guy. "Might be a while. He shipped out for a few days.

"Oh," Jerry said, looking critically at Bomber. "Well, when he gets back then. That'll be fine. Don't forget."

Bomber glanced at the card in his hand, "Sure thing...ah, Jerry?" He shut the door and put the card on the window sill by the door. He didn't like it, didn't like the owner showing up first thing in the morning. Rent's paid. Then he wondered if that was true and felt uneasy. In the living room he turned on the TV and settled in to watch "Good Morning Seattle." He listened to breathless accounts of armed robberies and explosions, along with stories about pickup trucks wrapped around trees.

*"Slow going on the floating bridge into downtown,"* the blonde with puffy hair said. *"And, now, from our nation's capital. President Nixon, in another unexpected turn of events in the ongoing Watergate investigation, has canceled tonight's television address to the nation. The President will instead hold a news conference tomorrow. Tune in for full coverage."* Bomber farted, patted his breast pocket for smokes. *"We now go to a special report on the depressed Seattle housing market. With foreclosures soaring, King County officials say homelessness is on the rise."*

"No shit," Bomber told her under his breath, then pondered this: No one in the Dog House had ever seen the landlord, not even Rocket. He knew Rocket paid Sandy the rent and she gave it to the landlord, a transaction that he'd helped support, but had never seen. Rocket collected donations from whoever was sitting around on the first of the month and Bomber always chipped in a chunk from his VA check, which wasn't much considering the cost of his habit. The drugs helped ease the pain from the bullet he took in Nam. He knew Rocket added to the rent collection from his own pay, after he took care of Cadillac Carl, their drug dealer. He also was aware that sometimes Rocket ate corn flakes three meals a day to keep the finances going.

Bomber gratefully fingered Rocket's ten dollar bill in his pocket. *Don't seem, right,* he thought. *Landlord showing up first thing in the morning. It ain't even light yet.* He wobbled down the basement stairs to the mattress he'd put in the corner and crashed long before Rocket ever got to the docks.

# FOUR

**ROCKET WORKED IN A LIGHT RAIN.** He uncoiled the *Sea Wolf's* lines from the cleats, prepared her to shove off. A silvery light glazed Lake Union's surface and made it easier to work. He looped a length of rope over his stiff fingers and threw it to the tug's deck, steam from his breath matching the spew from the *Sea Wolf's* smokestacks.

Gilly, the first mate stepped out of the galley house and stretched his arms overhead like a sleeper unwinding from a dream. He watched Rocket sidestep along the securing lines and yelled across the breech to shake a leg. Rocket ignored the old man, kept coiling line, licked frozen salt from his lips. He knew they were late for the rendezvous with the sea barge hauling gravel out of B.C., that the slow start was his fault. Hung over and late again.

Timing the water's upsurge, Rocket jumped lightly to the boat's deck. "What the hell took so long?" the old man huffed, working his cigar stub between tobacco-stained lips. "Get some coffee, kid. It's gonna be a long day." Rocket shouldered past him.

"Saved you some sweet rolls," Gilly said as they single-filed into the tight, steamy galley. "Grab some grub." He poured coffee into a thick mug, shoved it at Rocket. "Think we'll see that goddamned killer whale again?" He sucked in his round belly to fit between the bulkhead and table. "Damnedest thing," he said. "We never see that whale unless you're working. It's like the thing follows you around."

"It's an orca," Rocket said, his mouth full. He munched a raisin snail, wiped his mouth with his hand. The captain gunned the *Sea Wolf's* engines, eased away from the dock, rolled into the swells. The rocking sloshed coffee over the rim of the men's mugs. Rocket grabbed a rag, daubed at the spills. "Move your elbow."

He wiped in front of the first mate, wondered about the orca, too. Rocket knew the American tugboat guys called the orca "Looney," like the Canadian quarter, a dig at the currency and the Canadian boatmen who worked Puget Sound. The Americans complained that Looney popped up like a jack-in-the-box in the shipping lanes, put the Coast Guard on alert, or trailed salmon fishermen. Orcas were famous for tearing into fishing nets and stealing from catches, creating hazards and getting shot for causing trouble.

"Gonna hit the rack," Rocket said, sliding out from the table. He pulled the illustrated guide to dolphins and whales from the slot where the marine navigation maps were stowed. "I've got second watch. Make sure I'm up by five so I don't miss chow."

"We'll rattle your rack," Gilly answered, spreading the wrinkled *Seattle Times* sports section across the table. "But, it's not even noon."

"Long night," Rocket said. The first mate fingered his wedding ring, let out a dirty chuckle.

Riding an ebbing tide, the *Sea Wolf* made for the Strait of Juan de Fuca as Rocket took off his boots, grabbed a gray wool blanket from the stack on the floor, and settled into the narrow bunk. He tucked a small pillow under his shoulders and opened the book, flipping to the section on orcas.

*"With orcas, mating and reproduction is basically the same as with other marine mammals,"* the book said. *"They come together and match bellies."* Rocket rubbed his stomach under his thermal undershirt, twirling the hair around his belly button. *"A female carries her calf for 9 to 12 months. Babies are born in the water. They can swim from the moment they are born. Sometimes an orca mother will support her newborn from beneath, allowing the youngster to breathe without tiring."*

Rocket studied the familiar pictures of the mothers and babies, the pod swimming among ice flows. *"Orcas are the fastest mammals in the sea. Although they can weigh up to 13,000 pounds, they can swim up to 35 miles an hour, which helps them catch food.* Rocket read the words again, mentally calculating the speed at about 22 knots, figuring the Sea Wolf did 10 knots when she was underway on a calm sea.

*They are curious and sometimes attracted to boats,"* he read. Rocket knew Looney was what they called a rogue, lived separate from the family pods of killer whales that hunted around the San Juan Islands. Rocket had watched him shadow a tug as it escorted a freighter toward port. He believed the playful animal wanted to join in the fun, be a part of the game, go with them like he was part of the family.

Rocket closed the book, its cover smudged from years on the tug and the greasy hands of boredom. He dreamed of swimming, his arms by his sides, drawn through the water in an iridescent slipstream, Looney's tail just beyond reach, undulating as they powered through the unresisting water.

"Hey man, roll out!" Rocket startled awake and the whale book hit the deck with a flat pop. The second mate banged on the metal door again. "Hit the deck, Rocket. Chow's on." The guy opened the door and leaned in, his blood-shot eyes scanned the room as if checking for a stowaway, then he twisted his lips into a pleased smirk at the jolt he'd given the sleeping deckhand. "Hurry up, man, if you want some."

At five, Rocket went on deck to stand his watch. They were still miles from the rendezvous with the ocean tug towing the gravel barge. He fretted about the complicated tie-up they'd have to do in the dark to secure the load. He watched the gulls swoop in tangents, skimming the water's surface as night clamped down. Leaning over the side, Rocket spotted Looney in the last glimmers of light. The orca paced the tug, the tug's wake washing over his black-and-white body. He came abreast, his long dorsal fin sporting above the whitecaps. He dived, surfaced, and raced ahead of the *Sea Wolf*. Rocket gripped the top of the gunwale and laughed into the wind, inflating his lungs, electrified.

Rocket knew Looney's tricks, how he often crossed under the hull, popping up on the opposite side of the boat, tossing his big head, waiting for him to chase across the deck and lean over the railing to find the teasing orca, water frothing around him. When Looney submerged, Rocket hustled starboard for the game of hide-and-seek. The tug listed unnaturally, the spinning props sputtered.

The *Sea Wolf's* engines throttled down. The men scrambled on deck, knowing instinctively something was wrong, that they'd run over something and needed to do a hull check. The Sound was littered with big logs that had come loose from carelessly tied barge loads and other boating debris. The tug's engines reversed, sending the men lurching as they charged for their stations. The loudspeaker needlessly called, "All hands, All hands." Rocket ran to the stern, released the winch and dropped the dinghy to the water. The mates scrambled down the metal ladder aft and jumped on board.

"We got something," the first mate hollered and yanked the cord to fire up the weather-beaten outboard motor.

They signaled for line. Rocket threw to the men bobbing in the darkness and, in the fluster, missed his target. The captain flipped on the floodlights, which made Looney's broad side glisten in the water. Rocket hauled the wet rope back in and prepared for another toss. The first mate pulled out the grappling hook from the bottom of the dinghy and sunk it into Looney's side, poling closer to prevent the carcass from drifting. Blood like warm cherry Jell-O feathered the water. Rocket kept hauling line, hand-over-hand, looking at the whale's blank eye, seeing that the curtain was drawn. At the end of the rope, he grasped slick blood. It ran through his fingers and down the back of his hands. He choked, kept hauling.

"What the heck you doing?" Gilly shouted from the dinghy. "Throw the line, man. Goddamned thing got caught in the prop."

Rocket picked up the coil and threw it again, hard, hitting the second mate in the chest, knocking him overboard. With the emergency lights on, Rocket saw where the propellers had sliced into Looney. The first mate maneuvered the dinghy around the animal's tail and tossed a life bouy to the man gasping in the frigid water. He hauled him to the side, pulled him up by the shoulders of his peacoat, hoisted his leg over the side and rolled him onto the bottom of the skiff like a big fish.

They called for more line to secure Looney's body until the Coast Guard got there to haul the carcass from the shipping lane. Rocket ran around on the deck, heaving line, tightening slack, tying off, wiping salt from his wet cheeks with his sleeve. Looney's flukes lifted out of the swells and flapped listlessly, then the animal eased free of the lines. His sleek back disappeared beneath the water's ruffled surface, created a hole in the sea that rapidly filled. The men stood for a moment in shocked silence.

Dripping wet and shivering in the wind, the mates quarreled in the rocking dinghy. Rocket dropped the useless lines he held in his hands. Over the loudspeaker, the captain ordered the men back aboard. They came around, aligned the dinghy to the tug's stern and climbed the slippery rungs to the deck. The winch snapped as Rocket lifted the dinghy out of the water and it took a half hour to fix it. Then, in the night slit, where black meets black, between sky and water, Rocket walked the deck, stood his watch, scanned the rolling sea looking for any sign of his orca.

# FIVE

**A FEW DAYS LATER,** Lizette heard a car pull up in front of the house on Franklin Street and went to Sandy's bedroom window. She watched Rocket lean into his car and haul out his sea bag, then bounce up the walk to the Dog House and disappear inside.

"Rocket's home," she told Sandy, who lounged on the bed. "Wonder if he'll notice?"

Sandy rolled onto her side, didn't answer.

Next door, Rocket dropped his bag at the foot of the stairs and greeted the Dogs, surveyed his house and friends. The Dogs grunted at him and turned back to the TV. *Something's different,* Rocket thought, but couldn't put his finger on it. He sensed things had been moved while he was gone, but wasn't sure what. He took a sniff. *Furniture polish?*

In the kitchen, he found the sink empty. The cracked linoleum had green and white swirls, a pattern he hadn't noticed before. When he tripped over a garbage bag near the back door, empty beer bottles clinked. Going into the dining room, the piano gleamed. "What the hell happened here?"

"The nut job from next door," Bomber huffed, tucked his chin into the collar of his Army jacket. Rocket looked puzzled. "You know? Lizette? The one you told me to go get? The one you hired to clean the shitter?"

"I offered to pay her for doing the dishes." Rocket said, looked confused. "That's all."

The Dogs sat in stiff silence. Finally, someone mumbled "Lizette's a crazy lizard, man."

Rocket glanced around. The pizza boxes and potato chip bags were gone. The floors were swept and mopped. He searched the crowd, settled on Bomber. "Where is she?"

"Next door," Bomber said. "She wants money, man." Then added, "Jerry the landlord came by."

Rocket headed out and jogged up the sidewalk. At Sandy's house, he looked into the empty living room, yelled up the stairs and heard a muffled reply. He thundered up the stairs, burst in, found Sandy stretched out on her bed, honey-blonde hair fanned across a pillow, Lizette fluttering over her.

"What's up?" Rocket stepped to the edge of the bed and scanned Sandy's short, shapely body. "You sick?"

"Naw, just tired." She propped herself up. "Quit my job."

"Bummer," he said. "What about the rent? Did you pay it? Bomber said the landlord came by."

"It's cool." She settled back into her pillows and covered her eyes. "Would you guys get out of here? You're making me uptight. I need space. OK?"

"Yeah, sure," he said and reached for Lizette's elbow to usher her out, but she avoided his grasp. "You want anything?"

Sandy shook her head as they left.

After about three weeks, Rocket and Lizette had worked out a routine. They slept together sometimes, for comfort, like brother and sister because Rocket was usually too wasted to do much else.

But, when he shipped out, he sent her back to Sandy's, didn't like her snooping around when he wasn't there, stirring up the Dogs. While he was gone, Lizette went over and cleaned, hung out in the dining room with Fisher at the piano, sketched cross-legged under the windows, slept under the basement stairs sometimes, skipped Sandy's place except to take baths and wash a load of clothes. For their part, the Dogs flicked cigarette butts at each other and spit in the dishes. She ignored them.

The house plants had perked up during the past few weeks, Rocket thought, as he relaxed on a day off. He liked the arrangement with Lizette, liked the smell of lavender on his sheets and the sketches she left on his dresser, the folded laundry she put on his bed, his socks actually mated, although not always matched. It felt comfortable, more like a home than a house.

But, except for Fisher, the Dogs were not OK with Lizette. They said she chirped and hummed, usually snatches of Vivaldi, according to Fisher, but as far as the Dogs were concerned, who the hell knew? The men found her several times warbling half naked in front of the dining room windows. Stinky growled, "Chick's loosing it, man."

She muttered things about good karma and bad chi. When startled, she squawked like a parrot and flapped her arms, other times she warbled like a canary or clicked like a dolphin. *Built like a lizard, quacks like a duck*, is how Bomber described her. They all agreed she was off her rocker, which straight-up creeped them out.

They noticed she pulled herself together when Rocket came home, stopped dolphin clicking and bird chirping so much. He didn't see the worst of it, they said. Rocket fed her like a stray cat, leaving dishes with small amounts of food on the stove for her to find. She continued to sort of clean and water the house plants to earn her keep with Rocket. She'd sink into her hidden nest under the basement stairs when Rocket spent the night at Sandy's.

During the day, she went on walks and collected flowers and foliage from empty lots in the neighborhood and brought them back to the Dog House, put the weedy bouquets in old jars, the floral decay eventually making the house smell like shit, the Dogs groused. Once she put a jar of yellow chrysanthemums on top of the TV and somebody knocked it off while changing the channel, almost shorted it out. They were ready to give her the heave-ho on the spot, but got it working again.

This is what finally did it for the Dogs, what pushed them over the edge. Lizette set a big, old mayonnaise jar on the counter next to the kitchen sink and used it, she explained to Gizzard, who was jonesin' hard at the time, to develop her special plant fertilizer. The liquid was enriched with egg shells, she said, shaking the emulsion, and jostling the used tampons on the bottom. She told Gizzard, who stared at her with his Adam's apple bobbing like a turkey, that this was how she captured the iron and minerals her body shed so she could recycle them back to Mother Earth.

He sat down hard and missed the chair, hit the floor like a satchel of rusty tools. When the Dogs heard Gizzard crash, they charged in, thinking he'd seized out. He was moaning "mayonnaise" when they helped him up. She told them the poor guy fainted while she was talking about house plants and waved toward the jar by the sink. The Dogs backed away. They huddled and decided they couldn't take it anymore. She had to go.

So, when Rocket got back to the house, the Dogs, like always, were sitting in the living room on the mismatched sofa and upholstered chairs, unconcerned about the stuffing popping out. They'd tossed chip bags and pizza crusts on the bare floor like usual, and they'd made up their minds. They focused on the TV and ignored the Christmas tinsel Lizette had hung throughout the house in March.

Nobody said anything to Rocket now. He stood there and they ignored him. Someone got up and fussed with the scrap of tin foil pinched to the tip of one rabbit ear on the antenna to improve the TV's reception. They all sat with folded arms. Rocket was going to be the one to put her out. They'd decided. It was his idea to bring her in. He would get rid of her, but this time for good. They'd checked with Sandy, who said she didn't give a rip what they did with her. She agreed Lizette was out to lunch and said she didn't want to get involved.

Rocket saw it was no use, not worth fighting the Dogs over, and drove Lizette to Pike Place Market on a rainy Friday morning, handed her the forty dollars he owed her for cleaning. She cried, asked if it meant they were breaking up, put her head against the car window, rubbed her eyes, pulled at the little gold hoop in her nose, chirped, he thought, like a broken-winged sparrow. He told her no, but didn't have the heart to tell her they'd never actually been a couple and that he didn't know what she was talking about. He thanked her for helping around the house, said she'd done a good job, gave her another ten dollars, reached across her and opened the passenger-side door. He watched from the car as she moved on her stilted crane legs through the crowd of shoppers before he lost sight of her. He sort of liked the skinny little bird, he thought, and almost got out of the car to call her back, thought about the Dogs, shook off the impulse, drove away.

# SIX

IT SNOWED A FEW DAYS LATER, dropped about a half foot on the city. The folks under the freeway built a fire in an old barrel and Lizette huddled with them, her hands extended to the flames to melt the numbness before she rolled up in the moving blanket she'd copped from the loading dock of a furniture warehouse down the street and slept fitfully. In the morning they found the old man everyone called "Funny Sonny" dead in his bedroll. Somebody called the cops to pick up the body. They came, took a look around at the camp, said something about vagrants, and called for a paddy wagon. They were loading people into the back when Lizette slipped away and headed back to the Dog House, nowhere else to go.

She climbed in an unlatched basement window and settled into the pile of blankets she'd ditched under the basement stairs, eventually thawed out and fell asleep to the furnace's low humming. A commotion upstairs rattled her awake and she crawled up the dusty stairs to check it out through the door crack. Cadillac Carl, the dope dealer, had blown in and stood in the hall with two brown paper bags in his arms, frosty March air trailing him from the front door.

She watched him eye the Dogs, who sat bunched in front of the TV, and pull his lips into a sly smile that cloaked a missing tooth.

Somebody wheezed, "Hey Carl," and he tossed a nod to the room, rubbed the blood-stained gauze wrapped around his right hand. He held out the greasy bags. The Dogs leaned toward him, squinting in the blue light from the TV. He tipped his head toward the piano and set the bags on top.

"Chow fun, knuckleheads." He broke off a hard laugh, pulled white containers out of the bags, lined them up on the piano's sleek ebony surface, said flatly, "Belly up, boys."

Mesmerized by the unexpected appearance of their dope dealer, the Dogs roused and waved beer bottles. Cadillac Carl opened one of the cartons and the brassy smell of garlic and broccoli escaped. All at once, as if executing a long-practiced play, swearing and laughing, the Dogs jumped up and rushed the piano, Gizzard tried to pump Carl's bandaged hand, which he held to his chest.

Bomber clapped him on the back, said, "When'd you get out?" Not waiting for an answer, he jockeyed for position around the piano and the food.

In the excitement, no one noticed the basement door ajar, didn't see Lizette lying on her belly at the top of the stairs, holding a wool scarf over her mouth to stuff any stray sounds. She waited, hoped there'd be something left to eat when they all finally fell asleep. Then she'd grab it and slink back under the basement stairs, eat and sleep until the coast was clear again.

"You sumbitch, Carl, why didn't you call?" Rocket said, peering into a carton, finding only white rice, reaching for another one. "We heard the cops picked you up last night, man. Thought if you were holding, you'd be goin' down, for sure."

Cadillac Carl cracked wooden chop sticks apart and poked around in the steaming cartons.

"They couldn't hold me." He pulled a fried prawn out, held it neatly in the pincers, and bit the body in two. "Didn't have nothin' on me."

He looked Rocket in the eye. "I never touched that bitch. I don't care what she said. Don't even know her name."

"Sure," Rocket said, blinking, smacking his lips.

Cadillac Carl stopped talking, put the greasy prawn on the piano, rocked back on the heels of his scuffed cowboy boots, rubbed his knuckles under the bandage with his good hand, scanned the stubbly faces. A Dog threw down a grimy knit cap on the piano to mark his place and charged for the kitchen, returned with a cracked plate. The others peeled off the rim and went to the kitchen— jerked drawers open, ran water, rattled dishes, returned with bowls and cups and twisted forks.

Cadillac Carl stepped back from the pack and let them have at it. He took a mental head count: Stinky, Bomber, Gizzard, Rocket, Slick and Rainman. Toothless Smiley. Pee Wee. Almost all here, he thought, then saw Fuzzy squeezed into a corner, eyes downcast, avoiding his gaze.

"Looks cleaned up in here. What happened?" Carl glanced around.

Somebody spat, "Lizette."

"Where's Lizette?" he said, checking faces. "I heard she was crashing here."

"Doing thirty days in county for vagrancy," Pee Wee said. The Dogs laughed. Lizette watched, anger flickering in her empty stomach.

"Not really," Bomber said. "Rocket threw her out last week."

"That's a lie, douche bag," Rocket grumped. "You guys wanted her out, said she was nuts. So, now she's out. It wasn't my idea. I thought she was kind of handy to have around. Cleaned the crapper, which is more than you guys do."

Lizette choked on her scarf, almost got up from the dusty landing and stormed the piano, but fought the urge to bust in and throw broccoli beef in their stupid, junkie faces. She willed herself to stay calm and swallowed her chirps and clicks. She vowed to bide her time and find a way to get even with all of them, except Rocket.

Cadillac Carl looked the men over. *Desperate junkies ain't good for business,* he thought, chasing a rice grain across the piano top with his chopsticks. *They do stupid things. Knock over old ladies for purses, boost cars, attack pharmacy clerks, hold up banks.* He remembered one client who went into a Washington Mutual branch downtown and wrote a stickup note on the deposit slip for his own account. The cops were waiting when he got home with his fix. They wanted to know who he bought his shit from. Cadillac Carl took a quick Mexican vacation, which turned out to be a lucky break because he hooked up with some big-time connections down there who now were his steady suppliers.

The crowd roared on the TV and a few of the Dogs went to check out the action. The Sonics scored, pulled ahead. The game paused for halftime. With curses and beers and laughter bubbling all around, they came back to the piano. Cadillac Carl explained in a sarcastic tone that the barfly, who claimed he hit her in the eye last night at the tavern, changed her story, went into the police station and told them she'd decided not to press charges after all.

"Smart," somebody said under his breath.

"Yeah, but when'd they let you out?" Fuzzy asked, checked Cadillac's face to see how the question went down.

Cadillac Carl studied Fuzzy's tousled hair and bloodshot eyes, pants sagging loosely from his skinny waist. He set his jaw, narrowed his eyes to hot blue vents. Fuzzy hoisted his pants, scooped fried rice into a mug with quick spoon strokes, like he wasn't afraid, just busy eating.

They called him Fuzzy, not for what was growing wildly on his head, but for the tangled thicket elsewhere. His fuzziness used to delight the ladies, but that was before his world narrowed to the point of a needle and all his thoughts focused on his next fix.

"Got out about five this morning," Cadillac Carl said to the group. "After the coroner carried out the guy who OD'd in my cell. Real blabber mouth until he checked out."

On the TV, the announcer droned, *"And, now a news break. NASA says Skylab, the nation's first orbiting research station, is being prepared for launch. Once in place, the station will be operated by three-man crews. The value of the dollar has dropped more than ten percent and economists see a worsening recession . . . Officials say young voters are failing to register now that 18 year olds can go to the polls . . . Now, back to the game. More news at eleven."*

The front door rattled and Lucky, dragging a leg after an electrical accident when he worked for Puget Power and Light, shuffled in, puffing hard from stumping with his cane the few blocks from his mother's house. Seeing the grub on the piano, he grabbed a bowl from the kitchen, loaded up, and dumped his chow mein on the rug. Somebody said, "Bummer!"

"Where's Greg?" Cadillac Carl asked, checking the mess on the floor. Everyone glanced around.

"Next door, at Sandy's." Rocket finally said, stuffing a broccoli floret into his mouth with his fingers, crunching, swallowing hard. "Marian's down from Orcas Island. Got here this afternoon. She's looking for Lizette. That's her truck outside."

Because Lizette had scurried around the backside of the Dog House and shimmied in the basement window, she hadn't noticed Marian's truck out front. She felt a head-spinning urgency to talk to Marian now, thought about slithering down the dusty wooden steps and slipping out, making a run for Sandy's house, but didn't want to risk calling attention to herself or having to deal with Sandy, who'd pretty much given her the shaft.

Cadillac Carl leveled a look at Rocket hot enough to melt gum on the sidewalk in January. "The guy owes me, man."

"He's good for it, Carl . . . Lighten up, would ya? He's a friend."

"Yeah, well I'm not the Bank of fucking America." Cadillac Carl smeared a grease smudge on the piano with his pinkie, sucked it, worried that Greg was getting dangerously strung out, too. He'd been asking for dope on credit, paying late.

"How much you need?" Rocket looked around. The Dogs stared at Carl in the sallow light, chewing suspended.

"I'll take a hundred now, catch up with Greg for the rest later," he said in an ominous tone. The Dogs resumed chewing after Rocket went upstairs, but didn't say much. He came back and counted five twenties onto the piano top.

"Got a little surprise," Cadillac Carl said to the huddle around the piano. "Dessert."

He felt in the bottom of one of the paper bags pushed into a heap in the middle of the piano top. He pulled out a length of amber-colored rubber tubing and a small waxed paper bag with white powder. He unfolded a paper napkin to reveal a silver spoon, syringe and clean cotton balls. Stinky wheezed, "Far out, man!" and belched.

"Who's first?" Cadillac Carl smiled, surveyed the crowd. The Dogs jostled and nipped. One by one, Cadillac Carl tied off the Dogs. They rolled up the sleeves of their old flannel shirts, took a hit, mumbled "Thanks, man," and staggered back to the TV, plopped into their regular spots as the Sonics began the third quarter. Lizette felt the house's energy settling, prepared to slip quietly back down the stairs and wait some more before going next door, but watched a moment longer.

Elbowed out, only Fuzzy hadn't gotten a taste. Speaking in a low tone across the piano to Cadillac Carl, head down, he said, "My turn." He scratched himself and wiped his nose. The whites of his eyes were yellowed. His once fuzzy blonde hair had thinned and a bald spot showed on top when he bowed before Cadillac Carl under the dim bulb.

"You burned me man," Cadillac Carl said right out, toying with the syringe, rolling it between his fingers. "I looked for you last night at the bar. Before I got picked up. You know that . . . You were trying to avoid me, man."

Carl breathed in and puffed out like a viper. "You haven't paid up. . . . I don't like being messed with." He looked Fuzzy full in the face. Fuzzy pushed back from the piano.

"Hey man, you know, I got bills," he said. "I got loitering tickets and court shit. If I was in jail, how would I pay you?"

"I don't give a rat's ass what you do with your money," Carl said, stepping up to Fuzzy. "All I know is . . . I get mine."

"Yeah, I know . . . I know," Fuzzy said nodding like a puppet, waving down Cadillac Carl's volume with outspread hands.

He pushed Fuzzy's skinny arms away, "Don't I always come by with good stuff?" Fuzzy nodded. "Can't you count on me to be here?" Carl spoke louder, sharper.

"Sure . . . You're great." Fuzzy said and kept gesturing to turn down the sound.

One of the Dogs got up and turned up the volume on the TV. The game announcer explained the fine point of a rule after a play was whistled dead, his toupee sitting askew like a wrecked hamster.

"What're you doing here . . . anyway?" Carl said.

"Come on, Carl. For chrissakes."

"You don't pay, you don't come around."

"I swear. I got the money, man." Fuzzy's body shook, his teeth chattered. "I'll get it right after the game."

"You'll get it now!"

"I just need a taste, Carl. Come on, man. I'm sick. Just a little bit to keep me going . . . I feel like I'm dying, man."

"Fuck you."

"Let me do the cotton. It don't cost nothin' to do the cotton, just strain me up a little from what's left in the cotton," he begged and wiped his nose on the sleeve of his dirty shirt. "Keep me going, man. I'll pay you. I swear it. I always pay you." Fuzzy wiped pooled tears from his eyes. "Come on, man."

"You don't get squat til I get paid," Carl hissed.

Fuzzy stumbled to the corner of the dining room like he'd taken a shaft to the gut and slumped to the floor. He sniffled and rocked, scratched himself some more. He made himself so small it looked like he was melting into the floor. Lizette watched, melded into the wooden landing, held her breathe. The Dogs nodded in and out. Fuzzy whimpered and noisily sucked snot from his sinus cavities, swallowed.

"OK. OK. You can do the cotton," Cadillac Carl said quietly. "Come on." He reached down with his good hand and tugged. "Just don't want nobody thinking I'm going soft . . . That's all . . . Sets a bad example." Fuzzy rubbed his chin, nodded, acted wise.

Cadillac Carl prepared the spoon, added a drop of water and made like he was going to suck the moisture into the syringe, but he added some extra candy under the cotton. He dropped more water into the spoon's bowl with the eye dropper, then cooked it, boiling away the impurities.

Lizette smelled the sulfur from the matches, watched Carl wave the flame under the spoon. He filled the syringe all the way and tied off Fuzzy's skinny, outstretched arm, palped a scarred vein, pierced it. A spurt of blood flushed into the syringe, glowing red-orange in the glass tube. Cadillac Carl firmly pressed the plunger, smiled gently into Fuzzy's hazy eyes. "How's that?" Carl asked.

Fuzzy's face softened, his eyes rolled back. "Far out. Good shit, man. Good."

He crumpled to the floor under the piano. Lizette gasped into her scarf. Cadillac Carl looked around like he'd heard something and went and stood in the dining room archway, assessed the dozing Dogs in the living room. He watched the end of the game by himself, clapped once for a good layup. The Sonics lost. Fuzzy turned blue, stopped breathing.

Lizette studied Cadillac Carl's dark form through the crack in the basement door, saw evil standing upright and unashamed. Her heart curled shut like a tide pool anemone protecting itself. She slipped backwards down the stairs on hands and knees, covered herself with the blankets she'd tossed there, squinched her eyes and forced herself to think about damp green forests, fairies dancing among blades of grass.

Cadillac Carl stepped outside when the game ended and lifted a case of beer from the trunk of his car, ice cold from the crisp winter air. He roused the Dogs with the cold bottles under their chins, pulled a rotten, dusty curtain from a dining room window, and rolled Fuzzy's body into it. He signaled Bomber to help him. The Dogs watched bleary eyed as they worked the load out the front door and piled the wadded drapery into the open trunk of Cadillac Carl's Coupe de Ville. Without a word, Bomber went back inside. The Dogs said nothing.

Lizette heard the Caddie hum to life outside and pull away. She waited a long time in the dark, waited until there were no more sounds overhead and slipped out the basement window, panted along Eastlake, took refuge in a crease where dirt met cement under the freeway. She pulled flattened cardboard boxes over her and waited until first light. She caught the bus to Anacortes, took the ferry to Orcas Island.

# SEVEN

ORCAS ISLAND emerged from the mist like a fairy world in a children's book. Lizette watched the shoreline sharpen as the state ferry *Kalama* churned toward the landing, its decks bucking against the rolling current. The island rested before her, unchanged since the beginning of time. Trees blanketed the hills above verdant plains and spired along the dark hump of Turtleback Mountain. The foamy sea sloshed ashore in ebullient waves.

She bounced her ankle on her knee, bone striking bone, and puffed her hair, anxious to see Marian, eager to get to the ranch and her studio. Only conscious restraint kept her seated. A smile broke out on her face as she smelled the cedar and seaweed, the lush rot of the sea feeding new life. She touched her face with her fingertips, traced the stiff muscles around her mouth, surprised by a joyful stirring she hadn't felt in years, in forever.

The engines shuddered into reverse and the ferry slowed. Passengers gathered their belongings and prepared to disembark. Those remaining for the ride to Friday Harbor and Sidney in British Columbia looked bored as they watched the jumble of bodies gather around the car ramp. The wide-bodied boat nudged the dock, bounced against the pylons, settled into its berth like a lumbering beast nestling into a safe burrow. Cars shot off the ramp and accelerated up the hill, hurrying home in the waning afternoon light.

Locals on foot trudged off the ferry, indifferent to the magic that hovered over the Salish Sea, its islands scattered carelessly across the far Western edge of America. When it rains on the mainland, the sun shines on the islands. Canada's Vancouver Island shields the outcroppings in the straits of Juan De Fuca, Georgia and Haro further south. Sparkling light falls across the tree tops, roves the flower-dotted meadows and turns moisture to mist. Fierce winds glance off the mountains and cartwheel sea birds into a carnival of fishing and hunting. Lizette felt lighter, puffed by the wind, but at the same time more balanced. Safe.

When she was a child, she sensed the fairies living in the crevices on Orcas Island, their iridescent wings folded, sheltering in tiny hideouts. When storms swept over the mountains, she used to imagine the little creatures shielding their delicate bodies from the raindrops with tiny wildflower parasols.

Now, with the rain clouds clearing and every surface refracting light, Orcas Island shimmered with faint rainbows. The island pulled with its own gravity, held life differently than on the mainland. The *Kalama* blew a goodbye horn note and Lizette turned and waved. It revved its engines and slipped slowly back from the landing. A small child in a puffy jacket and red cap waved back to her.

As the ferry plowed into the swells in the strait, she scanned the water's surface ahead of it, looking for orca pods, their distinctive dorsal fins and sleek bodies breaching in the roiling sea. She knew the tidal energy of these waters nourished tiny crustaceans that launched a complicated food chain, provided abundant prey to nourish the ravenous appetites of these black-and-white hunters.

In the ferry slip, Lizette saw a dead gull, its legs wrapped in shredded fish netting. She could smell the creosote that oozed from the dock's pilings, leaking poison into the water where schools of smelt made synchronized turns, flashing their silver sides. She saw these losses and sensed the everyday carnage of sea lions clubbed or shot by fishermen defending their catch and ensnared birds flapping helplessly in the surf. Lizette did not know—but she wouldn't have been surprised to learn—that a gill net lost from a trawler in the San Juans the week before had killed a harbor seal, two white-sided dolphins, five Chinook salmon, 25 sockeye salmon, 30 ling cod, and 68 red crabs.

But, this sadness didn't dampen the joy that now had the upper hand in her consciousness. She moved closer to comfort and safety with each step she took toward the ranch, she wanted to call out for Marian and loosen the rubber band of tension gripping her skull. Her lips made quiet kisses.

In back of the Full Moon Saloon, Lizette pulled a battered orange bicycle from behind a green dumpster. Trash spilled onto the ground, damp napkins blew on a light breeze, carrying the stink of beer and onions out across the water. A few gulls picked at morsels, unconcerned with her presence. The sweet smell of garbage mixed with the rich odor of dead fish comforted her.

The bike, one of several stowed there, was used by island residents and farm workers who traveled to the ranches in an endless shuttle. She slung herself over the bike's heavy frame, checked the coaster brakes she hoped still worked and pushed off, pumping, standing to gain momentum, getting off to push the bike up the steep hill from the landing. On the flat road, Lizette pedaled, following childhood rules, listening for engine sounds that would warn her to pull over or stop on the narrow shoulder until it passed. With a chattering chorus of clicks and tweets yammering away in her head, she used her last bit of energy to pump, pump, pump along Horseshoe Highway.

Lizards and voles ducked for cover as she huffed along, taking deep breaths, transporting in her mind to the time when Indians used the islands as fish camps, catching salmon in reef nets around the inlets, working with the orca pods as they drove the salmon schools toward shallower water. The fishermen simply opened their nets to accept the abundance and thanked the Orca god. She thought about the legends of men who befriended orcas or transformed into them while they paddled in the sea, how they'd join the pack to feast on endless, writhing salmon banquets.

Her father had told her these stories of the first people who walked the island. He explained that later the white man came to trade and took over the sunny coves and snug harbors, feeding their hunger for land and animals, leaving behind disease. The old ones, like the parents and grandparents of Poland and Abaya, remembered the taking of their land and being pushed onto the reservation on the mainland. They went to Indian schools and worked odd jobs, hunted and fished, drank and fought among themselves. Now archaeologists and anthropologists, like her father and his students at the university, dug in the middens, trying to piece together the broken history of the Lummi from what was discarded or destroyed.

Rounding the bend, she headed down the sloping road, the old bike picking up speed. The gate to Cutler Ranch, its battered white arch with the rusted Circle-C, welcomed her. Lights in the main house cast a warm glow across the front yard in the growing darkness. She knew Marian had made it back to the ranch from Seattle ahead of her. The bike's fat tires crunched the gravel driveway and she pushed her knees into the pedaling, reached the dooryard in a flurry.

Standing down, she felt lightheaded, nearly fell when she dismounted and her sack shifted from her shoulder. Leaning the bike under the eave of the old red barn, she crossed to the back door of the main house. The evening news blared from the TV in the living room and she caught snatches of *"Watergate"* and *"Wounded Knee."* Through the backdoor window, she watched Marian standing at the stove, leaning over the rim of a big pot, stirring, putting the wooden spoon to her lips, blowing, biting a small amount. Her long black hair was tied in a knot on her head and she had on a big, gray flannel shirt and jeans. Lizette pushed the door open.

Marian wheeled around, broke into a big smile. "You're just in time!" She wiped her hands on a towel, rushed to wrap Lizette in a warm hug. "I was in Seattle, at Sandy's. I've been looking for you. Where've you been?"

She pushed Lizette back to look at her. "God. I've missed you." She laughed and clasped Lizette to her again, pushed her away. She searched Lizette's face, noted her stiff grin and wary eyes.

"Tell me everything." She shooed her to the kitchen table with the towel. "Sit down."

Lizette collapsed in a chair by the window and tucked her bag under the table. Marian saw the facial tic working under her right eye, the chipped and dirty fingernails, the broken lace on her worn boot. She saw lean thigh bones under dirty jeans. Her blond hair was broken and dull, matted from sleeping, she guessed.

*The skin on her face is sallow, the color of old pearls,* Marian thought. Small purple veins in the folds beside Lizette's nostrils told of too many nights at the tavern, too many strangers, too many days of wandering the streets without food, her Nordic beauty in tatters. Suppressing her pity, Marian put a bowl of lentils and lamb before Lizette, who looked at her, confused, as if she hadn't ordered it.

"How long since you've eaten?"

Lizette looked out the kitchen window into the yard, scanning the ground along the weathered picket fence for signs of crocus. *Not spring yet*, she thought. "What month is it?"

"What did you eat today?" Marian waited, silence yawned.

"Pfeffernüsse."

"All you've eaten today are cookies?"

"Just one . . . Only a bite. I bought it at the Swedish bakery before I got on the ferry in Anacortes."

"Liz, you can't do that." Marian took short paces in front of the stove, tossing her head, loosening her hair, pulling it back into a bundle at the nape of her neck, releasing it to flow around her shoulders. "You can't stay here if you don't eat. I can't be responsible. Where've you been? Sandy said she hasn't seen you in weeks. Neither have the Dogs. Greg told me."

"Sandy's. Rocket's. The hospital before that. . . . For a couple of months. I don't know how long."

"Well, you're going to collapse if you don't eat." Marian realized she'd upset her and turned to the cupboard and pulled down a wide, flat bowl. She ladled hot lentils and tender lamb chunks into it. She brought the bowl and a board with a half loaf of fresh baked whole-wheat bread to the table. Settling into a chair, Marian fussed with a stick of butter still wrapped in paper, cutting a stiff pat into pieces on a slice of bread. She snuck a glance across the table at the thin woman she'd known since she was a girl. Their parents had been friends. They were raised nearly like sisters, dividing time between Orcas and Seattle, but now Lizette seemed like a broken stranger.

"I'll run some bath water," Marian said between bites. "Want to jump in?"

She nodded OK and nibbled bread. The overhead light bulb caught the blue circles under her eyes and Marian felt the painful intensity of her ordeal, whatever it was. She looked away to shield herself from Lizette's hurt.

Marian got up and went to the bathroom, switched on the light. She'd hung her nursing degrees and midwife certificate from the Frontier Nursing Service in Kentucky above the toilet. She rarely thought about the arduous training, in nursing school at the University of Washington and later in the saddle, riding horseback from holler to holler in the Appalachian Mountains, attending births and doctoring poor families. These framed mementos hung above an Andy Warhol quote her father had cut out of a magazine and thumb-tacked to the wall: *"Having land and not ruining it is the most beautiful art anyone could ever want to own."* Above the light switch she'd taped a quote of her own from Gloria Steinem: *"Childbirth is more admirable than conquest, more amazing than self-defense, and as courageous as either one."* Like faded wallpaper, these things had long since escaped Marian's notice.

The hot water steamed the room as it filled the claw-foot tub. Marian switched on the baseboard heater and it pinged to life. She poured rose-scented oil into the water, the beads breaking up and dispersing as the water shot from the faucet. She got baby shampoo and cocoa butter from the medicine chest above the sink and a stack of thick white towels from the linen closet in the hall. She went into the kitchen. Lizette sat slumped over her bowl. Marian took her by the elbow, grabbed the canvas bag from under the table, led her gently down the hall, toward the smell of soap and roses.

Closing the door, Marian unbuttoned Lizette's green plaid jacket, starting under her chin, working down the row, lifting the cloth between nimble fingers, peeling it back from her shoulders, catching a whiff of wet dog fur, as she took it off. Finding a thin pink and yellow stripped sweater underneath, a dark stain on the front, she rolled the sweater from the bottom over Lizette's head. Her small, round breasts plopped softly on her chest. Leaning in Marian kissed the top of her right nipple, licked its tip. Lizette stood indifferent.

Marian unbuttoned Lizette's jeans and pulled them down to mid-thigh, baring her hard belly and round hip bones, v-shaped blond hair between her legs. Lizette bent her knees, slightly opening her thighs. Marian tugged down and lowered her jeans to the knees and, bending, loosened Lizette's boots, signaled, like a farrier shoeing a horse, for Lizette to lift her foot. She slipped the shoe off, doing the same on the other side. Then she slipped her jeans off the same way, one leg at a time. Lizette stood naked in the blue-tinted light and Marian stepped back, examined her—medically, compassionately, thoroughly.

Lizette turned and put a toe in the water, pulled back from the heat, tried again, put both legs in the tub and settled mantis-like into the bath. Marian soaped her back, outlined the vertebrae with lather, Lizette leaned forward, arched her spine to feel the tracing. Then Marian soaped her neck and chest. Pulling a leg over the side of the tub, she scrubbed Lizette's toes with a brush, clipped her nails, lifted her leg back over the side and lowered it into the water, signaled for the other foot.

Tugging Lizette to her feet, she soaped her shins and calves, scrubbed around her knees with a loofah. Lizette spread her thighs and Marian slipped a handful of lather between her legs, lightly tickling her clit, small and tight. Lizette let out a soft "um" and opened a little wider for the caress, relaxing her knees, lowering into the comforting touch, languorously extending her arms above her head, sliding her hands down her chest to roll her nipples in her fingertips.

"Good," Lizette murmured. The kitchen door slammed and startled her.

Marian helped her sit down in the water before going to see who'd come into the house.

"Hey! Marian? Where the hell are you?"

Greg banged the refrigerator door, followed it up with the hissing sound of a beer bottle popping open.

"What's up?" he said as she entered the kitchen. "You on the can?"

"No," she whispered, sitting down at the table. Greg joined her. "Lizette's here. I was helping her get a bath. Getting her to relax, open up. She's in pretty bad shape. Just got out of Westside. She needs sleep."

"The loony bin, again?" He belched, took another swig. "Chick's a tripper, man. Can't you get rid of her? I hate head cases."

"Lizette's my friend, she's part of me," Marian said firmly. "She needs soothing."

"Look, the Dogs already kicked her sorry ass out, at least twice. Sandy, too . . . Shit."

He got up and went to the stove. "What's in the pot? Smells pretty good."

"How long are you off?" Marian said as she got up, elbowed him away from the pot, filled a bowl and set it on the table. "I thought you were working on the tugs with Rocket."

"I'm working on the *Sally B*. Rocket's on the *Sea Wolf*." He took a swig of beer, rotated the bottle to read the label. "I'm off for a couple of days."

He took a spoonful of lentils, leaned back, "Rocket's comin' up when he gets off. He has some business with Cadillac Carl at the Dog House, but he'll be up after that, probably tomorrow or the next day. Barge they were towing got wedged in the Ballard Locks this morning. Slowed 'em down. He'll be awhile. But, I doubt he's gonna be glad to see the Lizard when he gets here."

"Did he have a thing with Lizette?" she said, alarmed, thinking about the scruffy Dogs.

"Naw. They just fooled around once in a while. You know how Rocket is, always taking care of everybody, bringing in stray cats. I heard the Dogs are the ones who threw her out."

He reached across the table and grabbed Marian's forearm as it rested on the table, grinned at her, lavished his ice blue eyes on her. "But, you're not too weird for me. Kinda kinky, which is cool, know what I mean, mamma?" They brushed lips over the table.

Scraping his bowl, licking the back of the spoon, he got up and went to the refrigerator, got another beer. Marian leaned back in her chair and looked at his shape, *Thin*, she thought, noticed his black hair curling over the collar of his work shirt. *Needs a haircut*, she thought. He stood in the middle of the room and guzzled. She held herself back from going to him and wrapping him up, warming his bones, feeling him respond. *He just needs to clean up*, she thought.

"Have another bowl," she said. "You're getting skinny." She got up, patted his boney behind on her way to the sink, pulled down a plastic pitcher and filled it with hot water, measuring a half cup of apple cider vinegar, dumping it in. She headed down the narrow hall to the bathroom.

"How ya doing in here?" she said as she set the pitcher on the bathroom floor, shut the door. Lizette was on her belly, long legs bent, ankles dangling in air, water barely covering her backside. "Let's wash your hair," she said and Lizette rolled over. "Dunk your head and get your hair wet."

She reached for the shampoo. "OK, now lean back. Rest on my arm and lay your head back. I've got you. Relax."

She cradled Lizette's shoulders in her left arm and lathered with her right. "Close your eyes so you don't get soap in them."

Marian reached for a towel and wiped around Lizette's eyes. "OK, hold your breath. Go under. I'll wash the soap out. Ready? Under you go!"

Lizette sputtered when she came up for air. Water ran off the end of her nose. Marian gently wiped it away. "Lean back some more. I'm going to give you a vinegar rinse. It'll make your hair shiny."

She poured the solution from the pitcher, slowly covering Lizette's head from forehead to the nape of her neck. Sensing a presence, Marian glanced over her shoulder as she held Lizette. Greg was standing in the doorway, big-eyed, leering.

"Get the hell out of here, pervert!" Marian said it with enough force to cause Greg to smartly shut the bathroom door.

She helped Lizette out of the tub and toweled her off, handed her a second towel for her hair. Digging in the canvas bag, Marian found only bits of cloth and paper, some bright colored scarves, a heavy sweater and a picture frame, a stack of sketch books. "Don't you have anything to sleep in?"

Lizette shrugged and Marian pushed up from the floor and headed to her father's bedroom, mostly undisturbed since his death more than a year ago. She flipped on the overhead light where she'd nursed him to the end and pulled a soft flannel shirt from a hanger in his closet. She dug some thermal underwear bottoms out of his dresser drawer, held them up to check the size and decided they'd have to do. In the bathroom, she helped Lizette pull the oversized clothes on and bent her at the waist to finish drying her hair. The temperature outside had dropped toward freezing. Marian wanted her bundled up.

"Where are you sleeping tonight?"

"In the cabin," Lizette said.

"I thought so." Marian frowned. "There's no heat down there. No wood. It's musty, closed up since you left last October. Probably varmints in there now, too. You can sleep here if you want. It's warm. Greg won't mind."

"I just want to be alone," Lizette said flatly. "I've had a lot of people lately."

"OK. Get some rest." Marian stroked Lizette's cheek and she offered her a weak smile. "I'll check on you, but I'm making rounds in the morning. Looking in on my mothers. Should have some births in a few weeks. Want anything from town? Greg wants beer and smokes. I'll pick them up while I'm out."

Lizette shook her head and gathered her bag from the bathroom floor, hugged Marian, smirked at Greg as she passed through the kitchen, grabbed the flashlight from the hook by the back door and headed out.

# EIGHT

SETTING HER BAG ON THE CABIN'S NARROW PORCH,
Lizette felt along the top of the window frame, found the padlock
key, popped the lock and threw the hasp, pushed the door open,
shined the flashlight around. The room was the same as she'd left
it last fall. She'd sensed the beast of winter panting hoarfrost in
the night and fled to Seattle, sick of her work and the self-imposed
confinement.

She saw her large canvases were still tipped against the wall, the
way she'd left them, their faces turned modestly from view. Paints
and brushes lay scattered on the rickety bookshelf in the corner. She
ran her hand across the rough plank table, rubbed the gritty dust
between her fingertips, smelled them, breathed the particulates of
home, sneezed. She wiped her eyes and arranged candles in rusted
jar lids. She lit them with a wooden match, coaxed the seared wicks
to catch fire. The dull yellow light cast a circle around the table, but
didn't penetrate into the corners of the room.

Along the opposite wall, a narrow camp cot sagged under
the slight weight of a faded mattress. The cabin's big windows
faced a small cove. The wood-burning stove, its door gaping

open, stood cold in the corner. She went to the alcove where sheepherders had once stowed gear—boots and jackets, shears and combs for skirting wool—and pulled a big plastic bag from the back. Untying it, she tugged out her sleeping bag, freed a pillow from the bottom, its case delicately edged with Mrs. Cutler's feather-stitched embroidery. She arranged them on the cot, blew out the candles, and lay down.

In the quarter moon's dim light, Lizette looked through the window panes set floor to ceiling, to the inlet where the Salish Sea lapped the beach below the cabin. She scanned the meadow that sloped to the sand and, in the faint moonlight, saw woodland star flowers peeking through the salt grass. She turned on the cot, heard the springs creak, and relaxed into the peace and privacy.

When she woke, it was light outside. A water jug and tube of rice cakes were on the floor beside the cot. On the table she saw a jar of peanut butter and a bear-shaped plastic bottle of honey. *Marian*, she thought, and got up to pee in the porcelain chamber pot by the door. She nibbled at a rice cake, got back into bed, stretched the sleeping bag over her cold shoulders. She slept on the razor's edge of a black pit, unconsciously checking twitches that would send her over the precipice and into convulsive free fall.

She fought it off, but the memory roared in, flattened her on the cot. The Twisted Owl. Men in dark clothes. Smoky haze. She'd looked for Fisher, tried to find him sitting in with the band. In her head, Marvin Gaye blasted "Let's Get It On" from the juke box. She felt hungry. She fought for unconsciousness, tried to submerge, searched for a blank canvas, sleep, couldn't find it.

He touched her thigh, gestured for a dance, clutched her to him. Smelled of grease and sweat. She'd gagged and felt his hands slip below her waistband. Peeking over his shoulder, she saw a man watching them. He caught her eye, leered, pushed toward her in the crowd, she pulled away from her chubby partner, looked for the door. Her mind slipped into a blank place.

Then snatches of angry yelling gripped her in her sleep. *Stabbed! Bleeding! Damn! Call an ambulance!"* She felt crushed as the crowd rushed the door. The chubby guy turned her loose and moved away. She slid to the side wall and threaded her way to the window, found a spot that looked onto the street. A man lay on the ground in the rain, his legs twisted, blood from his belly running thin across the wet sidewalk. Another man staggered to the window, leaned against the glass and braced his hand against the surface, blood leaking through his fingers, smearing the window in front of her. She touched the glass, momentarily fascinated with the carnal, translucent hue, then turned and pushed back through the bodies clogging the tavern's front door.

She went to her table, fished her canvas bag out from under it, and ran for the rear door, paused to listen, catch her breath before turning the knob. The door swung into the alley, in her dream the step down felt like falling from a high ledge. She looked over her shoulder, then up and down the alley to make sure it was clear. She decided to take the long way to the next street, avoid the commotion. Sirens, getting closer, screaming. The buildings looked slimy. Boarded up windows and metal doors stared blindly into the narrow darkness. She floated toward the streetlight at the end, rain sparkling in the glow.

He shoved her from behind, wedged her into a doorway, black overcoat dropping around her, hand clamped over her mouth. He snapped her head back, put his head beside her cheek, breath smelling like rotten fish. He ripped down her loose jeans, spread her legs with his knees. She flashed on his sure moves, knew he'd done this before, screamed *"Help!"* into his thick, calloused fingers. He pulled her sideways, hit her open-handed, full force on the side of her face, stunned her silent, shoved her chest against the metal door.

She shook it off, turned, put her arms up to fight. A jab to her side. A bone snap took her breath away. Flattened against the door, hips pulled out, head banging steel, he ripped her. Something, anvil-heavy, swung against her head, in her dream she sank beneath the water.

Cold, greasy moss on cracked pavement against her cheek. A wad of chewing gum by her nose. She puked, tried to get up. Before she blacked out, she watched a dog lapping her vomit, then felt it licking her bare thighs, its tongue warm and comforting.

Her own screaming and crying startled her awake in the dark. Sweating, heart pounding, she got up from the cot and lit a candle with shaky hands, drank some water and went to her large canvases and turned their faces to the flickering light. The sounds in her head slowly quieted and her hands steadied. The hard, greenish fluorescent light of the hospital faded from her mind, the probing questions stopped.

She put her big canvas on a rickety easel, saw the empty places in her painting that cried for color—vermilion, ochre and verdant greens, azure. Tree branches tapped impatient fingers on the cabin's roof as she cried and rummaged through her bag, she found the pill bottle Dr. Finch gave her at the hospital, poured water into a chipped mug. She fished out a powdery pill, threw it back, took a swig from the mug, swallowed, then blew out the candle and got back in bed, shivering.

In the echoing well of sleep, Lizette heard, "You've been out for days." Marian stood over her. Stretching, Lizette mumbled, opened her eyes and hoisted herself onto an elbow.

"I brought chamomile tea and scrambled duck eggs," Marian said, motioning to a plate and thermos on the table. "Wake up before they get cold. I want to do Sun Salutations with you. This yoga teacher came to town a few weeks ago and gave some classes at the Grange Hall. I want to show you some of his asanas. They're really far out."

Unzipping the sleeping bag, Lizette put her feet on the floor and looked resentfully at the bleary figure moving too quickly around the cabin, plaid shirt, tights and high-top work boots, wild hair.

"Give me a break. I just woke up."

"Did you take your medication?" Marian said, twirling slowly toward Lizette. "Let me see the bottle." Lizette stood and yawned.

Marian grabbed her own wrist and arched her arm overhead, stretching to the left, doing the same on the other side, folding forward, pulling her head to her knees. She straightened and took the pill bottle Lizette offered, went to the windows to read the label.

The lithium dosage was mild. *Maybe not too deep into her mania,* Marian thought, *or whatever the hell it is that makes her go crazy. Maybe I can help straighten her out, get her back to work.* She looked around at the canvases and it struck her that she hadn't heard Lizette laugh in a long time. She flipped through her memory but couldn't conjure the sound.

"Poland built me a platform on the beach," Marian said and turned back to Lizette. "It's a few feet off the sand so it stays dry. Great for yoga. Wind blowing from the water helps with breath." She pinched her nostrils and exhaled noisily through her open mouth.

Setting a wooden fruit box on end, Lizette scooted it up to the table and, elbows propped, she began to eat, ignoring Marian. The eggs had gone cold, but she shoveled. Marian dropped onto the wobbly wooden stool on the opposite side.

"Where's Poland?" Lizette asked and watched Marian wrap her short legs around the stool's nicked and paint-splattered legs.

*Still sits up straight*, Lizette thought. *Like a kid reminded at the dinner table. She hasn't changed, still a goody two shoes, looking down on everyone, thinking she can fix them and tell them what to do.*

"Poland's up in the east pasture," Marian said, getting up to look out the window. "The lambs are dropping. He says my father would have wanted us to keep running sheep so we keep a small flock. I told him it's too much work. Market prices are lousy right now."

Pulling up onto her toes, stretching and scanning the water's surface, Marian said, "Looks like an orca's hunting in the strait. I see a dorsal fin."

Turning back to Lizette, she babbled on, "One of the ewes prolapsed this morning while lambing. Greg went up to the pasture with our new dog Tucker to catch her and put her in the jug for safekeeping. I'll take a look later. We may have to bottle feed a few of the babies. You up for that?"

Lizette looked at her, head aching, indifferent.

"You used to like that job. And we need to bake bread. We're completely out, nothing in the freezer." Marian got up to pace. "It's cold in here. I'll have Poland bring down some stove wood."

"What's today?" Lizette said, staring into the plate, pushing at the food scraps with a bent fork, and feeling overwhelmed.

"Thursday."

"When did I get here?"

"Tuesday." Marian looked perplexed. "You've been asleep for two days. It's the middle of March. You've been gone about six months. What did you go through at the hospital this time? You seem totally out of it."

"Well." Lizette held her head in her hands and wrapped her fingers around her skull, picked her words before she spoke, skirting what really happened to avoid Marian's horrified response and inevitable probing. She couldn't talk about it now, maybe never.

"This skinny old woman, must have been seventy. She was in the room next to mine. She kept yelling in Swedish, said she was having a baby. She took off her hospital gown and got on her bed and pulled up her knees. Like this."

Lizette went to the cot and lay on her back, pulled her knees to her chest in a tuck, stretched out, stared at the cabin's soot-covered ceiling.

"The nurses didn't know what she was saying. I could understand a little because she talked like my grandmother. She rocked back and forth, like this, and pushed. It went on all night. Panting. Grunting. Wailing. When it was finally born she balled up her hospital gown and rocked it as if it was a baby, singing lullabies and stuff."

Lizette got up and went to the chamber pot, squatted, peed. Marian turned her back, looking out at the water.

"Thank God she didn't think it was twins." Lizette said. Marian snorted, shook her head in wonder.

Lizette got back in bed and continued in a flat tone, propping her head in her hand.

"This other woman started screaming she was on fire. It went on all morning. She started right after breakfast. She was in the day room. They were watching cartoons on TV and she just went off. Finally they got some male orderlies and a couple of nurses and carried her to the shower room. She was kicking and screaming. They put her on the tile floor and turned on the cold water. That put the fire out. She stopped yelling, just lay there and slept until after lunch."

"Were you in a private room?" Marian said, studying Lizette for damage, gathering her hair into a pony tail with both hands and wrapping a rubber band around the bunch. She stepped closer and examined Lizette's skin and long neck, looking for puffiness, lymph node swellings, trying to assess the physical impact of the hospital stay, making metal notes like she was charting a patient.

"Yes, the whole time . . . well, not at first," Lizette paused to collect her memory. "I was by myself, then they brought this young one in, hair all black and curly, standing on end. She lay on the bed on the other side of the room. Put her face to the wall. That was OK with me. I fell asleep reading. When I woke up she was standing over the toilet bowl dangling dental floss with a tiny safety pin tied to the end."

"What was that about?"

"Said she was fishing."

Lizette pressed her lips together to keep from smiling. She hoisted her long legs over the side of the cot, leaned forward to tell the story.

"I looked at her and her eyes were like BBs, hard and black. Evil. I saw it. Teeth like a shark. Really bad chi, scary."

"Did you tell the nurses?"

"No. I took ripped pages from the book I was reading and crumpled them up on the floor. I'd found matches hidden under the mattress when I first got there and got them out, set the paper on fire."

"What?" Marian said wide-eyed.

"The girl started yelling and freaking out," Lizette went on, rocking on the side of the cot, laughing in soft tinkles that started Marian giggling. "She called me a crazy bitch and said, 'What the hell're you doing?' I told her I was building a fire. She goes, 'What for?'

I said, "To cook the fish when you catch it."

"My God, Lizzie. How did you think of that?" Marian crossed the small room to the cot and hugged Lizette. "What happened to the fisherman?"

"They told me later she always tries crazy stuff like that to freak-out roommates so she can get rid of them and get a private room. They knew all about her. She has had multiple involuntary admissions."

"She stomped out the fire and called the nurses." Lizette pulled the neck of her flannel shirt across her lips to contain her laughter. "She told them I was nuts and she wanted to be moved to a private room."

"What'd the nurses do?"

"They took her out and put her in with a girl they kept in diapers because she rubs shit on herself. A couple of days later the black-haired one slashed the baby girl with broken glass. I think they finally took her to jail because she was too crazy to keep in the nuthouse."

Marian burst into laughter. Lizette offered a sly grin because she knew Marian would misread her smile and be satisfied by her stories, wouldn't probe any deeper.

"Well. It's over now," Marian said and sighed. "You're safe here."

Marian picked up a hair brush from the shelf and lifted Lizette's wispy hair, made quick swipes at the ends to get the snarls out, then took long strokes down the length of her hair from the scalp to the middle of her back. Lizette pulled away from the strokes, her eyes watering from the pull. "When do you have to go back to see the doctor?"

"Never."

Marian frowned, figured they could call later and find out.

"Let's go stretch." She headed for the door. "Get your sandals on. You need to get the kinks out."

The sun spread across the damp skirt of the meadow below the cabin, soft wind breathed through the grasses. Lizette, towering above Marian's petite, round shape, trudged to the platform, groggy and still sore from the beating in the alley. Sometimes her rib ached and her vaginal muscles went spastic at odd moments. She climbed the crude stairs at the platform's side. Marian sat in Lotus position and began to breathe loudly through her nose.

"I'm doing Ocean Breath – Ujjayi Pranayama," Marian said, hissing air through her sinuses. She sat on the platform facing the sea and Shaw Island in the distance, its outline gray-blue in the mist.

Lizette kicked off her sandals, sat down, put the soles of her feet together and bounced her knees. The waves roiled and spread water across the sand in front of them.

Open to the morning," Marian said. "Let it dissolve your barriers, embrace the healing."

She pushed forward and stretched her arms over her folded legs and missed Lizette's scowl. Marian slipped back into *Child's Pose*, her back lifting and falling with easy, noisy breath. Lizette followed, keeping an eye on her. They pushed into *Downward Facing Dog* together, pulled forward into *Plank*. Lizette collapsed into a rumpled pile when she tried *Crocodile*.

"Go to *Child's Pose*," Marian instructed like a fussy schoolmarm and Lizette was on the verge of telling her where to stick it. "It's a recovery position. It'll take you a while to regain your strength and be able to do *Crocodile* again."

Lizette huffed as she pulled back, rested her hips on her heels, felt the rub of sit bones on heel bones, her pelvis aching. She heard panting and looked sideways. A black and white sheep dog, tongue flapping, bounded across the sand and up the steps to the platform, jumping up on Marian, who was standing one-legged in *Tree Pose*.

"Hey, Tucker dog," Marian said, tipping sideways, bending to scratch behind the dog's ears, playfully clamping his muzzle and letting him wiggle free. "What're you doin' here?"

She saw Greg waving to her from the edge of the trees and checked her watch and saw she was late for her rounds. That's what she called her midwife visits to the pregnant women she helped prepare for home births. Marian pulled on her boots.

"This could take a while," she said. "I've got a first-time mom. She's young and scared, looks like she's going to deliver early. I've got to hike up to her place. Hippies! They built a lopsided cabin up on the mountain." She patted Tucker on the head. "She and the father are clueless."

Lizette watched the two bounce across the meadow to Greg, who stood with his hands on his hips, whistling a command to Tucker and turning his back on Marian as she caught up with him. They disappeared into the trees and Lizette stretched out on the platform, relished the solitude.

# NINE

EYES CLOSED, lulled by the water's rhythmic slosh, she awoke on the platform and heard a goose honk and, fading away, the sound of a ferry rumbling toward San Juan Island. In the distance, a truck's engine growled, a gull mocked. Sounds pulsed up through her body and exploded out the top of her head. Her left eye throbbed, her arm ached, her pelvis burned. When she couldn't take it anymore, she sat up and looked out on the vast, undulating sea, felt queasy.

At first it was just a black line cutting through the water. Then she noticed the slight bend at the tip. As the line got closer and changed direction, she realized it was a fin, attached to a broad back, an orca making for the beach, its dorsal like a knife blade aimed directly at her. She flapped her hands rapidly to release energy, put on her sandals, and hurried back to the cabin, looking over her shoulder at the orca's humped back and the vapor puffs from its blowhole as it closed in on the beach.

Settling into her cot, out of breath, she pulled the sleeping bag over her and confronted her fear of the orca, as if watching it from underwater. Her ribs hurt when she moved on the narrow bed. Memories washed over her. She saw herself, stepped inside the memory, saw the flat, steely sky from the small window in her hospital room with one eye, the other swollen shut and bandaged. They said the vaginal tears would heal. Voices imparted these details with words that clacked like marbles, random sounds popping together in her head. She submerged, drifted from them to the place below, the place protected by "Watches Underwater."

"Are you hearing voices?" In her half dream, the doctor sat beside Lizette's bed, clipboard on his knees, tweedy and reeking of cigarette smoke. She clicked her tongue and turned to the wall. "We see you've been admitted to the mental health facility at Westside Hospital in the past. We have those records. Can you tell us something about that experience?"

He tried to gently draw out an explanation for her present condition, her past problems, but it felt like she was at the dentist, the doctor working without Novocain, fingers down her throat, indifferent to her pain. The toxicology report showed no drugs in her system when she was admitted, he told her. Her anger flared. She turned and showed it to him, showed him the flames behind her good left eye.

The cops tried to take a report, sent over a nice young officer in a crisp uniform and sparkly badge. He stood by her bedside and spoke slowly, in baby words, like she was a dimwit. He tried for a description of the suspect – height, weight, hair color – tried to establish a motive, figure out if she was somehow involved in the stabbing in front of the Twisted Owl that night, but she couldn't give him anything concrete. After a half hour, he gave up.

"Miss Karlson?" Lizette did not respond. "You've got a visitor," the nurse said sweetly, the fat one with the gaping buttons across her big tits. "Are you up to a visit, dear? It's your father."

Lizette turned and stared at the woman, focused on her chubby knees, the run in her white stocking, and leaned over to the bedside table. She picked up a small plastic water pitcher and hurled it, hit the door frame just as the nurse cleared the threshold, splattering water into the hallway. Lizette heard them paging her doctor over the loudspeaker and started screaming. The nurses sent her father away and threw out the flowers he'd brought.

She took a shot of sedative in the butt while they cleaned up the puddle, two orderlies standing by for safety, just in case. They said she was a danger to herself and others, called her "gravely disabled," which she knew meant they thought she was crazy.

They took her by ambulance to Westside Hospital, a locked facility in Ballard, told her she'd be there seventy-two hours. She liked the ambulance ride. Colors flashed by like she was riding a carnival tilt-a-whirl, she remembered feeling exhilarated to be moving again, moving anywhere. The water on Lake Union reflected light like rumpled tinfoil, the leaf-barren trees twisted into wire sculptures in December. When she got to Westside, some of the staff recognized her, called her by name while she was being processed.

They laughed, she remembered, patted her on the arm like being there was no big thing. They medicated her, and put her in a private room. She slept a lot at first. She agreed to stay, stabilize, as they called it. She wanted to escape the grind of the streets—the cold, the hustle, didn't care where she ended up.

After a couple of weeks, she dressed herself in a bathrobe and sketched on her bed. They tried to draw her out to mingle with the other women, join the group activities, but she refused. She met with Dr. Finch, a silly woman, Lizette thought, but harmless enough, as long as she didn't ask too many personal questions. She didn't feel like reliving her childhood or her mother's death, or the assault in the alley for the benefit of a prying stranger.

Then one day a nurse popped her head in, said Finch was waiting, told her to dress, gather her belongings. Lizette pulled her things together, it wasn't much. They tripped the door lock and she hurried down the stairs. Outside Dr. Finch's office she knocked, tried the doorknob. She could see a dark shadow moving on the other side of the door's wavy glass. As she took her hand away, the door opened and Dr. Finch stood there holding a blue plastic watering can, wisps of gray hair escaping from under the bifocals on her head. She waved with the can for Lizette to come in.

"Sit," she said, nodding toward the center of the small room where a wooden chair was pushed against the big desk. Lizette had sat there many times, but today noticed the chair's shining seat, polished over time by the rub of many twisting bottoms. She set her big canvas bag on the floor, propped it against the desk.

Seated, she braided her fingers and looked down to study the bare threads where the carpet pile was worn from the scuffle of troubled feet. The doctor finished watering the wilted plants along the window sill and settled into her coffee-colored leather chair. She lowered her glasses and peered at Lizette over the rims before scanning her file.

"You're being released from this hospital for the third time in five years," the doctor said flatly. "You've only been with us about six weeks, but in the future a court might not be so lenient about length of stay. Do you know that?"

Lizette lowered her head. A smile sneaked across her lips at the absurdity.

"This is no joke. You have to take your medication, consistently." Dr. Finch leaned back in her chair, leveled her look at Lizette. "You can't stroll around half naked in rough-neck bars twittering like a bird. The medication will help keep you stable, but you may experience tremors and tics, rhythmic contractions of the soft palate, slight nausea at times."

Lizette hung her head as if in prayer.

"This isn't hard, Elizabeth. Look at me," she commanded. Lizette lifted her head, but hooded her eyes.

*Bird-brained bitch*, Lizette thought.

"Take one pill a day and enjoy the rest of your life," Finch said. "There's no reason you need to come back here. You need outside support and counseling, that's all."

She rocked forward and pushed a pill bottle across the desk toward Lizette.

"Thousands of people suffer from destabilizing conditions and they're able to hold jobs, lead relatively normal lives," the doctor continued. "It says here you've been approved for public assistance, that the checks will be sent to your father's house. Is that where you'll be staying?"

"Yes," Lizette said, looking out the window. She'd had a couple of months to think about what to do. She'd go out to Orcas Island, stay with Marian again. She'd watched gray clouds gathering above the treetops, winds rattling the branches, making way for rain.

"I get my county checks at my father's house. That's how we've done it since the first time."

"Do you mean the time you broke out all the windows in your father's home?" Finch waited, tapped the desk lightly with her fingertips.

Lizette nodded, but did not mean that time. She meant the time before that when she'd let her mother's canaries out, freed them from the cages that hung from hooks in the kitchen. They had warbled pitifully, begging for freedom. She'd rolled over in her bed one morning, pulled her pillow around her head and still the canaries' lamenting pierced her ears, twisted her heart and she couldn't stand it.

That morning she'd released them, watched their bright yellow bodies fly into the welcoming green leaves of the apple tree in the backyard and disappear over the neighbor's fence. Her mother had freaked out, said canaries were supposed be caged so they'd sing. Lizette called her a Nazi and began chirping, running around the kitchen, grabbing dishes, shattering them on the floor. That was when her mother ordered her out of the house. That was the first time they decided she was crazy, the first time they locked her up when they found her living on the street. After that they stopped chasing her.

Eventually, her father said he'd convinced his wife to allow Lizette to continue getting mail at their address, to stop by occasionally so they could see her. Her mother barely spoke to her, treated her like she had some disease that was catching. She hated the pitying, disappointed look on her mother's face, the suffering on her father's, couldn't stand being around them, preferred the freedom of the streets to their suffocating, self-motivated concerns.

"Well, you're going to need to check in somewhere," the doctor said. "Your progress needs to be monitored or you'll turn up here again. Frankly, you may not be free to go next time. Here's a list of private counselors."

"What am I supposed to do with it?"

"Don't interrupt. I know you understand. I'll expect to meet with you again in ninety days, before the pills run out, and we can confirm your private treatment plans. We've talked about all this before. All I can offer now is: Good luck. You're free to go."

Lizette saw herself pushing up from the chair, gathering the straps of her bag, dropping the pill bottle into it. She left the office, pulled the door firmly closed. In the hall, she looped the bag over her shoulder and headed toward the stairs. She remembered that she held back from running, tried not to draw attention from the staff, making for Westside's main doors and the bright light beyond. On the way out she'd heard banging on the ward, someone whining loudly, growling between breaths. She nearly stumbled as she rushed outdoors, charging for the green lawn outside, running across the wet grass, her bag flapping against her side, laughing, laughing, choking, stopping to bend over and catch her breath, coughing, laughing some more, running.

She remembered she huddled in the bus shelter down the block from the hospital and watched a light rain fall, turned to study the leaves of the hedge that protected a garden and a neat white house beyond, where she guessed normal people lived. The leaves of the hedge reached toward each other, but did not touch, mist gathered in the leaf creases, collected into heavy drops and fell, splattering like mercury across the sidewalk. She'd dug in the bottom of her bag for change and got on, transferred to a trolley going downtown. She let the memories fade and slept.

Sweating, she got up now and peered through the cabin windows, moonlight glimmering the sea, guessing the time—about midnight, she thought, surprised that she'd slept again. She scanned the sea's riffles, looked for the hunter. Embers glowed in the stove, cast an orange sheen over the room. She noticed neatly cut wood stacked beside the stove. She went and opened the stove door, fed the dampening coals a few sticks. Flames licked the edges of the neatly split wood.

Poland, she thought, comforted that he'd watched out for her, and went to her large canvas and turned it to face the room. Sitting on the rickety stool, resting her arms on her thighs, she studied the painting. After a while the gaps began calling to her, begging for color. She got up and gathered brushes, looked into tins, shook oil and thinner cans, fished her mother's palette knife from the bottom of her canvas bag. On a square of thin plywood, she mixed a small amount of paint, working it to the right fluidity. Feeling the brush handle in her fingers, she twirled it slowly to balance the paint load. Leaning into the canvas, she stroked the color into the places it wanted to go, got up, stood back, went to the stove, added a couple more logs to the fire. Humming, she sat back down, considered, listened to the white spaces, waited for the call and mixed manganese violet on her palette, feeling the color's richness like a weight on her fingertips.

Sometime during the musing and mixing, dawn arrived, flattening the sea to sheet-metal gray, deckling its edges with iridescent black. On the beach, black cormorants skittered along the sand. A seal's sleek head broke the water's surface and periscoped the cove. Lizette wiped her hands and went to the window, tried to make contact with the creature. He slipped below the metallic surface, popped up, twitched his whiskers, blinked. Further out, she saw the straight black line heading for the cove. The orca blew steam, glided, disappeared. Lizette watched, looking for the seal, scanning the water's surface. Glancing down at the beach, she saw it had hauled out and waddled across the sand, plopped into its own puddle of fat, rolled over to accept the sun's early warmth on its belly.

Lizette watched the orcas' dorsal fin cutting the water's surface, shifting direction, relieved the little monk seal was safe. She giggled to herself at the memory of her father making lunch, tickling under her chin, thinking it would be fun to tickle the seal, feed him tuna fish. She pulled on a jacket, put the flashlight into her pocket out of habit, and headed up to the main house.

# TEN

GREG SLOUCHED BAREFOOT IN A KITCHEN CHAIR, his leg hooked over the edge of the table. Coarse ankle hair poked out around the ragged hem of his jeans. He grunted when Lizette walked in. Jimi Hendrix blasted "Purple Haze" from the stereo in the living room, the sound rocking the kitchen. He raised his head and focused on her through narrowed eyes. *Satyr*, she thought. *Half goat.* She recoiled from his smell.

"You finally up?"

She plucked energy from the pit of her stomach and stiffened her spine to deflect his disrespectful gaze. "Where's Marian?"

"Still at the birth. Some half-breed squaw. Said it could be a while, when she called."

He put his foot on the floor and twisted in the chair to look at Lizette, assessing her body in a way that made her cover her breasts with her arm.

"Just hope they pay her. She can't take care of them for free. Nothin's free, man. You know?"

"Where's Poland?"

"How the hell should I know? He said something about helping his wife get ready for a potlatch, some kind of family reunion. Abaya's always out digging roots and weaving baskets. We got guys walking around on the moon for chrissakes and she's carving bones? It's the goddamned 70s, man. You gotta wonder. Know what I mean?"

Lizette had known Poland and Abaya since she was a child. Their ways made perfect sense to her. What scared her and made the ground feel like it was shifting away from her feet was that beasts like Greg existed. She didn't know how to speak to him, it was as if she were watching a bear at the zoo, fascinated by him in a frightened way. She twittered at him, clicked her tremoring tongue, glanced over his head to the windows that faced the front garden. She caught him smirking as she cast her gaze beyond him.

"Anyway," Greg offered, "Poland said they're getting ready for some big Lummi thing. You'd think the guy would do some work around here. Marian pays him enough."

He got up and went to the refrigerator for another beer. Lizette moved aside, leaned against the sink.

"I heard him tell Marian a bunch of war canoes are paddling over from Bellingham for the party. They could save the sweat and take the ferry. He said they're gonna do the whole thing—funeral, couple of weddings, baby christenings, dance, swap meet. A lot of food and camping out."

Popping the cap, he tossed the bottle opener into the sink with a clatter, took a long pull on the bottle, bobbling his eyes at her as the slug of beer went down.

She watched Greg like a dangerous animal and thought about one day last fall, before she cut out for Seattle, when she'd overheard him speak rudely to Poland while they were working in the barn. Lizette was sitting in the sun, outside the door, sketching, half listening to them talk as they cleaned sheep pens. The old man ended the exchange by walking away from Greg and came to stand outside the barn near her, raking his thick silver hair, tugging on his long goatee.

"Coyote shows off to girls, juggling his eyeballs," Poland said out loud to no one and spat. He saw her and went on, "One day he threw one so high it stuck in the sky. Now it winks first when the sun sets. It's the light that guides drunks and lazy bones to the tavern."

That's how she pictured Greg now, his ice-blue eyes bobbing in their sockets. She saw coyote—yellow teeth, mangy coat, snapping jaw. Shaken by the strength of her vision, she turned away from him and opened the refrigerator, grabbed a bottle of milk. Jimi Hendrix sang "All Along the Watchtower" from the living room and went into a guitar riff. She took a hunk of Jarlsberg cheese from the shelf and got a knife from the drawer.

"No bread," Greg said, holding his arms and hands as if playing an electric guitar, leaning into the riff. "Marian says you're gonna help make some. You could get started without her, you know? I love the smell of bread better 'an I love the smell of pussy."

Lizette gagged, turned her back to him, and poured milk into a glass, took big swallows, as if he might come and snatch it from her.

He worked his hands like drumsticks, keeping time to the beat, tapping an imaginary cymbal, picking up his air guitar again, smug about having bugged her.

"You know my man Rocket? Works the tow boats with me?" he needled her.

"I know him," she said softly.

"He might come up this weekend, if he can lay off Sandy," he said and laughed sly like. "My man likes his China white, if you dig me? Helluva jones." Greg looked straight at her. "You holding anything or did they take your stash when they put you in the loony bin?"

Lizette clicked her tongue, pulled her head into her shoulders, trembled at the thought of Cadillac Carl. Jimi Hendrix sang "Hey Joe." Greg looked smug and the silence under the music hardened to steel.

"Where's Tucker?" she asked, unbending, turning to face him.

"The dog?" Lizette nodded. "How should I know? Probably chasing ewe," he said and cackled. "Get it? Ewe?" Lizette felt sick.

A truck came scrunching up the driveway. She caught the sound first, then a flash of green from the window. Poland opened the kitchen door and scraped his boots on the mat, stepped inside. Looking up at her from under his shag of gray hair, he smiled, the creases deepening around his eyes. "You come like crocus in the spring," he said, grabbing her hands, dancing her around, making her giggle.

"I haven't seen any yet," she said.

"It won't be long. Already blue-eyed Marys and buttercups are popping up in the hot spots."

"Where you been, chief?" Greg stretched his arms overhead, interrupting Poland. The old man veiled his eyes and squinted, as if trying to see a speck of dirt.

"Errands for the wife, checked on Marian at the birth. Dropped off some fresh sword fern for the mother to chew. Abaya says it helps things along. Marian says maybe a couple more days before the baby comes. She has everybody at the house calmed down now. False alarm. She's cooking beans and soothing the mother. They're just kids. He works at the marina. Good with engines, but don't know what to do about babies. It was quiet when I left."

"Shit," Greg said, bending to pull boots from under the table, slipping his bare feet in and tugging on the laces. He stood to leave and Lizette noticed how thin he'd become, how strung out, and flashed on Fuzzy and the Dog House.

"I didn't come all the way out here from Seattle to sit by myself. I could've stayed in town with the Dogs, gotten in some hitting and fielding practice. It's almost spring, ya know, baseball season?"

"I need a tooth brush," Lizette said.

"Yeah. Well, don't use mine. It's the blue one on the back of the sink," Greg said, heading for the back door. "Use Marian's. It's the yellow one in the holder."

"OK," she said, taking a box of baking soda from the shelf and going into the bathroom, locking the door.

"Go easy on the toilet paper, huh?" Greg yelled at her before he went out. "Septic tank's backing up. Marian needs to get somebody out here to pump it." The back door slammed.

Lizette took the tooth brush from the holder, shook baking soda on the bristles, and scrubbed her teeth, swished with water from her cupped hand.

She replaced Marian's tooth brush and picked up the blue one on the back of the sink. She went to the toilet and squatted, using it to scrub the mineral ring that had accumulated at the water line in the bowl, reaching down for the brown stains at the bottom. She stood and put the tooth brush back where she'd found it.

"Do you want to come see our garden?" Poland asked as she came into the kitchen. "Abaya's putting in lettuce and bedding flowers for the summer bouquets. Right now we've only got carrots and radishes, broccoli and chard for the farmer's market. Tomorrow morning will be the first market of the year. Probably the whole island will show up to buy, if it don't rain. Not too much is ready for market yet. Come on."

Lizette pulled one of Marian's old jackets off a hook on the back porch and hopped into the cab of Poland's rusty truck, the passenger-side visor flopping loosely as they hit ruts. They bounced along, both of them scanning the woods and meadows for the tell-tale signs of spring.

"Lavender!" Lizette shouted as they rounded a curve. The slope beside them was thickly carpeted in dusty gray-green spikes that would flower purple across the hillside the moment it warmed it up.

"Abaya worked on the lavender farm last summer, helped with harvest," Poland said, a hint of pride in his voice. "She did it for no pay, too, so she could get the boxes of soap and lotion, must have got a hundred of em.

"Why'd she want all the boxes?"

"For the potlatch. We called one to honor our sons and our family."

"Greg told me," she said, hating to mention his name.

"Something's wrong with that guy." Poland frowned. "If Hal Cutler was alive, he'd run him off. Trash. I don't like him around the place, around Marian. She's a good girl."

"He's a Dog," Lizette started to explain, thought better of it. "He uses drugs."

Poland didn't comment, but Lizette could tell he'd tucked the information away, confirmed his own suspicions.

"Abaya has been working on the potlatch for a long time, making baskets, carving, weaving, beading," he said, changing the subject. "She never stops."

"Why'd you call a potlatch?"

"It's been a long time since the tribe called for one."

He gripped the steering wheel tighter and leaned forward, studying the winding road he drove every day, swerving to miss potholes. "You know we lost Johnny, our middle boy, in a logging accident a couple of years ago. That's three sons lost to accidents, one went to Vietnam."

Lizette looked down, bit her lip. The whole island heard what happened to their sons. She said nothing about Raven being in Seattle.

"After Johnny, that's when Abaya wanted a potlatch," Poland said. "She said it was time."

"She couldn't stand the pain anymore, you mean." Lizette looked at him sideways to see how her comment went down.

Rounding a curve, the driveway to the Moran Mansion branched off from the road, the massive slate gray roof and white sides visible through the trees. Built around the turn of the century by the mayor of Seattle, the house was known to locals not just for its size and view of the water, but also for the famous people who came for lavish parties. Sometimes they'd drive their fancy cars and use the ferry or they'd come by boat, tying up their yachts at the harbor below the big house, causing a flutter of conversation at the hardware store the next day.

"Suzie Two Deer used to work there as a maid," Poland said as they flew by the entrance. "Says they have an organ in there with big pipes and carved wood from ships. Old man Moran built ships in Seattle. You know?"

Lizette nodded, having heard the story of the Morans many times since she was a girl, locals never failing to mention the estate's history. She'd seen and heard the organ because the estate had been a hotel and restaurant for as long as she knew.

"Very rich people go there," Poland continued like she was a tourist. "The place sits on my grandfather's old summer hunting ground."

Lizette knew this, too.

"The deer liked to browse the grasses on the flats. But, now it's a big hotel. Robert Redford, the movie cowboy came once."

"Did you meet him?" She stared out the truck's window as trees and water whizzed by, bored by the conversation.

"Naw, but me and Abaya saw one of his movies once in Bellingham."

Lizette knew they were close to Poland's farm when they came to a long line of split rail fence. She'd watched Poland and his sons build the weaving fence in sections over several summers. Then the white, single-story house came into view. They turned into the dirt driveway and followed the fence line to the dooryard. Smoke puffed from the chimney and Abaya stood on the front steps in a blue-flowered apron, abalone shell earrings the size of saucers hung from her stretched lobes. She held her arms out and Lizette released herself into the warmth of Abaya's embrace.

# ELEVEN

**IN THE MORNING,** Lizette and Abaya went to the garden. Abaya bent over a raised bed, the dirt boxed in by rough logs, and plucked weeds, tender in this early season. She worked her knobby fingers along the rows of green radish leaves, pulled up a big one, knocked off the dirt, offered it to Lizette. "Easter egg," she said and moved on with her weeding.

Lizette took the pink and white root, wiped it on her jacket, put it in her mouth and crunched, feeling the sweet, hot taste explode on her tongue.

"When will these be ready for market?"

"By Easter, if it warms up and don't rain so much," Abaya said, looking at the dark clouds rolling overhead. "Easter comes late this year, that's better. Vegetables have more time to get big." She pulled another radish, studied it. "They're like painted eggs." She laughed. "Good for kids. The colors mix them up. They think candy, but no."

"Poland says you're almost ready for the potlatch," Lizette said, watching her weed.

"Not yet. The store house's filled up, but there's still a lot to do."

"How many people are coming?"

"Hard to say." Abaya stood and stretched her back. "At first only a few people said they'd come. That was a couple of years ago, when Poland first put the word out. Now, I don't know. The tribal office in Bellingham tells me hundreds. Maybe some people will come by canoe from Queen Charlotte Islands in B.C. And, I hear some cousins in Alaska might show up."

"Wow." Lizette looked around at the garden and small cottage. "Where're you going to put them? They can't all stay here."

"No, not here. Our pasture goes down to the water in the back. If you follow around the shore you come to the state park. There's camping there. I already talked to the park people. They're going to set aside space. Poland's getting those outhouses they move around."

"Porta Johnnies?"

Abaya shrugged. "He had to get a permit from the county. Made a road around the meadow for the truck to deliver 'em. See, over there." She waved her arm in the direction of the open, grassy field. "He made a big fire ring there and he's building a sweat lodge, too."

At the end of the garden, Lizette saw the berry trellises and walked to them, lifted the leaves with the back of her hand, careful of the thorns, looked to see if any raspberries were ripe, but knew it was too early. The vines were blooming and, even in the chill, a few bees darted in and out collecting pollen.

"Let's go see the storehouse," Abaya said, an edge of excitement in her voice. She walked out of the garden, closed the gate behind them. The white barn beyond the house had once been used to milk cows. Sliding the door back, they entered the darkness. When Lizette's eyes adjusted, she saw hundreds of cardboard boxes stacked in all the milking stalls, more along the back wall and in the hayloft.

"Amazing!" Lizette spun around in the old dairy barn, taking in all the corners. "What's in all these boxes?"

"Blankets, baskets, medicine bags, straw dolls for children, flutes, drums, spirit charms."

"Poland said you have lavender."

"Yeah." Abaya drew her lips into a pucker and smiled modestly around the edges. "You bet. Lots. For the ladies. The boxes have little flowers on top and purple ribbons. Inside is soap and cream. Pretty. My cousin's daughter is getting married while everyone is here. They're going to spend the wedding night over at the Moran Hotel. I'm giving the bridesmaids the lavender boxes, and some other special ladies. The minister's coming from Bellingham."

"What's in the tool room?"

"Tools," she said, rolling her eyes. "What else you'd expect? Gold? My old husband still needs to work around this falling-down place. He's a lazy bones, driving all over the island, getting in everybody's business like an old woman. I warn him, but he don't listen."

"But," she said, shifting back to an excited tone. "The good stuff's in the house. We got totems and scrimshaw, paintings, special baskets. Drums. Masks. Button robes and Chilikat blankets. Some things are very old. We'll only show them, not give them away. Poland will bring out his copper shield. It's very old, from his father and his grandfather and before that way back. You break off small pieces and give em to the big guys, the ones with lots of sons. That's Poland's job."

Walking around, looking at the stacks of boxes, Abaya seemed almost girlish. "This gathering is to honor my sons," she said, sounding fragile. "I had four sons. Now they're all gone. Dead or lost."

Lizette kept quiet about Raven, honored her promise again not to say she'd seen him or tell anyone that he'd gone to Wounded Knee and not mention the trouble he and Dennis Banks and the rest of the American Indian Movement were having with the FBI.

She watched Raven's tiny mother, her big earrings bobbing, wipe her hands on her apron, pace and embrace the depth of her loss. Lizette could barely stand to watch her.

"The spirits have taken all of them and this potlatch will honor that," Abaya said, walking softly, her feet barely disturbing the floor's fine dust. "Sometimes in the night, I hear them laughing outside my bedroom window, like when they were kids. Then I hear a thud and know they're fighting. Then they laugh again and I go back to sleep." She turned and walked out of the barn. Lizette waited behind, gave Abaya space in her rarely expressed grief, pulled the heavy door shut and walked to the house.

While they prepared breakfast, Abaya pointed to the things she wanted Lizette to do. Lizette, understood the gestures, grabbed plates and glasses, pulled spoons and knives from a battered drawer. Sliced potatoes, salted the water. Turning on the burner—whiff of propane. Splash of oil, dash of garlic powder. Abaya waved her meat fork here and there, like a symphony conductor with a baton. Fat salmon steaks sizzled in the skillet, potatoes fried on the back burner. When it was ready, Poland appeared like magic. Lizette ate everything on her plate, got up to clean the last of the potatoes from the skillet, going into the refrigerator for ketchup, which she guessed the old people didn't use much judging from the crust around the lid. She reached into her bag and took a pill from the bottle Dr. Finch had given her, washed it down with a big bite of fried potato.

"Whose pajamas you wearing?" Abaya asked as they washed dishes together, Lizette drying as fast as she could, but not keeping up. "You look like a bum."

"Marian's father's. My stuff was all dirty. I'd been on the streets for a while, hanging out."

"Where do you sleep on the streets?"

"Wherever. On pallets, if I can find them. It keeps you off the ground when it rains. I put plastic down and then newspapers, layer them on, roll up. I take the papers from the free boxes on street corners when nobody's looking. It works pretty good, especially if you find a guy with a dog." Abaya rolled her eyes and Lizette laughed. "Dogs are always warm, the guys not so much."

Abaya snorted and scrubbed the skillet. Lizette wrapped the dishtowel around her slender fingers to dry inside a glass, noticing orange paint on the heel of her hand from last night.

"You stay here tonight. In Raven's room. Help me pick and sell at the market tomorrow. We can buy you some clothes, Scarecrow," she said, throwing Lizette a disapproving sideways glance.

In the dark, the next morning, Lizette helped the couple load boxes of winter vegetables—carrots, chard, potatoes, broccoli—for the farmer's market. They fussed at each other, elbowed over the tailgate, one putting in a box, the other turning it a different direction. They put in a long folding table, a bundle of paper bags, a produce scale. Abaya slipped the cash box under the front seat. Poland ran back to the barn for the beach umbrella.

They pulled into the parking lot beside city hall and joined the flurry of people setting up in the early morning mist. People came by and clapped Poland on the back, others hugged Abaya, asked what they were selling, said they hoped the rain held off. The smell of coffee and cinnamon filled the air. Lizette took five dollars from the money box under the truck seat and bought coffee and a fat, frosted cinnamon roll for Abaya, who fluttered her hands, waving it away. "Goo kills you." Lizette took a big bite and warm frosting dripped on her chin. Abaya tsk-tsked in disapproval.

Sunlight peeked between rain clouds and plumped the market's colors. Lizette sat on a log licking her fingers and drinking coffee, watching the scene come to life. By nine o'clock the parking lot was full of shoppers. Lizette bagged produce as fast as Abaya passed it to her, hardly looking up. By noon it was over and the vendors began cleaning up, laughing, loading, counting cash.

"You need pants," Abaya said, taking her by the elbow. "Let's see what that stinky hippie girl has for your long legs."

Folded clothes were piled on a table at the clothing stall. The hippie woman chatted with a cluster of friends. A couple of rolling racks stood unevenly in the dirt behind them, garments hung in a jumble of color.

"We need pants," Abaya said, interrupting the conversation, commanding attention. "You got any to fit this girl?"

Looking Lizette up and down, the woman dug down in a stack, pulled out a pair of blue jeans, handed them over.

"These might work."

Lizette took the jeans, looked uncertain.

"Wanna try?" she said. "Go behind the screen by the van."

Lizette sat on the van's bumper and slipped out of the thermal underwear, dirtier now from the garden and the farmers' market. She pulled on the jeans, which fit fine, but were frayed around the bottom, like stupid Greg's, she thought. *Probably belonged to a shorter person.* She balled up the thermals, stuffed them into her bag and came out from behind the screen.

"You need a top to go with that?" the woman asked her.

"What?" Abaya huffed to the woman, before Lizette had a chance to answer. "You think you're Seattle Nordstrom's? We don't got money for tops. Where'd you get that skunk oil you got on?" She put the flat of her hand to her nose so the woman would see.

"It's patchouli, helps balance energy," the woman said impatiently

"Maybe I should buy some of that stink and use it to scare deer away from my garden. I call that balance."

The woman pulled at her chin hairs and looked down her nose at Abaya, moved her rough hands over the stacks of tops, arranged by size and color, scowled and said nothing.

"Maybe these shirts," Abaya said, pulling out a red turtleneck, then a yellow blouse, a brown sweater. "But, only if it's three for one price."

She handed the woman two dollars and took the folded tops in her arms. She pulled a ten dollar bill out of her apron pocket, sniffed at the woman, waved the money briefly to show the woman she'd beaten her in the deal, gave it to Lizette.

"You worked good today," Abaya said to Lizette. "I owe you at least twenty." She looked the hippie woman up and down disapprovingly, turned and walked away.

"And, you don't go out in public stinking, like some people!" She headed back to the stall where Poland was packing up.

Lizette hurried after Abaya, grabbed her arm and made her stop. "You didn't need to talk to her like that. I don't need the money. I took five from the cash box before we started."

"I know. I saw you. You think I don't see?" Abaya grumped. "Next time, ask! But you worked. That's honest. You work, you get paid," she said. "You want to work next week?"

"I'll help, if you want. Sure."

"OK. Now we have to go home and unload. Get ready for next week."

They pulled onto Main Street, rain splattering the windshield, people hurrying to their cars. Wind whipped the town's one dangling traffic light, which Poland ignored when it turned red.

"Criminal man," Abaya muttered under her breath as they blew through the intersection. A pickup screeched its brakes to keep from hitting them, the driver laying on the horn.

"Jailbird wife," Poland said, grinning, stepping on the accelerator, shifting the empty boxes in the truck bed.

After they unloaded and closed up the barn, Poland said he had to go to the ranch. Lizette hugged Abaya, who reminded her about working the market next week, then she climbed into the cab. When they pulled into the Cutler Ranch, they saw strange cars parked next to the house. Lizette noticed Rocket's 88 and the open barn door, guessing he was inside.

"Looks like Rocket's here," she said, trying to keep her voice steady. "That's his Oldsmobile. Greg said he might come up. And, Marian said a bunch of other people are coming from Seattle. She said they could crash in the hay loft."

Poland tisked with the sharp edge of his tongue. "Bums . . . Coyotes . . . Always sneaking around here. Her father never would have let them on this place. They'll set the barn on fire with the smoking. Stupid!"

Rain poured and puddled in the ruts where the driveway gravel had worn thin. Poland slammed the truck door when he got out and stormed into the barn. She could hear him slamming tools around. She took her bag, waved a hasty goodbye, which Poland ignored, and hurried down the trail to the cabin.

# TWELVE

**PUSHING THE CABIN DOOR OPEN**, she found Rocket sitting on the stool in the middle of the room, staring at her paintings. "Hi." He stood up, smiled crookedly. "How ya doin'?" He rocked back, took a long look at her. "Marian said you've been sick."

"What're you doing in here?"

"Sorry. The rain started coming down . . . hard." He flapped his black and white flannel shirt against his muscled chest to show it was wet. "I was gonna sit down by the water. Greg told me you were staying in the cabin. The door was unlocked. I was just getting out of the rain."

He moved toward her, nodded toward the rain rolling off the eaves through the open door. "Doesn't look like it's letting up."

He extended his hand to her as if to shake and Lizette pulled back. He dropped his hand.

"Nice paintings," he said, preparing to leave. "I like that one." He stopped and went back to the canvas she'd been working on the past few days. He brushed its surface with his hand, touched a moist impasto, flattened the movement and energy she'd built with careful brushstrokes. She frowned and kept quiet

"What is it?"

"Nothing," she said, folding her arms, standing aside, gesturing with her head for him to leave. "Don't touch it . . . It's not dry and you wrecked it."

"Well, it looks like something," he said, turning back to the canvas, wiping his fingers on his jeans, "I just don't know what. Want me to build a fire? Might help it dry."

Lizette scowled. "I want you to go."

"It's damp in here," he said. "There's wood."

He went to the stove and knelt, gathered kindling from the wood box, popped small scraps into the firebox and struck a match, dropped it in. The fire flared. "That'll warm things up." He blew into the stove. The wood crackled.

"Marian says you been sick," he said again.

"Marian's not a doctor," she said through clenched teeth.

"Put your bag down. Relax."

Lizette set her bag in the closet. Turned to him, said, "You have to go."

"Don't be so uptight." He stood and put up his hands in defense. "I'm just getting out of the rain, not hurting anything."

"Is Marian back?"

"Yeah, but she's asleep. Up all night. The woman she helped had a baby boy this morning. Tough time, Marian said. She's taking a nap . . . with Greg. That's why I left and walked down here."

"Who else's here?"

"I don't know. Some cat from Seattle. Friend of Greg's. Never met him before. He's a poet, something weird like that. Fisher's with us. He's sleeping on the couch, half loaded. More people are coming later, a couple of local guys said they'd stop by." He went back to the stove, put more kindling on the flames. "A good band's playing in town tonight. You wanna go?"

He moved to the window and looked out on the little bay. "Hey! Did you see that?"

"What?"

"A black fin. Huge. It's an orca"

"They live here, mostly in the summer though." She joined him at the window. "It's kind of early for them, but some rogues have been hanging around here for weeks."

"Look! There it is again. Shit, man!"

"It's hunting," she said calmly, scanning the water's surface.

"That close to shore? What the hell?"

"They live here," she repeated and turned from the window, tended to the fire. "The water's deep close to shore in the cove, bottom drops off."

"It's Looney!" Rocket shouted and Lizette peered through the glass at the water.

"Looney!" He bounced up and down. My orca! See the gashes on his back!"

He stabbed the glass with his thick fingers. "Christ. I can't believe it! He's alive! Oh, my God! Look! There's a seal out there."

He banged on the glass with his knuckles, looked around for Lizette, but she was already out the door and running down the path to the beach.

"They're swimming this way!" he called to her, following down the trail. "This is so far out!" He stopped and slapped his knees, laughed out loud.

Marian's border collie pup Tucker, ran barking onto the sand, circling Lizette, running up to Rocket and back to the water's edge. The dog came back again, circled them, bounded back to the water, covering the short distance in a flash.

"Tuck! Come!" Lizette tried using commands, then begging, "Come boy! Good boy!"

She stopped calling when, in the roiled surf, she saw her gray speckled seal pop up, dive, pop up. She saw terror in its eyes and clutched her throat, screamed. The spooked seal made a run for the beach, cleared the water's foamy lip, waddled up the wet sand, the dog nipping at its hind flippers.

A mass of black and white, clicking and gnashing, roared out of the water, just missing the seal's flippers. Lizette jumped back. Tucker lunged forward, lowering his body, barking into the swirling surf. The orca's beaching sent water surging around Lizette's ankles, knocking her off balance. She saw its pink tongue and conical teeth, it's searching, hungry eyes. She shrieked. Rocket grabbed her, pulled her higher up the beach, onto the spiky salt grass.

"See the scars?" he yelled into her ear, yanking her arm. "Propeller marks. Jesus! Christ! He's alive! I can't believe it!"

Tucker bounded into the water beside the beast's snapping jaws. He took a sideways blow from its head and was swept deeper into the surf, then leapt back onto land, whirled on the orca, barking in a high, angry pitch.

The seal, stunned by the gush of water, struggled for traction, clambered for higher ground, barking hoarsely, paddling the sand. It didn't see the open mouth, teeth homing in from behind. Jaws clamped. Bones crunched. Blood spurted in a fountain, sprayed the sand and the dog, lipsticked the orca's mouth. Tucker yelped and grabbed at the seal's gray body dangling from the orca's mouth as it slid back into the sea.

It surfaced by the jagged rocks at the edge of the inlet, the seal's body gripped in its teeth, still barking. Tucker gained the rocks in a bound, snarling and snapping. Water surged from the orca's thrashing and washed over the jagged rocks. Tucker lost his footing and fell into the frothy surge, caught his hind leg in a crevice, yelped madly. Rocket leaped onto the rocks and a wave swept him into the orca's wash. Lizette watched him clutch at the outcropping, edging toward Tucker. The orca threw itself against the rocks, pushed a surge of water over them, creating enough float for Rocket to free the dog's leg.

Then the orca was gone in a black and white streak, dorsal fin erect, tail flipping defiantly as it swam away. Further out, the huge animal tossed the seal's body into the air, snatched it, tossed it, snatched it and sounded, tail flukes lifted defiantly.

The water flattened. The pelting rain washed away the blood on the sand. Tucker whimpered at Lizette's feet, covered in blood. She knelt to look at his wounds and saw his paw and front leg were cut, but his hind leg was the worst. Rocket ripped off his shirt, picked Tucker up and wrapped him, holding a wad of sleeve tight against his hock.

"Let's get Marian," Lizette said as they ran through the trees toward the main house.

"Marian! Marian, wake up!" Lizette gasped, charging into her bedroom. Greg was sitting astride her and she was tangled in the bedsheets

"It's Tuck," Lizette said, shaking the end of the bed, dripping water on the floor, gasping for air. "The orca got him. He's bleeding,"

"How the hell did that happen?" Greg demanded, falling to one side, rolling onto the floor, standing, pulling his pants over his feet, hopping as he hoisted them up.

"He was trying to protect the seal," Lizette explained.

"He's a fuckin' sheep dog," Greg yelled at her. "He's supposed to protect sheep. Dog's a head case, man. Now, get the hell out of here."

Marian pushed past them, pulling a loose dress over her head as she went. In the kitchen, Rocket held the whimpering animal against his bare chest. Marian cleared the table and put Tucker on it.

"Get me some towels from the hall closet," Marian ordered. "Greg, get my black bag from under the bed. Put him on the table. I need to take a look."

She worked Tucker's leg, checking for fractures, torn tendons, any sign of irreparable damage. The dog whined and lay his head down. Greg put the medicine bag on the table. Marian reached inside for a syringe and a vial of Novocain. She gave the dog a quick shot and he relaxed. She shaved the fur from his leg, while Rocket held his head steady, and she looked more closely at the wounds. Lizette slid down the cabinet to the floor, sobbing. Marian looked up, saw that in the commotion Poland had come in.

"Poland, get Liz out of here," Marian said. "Take her out to the barn. Show her the new lambs. Do it now. Greg, put a pot of water on the stove to boil. Hold him steady, Rocket."

Lizette leaned on Poland as they sloshed through the rain to the barn, going into the cold darkness, smelling the sweet hay and manure. In the pens around them, hungry lambs bleated and nursed.

"The seal was my friend," Lizette sobbed. "He came to me when I first got here. I tried to talk with him, but he was so shy." She stopped to catch her breath, explain. "He played outside the window while I painted. The orca threw him around like a dog's chew toy."

Poland led her into a lamb pen and pressed her down in the straw. He went and got a blanket and a couple of bottles with heavy nipples and came back to sit beside her, wrapped her legs, handed her a bottle and a lamb.

"My cousin married a Tlingit woman," he said. "He lives up north with her. They got three kids, all girls. They're grown up, married now. My cousin, he said his wife tells a story about how, in a time before killer whales, there was a hunter and totem carver named Natsilane. See?" Lizette nodded that she understood.

"So, he got a wife on Duke Island. A chief's daughter. Beautiful. Big chest." Poland put down the lamb he was feeding and bobbled his hands in front of him. Lizette giggled and sniffed.

"So," Poland continued, "he lived with her people. At first the village people didn't like him, but then they saw he was a good hunter and he shared his kills with them. But his wife's brothers didn't like being shown up by an outsider.

"They decided to get even, teach him a lesson. On the day of the big seal hunt they paddled near rocks, and Natsilane climbed out of the canoe and plunged his spear into a big bull seal that bellowed into the wind." Poland suddenly trumpeted like a seal, startling Lizette and the lambs, making her burst into tears again. Poland hugged her, stroked her head.

"Sorry," he said. "I got excited. So, his spear point broke off in the seal." Poland showed how it snapped with his fists, startling the lamb cradled in his arms. "The sea lion charged into the water. But that wasn't the worst part. The brothers were paddling away as fast as they could, leaving Natsilane on the rocks."

Speaking softly in the half light of the barn, Poland said, "What they did broke his heart." He reached over Lizette and tucked the blanket tighter around her legs. "He pulled his cape over him and slept on the rocks, but woke up when he heard his name whispered on the wind. He saw a sea lion that looked like a man and followed him into the water, down beneath the waves and into the Seal Chief's House."

"Where was Watches Underwater?" Lizette asked. She snuggled tighter against Poland and let the lamb suckle her fingers. "Couldn't she help?"

"I told you. It's a Tlingit story, not Lummi." He cleared his throat. "No one's watching in this story. Now, when they got to the great house, the chief asked Natsilane if he could help his injured son. Natsilane pulled his spear point out and sewed up the wound. The sea lions formed a raft with their backs and took him home. The seal son healed and, later, the chief granted Natsilane the power to create life."

Lizette shifted the lamb on her lap. "Then what happened?"

"Well, the boy carved a black and white fish out of spruce, the first killer whale. It was big and beautiful and no one had ever seen anything like it. When he put it in the water, it came to life and swam out to sea, sleek and black with a white saddle. It came back whenever Natsilane called."

"This is a long story," Lizette said, yawning.

"No, it's a good story," Poland said, putting down his lamb and standing up. "I told it to your father once. He wrote it down. It was the first orca and Natsilane taught it to hunt and help the people. It brought schools of fish to the families and they feasted everyday."

"Then what happened?" Lizette asked

"Happened?" Poland looked disappointed that she didn't get the point of the story.

"Nothing happened. Now orcas live in the water and help the people. I'm telling you this so you understand the orca's job and don't get scared. Seals eat the fish, orcas eat the seals. We eat everything. Sometimes we work together, sometimes not. They're hunters just like us."

"My father used to tell me stories when I was little," Lizette said. "But, his stories were shorter." Poland puckered his lips, suggesting he didn't approve of abridgement, and took the sleeping lamb from her.

"Your father is a good man," he said, placing the lamb in a nest of straw. "He's just hurt right now. I've known him a long time, your mother, too."

They looked up to see Marian come in carrying Tucker, his hind leg wrapped in a big, white bandage.

"I did the best I could, but the gash is pretty deep," she said. "He's a good sheep dog, but he may not be much use anymore. He may end up with a bad limp. Hard to tell if the tendon was nicked and how well he'll heal. He's still a pup."

She handed the dog to Poland. "Can you take him home to Abaya? She'll know what to do."

"No." Lizette stood up, folded her arms across her chest to block any argument. "I want to keep him with me."

"Nursing an injured dog is a lot of work," Marian said. "You're not well yourself. But, if you want to try, get a box and a blanket. You'll have to keep him quiet. I don't want the bandage getting dirty. There's food in the cupboard. Take a bowl for water."

Poland shuffled through the supply room off the main barn, holding Tucker, while Lizette went to the house for food and bowls. They met outside the barn, Poland carrying the dog in his arms, Lizette leading the way down the trail.

"I've got rounds tomorrow," Marian called after them. "I'll be gone early. Then errands in town after that. Stay out of the barn until Greg and Rocket get rid of everybody. I told them they have to clear out first thing tomorrow."

# THIRTEEN

BACK AND FORTH, FROM FIRST LIGHT, the rogue orcas patrolled the mouth of the small inlet below Lizette's cabin. They rolled through the water, black dorsal fins cutting a swath in the chop. Back and forth, like ominous sentries. Back and forth.

Lizette stopped working and watched their rhythmic undulations, paint brush suspended in mid-stroke. The muscular young males, distinctive white splotches flashing on their backs, herded prey toward shore, then closed in for the kill. They plucked fish swimming frantically near the water's surface and tossed them aside, trolling for bigger game. They came like this every few days, cruising, killing, departing.

Three long, black dorsal fins sliced the surface in even formation. She put her brush down and headed to the platform above the beach, lugging Tucker, careful not to bump his healing hind leg. She saw a salmon tossed into the air like a bath toy. One orca bludgeoned a baby seal with his powerful head and fins. "The hunting party's small today, she told the dog, scanning the water's surface. "But, where's Looney?"

Poland told her rogue males were driven from the pod by their mothers, forced to roam and feast, but never again to suckle. She didn't like the rogues, but felt like she understood their ruthless need, their loneliness. She sat mesmerized by their primal force.

She rubbed Tucker's ears while they basked in the morning's warmth and nuzzled his sweet black and white face. Harlequin ducks, Canadian geese, teels and gulls, suspended their flights as the orca pack pressed closer to shore. The birds settled high on the sand, folded their wings, held their chatter.

When the menace moved off, the air expanded in quiet relief, like a town's exhale after motorcycle thugs ride away—gunning their engines, rattling storefront windows, leaving behind a grateful peace. The birds took flight then and wheeled above the cove, chastising the departing invaders with honks and cries.

"There's bread," Marian called across the meadow, her body shadowed by the trees, but Lizette could see her hands cupped around her mouth, hear the words "Whole wheat . . . have some." Lizette waved and walked toward her, hugging the dog to her chest. When she got closer, Marian shouted again, "Cream cheese, lingonberry jam!" trying to entice her.

"My favorite," Lizette told Tucker. She followed Marian up the trail to the main house. Along the way Marian pointed out plants, called them by their Latin names -- *Polypodium glycyrrhiza, Asarum caudatum.* "Show off," Lizette said as she legged up the hill, puffing from Tuck's extra weight. "This dog weighs a ton. You could just call them licorice fern and wild ginger."

"I need to go to Bellingham," Marian said flatly as they hurried along.

"OK. What for? . . . Grocery shopping?"

"Yeah. For the equinox party Greg wants to have. And, I have an appointment at the free clinic," she said. "Did you take your meds?"

"I forgot," Lizette said sheepishly.

"You're getting better, but we've got to be consistent with the meds, otherwise they don't work right," Marian scolded. "We've talked about this before."

Marian paused before they got to the house, gazed toward the orchard planted in the wide swale that stretched away from the house to the cliffs over the water on the western side of the ranch. Cedar forest rose on the low hillsides and sheltered the fruit trees, gathered warmth into the orchard.

"Poland says we'll have fruit pretty soon," she said collecting herself, turning back to Lizette. "It'll sell fast at the market, once it's ripe. Poland says we have to pick at the right time, otherwise it isn't good, too hard, doesn't sell. We'll probably have a good cherry crop, too."

Lizette put the dog down and he snuffled at the grass, bejeweled with dew. She knew all about the orchard and the fruit, worked there with Poland all the time, which is more than she could say about Marian. She squinted at her, couldn't understand why she was talking like this, pointing out the obvious.

"Last year's cherries were light," Marian said. "The trees are alternate bearing, you know. They'll be ready in a few months, a bigger crop. Then the apricots and peaches follow, if we get enough heat." She shaded her eyes with her hand, scanned the blue sky as if looking for heat. "Apples and pears in the fall." Then she fell silent and looked sad.

"Poland says you have to be quiet and listen to the orchard," Lizette said, standing beside Marian, studying the trees with her. "He says you have to feel the ripening. That's why we walk in the orchard so much. The trees still haven't fully bloomed. It's too cold, you know that." She gave Marian a questioning look. "The trees are like sleepy kids, just waking up."

Marian shrugged and headed for the house. In the kitchen, she cut thick slices of bread from a fresh loaf, releasing a warm, yeasty smell. Lizette sat at the table, content to smell and look out the window, scanning the base of the picket fence for crocus, searching for spring. Tucker snorted in the food bowl on the back porch, lapped water.

"I washed your clothes," Marian said in a tone that reminded Lizette of her mother. "A couple of things were so shredded I threw them out. The rest I folded and stacked on the dryer. Take the stack down when you go." She buttered a slice of bread and took a big bite, buttered another slice for Lizette, handed it to her.

She tidied the kitchen, more movement than purpose, brushing bread crumbs into her palm, folding the dish towel, checking that the cabinet doors were closed and tightly latched, running her hand across the top of the refrigerator, checking her fingertips.

"What's wrong, Marian?" Lizette said. "You're acting funny. Is it the party? I know it wasn't your idea."

Lizette got up from the table and put her dish and cup in the sink, felt stiffness in her neck, and twitching. Dr. Finch said these were signs the medication was working and that she'd have to learn to live with it. And, she'd have to get used to the dull, sleepy feeling. Without answering or even a bye, Marian went outside and got into her old white Chevy truck, gunned the engine and fishtailed down the driveway to the road.

When Marian got back, Lizette stopped cleaning the kitchen and went out to the truck to see if she needed help unloading. Marian had her head on the steering wheel. "Chicken-shit bastard! Son of a bitch!"

"What?" Lizette said, rearing back then reaching in to rub her shoulder.

"The clap! He gave me goddamned gonorrhea! It shows up sooner in men. Their dicks drip. He has to know. He hasn't been up here in two weeks. I talked to him on the phone a few days ago. He never said anything about it."

She hit the steering wheel hard with the palms of her hand. "I looked at the stain through the microscope myself. I've got a huge bacterial load. The bastard! I could lose my fallopian tubes, never have kids," she ranted. "Who'd he get it from? Not me, that's for sure!"

Marian threw things into cabinets as Lizette brought the supplies in, Tucker stumping in and out with her, bumping against her legs. She hefted the fifty-pound lamb chow bag onto her shoulder and took it to the barn. She checked the new lambs nosing around in their pen, filled up their water feeder, added food pellets. One curious lamb came to nuzzle her hand as she reached toward it through the pen slats. When she came back into the house, Marian was sitting at the kitchen table crying.

"I'd like to know who he's banging," Marian said, hiccupping and getting up for a glass of water. "What Skid Row whore is he messing with? The clap! I trusted the bastard and he gave me gonorrhea! I never guessed. Jesus. I'm so stupid."

"OK," Lizette said.

"What's OK?" Marian turned to her and shouted. "Are you stupid, as well as crazy?" "It's not OK! Are you an idiot?"

Lizette felt a sting across her face from the words, as if she'd been slapped. The energy from Marian felt like hot iron filings thrown in her face. She went out the back door and down the path to the cabin.

When she opened the door, Tucker hobbled inside. She sat on her cot and stroked his head, scratched behind his ears. Tears leaked down her cheeks. She got up and went to the closet, kneeling and reaching way back to the crack between wall and floor. With her fingernail she scratched out a small bit of tin foil, unfolded it, checked inside, a multiple hit of LSD she'd been saving, enough to send several people tripping. She carefully refolded the foil and slipped the packet back into its hiding place.

She went outside to the platform, Tucker limping after her. She waited for the hunters, but they did not return. When it got too cold and windy to sit there any longer, she went back to the cabin. She lit candles, started a fire in the stove, filled the dog's food bowl and lay down. Tapping at the door woke her. A curtain of black covered the window. The moon hadn't come up yet. The candles had burned out.

"Liz, I'm so sorry," Marian said as she came in. "Did I wake you?"

"Yeah. It's OK."

"Honestly, I'm sorry. Really."

Marian found a candle butt and struck a match.

"I'm just freaked out. I didn't mean what I said. I made dinner. Come and eat with me? I don't want to be alone, especially if Greg calls. He's supposed to be off for a few days after tomorrow. He's the one who wanted this party . . . Wanted to invite the Dogs. Like we've got something to celebrate! It's just an excuse to get blasted."

"What day is it?"

"Thursday. What does it matter?"

"I don't want to miss the Saturday market. I'm working. Poland's picking me up early tomorrow. I'm spending the night with him and Abaya so we can harvest on Friday and set up early on Saturday."

"Oh. Well, you can have dinner with me tonight, right?"

"I guess. It's just that I can't help with the party. I've got stuff to do."

"Don't be like that, Lizette. I'm sorry for what I said. I didn't mean it. I'm upset."

"I know. I see it. It crackles, feels like burnt orange."

"Please," Marian begged. "Can't we at least have dinner? You don't have any food down here and you're almost out of dog food.

Tucker needs to eat and have his leg checked, the bandage changed. Come on. Pretty please."

Marian scooped up Tucker. Lizette got his empty feed bag, grabbed the flashlight, and they started up the trail, Lizette swinging the light side to side to show the way.

They ate dinner in silence, the tick, tick of the clock marking the stillness.

"I'm going to make brownies for the party and I bought vanilla ice cream." The brightness in Marian's tone sounded forced. "Sandy's coming up from Seattle tomorrow. She can help me get ready." Lizette smirked. Taking a deep breath, Marian pushed up from the table and gathered the dishes.

"I bet she knows who Greg's been humping. She has to."

She ran water in the sink and sloshed dish soap around, talking mostly to herself. Later, the two women boiled potatoes and peeled them. Lizette chopped onions and celery. They listened to the radio, Top 40. Marian got down a big blue enamel bowel and mixed chunks of hard-boiled eggs, sweet pickles and celery together, tossing the mixture with mayonnaise and onions. They counted hot dogs and buns, stacked the bags of chips.

Afterward, they fell into Marian's bed, their hands smelling of onion and garlic. Marian said Mrs. James from the neighboring ranch hit a deer with her old Nash Rambler on the way to Bible study that morning. She stopped to help, put gauze and a bandage on her forehead.

"She just got back in her yellow and black station wagon, thing's a tank, didn't have a scratch on it." Marian laughed in the dark. "She continued on to church like a fat bumblebee."

She rubbed Lizette's hips, making swirls around her sockets, felt her relax, heard her sigh. She reached under Lizette's shirt and softly traced the vertebrae up her back, then rolled over and rested on her own back, hands folded under her head.

"What do you see in Greg?" Lizette asked, her voice sleepy. "It seems like men are animals, like goats and pigs and dogs. I don't know why you bother."

"I don't know." Marian rose up and rested on her elbow. "I like his body. It's lean and strong. But, lately he has been dipping toward the scrawny side, I have to admit."

Lizette knew he'd rather get loaded than eat, but, in her drowsy state, didn't say so.

"He just needs to eat more," Marian said. "And, stop hanging out with the Dogs. I love to feed him. He always likes what I cook."

"No, he needs to lay off . . . " Lizette started to say *drugs*, but decided against it, waited.

"He doesn't crowd me," Marian finally said. "I come and go as I please. I don't worry about him getting uptight. Some midwives have had to stop because their husbands don't want them running out the door all the time, especially if they have kids. He doesn't tell me what to eat and drink, who to be friends with, what time to be home. Basically, I love him because he doesn't have any expectations of me. But, I expected he wouldn't have sex with some other chick, at least not without a warning."

"What about you?" Lizette mumbled, pressing her butt against the warmth of Marian's thigh.

"I'm so busy, it's not an issue," Marian said, snuggling closer to Lizette. "I've been known to have some pretty hot pants, but I haven't been interested in anyone since I've been with Greg.

*Since your father died*, Lizette thought.

"I'm lazy." Marian rolled onto her side. "Obviously, I can't say the same for him. I mean about seeing other people. Wouldn't you agree?"

She waited for Lizette to respond, heard the steady rhythm of her breathing and got up to pace the dark house.

# FOURTEEN

"WAKE UP, SLEEPYHEAD." Marian stood in the bedroom door-way, a steaming coffee mug in each hand. "We've got lots to do this morning. Sandy called. She's on her way, coming up with Fisher, says she has some news. Fisher's working at the Moran tonight, playing the organ, filling in for the regular musician. But, he said he'll switch back and forth from the organ and the piano"

Lizette took a sip of coffee, so hot it made her eyes water. She blew into the cup. "He's nice. I love listening to him play the piano. At the Dog House, we'd be alone a lot in the afternoon and he'd play things that made me smile."

"He's supposed to bring up some Sumatran coffee beans for the party. Said he'd stop by Pike Place Market on the way."

"He's working out here now, I mean, on Orcas?"

"Sometimes. Comes up on weekends. Gigs at the tavern in town in the summer, plays Bluegrass banjo. They give him a room in back of the Moran when he plays at the hotel, but he usually sleeps here."

"My parents used to take me to the Moran once in a while. Once they got into a fight there. Not an out-in-the-open argument, but

I remember tight-lipped hissing, like snakes. Made my sandwich stick in my throat."

"Well," Marian said, choosing not to comment on her parent's unhappiness. "They say Fisher played with the Seattle Symphony or something, but got messed up on drugs, started playing in jazz clubs, dealing dope on the side. Got busted for possession. He has a following. Did you know that?"

"You mean fans?"

"Yeah. People who go out of their way to hear him play. Mostly old people."

*Is he famous and I just didn't figure it out?* Lizette thought and wondered what else she'd missed in her confusion.

"Not like the Rolling Stones," Marian added, shaking her head, amused at Lizette's perplexed look. "Just local folks. Apparently his family's pretty nice, too. They have a glass shop in Kent. His father and brothers fix windows. But they're kind of Christian, wanted him to play at church. Then, after he got busted, they didn't want him around anymore. Sweet guy, really. Great hands. You might consider . . ."

"Consider what? He's a Dog!"

"I guess." Marian sat on the side of the bed and fluffed Lizette's tangled hair. "If you call crashing at Rocket's house so he can play his piano being a Dog. He doesn't even play softball that I know of. I'm not even sure he's on the team."

"No one else can actually play the piano, except him." Lizette said. "He's his own team. Rocket plays chopsticks and acts like he's some kind of maestro. But, Rocket and the Dogs don't know the first thing about music."

"Or anything else." Marian said and bent to pull Lizette's jeans from the floor, handed them to her. "Only Fisher can play, like I said. He'll be here in a while with Sandy. They've been hanging out.

But, I already told you that, didn't I?" Lizette looked blank to mask her surprise that Sandy and Fisher were spending time together.

"You're wooly," Marian said. "Drink your coffee. Wake up!"

From the kitchen they heard footsteps and Poland's familiar "Hullo." Marian hurried down the hall to greet him. Lizette heard them talking while she dressed. She splashed water on her face in the bathroom and combed her hair with her fingers.

"Good morning, sleepy girl," Poland said when she came into the kitchen, pinching out a grin. "We got work, Elizabeth. Some guys are coming to help shear sheep. Gotta get the flock ready." He worked the blades of the shear he was holding, the edges scraping. "May take two days to finish. We need your help with the lambs, you work the dogs."

"Where's Tucker?"

"Oh, don't worry about him," Poland said. "He's already in the barn. He wants to work. Come on."

"She hasn't had breakfast," Marian said. "And, get that dog back in here. He's not ready to work."

"Plenty of time to eat—when work is done," Poland said, heading out the door. "Dogs are happy when they're doing something. You'll ruin him."

In the barn, Tucker limped up to Lizette, wagging his whole back end. He had on a clean bandage, smaller than the last one. *Marian*, she thought. *Fixed it while I was sleeping.* Tucker jumped up and Lizette examined his front paws, his injured hind leg buckled under the weight.

"Down," she commanded and agreed with Marian that he wasn't ready to work. Tucker looked hurt and sidled off.

"Marian checked him this morning," Poland said. "Said it's healing, but maybe he won't ever be able to herd, may drag a leg. Can't tell yet, but you can see he wants to get out there."

Marian was standing at the barn door, watching them, light playing behind her head, veiling her face.

"Tucker's doing pretty well," she said. "Considering he was attacked by an orca."

She laughed and Tucker came to her, rubbed against her leg, as if pleading his case.

"Take him down to the cabin, Liz, and feed him. Lock him in while the other dogs work. He'll just get in the way and re-injure his leg."

Lizette picked Tucker up and started to leave, the dog barking in protest, the other sheep dogs coming into the barn, circling Lizette, ready to help him out.

"And, Liz, don't forget your pill," Marian said. "You're doing pretty good, too."

"I sleep too much."

"You're better," Marian said, nodding approval. "Your father called this morning."

Lizette shifted Tucker for a better grip.

"He wanted me to remind you about the checks from the county in your mailbox."

She spoke louder to be heard over Tucker's barking, said, "He wants to know how you're doing. Remind you about your appointment with Dr. Finch. Apparently the hospital called. I told him you're good, invited him to come out."

"What did he say?"

"Put Tucker in the cabin." Marian shooed at Lizette. "The barking is driving me crazy. "

When Lizette returned to the barn, she could see Poland and a couple of men far off in the meadow. The young black and white collies worked the edges of the flock with their mother, Old Mollie, pressing the sheep closer and closer together. Lizette went into the meadow and began gesturing with her hands and whistling to the dogs, directing them when they veered off course. They herded the animals toward the open pens beside the barn, moving quickly along the line of sheep they were forming, working front to back, side-to-side, nipping, bumping. A big lamb stopped to graze and was disciplined with a snap to the neck. It kicked out its hind legs, joined itself to its mother's flank and they ran as a single unit, shoulder to shoulder. The men ran behind the flock, trying to catch up.

"Open the pen gate!" Poland shouted to Lizette.

The flock moved down the meadow, picking up speed. She unlatched the gate to the outside pens, lifted it from its sag, swung it wide and stood out of the way. The flock hung together as the dogs brought them in, moving as one. They crushed into the pen, making pretty little leaps before settling down. Lizette latched the gate behind them.

"Wool's too wet," Poland said when he reached her, panting, leaning over the pen and grabbing handfuls of wool.

"Can't shear today. Open the barn doors and let them inside."

With the flock secured, Lizette hurried into the barn, swung the door wide and the dogs pressed the sheep into the sheltered pens.

She heard Poland tell the men, cousins of his, it looked like, "Naw. They gotta dry out. A day or two. I'll let you know."

The sheep jostled around the water trough, the dogs slipped back into the pen, nudged them as they drank. Poland whistled and called the dogs off, shamed them with his tone for needlessly harassing the penned animals. They slipped away and found the food bowls Lizette had set out for them. Poland went back outside to the men in the driveway. They shook hands and got into their pickups and drove away.

"Too much rain," Poland said.

He came to stand beside Lizette while she patted the lambs bumping around in their separate pen. He chuckled at their antics.

"It doesn't take so long for Southdowns to dry. Wool's not thick, not worth much either. But, we can sell some at the market. The spinners like it. Abaya needs to card it though, clean off the dirt and poop before they can make yarn."

A car tooted as it came down the drive, a blue Volkswagen with bug-eye headlights, luggage rack on top. It rolled up in front of the barn's open doors. Sandy got out from the passenger seat, round belly showing first, long blonde hair, to her waist, thick and healthy. *Bug eyes, like the car*, Lizette thought as she watched her. She was wearing a man's white dress shirt and a long denim skirt, hiking boots showing below the hem.

"Hey. Lizette! How do ya like my belly?" She turned sideways and smoothed the shirt over her round bulge.

Lizette smiled and backed away. Fisher grinned with yellow buck teeth as he unfolded his long frame from behind the wheel. She thought his thinning hair looked like crumpled brown grass. *He can't be the father*, Lizette thought. *She's too pregnant for that. I would have known.*

"Where's Marian?" Sandy looked around like she expected Marian to pop up from a rabbit hole.

Lizette pointed toward the house and retreated into the barn. She checked the orphan lambs, again, added feed and water, then walked down the trail to her cabin. She wondered who the father might be, heard laughter coming from the house, the phone ringing, rock music—Janis Joplin wailing "Down on Me."

Inside the cabin, she settled on the stool and spread peanut butter on a rice cake, took a swallow from the water jug, stared out the window, scanning the water's surface, waiting for them to come, watching for flashes of black fin gliding through the chop, searching for Looney.

"Elizabeth?" Poland called from outside. She got up and opened the door. "Abaya wants to sell at the market tomorrow. Are you gonna come?"

"Sure. I told you I would."

"Good," he said. "We need help and you need money, lazy girl. We can go home in a while and harvest in the afternoon. Now I need to do some orchard work. Won't take long."

She followed him along a side trail, through the fragrant cedar forest that protected the fruit trees, past the littered ranch dump, over a small hill, Tucker stumping behind them. They stepped into the bright nimbus that wrapped the cherry trees in golden light. Blue jays argued over perches on the budding branches, a falcon swept overhead, waiting for a clear shot at the noisy jays, jabbering away, innocent of the hunter.

"Put the ladder up on the trunk," Poland said, showing her how he wanted the ladder set.

"Check again that the ladder is planted, steady before you go up. Always check twice."

She climbed, steadied herself on a sturdy branch.

"Here are the clippers. I'll hold the loppers. Clip, right there."

"Here?" She had the clippers set on a thick branch.

"No. More toward the end, at the fork." He stood beneath her gesturing. "Go out more to the end. I just want the branches lightened for when the fruit comes, so they don't break. You need to learn pruning, silly girl. Marian's too busy to know. That way you can show the crews what to do, when I'm not here."

"You never go anywhere," Lizette said.

"Someday I won't be here. The crews won't listen if you don't know what you're talking about."

She went after a branch, the leaves brushing her face, the birds taunting her on the higher branches. She clipped steadily as he pointed from the ground, her fingers cramping after a while, the tender skin on the inside of her thumb burning.

"If you eat too much fruit, you poop," Poland warned her as he steadied the ladder. He made a putt-putt sound with his lips and laughed at himself. Lizette laughed too at his silliness, snipped and dropped a cluster of leaves on his head.

She reached for the loppers and took out a heavy branch, dropping it to the ground, just missing Poland's boot. "Watch out! You wanna kill me?"

In a few of hours they'd trimmed and shaped a dozen trees. Poland went and got the truck and she kept working, her arms and back aching. They loaded the prunings into the truck bed and then they bounced along the rutted orchard road to the ranch dump, heaving the load into the big hollow. They were unloading tools into the barn when Marian came out and called them to lunch. Poland waved to Marian, shook his head "no," told Lizette to go, that he'd come back and pick her up on the way to the Saturday market. Before daylight, he warned, and got into his truck and headed down the driveway to the main road.

"Liz, come on," Marian urged, beckoning with her arm.

Lizette hunched her shoulders and went in, sat in the kitchen chair closest to the door, studied the blisters on her thumb from squeezing the pruning sheers. She still felt ticked about Poland leaving her, about the way Sandy had treated her in Seattle, pissed about her refusal to let her stay at Franklin Street. She felt a twinge in her side, her rib still mending from the attack at the tavern – how long ago? She tried to remember. Before Christmas, more than four months ago. She realized she'd been back at the ranch for two months now. Sandy sat rubbing her belly. Lizette ignored her, realized why she'd quit stripping, understood what she was hiding back then.

Fisher slouched in a chair across from her, a bowl of navy beans steaming in front of him. Lizette felt him look her over. Marian set a bowl of beans in front of her. Fisher smiled his yellow beaver smile. Lizette studied her dirty hands.

"Fisher has to eat and take a nap," Marian said. She popped open a jar of Abaya's homemade blackberry preserves and put it on the table with a spoon beside it. "Sandy and I want to go down to the Moran for dinner and hear him play. You need to go, too. I made reservations. Do you have a skirt?"

Startled by the suggestion, Lizette shook her head, stared into her bowl, took a taste, put the spoon down. She looked up and found Fisher staring at her, again, intent. She blinked, adjusted her body in the chair, focused on the thumbtack holes in the wall by the window. Her face ticced, rain fell outside, dropping from the sky, shattering on the ground, the thunder of the falling water getting louder in her ears, terror clawing her stomach and clutching her chest. Her pelvic muscles convulsed.

Shoving back her chair, she fled the kitchen, slipped on the trail, fell once, bounded muddy onto the cabin's narrow porch, threw open the door, slammed it behind her, fell onto the cot, held her head in agony, wondered what triggered the panic. The smell of moss and vomit came to her. The alley. Men grabbing her. When the fear smoothed out, she got up and took a pill, checked the supply inside the plastic bottle with a shake. Nearly empty. She had to go back to Seattle, hated the thought.

Tucker scratched at the door. She opened it and he went right to his box and curled into a ball. She wiped water from his coat with a rag as best she could, carefully rubbed his bandage clean. They napped.

# FIFTEEN

THIS COLOR CAN'T BE REPRODUCED, Lizette thought, as she crossed her ankles under the table and folded her hands in her lap. The warm yellow glow in the Moran Hotel's dining room fascinated her, but frustrated at the same time. She couldn't figure out how to create color that was like the burnished gold in a pawnshop jeweler's window—worn wedding bands and cuff links glowing with memories lost, precious metal tinged with emotion. How, she wondered, could she cast that color onto canvas. *What color is it?* she wondered, and tried to figure out a combination of pigments that would create it. Maybe lily pollen, glistened with egg white.

"Hey, wake up!" Marian nudged her under the table. Lizette smiled at Marian and Sandy. At least she thought she did. Her tongue felt numb, her body stiff, only her mind remained limber enough to move. Sometimes lily pollen is too brown, she thought, if the flowers are old. She fretted and sorted through the color wheel in her mind.

Marian and Sandy had come down to the cabin that evening and awakened her from a slick, black dream – broad backs, suffocating overcoat, dark water, a scream that stuck in her throat. They handed her one of Marian's skirts, dressed her and combed her snarled hair in the candle light, twisting it into a chignon on her head, securing it with long pins decorated on the ends with lacquered sea shells, making tendrils in front of her ears to soften her gaunt cheeks. She wore the brown sweater Abaya found at the market, more low-cut than they'd realized at the time. Marian and Sandy smiled at the sweater's snug fit, said they liked the way it showed off her collar bones.

Walking into the dining room behind Marian and Sandy and the maitre d', she felt like she was being led by circus midgets. People stopped between bites to stare at her and she could almost feel the St. Lucia crown of candles on her head, like at church. She heard the organ music rolling through the open roof timbers, sensed the feeling of her parents nearby, feeling as if they were smiling from a pew near the front.

Marian leaned over and whispered behind her menu. "Fisher's playing." Lizette listened more closely. A Chopin etude, warm and billowy, hovered above the dining room's clink and tinkle, flowed from the music room in waves, filled gaps in the laughter and conversation. Her father's spirit came to her, hovered beside the table. He loved Chopin.

She picked up her menu and looked out the windows. "Sounds great," she said, overcome by sensations and memories. Outside, black was broken only by an occasional whitecap, suggesting a surging tide in the tiny harbor below the hotel. The white masts of sailboats bobbed and rigging pinged as the wind gusted.

Lizette remembered her father bringing her and her mother here a long time ago. In the summer. They ate on the deck overlooking the boat harbor. Her father, excited by the finds during the week's dig for artifacts, talked about the Lummi tribe and its history, as if he held time in his hands, recaptured and repossessed. Her mother gossiped about local artists, a new clothing boutique in Eastsound, plans for a group show at the Seattle Art Center in the fall, about including a few small pieces of her own she thought might sell.

Her father, always the teacher, leaned over to Lizette and explained the mansion's design was an example of the Arts and Crafts Movement, part of the hand-crafted reaction to mass production factories and the fussy Victorian style that came before it. Lizette didn't care, but loved the Tiffany lamps. She remembered the mahogany piano in the music room, the walls of pipes for the organ, the ox-blood leather chairs where she'd sat with her parents, legs too short to put her feet on the floor.

"Excuse me, ladies. Ready to order?" The waiter was speaking to her, his head cocked. Pushing up from the depths of her mind, Lizette squinted at him, couldn't figure out what he was saying, panicked, nearly burst into tears as the memories receded.

"He wants to know what you want to eat," Marian prodded, seeing her confusion, looking worried.

"What?"

"What do you want to eat? I'm having salmon," she said.

"OK."

"Make that two orders, please," Marian said. Sandy ordered lamb chops with mint jelly. Another man came and filled the water glasses. Marian ordered a bottle of wine, Mateus rosé.

Lizette scanned the room's blank walls and remembered her mother complaining long ago that this lovely old mansion had no art, wondering aloud if perhaps her agent could arrange a sale of her work. She said she'd just finished a large seascape that would go perfectly over the fireplace mantle in the lobby. The blues and sand tones would complement the inlaid seashell design in the casing around the firebox, she said, and a good hearth rug in just the right hues would tie it together. Her father said no, that old Moran had considered the view from the windows to be art enough. No painting could ever compare with God's handiwork, her father had said in a pompous tone.

Lizette remembered the smile sinking on her mother's face, her father's smug look as he gazed from the deck to the water, the breeze riffling his hair.

"Do you always have to act superior?" her mother had said in a leaden voice. "You enjoy putting me down, trivializing my work."

Lizette remembered that her tuna sandwich had started to taste bad, stuck in her throat, and she put it down, refused to eat another bite, although her father pressed her to finish. Her parents fought quietly over this, too, her eating, the way she sat, which hand she used to reach for her glass of milk. It was pressure against pressure, rather than outburst, with her stuck in the middle.

"Do you want wine?" Marian asked as she filled Sandy's glass. "A little drop never hurt a pregnant lady."

"This kid has had more than a glass of wine," Sandy said, picking up her glass and emptying it in two big gulps, patting her round belly, giggling. Marian frowned and poured a half glass for Lizette.

"Once Rocket brought over some tequila and weed to cheer me up," Sandy said. "We got messed up, I mean really! Rocket pissed the bed. That's how bad it was. That happened after Al got his sorry cholo butt thrown back in jail. I'm sorry to talk that way about the father of my kid, but the jerk was always coming in loaded and knocking me around."

She turned sideways in her chair, pouted. Lizette vaguely recalled Al, met him once or twice at the Twisted Owl. She remembered he'd been there with Sandy and Rocket.

"I'm glad he's not around," Sandy said. "But, I did like riding his Harley. We rode all the way down to Ellensburg once to meet up with some of his Hell's Angels buddies. They were at Alta Monte when things started going down. Guy got killed, did you know that?"

Both Marian and Lizette sat watching her. Marian moved her lips to show she was paying attention. Lizette scanned her memory, recalled the Rolling Stones, but couldn't remember the year of the Altamont Concert, maybe '69, she thought.

"You heard about that, right?"

Marian nodded her awareness of the concert, but Lizette doubted her. Sandy prattled on.

"The Hell's Angels tore the place up. Anyway, that was before we stayed at this place, the Antler Motel, in Ellensburg, that was last year. It had this far out vibrating bed and a stuffed deer head on the wall. I thought the stupid thing would fall off and kill me in my sleep. It was far fuckin' out."

The gray-haired couple at the next table looked sour about the way she was talking, flapped their napkins as if to dispel a bad odor.

"Here's dinner," Marian said, drawing Lizette's attention back to the table.

"Got ketchup?" Sandy asked as the boy refilled water glasses. "And how about some more wine?" Marian poured the last of the bottle into Sandy's glass and shook her head "no" to the waiter. "Too bad Fisher can't bang out some rock. He's not too bad for a bald drunk with thick glasses. But, he probably has a beanpole dick."

Lizette got up, looked down on Sandy and almost said something, but couldn't figure out what. She turned and walked to the mansion's music room, settled in a leather chair just like the one she remembered from when she was small, *but this time her feet touched the carpet*, she thought. On the table in the middle of the room, a big vase of white star-gazer lilies dropped powdery yellow pollen from their stamen and she studied the color on the polished surface.

Fisher bent over the piano keyboard, just his head and shoulders visible as he played. His glasses had slipped to the end of his nose and he'd rolled up the sleeves of his rumpled dress shirt, loosened his tie. Lizette closed her eyes and floated on the music, soaring with Ravel's Bolero, her breath rising and falling with the notes, seeing swirling red in her mind, following the sounds to crescendo, lolling in the silence that followed. Her hand lifted and warm fingers wrapped her palm. She opened her eyes and Fisher stood in front of her.

"Your hands are beautiful," he said. "But, I already told you that, didn't I?"

Lizette focused on remaining calm, wondered why people always needed a response to their slightest comment, when basically she didn't care, was usually preoccupied with her own thoughts about color and light and her canvases.

"Come sit with me. I'll teach you to play Rachmaninoff."

She pushed up, stretched to her full height.

"How tall are you, anyway?" he asked as he led her to the piano bench.

"Five eleven."

"I'm six three."

"Oh."

"Ever think about modeling?"

Lizette sat on the edge of the bench, pondering a question she'd been asked many times in her life, but never had an adequate response beyond "No." The idea of parading around in front of strangers for money never even seemed like a remote possibility to her.

"Don't talk much, do you?"

Her exasperation eased when he began to play, his fingers rushing up and down the keyboard, his skinny legs pumping the pedals, sweat beading at his temples.

"Are you a Swede?" he asked. She nodded, watched his fingers fly.

"How do you know Rocket?" Lizette asked, batting away his question.

"The guy saved my life," he said, running through an arpeggio. "He let me sleep at his house when I first got out of jail. His piano saved me. I would have gone crazy if it wasn't there. He even got it tuned for me so it sounded better. I practice at the Dog House all the time, hang out with the guys."

"I know," she said, wondering if he even remembered her being there, feeling like a ghost. "But I hardly ever saw you doing things with the Dogs. I mean getting high, going out to the taverns with them, and stuff."

Lizette started to get up, but he put a firm hand on her forearm and pulled her down. She panicked, felt his touch like a stab.

"There you are," Marian bubbled into the music room, Sandy on her heels. "An old guy in the dining room gave me this ten dollar bill. Asked me to bring it to you. His wife wants to hear something from *My Fair Lady*. Do you know any of those songs?"

"Sure," he said, pushing his glasses back on his nose and launching into "The Rain in Spain," but with a jazzy twist. "I'll throw in some *Oklahoma* too. That always gets 'em."

"You hardly ate anything," Marian complained, standing behind the couple and putting her arm around Lizette's shoulders, slipping the money into Fisher's shirt pocket. "Weren't you hungry?"

Lizette shook her head and fingered the base keys in front of her.

"You going to the tavern when you get done here?" Sandy asked Fisher as he launched into "I Could Have Danced All Night."

"Maybe," he said. "Whose playing?

"Some group from Bellingham," she said. "I think."

"I get off in about an hour. Want me to meet you guys there?"

"Not us," Marian said. "Lizette works at the farmers' market on Saturday mornings. She's already picked the vegetables, right?"

Lizette shook her head, shrugged, knew Poland and Abaya had taken care of it. "And, I'm getting ready for the equinox party tomorrow."

"Far out," Fisher said, pounding away on the keys.

"I'm here to party," Sandy interrupted. "I don't need to get up early. I'll ride back to the ranch and get my car. Pick you up here in about an hour?"

Fisher gave her a two-finger salute from his forehead and kept playing. The women found Marian's truck in the parking lot and squeezed into the cab. When they rounded the bend and headed down the hill to the ranch they could see lights on in the house and a couple of cars in the driveway. In the kitchen Greg and Rocket were making sandwiches, helping themselves to potato salad.

"Hey, shithead," Marian said to Greg as she came in the door. "That salad's for the party tomorrow. Don't come in here just taking whatever you see."

"Don't get uptight. There's plenty. Where've you been?"

"None of your business. Balling every guy on the island. Where have you been? Or should I say *who've* you been with? I'd like to know whose disease I'm sharing. Buy 'em a get-well card."

Rocket turned to Lizette, who stood frozen in the doorway, asked her quietly, "Mind if I eat down at the cabin?" Lizette grabbed a flashlight from the hook by the door and Rocket took his plate of food. He took a rumpled sleeping bag from the shelf above the washer on the back porch and they headed for the trail. They heard dishes breaking as they picked their way down the slope.

"Hey! Hey! Get down you beast," Rocket said, pushing Tucker away from the cabin door with his foot, going to the table and setting down his plate and fork, the dog followed, looking for a handout.

Lizette lit the kerosene lantern, turned down the wick and went to the stove to build a fire.

"I hate beggars," he said to the dog and dangled a piece of salami just above his head, teasing the meat up and down as Tucker snapped at it. "You been working?"

"Yeah," she said.

"I was talkin' to the dog. But let's see what you've been doing. What's that painting? The water?"

"No," she said, glancing at the canvases tilted against the wall, getting up to take her new piece off the easel.

"Are you just going to hide this stuff down here and not show anybody?" he said, taking a bite from his sandwich, a piece of cheese hanging from the bread. He stuffed it back in with a dirty finger. Tucker whined.

"It's private," Lizette said. "It's how I talk. Through my hands. It's what I feel. It's nobody's business."

"Don't you want to sell them?" he said. "Looks like you could use the bread."

"No," she sighed. "My mother sold hers. One of her paintings, a seascape, is in the Seattle Art Museum. I visit it sometimes, but I don't like it. It's just paint. It doesn't talk to me. What I'm doing isn't about money like it was with her."

"That's too bad," he said. "My mother's an artist, too. In San Francisco. Well, mostly an artist, when she's not crazy or drunk. We grew up with canvases and brushes all over the house. Me and my brother. For a while she thought she was Jackson Pollock, flinging paint all over the floors and walls. Sometimes she even hit the canvas." He started laughing, coughing at the same time, nearly choked. Lizette got up from the stove, pounded him on the back.

Recovering, he wiped tears from his eyes. "The landlord came in one day to check the place and found garbage and paint spilled everywhere. He wasn't much of an art lover, if you know what I mean," and let out another hacking laugh. "We had to move out the next week. Found a place in the Panhandle, next to Golden Gate Park. You ever been to San Francisco?"

"No."

"Great place until the hippies showed up," he said, flinging some cheese to the dog. "We used to hang out at the park at night in high school, smoke weed, drink a little beer. It was cool. Go to the Fillmore and hear music, Jefferson Airplane and Sopwith Camel, do you like the Camel?" Lizette stared at him, seeing him move like a marionette, strings lifting his hands and turning his head, working his wooden lips.

"All these freaks and weirdoes started hanging around," he continued. "Dancing, going 'far out man' and 'righteous brother.' Like anybody from Michigan or Salt Lake City would know far out from their assholes. Then the cops started rousting us from the park, came riding in on horses, said we couldn't stay there anymore. Then the freaks started ODing, raping and killing each other in the bushes. It was a bummer, man. Summer of Love, my ass. It was like the place exploded, nothing left but rubble. I got out just in time. But, shit spreads when you step on it. Now they're up here, all over the place, going back to nature, whatever the shit that is. I didn't know we'd ever left."

Lizette went to the stove and blew on the fire, added a few more pieces of wood. When it started crackling she got up and paced before the windows, looking out, trying to see the orca in the dark. The cabin warmed. Rocket finished his food. Lizette blew out the lantern and lay down on her cot. Rocket spread his sleeping bag by the stove, took off his jacket and rolled it into a pillow, stretched out. Tucker climbed into his box.

"You from here?" Rocket asked in the dark, his voice startling Lizette. She pulled her sleeping bag up, covering her shoulders and chin.

"Yes."

"How long have you known Marian?"

"Always. Let's sleep."

"When did you meet her?"

"One day I was sketching, in the far back meadow, near where my father and his students were digging. I didn't know I was on her family's land. I was sitting there drawing ferns and wildflowers. She walked up to me and we started talking. We were about seven or eight."

Her voice trailed off and she floated for a few beats, let the memories wash over her.

"After that we spent every summer together. She had an old palomino horse, Lightfoot, and we'd ride bareback together. We'd ride into town, get ice cream cones. Marian loves maple nut. I like pistachio. She's like a sister. We're both only children. Her father made her do chores in the morning, sometimes I'd help her in the barn. I liked to, still do. Then we went everywhere in the afternoons. My parents were working so they were glad I wasn't around to bother them. They fought a lot, anyway. They liked Marian and her family. My father hunted sometimes with her father and the other ranchers, after harvest. He'd come back up here by himself in the fall and hunt with Poland."

"Where'd you live the rest of the year?" he said.

"In Seattle." All the questions irritated her and she changed the subject. "Where'd you get the piano?"

"It was a gift from the Metzgers," he said. "The first people who took me in when I moved here in '68. Good people. Kept me off the streets."

"I know," she said, meaning anyone who'd give Rocket a piano had to be good.

"You know too much," Rocket teased. "What's Marian so pissed at Greg about?"

"I don't know. Let's sleep."

"OK. But, I want you to know I'm sorry about what happened to you . . . about the attack and all. I know the Dogs haven't been very nice to you."

"It's OK Rocket, really. I understand. I don't want to talk about it. Poland will come down early tomorrow and get me. Today has been too much. I feel swamped. But, I'm glad you're here, that I'm not alone. Let's just be quiet and listen to the water."

"OK." He walked on his knees to the side of the cot, leaned over and kissed Lizette on the forehead. "Goodnight."

She lifted her lips up to him, but he pulled back.

"Rest," he said gently. "I don't wanna start anything."

Lizette longed to be held, to slow her whirling mind, to melt into his body, release.

"See you in the morning," he said and settled onto the floor, closed his eyes to the moon shining over Orcas Island, knew Looney was breaking the water's surface somewhere in the night, hunting.

# SIXTEEN

GREG PULLED DUSTY PLYWOOD FROM BETWEEN THE BARN STALLS. Fisher gripped an end. They carried the sheets into the front yard and laid them on rickety sawhorses, then rolled out an extension cord and used the electrical outlet behind the washer on the porch to plug in the stereo. Marian brought a broom and swept the plywood picnic tables, spread torn tablecloths over the worst of the dirt and bird droppings.

"Already looks like a party and it's not even noon yet," Greg said, smoothing wrinkles from the faded yellow and aqua cloths.

"Looks like rain," she said, scanning the gray sky. "What time did you tell people to show up?"

"Hey!" Greg brushed past her, gestured at Fisher who was setting up the turntable and receiver. "Turn the stereo on, man. We need tunes."

He went back into the barn and got a big aluminum tub and rinsed it out with a garden hose in the side yard. A couple of cars, one with smoke puffing from under the hood, pulled up. He waved them to the side of the barn, signaling the drivers to park away from the dooryard and the front garden where they were setting up. He smoothed his curly black hair with his hands and wiped barn grit from his dark, girl-ish eyelashes, took a big swig of beer from the bottle he'd set on a hay bale and went to greet Bomber and Stinky.

Lucky was stuck in the backseat of Stinky's smoking Chevy Nomad and had to be pried from the car. The guys arranged him feet-first and tugged until his ass cleared the door frame, then let go and turned away. Lucky fell to the ground in a heap, feeling around him in the dirt for his cane. He was too drunk to find it by himself so Greg bent and picked it up, wrapped Lucky's fingers around the shaft. With the cane planted, he hoisted Lucky up, almost erect.

"Get a chair you knuckleheads." Greg had Lucky under the armpits, supporting his out-flung arms like sticks in a scarecrow, the cane dropped to the ground again. "There's one in the barn!" he shouted, could hear the men rummaging and knew they were looking in the wrong place, but couldn't let go of Lucky or he'd be on the ground again. "Help me get him to the house. Hurry up, assholes!" As he propped up Lucky, he looked down to find the man had wet his pants.

"Piss!" Greg let go. Lucky swayed for a few moments before going down. Stepping over his struggling body, Greg stormed into the barn, its weathered siding practically bulging from the hot words that spewed from his mouth. Bomber and Stinky saw an opening in the back of the barn, wiggled through the feed hatch, and ran for the orchard. Lucky writhed in the dirt, further soiling his pants. Another car tore down the ranch's long driveway, going too fast, spraying mud and gravel. Greg came out sparking like a welder's arc to see who'd arrived.

The man who got out of the car wore a three-cornered hat with a long white ostrich plume. With a bullfighter's flourish, he wrapped a black velvet cape around himself, flashing then hiding its fuchsia-colored lining.

"Toulouse!" Greg rushed toward the newcomer and clasped his hand. "Glad you made it. Nothin's going right today. Come on in and things will get better. Glad you could hang out. You know most of the guys here from Franklin Street. The Dogs? And, there's a lot of people from the island."

"Nothing but vain fantasies," Toulouse said. "What's the point of this soiree?"

Greg wrinkled his nose, showing the tiny scar he'd gotten when he fell against an open drawer in his childhood bedroom. His dad had been drunk when he shoved him. His mother apologized later. The doctor in the sorry mill town where his father had worked, and ground his mother to sawdust, laid in six stitches. Greg leaned back on his heels, rubbed his scar, and looked up at Toulouse, squinting as if examining a statue in the half-light of the wax museum near Pioneer Square.

Toulouse extended his arm and spread the fullness of his long cape around Greg's shoulders, pulled him against his chest. "I talk of dreams, child of an idle brain." He brushed Greg's hair with his lips. "From Shakespeare. Romeo and Juliet?" He unfurled the fabric from Greg's shoulders and let him go.

Greg shoved his hands in his pockets. He shot a glance toward the house. "Not here!"

Marian came out, stood in the dooryard with her hands on her hips, watched the men embrace, huffed under her breath as Greg and the so-called "famous poet," the one he'd been waiting for all morning, walked toward her.

"Glad you could come," Marian said, extending her mayonnaise-smeared hand without wiping it. "Do you want to take your things off?"

"No, if you don't mind," he said, pulling his cape closer with a sweep. "Is everyone here?"

"I don't think so." Marian rolled her eyes and looked over at Lucky lying in the dirt. "We're expecting a whole army of bums and winos before this shindig's done. We're celebrating the spring awakening, the vernal equinox."

"Hierogamy?" he asked, smiled at her slyly.

"Excuse me?" Marian said.

"The ultimate celebration," he said imperiously. "You know. The great mating of god and goddess. The rites of spring."

"Yeah, well, sure. Fisher and Sandy are playing music in the living room." She put her hand on his back and pressed him toward the kitchen door. "Come on in."

"Actually, I want to see Lizette," he said, pulling away. He smiled and Marian felt a sly vibe. Looks like a vampire, she thought. Marian studied the pinched creases around the man's eyes, the elasticity of the skin around his throat. "Lizette isn't here. She's still at work at the farmers' market in town.

"Where's Rocket?"

"I don't know." She wiped her hands on the dishtowel she was holding. "You seen him, Greg?"

"He was with Lizette last time I saw him. Check the cabin."

"Where's that?" Toulouse said, staring off in the wrong direction as he scanned the orchard and upper pasture.

"It's down there," Marian said, flapping the dish towel toward the trees. "Follow the path behind the house down to the cove." Toulouse moved off with a flourish, tipping a goodbye from the rim of his foolish hat. Marian watched him go, his self-importance shoved up his ass like a mop handle.

Over her shoulder she yelled at Greg, "Get that idiot out of the driveway before somebody runs over him!"

She went inside and slammed the back door. Outside she heard more cars arrive as she sprinkled paprika on the re-mushed potato salad, smoothed over the helpings Greg and Rocket stole. A horn honked, doors slammed, a glass bottle shattered. Marian stretched a kink out of her neck and covered the bowl with a chipped plate, took it outside to the picnic table along with a bag of potato chips.

Toulouse knocked on the cabin door and Rocket got up from the table where he was eating and opened it, Tucker barking around his knees.

"Hey man! What're you doing here?" Rocket said, recognizing Toulouse and extending his hand. He knew his real name was Henri Toussaint, but because he was French Canadian and styled himself an artist, the Dogs called him Toulouse, after Henri de Toulouse-Lautrec, the only French artist they could name. Somebody had tacked a torn, water-stained print of Toulouse-Lautrec's can-can dancers in the bathroom on Franklin Street, right above the cracked toilet. The joke was that Henri was long and tall, Toulouse-Lautrec short and stubby—both equally weird.

"You were bragging about Lizette's paintings the other day. Since I'm a bit of an art agent, thought I'd come down and take a look," Toulouse said. "Where are they?"

"Right here," Rocket said, showing him into the cabin. "I'll flip them around so you can see. They're really trippy, man. I don't know what they are. Underwater landscapes, fantasy, like some kind of acid trip?"

Rocket began turning canvases around to face the room, propping them against the walls as he spread them out. Toulouse gasped when Rocket turned the first, unfinished canvas to the light. "Mon Dieu!" he said. Then as the others were presented, he whispered, "Christ," and stepped back, bumping Lizette's cot, nearly falling into it. "These are fantastic. Has anyone else seen them?" Rocket shrugged.

The quality of light in the cabin changed from the sullen gray overcast that had grudged against the window, bursting now into a radiant glow that surrounded the canvases and heated the room, causing the men to rub their eyes.

Toulouse saw areas of abstraction mixed gracefully, sometimes jarringly, with traces of figuration. Much of the imagery reflected the coastal forests of Washington, with fanciful-looking flowers and plants, odd specimens used as organizing—perhaps disorganizing—principles. His main impression was the feeling of looking through veils, or at a fantabulous landscape compressed in a steamed, translucent terrarium. The water, the sloshing, the luminous Salish Sea were cast over this fantastic vision. Toulouse wiped sweat from his forehead.

"Beautiful, ineffectual angel, beating in the void her luminous wings in vain," Toulouse said, recovering somewhat from the effect and pacing in front of Lizette's paintings. "Lord Byron, you know?" Rocket considered his poetic outbursts gibberish. Toulouse pondered, asked: "Wonder how much they'll sell for?"

"She doesn't like people looking at them, doesn't want to sell them." Rocket quickly turned the canvases to face the wall again, slid them back together. "She gets upset. Throws things. Makes bird sounds. That's what she does when she gets scared."

"Then it's better you don't show them to anyone," he said. "Can you lock this place? When is she coming back?"

"Hey, I just woke up, man. How should I know?"

"OK. I'm going back to my car and get my camera." He went out the door and stood on the porch, turned to look Rocket in the eye. "I'll be right back. If she comes, get her out of here while I take some pictures. I mean, you're right. This is interesting."

"Why do you want pictures? That might freak her out."

"I just want to remember this," Toulouse lied.

"Lizette really is special," Rocket said. "Reminds me of my mother, but her stuff is way better. I don't wanna upset her. She's been through a lot."

Toulouse turned and hurried up the trail. As he passed the house on the way to his car, he saw people gathered around the picnic table in the front yard. Music blasted and he waved at Greg then looked for his car in the jam that now lined the ranch's long entry road.

Wind picked up some loose paper plates and sailed them over the picket fence into the wild grasses beyond. Greg grabbed a beer from the tub and flicked bits of ice from the label, went inside, knocked on the bathroom door, opened it.

Lucky snored in the tub. Greg locked the door behind him and reached above the medicine chest, felt in the dust curds for the screwdriver. In quick turns he loosened the screws that held the light-switch plate to the wall and plucked a plastic bag from the small recess beside the switch. Then he loosened the syringe taped to the back of the toilet's water tank, sat on the commode and cooked a bit of the white powder in the bowl of a soup spoon.

Lucky stirred, coughed, bubbled saliva under his mustache, turned his head to the wall. Greg singed his fingertips as the matches burned down. He loaded the syringe, shot up and stretched in relief. Someone pounded on the bathroom door. Lucky mumbled, "Buzz off" from the tub. Greg flushed the toilet. More knocking. He spritzed air freshener.

Lizette stood there when he opened the door. "You screwed up my rush," he growled as he pushed past her. Standing in the hall, she'd heard the scraping on the other side of he wall and then the chink of metal on metal. She locked the bathroom door, placed a hand towel over Lucky's head for her own modesty.

She checked the room, scanning the metal surfaces, feeling along edges, found the screwdriver and went to the switch plate, removed the already loose screws and pulled the plastic bag from its hiding place. She peed, and, before she flushed, she dropped the plastic bag into the bowl, watched it disappear down the vortex.

She washed her hands and dried them on the towel on Lucky's head. A few drops of water landed on his nose and he mumbled, "Shit."

In the kitchen, she checked her bag for sketch pad and pastels, headed for the trail that led through the orchard and along the rim above the cove before it looped back to her cabin, Tucker on her heels. She'd been working cooped up in the cabin and wanted to be outside

# SEVENTEEN

A SHARP WIND WHIPPED THE TREES and scattered leaves around Lizette as she sketched on a rough-planed log, gripping the edges of her pad to keep the pages from ruffling. The wobbly bench overlooked the cove and she could see her cabin below, smoke puffing lazily from the stovepipe. The little meadow in the cove fanned toward the water and the overcast sky melded with the horizon in a continuous gray tone.

Startled by the crack of a broken branch, she turned to see Rocket coming up the trail, his jacket collar pulled up to protect his ears in the wind. Tucker darted from under the bench and nudged at his knees until Rocket gave him a pat then the dog dived back under the bench. Lizette smoothed the paper, smudged the charcoal lines she'd just drawn with the side of her hand and tightened the muscles of her face into a half smile to mask her feelings. Only a small twitching beside her right eye gave away any anxiety.

"What're you doing?"

"Thinking."

"Doesn't look like thinking," he said, plopping down beside her, rocking the bench. "Let me see."

He reached around her and she pulled the sketch pad away and held it against her chest, rubbing black on her yellow sweater. Lizette lowered her pad and scanned her drawing, thought, *Why not? So what if he sees?* She let him have it, the pages fluttering in the breeze.

He studied the drawing, then reached up and felt the shape of his nose with his hand, traced his brow ridges, fingered his lips and earlobes, feeling the sketch's likeness. Looking squarely at Lizette, he captured her wandering eyes. She looked away. "Hate to say it, but it kinda looks like me. I mean a better me. Who is it, really? Talk."

Lizette started to say something, but instead picked up a twig from the bench and broke it into tiny sections, measuring, cracking, measuring, afraid, but wanting him to know that his face haunted her, the lines and contours, the dusty yellow shadows under his jaw when he needed a shave, his blue eyes, square body, crooked smile. *He almost makes it,* she thought. *Maybe, with time, he'll change and we can make it work together.* She threw the twig pieces over her shoulder, scattered her hope and crossed her leg, agitating her foot. He held the pad out at arms length, squinted at it with one eye, set the pad down between them.

He reached for her hand as she stood, but she pulled her arms behind her back. A seagull wheeled above the cove. She put her arms out and mimicked its graceful flight. From a tight place in her throat she called to it in a high pitch, "Skaw! Skaw!" Catching her breath, laughing, she glanced at him sideways to tease his hidden prude, but Rocket was gone. She saw a shaft of amber light dance around the crown of his head before he disappeared down the path. The clouds hunched over, covering up the light burst. She waited, then followed down the path to the cabin.

A dark figure on the porch surprised her and she stopped, half hidden in the green understory. His black cape meshed with the weathered, mossy color of the cabin's exterior, faded in and out in the afternoon shadows. A hawk's piercing cry startled her and she looked up, returned to the black apparition, sensed the man was leaving, that in the cape hanging loosely from his shoulders he was spiriting something away, but she could see nothing in the folds of the fabric, dismissed the thought, besides Rocket was there. He wouldn't let anybody take her things, if there was anything worth taking.

"I'll be up in a minute, man," she heard Rocket say from inside. Then the dark visitor turned and closed the cabin door. He looked up and saw her standing on the sloped trail like a startled doe, maybe twenty yards away, leaves clinging to her hair. He waved his hand and said, "Hey, Lizette," but she did not know him. Tucker lunged down the trail, barking a warning. The man held the top of his funny hat as he scurried off.

"Who was that?" Lizette said as she came into the cabin, dropping her canvas bag at the foot of her cot and going to the stove to warm her hands, turning to heat her backside.

"Toulouse."

She pushed Tucker away from her knees, nudged him toward his box beside her bed.

"The poet?"

"Yeah."

"I've heard of him, maybe from Fisher. What's he doing here? Somebody, maybe Greg, said he was in New York or something. Isn't he famous?"

"He just wanted to talk." Rocket sat on the wobbly stool and turned toward the window, avoiding her eyes. "I showed him a couple of your paintings. He has been hangin' around the Dog House lately. Mostly with Greg. They go out and get loaded sometimes. He must've said something about you're paintings."

"I told you to leave my stuff alone. That's the rule. Even the Dogs follow that one at your place." She stamped her foot, picked up a thin black paint brush from the table and threw it at the wall. "That guy has *way* bad chi! I can see it. Foul energy."

"Chi? What the hell's that?" He stood and studied her face, trying to find an opening in the maze of her mind, but gave up, knew he'd never get through to her. "Relax. It's no big thing. He liked them. He's an OK guy, weird, but OK." Rocket went to the door and spoke with his back to her. "I'm going up to the party. Are you coming?"

"In a while. Close the door."

"You don't have to pout," Rocket said.

"Close the door!"

The afternoon sun scattered silver sequins across the water. Lizette went to the big window and scanned the surface looking for the hunters, searching far out in the channel. Maybe, she thought, maybe it's them moving closer, she squinted, maybe it's an illusion, a refraction, a mind trick. But no. There they *were*, zigzagging closer, still a long way out. Turning back to the room, she saw her pill bottle on the table, lying on its side. She shook it and heard a weak rattle. Pulling the lid she saw there were only a few pills left and tried to think how long she'd stretched a one-month supply – five weeks? No. More. She needed a refill and had to check in with Dr. Finch. On her hands and knees, she leaned into the closet and scratched the tinfoil from under the closet's framing.

She put the acid tabs in her pocket and took her pill, followed it with a drink from the water jug on the table. Images of Dr. Finch and the hospital, her father, the streets, the rain and the moldy smell of the black raincoat, the arm crushing her larynx, pulling her pants down, kaleidoscoped through her mind. She sat on the stool, shaking. In a while, when her breathing slowed and her hands steadied, she got up and headed for the house. Music heaved through the air in gushes, Motown from the phonograph in the front yard mixed with honky-tonk piano inside, harmonica, tambourine, a slowing tempo, then silence.

A beat picked up, heavy bass, lots of piano. In the front yard people laughed and hung on each other, shaking asses. Someone called her name, but she did not respond, just looked at the scene. *Troll's banquet*, she thought.

"Lizette?" Toulouse sidled up to her in his musty drapery. "I want to talk to you. I had the opportunity to look at some of your paintings. Quite nice, astonishing, really."

"You nasty prick," she hissed. "Stay out of my cabin or I'll astonish you."

"You're right about my prick," he said, laughing. He pulled his cape around him like he was trying to keep germs from escaping. "Had kind of a green drip going for a while."

"What?" Lizette put her hands on her hips and saw him like a turd on the grass. She looked at the angle of his arrogant jaw and his burnt sienna eyes. *Hades in drag*, she thought. *Liar.* "Are you nuts?" she said. "You're telling me you've got the clap or what? I don't even know you."

"Sorry," he said, fingering the brim of his ridiculous hat, looking away, acting all innocent, annoying her further. "It just popped out. Sorry again. Pardon me, really. I mean I'm taking pills. Everything's OK. Kind of a nasty strain going around, though, that's what the doctor said. But, hey, listen." He reached out and grabbed her by the bicep. "That's not what I want to rap about. It's your canvases. They're wonderful. Can we talk?"

She pulled her arm back, let out an anxious chirp. All at once she knew who Greg had been sleeping with. She charged into the house, looking for Marian. The living room was thick with music. Marian sat withdrawn, as if shielded by a translucent curtain, brooding in her mother's old chair by the window, the place where her mother used to knit wool from the ranch's sheep and listen to the radio, tell them stories when they were girls. Marian sat immobile now in the party's swirl, Mrs. Cutler come to life, thinner and prettier, but a shocking likeness just the same.

She saw Greg, nodding out in the wing chair across the room from Marian, and tried to figure out what to do. She needed to talk to Marian, but realized Greg was not asleep. He was watching her with wary eyes, knees spread, arms akimbo, malevolence distilled. Sandy beat the tambourine against her baby belly and swayed on the leather footstool pulled into the middle of the room. Rocket blew the harmonica, tapped his foot, syncopated with his head. Sandy got up, offered a bump and grind from her strip tease act, gathered her milk-heavy breasts and thrust them toward Rocket, shimmied, spread her round ass.

It was Fisher she'd heard above the party noise, pouring out sounds like rain coming down, gutter down, funky low-down. Lizette folded onto the floor beneath the front windows, leaned against the wall, opened to the music *light rain, light rain, baby, pouring down*, and kept time with swishing knees. Fisher hunched vulture-like over the keyboard and threw Lizette a wink, a kid doing tricks on a bicycle, playing *"Six Days Upon the Road"* and singing like Taj Mahal in a gravelly roll *"I got ten forward gears and a sweet Georgia overdrive. I'm takin' little white pills and my eyes are open wide . . . Baby, Baby watch the way I shift my gears . . . I'm six days upon the road and I got to see my baby tonight."* Lizette watched him and offered an encouraging smile, felt lifted by the beat. She noticed Greg had roused and was studying her.

"Hey, Lizard." Greg said and flopped his arm. "Get me a beer." She ignored him and scooched away.

"Come on, Lizzy. Please."

"Pig," Lizette said under her breath.

He pouted his girlish lips, fluttered his long lashes. "Please."

"Get it yourself," Marian growled, leaving no room for argument.

Greg got up, steadied himself on the arm of the chair. "Gotta piss," he said, lurching forward and heading down the hall toward the bathroom. Fisher played some kind of honky-tonk version of "Candy Man." Sandy pulled the tambourine over her head and kept time with the heel of her hand, her belly swelling and extending. Rocket used the top of the old upright piano as a drum. From the bathroom, Lucky shrieked razor sharp from the tub and the music stopped. Rocket dashed down the hall.

"What's up man? Why're you hitting him?" Greg wailed on Lucky and Rocket grabbed him around the waist from behind, held his right fist above his head while Lucky cowered in the bathtub, hands in front of his face to defend against punches. "Lay off, Greg. Are you crazy?"

"Fucker stole my stash. He's the only one who could've."

"He's been passed out in the bathtub the whole time he's been here, dumb shit. Calm down." Marian and Sandy blocked the bathroom door, but Lizette could easily see over their heads. Greg sniffled, on the verge of tears. Rocket bent him over, pulled his arm behind his back, growled something into his ear.

Lizette went to the kitchen and got a beer, popped the top with an opener, set it on the counter and peeled open the tinfoil from her pocket, dropped a translucent acid hit into the brew. Back in the living room, she set the bottle on the small table beside the chair where Greg had been sitting.

When Greg calmed down, they brought him to the living room and pushed him into the chair where he'd been sitting, everyone settled back into their spots before the outburst. Fisher began playing again, Hayden. A riff from Variations in F Minor, Lizette thought, and smirked at Fisher's wise-assed incongruity, the shift from rock-a-billy to classical, she recognized the conceit in his virtuosity, shared his artistic frustration, and forgave him.

Greg wiped his nose and took a slug of beer from the bottle. Outside shadows lengthened and the wind kicked up. People began leaving, cars revving, doors slamming, loud good-byes. A horn honked at the end of the driveway and the driver turned on the car's headlights. Somebody backed into the fence, snapped a post before tearing off, leaving the pickets tilted. Fisher played "Happy Trails." Greg drained his beer bottle.

"Last call!" Marian said.

# EIGHTEEN

RAIN SPRINKLED ON THE PARTY'S REMNANTS, dampened Lizette's hair as she picked up paper napkins and cups in the front yard, stuffed them into a trash bag. Fisher fussed with the toppled fence, trying to prop it up, but it fell over again. She stepped over the fallen fence into the field, dampened her pant legs, and happily chased the escaping papers.

In the tangled bushes beyond the meadow she listened to a bird's tentative evensong, just a few notes, a few more, then it stopped. Along the fence, she saw one brave purple crocus beside a discarded beer bottle. She felt a pulse of gratitude that it hadn't been crushed during the party and picked it, ignored a guilt pang at breaking this tender promise of spring from its stem. She licked the drop of nectar that formed a dainty knob on the tubular end, put the flower behind her ear, slipped more beer bottles into her sack.

Throwing a leg over the low fence, she stood again on the clipped grass in the front yard and picked up more trash. It felt good to bend, to stretch out the backs of her legs. She squatted, gathered potato-salad-caked paper plates, and rolled up through her spine, took a yoga breath, giggled in relief that the party was over, trash in both hands. She put it in the bag and set it aside, extended her arms overhead, pulling out the kinks, one arm, then the other, Marian style.

Poland rolled up, his truck's windshield wipers flapping out of sync. She threw the plastic bag she carried into the truck's bed. He pointed to the flower behind her ear, smiled.

"You found spring." She fingered the delicate petals beside her ear. "Pretty," he said. After a couple of months, he thought, she looks plumper and pinker.

"How much more junk you got?" He got out of the truck, looked around. There wasn't a lot left to pick up in the yard, he saw. She'd done a good job. "Is there more trash inside?"

She checked, returned with two more full bags from the kitchen, beer bottles clanking as she walked to the back of the truck.

"There's more," she said. "Couple of bags left in the kitchen. These were on the porch." She wrinkled her nose. "Stinks. We should've made a dump run *before* the party."

Poland grunted and tied the tops of the sacks, pushed them against the back of the cab. "Where's Coyote?"

"Inside." She shrugged, pulled a frown. "They're in the bedroom, arguing."

"Not good." Poland shook his head. "They fight like fire and water, too much steam."

Lizette got the rest of the garbage. She heard angry voices coming from behind the bedroom door, went into the living room and stood there holding a garbage bag in each hand, listening, trying to decide if Marian was in trouble, needed help. It didn't sound too bad, Lizette thought, nothing Marian couldn't handle. But, to be sure, she knocked on the door.

Greg yanked it open, leaned his goat face into the hall, "Get lost!" he yelled and slammed the door. She went out to the truck and lobbed the bags into the back. Poland put in a gas can and some tools.

"Everything OK?" Poland said. Lizette threw up her hands, shrugged.

Nodding at Fisher who'd been putting chairs in the barn, Poland said, "You coming, Piano Man?"

Lizette got into the truck cab, scooting to the middle of the seat. The men got in on either side. They bumped along the orchard road, the tires slogging through the long grass. Poland gunned the engine in the thick spots.

"Sheep need to get to work on this grass," Poland said as they bounced along. Lizette bumped her head on the cab's roof and rubbed the spot. "Didn't want to move the flock down here, not with all those crazy people around."

Fisher smiled at Poland's assessment and showed his horse teeth. She looked at his long, pretty fingers resting on his knee, at his perfect, oval fingernails. Compared her hand to his. She felt his thigh brushing against hers and pulled closer to Poland.

At the back of the ranch, in a crease of land beyond the orchard, the dump was a deep cup that had been hallowed out long ago with a tractor. Over the years the hole had been widened and deepened as the hungry maw chewed up household garbage, broken equipment, old appliances, hunks of rotting wood, glass, even a rusting truck that might have been new in 1920.

Poland called it the bone yard. He'd taught both Marian and Lizette to shoot a .22 rifle there when they were teenagers, setting rusted soup cans and moldy fruit jars on an old truck radiator so they could practice their aim. Both girls liked the pull of the trigger, the kick of the stock against their shoulders, the explosion of glass and metal when the bullets hit their mark. They'd squeal and cheer and slap each other on the back.

But, Marian was the best shot, always had dead aim, whether it was pool, bowling or darts. Once she killed a rat at the dump with a Frisbee as it was licking a broken ketchup bottle. It toppled, hit cleanly behind its tiny ear, a red glob of blood suspended on a long whisker when they checked it. Lizette thought about that now, felt like taking some shots, wondered if Poland's rifle was in its usual place under the front seat.

Poland parked on the edge of the pit, pulled bags from the back of the truck, and started down the slope, holding his body sideways against the steep angle as he went. Fisher grabbed a full bag in each hand and followed him. Lizette took the rest. "Dump them over there," Poland said, gesturing toward a blackened place in the deep bowl. Two long tree trunks, set side by side, bridged a section of the pit's rim, about twelve feet above the bottom. They burned the household refuse there, using the big old trunks as a shield against the chance that embers would fly up and set fire to the cedar trees towering above the pit. They untied the bags and mounded the garbage. Poland went back to the truck and got a rake and hoe. He brought the battered yellow and black gas can back, too.

He looked up at the sky that was dropping thick mist onto their heads and doused the pile, a colorful confusion of waste. He picked up a stray napkin and lit the edge with a match and dropped it onto the pile. The fire whooshed into dancing flames. Lizette clapped and half whirled, took a couple of slow bops, right then left.

"Fire dancer," Poland said, laughing, clapping a rhythm with his hands. Fisher stood transfixed by the fire as beer bottle labels curled and flat black ashes floated heavily up to the underside of the logs. Waves of smoke snaked between the logs and disappeared into the moist and darkening sky.

Lizette called down from the tree-trunk bridge. They looked up to see her balancing there, one foot on each trunk, catching warmth from the fire between her legs, drying her pants.

"Watch out, Hummingbird," Poland warned. "Here comes fire!" and he doused the pile with more gas. Whoom!

Lizette threw back her head and cawed like a crow, wobbled, caught herself, looked down on the men in the pit, everyone laughing. From the black shadows of the cedar trees, Greg stepped forward, a wild-animal look on his face.

"Fucking bitch! Crazy whore!"

Spooked, Lizette lost her footing and fell hard across the trunks, knocked the air from her lungs. Greg made a small leap to the trunk nearest the pit's edge. He stepped along spider-like until he stood above her, his face glowing from the fire below like an evil orange lantern. Cerberus flashed through her mind, Dog of Hell. He pulled a butcher knife from his belt. She rolled onto the opposite log and inched backward. He stepped across and loomed over her, eyes dilated, shadowy red snakes of firelight writhed around his head.

He stared blindly, gripped by rage. Lizette heard Poland and Fisher's voices, but they sounded far away and musical.

"No. Stop. No. Stop."

Greg did not waiver in his advance on her and Lizette put her arms up to protect her face. Greg swayed over her, slashed, caught her pant leg with the blade, pulled up from the rip. He gathered all his power, raised the knife like a spear above his head—fell sideways.

Lizette saw the round metal disk strike Greg's abdomen and fall onto the tree trunk, tumble to the fire below. She turned to see Marian standing on the pit's opposite rim, her arm and wrist still extended from flinging the dented hubcap like a Frisbee. Greg tumbled down the side of the pit, rolled to a stop near the edge of the fire, howled, twisted, held his stomach, flopped side to side. Lizette stood and jumped to the rim, slid down the side of the pit on her butt.

"Move him away from the fire," Poland said. "See if anything's broken." He waved toward the truck. "Marian, get the tarp from behind the front seat. Come on, Piano Man, get his legs."

Fisher and Poland dragged Greg away from the flames. Marian ran, slipping on the side of the pit, crawling toward the truck on all fours, getting to her feet. The two men lifted Greg, who moaned loudly and spit a little blood. They moved him to a flat spot, next to an old, rusted refrigerator.

Marian spread the tarp, directed as they lifted him. Greg gagged and moaned. She took Greg's wrist, checked his heart rate against her watch.

"Where do you hurt?" Marian asked, getting her own breathing under control and straightening his arms, squaring his shoulders. "Lizette give me a hand! Straighten out his legs."

Lizette pulled away from the scene, slowly backing, as if from a poisonous snake.

"It hurts here, ahh, here." Greg pointed to his abdomen and tried to roll onto his side as Marian pushed on the spot. She ripped open his shirt and looked at the blue welt and swelling, gently pressing into his belly with her fingertips.

"Jesus!" He gasped like the wind had been kicked out of him and sucked hard for air.

Marian looked around at the worried faces. "I think it's his spleen! Maybe a rupture. We've got to get him out of here." They helped Greg sit up while he cussed.

"Can you stand?" Marian had her hands under his armpits, lifting, but not getting him on his feet.

"How should I know?" In tears, Greg craned his neck, pulled away from her and the pain. Poland and Fisher got on either side of him, Marian pushed. He swayed and the men braced him, pressed in to share their strength. Draping Greg's arms over their shoulders they eased him forward and he took a step, cried out.

Lizette paced a few steps to and fro, bent and picked up a round piece of glass, fingered it to stay calm. They staggered with him to the pit's slope and looked up, gauging the ten or twelve feet, to the top.

"Get his belt from the back," Marian said, looking over at Lizette, who was tweeting into the towering trees while her fingers worked the glass disk. "Snap out of it, Lizette. We don't have time for that shit!"

Lizette recoiled as if she'd been stung, grabbed Greg's belt and pushed from behind, the force catching Fisher off guard. He fell sideways against the hill, tripped over his own feet. Greg wailed.

"Take it easy!" Fisher said to Lizette and got his arm back around Greg. He glared at her from behind his thick glasses. "We know you're pissed, Liz. Knock it off."

"Go this way," Poland directed with his free arm. "It's not so steep over there. But, be careful, the dirt's slicker."

Greg let out a deep groan as they dragged him sideways, moving together, until a foot slipped and they all went down, flopping against the slope. Greg cursed as they grunted and huffed, regained their footing and moved him forward again.

"Lower the tailgate, lift him into the back," Marian ordered, stamping off the mud that had collected on her boots. The others did the same and piled into the truck's cab.

Marian got into the bed and settled Greg, jumped up and banged on the cab, signaling Poland to take off. He wheeled the truck around and tore through the orchard. Marian jumped over the side when the truck stopped rolling, ran for the house.

"Sandy, get your stuff!" she yelled. "Rocket! We gotta go! Greg's been hurt! We've gotta get him to Seattle. To a surgeon!"

Marian came out leading Sandy by the elbow and slinging her black medical bag over her shoulder, a blanket draped over her arm. "They can't handle a trauma case like this in Bellingham," she told

Poland. "We've got to get to the ER at King County Hospital. I know the docs there. When does the next ferry leave?"

"About twenty minutes," he said, calmly. "But we can't all fit in the truck."

"I'll drive Sandy in her car," Fisher said, looking sympathetically at her big belly and sleepy eyes. "That's how we got here."

"OK, let's go. Where's Rocket?" Marian said as she jumped into the back. Lizette got into the cab. "Gun it, Poland!"

Lizette looked through the rear window, saw Marian settle beside Greg and gently pull up the blanket, lean down and kiss his forehead.

"What about Lucky?" Lizette said, leaning out and yelling at Marian. "He's still in the bathtub."

Marian raked her hair and looked at the trees flashing by. "Shit! Can Poland get him later?"

Leaning over the steering wheel, staring straight ahead at the road, he said, "I'll get Abaya to help. Rocket's around there someplace. She'll check on them. I'll call home from the landing. They can't stay at the ranch by themselves. Too crazy." Lizette nodded "yes" to Marian through the rear window.

Poland banked into a turn on the Horseshoe Highway and Eastsound came into view. Lizette scanned the gray and black streets, caught glimpses of the water between white-washed buildings, the sea turning a murky jade in the last shades of evening. She strained her eyes, looking for the lights of the ferry.

At the landing, cars were lined up, hood to trunk, all the way down the hill to the loading ramp. Poland pulled in behind the last vehicle, Fisher on his tail in the V-Dub. The rain fell harder now and Lizette got out and went to Marian with a "now what" look. Greg shivered in the back.

"We can't stay here." Marian vaulted out of the truck bed and charged down the hill. "He's going into shock. Lizette, cover him with jackets!"

At the bottom of the hill, the dock attendant sheltered from the rain in a little shack. He listened to music, the sound intermittently drowned out by the crackling ship-to-shore radio that connected him to the ferries as they crisscrossed the Salish Sea, lumbering endlessly from one island to another.

"Hey, Marian, what's up?" The man recognized her standing at the door. She'd gone to high school with the guy, not long ago put a couple of stitches in his head after he got his skull cracked in a bar fight.

"Got an emergency. Guy injured at the ranch. I need to move to the front of the line. How long until the ferry gets here?"

"Probably ten minutes, everything's on time tonight."

The man stepped out of the booth and checked the long line of cars, put on an orange safety vest over his jacket. He got a couple of orange sticks and started toward the cars. Marian moved up the hill behind him. He signaled the waiting vehicles to pull over, slowly cleared a narrow lane. Marian ran back to the truck, jumped into the cab, said, "Go! Go! Go!" She waved at the cleared path and Poland eased the truck down the slope to the front of the line. Fisher followed with Sandy hanging out the passenger-side window, yelling, "How long? How long?"

"Ferry's just clearing Deer Point," the attendant hollered. "It'll be here any minute." He looked into the truck's bed and saw Greg pulled into a fetal position.

"Tell the captain to call ahead, have an ambulance meet us at the dock in Anacortes," Marian directed. "We're going to county hospital in Seattle. And, get the deckhands to bring more blankets as soon as we're onboard."

"Will do," he said and picked up a microphone attached to the squawking radio, passed on the instructions.

The ferry rumbled into its berth and the metal vehicle ramp had barely been lowered when Poland lurched the truck forward. The deckhands signaled him to the side, so the truck and V-Dub would be the first vehicles off when they landed in Anacortes. Marian got in the back, unwrapped her blood pressure cuff, called for blankets. She took a reading, turned pale.

Greg looked down at his arm and started yelling that it had scales, millions of scales. Marian hushed him, concerned about delirium setting in so soon. It wasn't a usual symptom with a ruptured spleen. The ferry fought through the surge, and finally, through the mist, they saw the flashing red lights of the ambulance.

As they docked, the ambulance attendants threw open the back doors of the old Cadillac station wagon and pulled out the gurney, popped its spindly legs into place, waited. Poland shot to the parking lot, backed up to the open doors. Cars moved off the ferry, drivers gawking as they passed the flashing lights and Marian instructing the attendants on how to transfer Greg to the gurney, her foot braced in front of the wheel to keep it from rolling.

Lizette jumped into the back of Sandy's car and Poland swung his truck around, waved, and got back in line with the other vehicles for the return trip to Orcas.

"Get his vitals," Marian yelled as she got into the back of the ambulance. "Roll, roll!" She realized the drivers probably didn't have more than first aid training and elbowed the man out of the way.

She pulled her stethoscope from her black bag and Greg looked up at her as she put on the blood-pressure cuff, "Light's like cracked crystals," he said wondrously. "Spinning . . . fast."

Marian tucked his arms more closely against his body and brushed his damp hair from his forehead. Siren on, they screamed into the night.

"Far out, man," Greg said in a vacant, amazed voice. "I'm flyin' man!"

The attendant looked suspiciously at Greg, then at Marian. He asked Marian what happened, why they were taking him all the way to Seattle, instead of Bellingham. She realized she'd have to explain Greg's injury and her decision to bring him all the way to Seattle.

# NINTEEN

POLAND PICKED UP MARIAN and Lizette on Franklin Street a few days after Greg died. He left the truck running outside Sandy's, making it clear he had no intention of visiting. He gave Lizette a shy hug in the front hall, whispered something in her ear. Marian clasped Sandy around the shoulders, Lizette patted her round belly, and they dashed for the truck. They rode the eighty miles to the ferry at Anacortes without saying much.

"You left a messy house!" Abaya said, hands on her hips, when they came dragging through the back door at the ranch. The kitchen smelled of onions and meat. "I made venison stew." Abaya moved past Marian and Lizette to peck Poland on the cheek.

"Silly woman," he huffed, embarrassed. She gave him a playful pinch and he rubbed his elbow in mock pain.

"Everything was upside down when I got here," Abaya groused. "You girls made a mess. Some caveman was moaning in the bathroom. I got scared. Then the Rocketman showed up and got the guy out. The toilet backed up." She pinched her nose to show the stink. "Poland called the pumper. The guy said you shouldn't wait so long next time. Big mess. Your father never . . . "

"Thanks," Marian cut her off, sounded weary. "I don't know what I'd do without you, both of you. Everything's jumbled right now. When I dream, my father comes to me. When I'm awake, I hear my mother. Greg is laughing. Lizette is dancing in the orchard. I've never felt blown away like this before."

Abaya wiped away the tears sliding down Marian's cheeks and turned to Lizette, who hovered by the table. "You missed work. What? You think good jobs are easy to find? I can get someone anytime who doesn't go running off to Seattle whenever she feels like it. We got business here."

Lizette bit her lip, sat down, crossed her legs and bounced her foot.

"You hungry?" Abaya snapped.

Lizette shook her head, put on a pout.

"We'll eat without you," Abaya said dismissively. "This old man always needs something for his belly."

She served up the stew, poured milk, and settled into a chair. They spooned through carrots and potatoes, breaking hunks of spiced venison with the sides of their spoons.

"I'm sleeping here with you tonight," Abaya said. Marian didn't argue.

After Poland left, they washed the dishes and Marian took a bath. They all sat on the couch in the dark watching TV, sharing the same heavy blanket, the screen's gray-green light flickering on the living room walls.

Drowsy, they listened to the late news. *"Dedication of the World Trade Center was heavily attended. New York Governor Nelson Rockefeller called the towering complex the centerpiece of the city's downtown redevelopment plans, a sign the recession is ending. In the nation's capital, the U.S. Supreme Court has ruled in Roe v. Wade, overturning states' bans on abortion, making it legal in the United States for the first time."*

Marian leaned forward to hear, got up and turned up the volume. *"The outcome of the controversial case could make abortion a constitutional right in America, a move hailed by leaders of the Women's Liberation Movement and many in the medical profession. . . . In South Dakota, the FBI and U.S. Marshals continue to struggle with armed members of the American Indian Movement, many of them highly trained Vietnam combat veterans."* Pictures of scruffy men brandishing rifles flashed on the screen, long pony tails, headbands, fists raised in power salutes, more footage of men in military uniforms and sunglasses.

"Crazy men," Abaya shook her head. "Somebody's kids are gonna get hurt. She flipped the TV off, throwing the room into darkness. Lizette thought about Raven, prayed he'd be safe, said nothing.

"Time for bed girls," Abaya chirped like a mother bird. "You need rest. The phone rang the whole time you were gone. You can look at the messages I wrote down in the morning."

"Anything important?" Marian asked, sleep in her voice.

"Sure. Why else call on the telephone? For fun?"

Lizette slipped out the back door and headed to the cabin. It felt like years since she'd picked her way down the path and she couldn't wait to get inside and shut the door. From the cabin's windows she scanned the water, watched the moonlight dance over the whitecaps, took a deep breath and felt her knees buckle. She dropped into her cot, pulled up the sleeping bag and crashed.

She awoke at first light with a gnawing hunger and hurried to the house. Marian and Abaya weren't up and she put a pot of water on the stove, searched the cabinets for oatmeal. The phone rang and Abaya, in a faded blue robe, grabbed the receiver off the wall before she could get to the phone. "No. She's asleep. She can call you when she gets up. What's your number? OK, OK."

"Who was that?" Marian stood at the kitchen door. Lizette stirred oatmeal, Abaya beside her.

"Sandy. She wants you to call."

Abaya turned from the stove and looked out the kitchen windows. "It's April and raining like January, cold. You just left her house . . . She's a dumb one."

"Did you make coffee?" Abaya waved to the copper-colored electric pot on the counter with her wooden spoon, and Marian got a mug from the cupboard. Abaya dropped a glob of oatmeal on the floor, bent gracefully and wiped it with a damp rag.

"Did she say anything else?" Marian looked at Abaya's small frame, at her narrow back. *Lizette's right,* she thought, *the world is filled with fairies and elves*, and went to her bedroom, returned with her black midwife's diary.

Marian leafed through the diary's pages, stopped when she found the notes on Sandy. *Belly measurement large for estimated gestation. Blood pressure a bit high, but within normal range. Firm cervix, strong heart sounds for both mother and baby. Most recent urine results normal for all panels. Next visit, one month.* She looked at the calendar and saw she was supposed to see Sandy in two weeks.

She took her coffee to the living room and dozed by the fire, thought about the ranch, its cross-fenced meadows and fruit orchards, how it looked in the spring when she got off the school bus and skipped up the road to the house, blossoms everywhere. She understood that she lived at the ranch, not just physically, but in her mind and spirit. She took the familiar smells of bread baking, the quality of light in the kitchen on a summer morning, the sound of bleating lambs with her wherever she went. The fertile essence of her family's land kept her grounded, a force she worked against and folded into. She realized she couldn't survive without the ranch, that she'd been lax with her heritage, her livelihood, and felt ashamed.

The image of her father, barrel-chested and gruff, came to her as she sipped from her coffee mug. She saw his dusty hat pulled down to shade his eyes. She pictured him talking in a knot of ranchers, laughing, offering advice while she spied on them from the dark shadows of the barn. She listened to the talk about fruit markets and flock management. Shepherds came and went. Old Doc McClellen made vet calls and they talked dosing and breeding. He always let her help him with the sheep. And, there were orchard workers and foremen, but always, throughout Marian's life, there was Poland, standing outside the circle of men, directing them without them realizing it.

"Chopped enough wood for a week," Poland said as he came in with an armload and laid it beside the fireplace. "Gotta go," he said to Marian, shifting from foot to foot. "How long you staying?"

"A couple of days. I've got a couple mothers at Friday Harbor to check on. After that, I'll be home more. Promise. Lizette can handle anything that comes up in the meantime," surprising herself at the easy answer, showing how much she relied on her friend.

Poland snorted and led Abaya out the back door. She heard Lizette's voice in the dooryard and Abaya's shrewish tones, caught words: "sick," "hurt," "confused," then giggling, and knew they were talking about her.

The phone rang, but before she could get up, Lizette burst in the back door and rushed to answer it.

"Hey, Sandy. Who're you doing?" She laughed and continued, "I mean what're you doing? Contractions?" Lizette went blank, checked in the living room for Marian, who got up, wondering first at Lizette's bubbly greeting on the phone, probably glad to be home, she guessed, and grabbed the phone.

"Are they regular?" Marian ran through her list of routine questions. "How many minutes apart? Are they in your lower back? Is the baby moving? Has it dropped? I don't know. It's too soon for labor. Wait, stop yelling." She knew mothers in labor were usually more subdued. "Start timing them. Is Rocket around?"

Marian covered the mouthpiece, said to Lizette, "Can you go back down there? She's all alone, scared. I know it's not time yet, probably Braxton-Hix contractions. But, I've got other mothers to check here."

Lizette dreaded returning to Seattle, but didn't complain. She got nods of understanding from Poland and Abaya, who were loading the truck and went to the cabin. She gathered her things into her canvas bag, pulled the sleeping bag over her pillow, scanned the water's surface for a sign of the long-finned hunters, then padlocked the door and set the key on the ledge above the window. Marian ran through instructions as they drove to Orcas Landing: "Get Sandy to the women's clinic, I'll call ahead. If there's any blood, call the women's clinic immediately. Make sure she rests, puts her feet up. Her blood pressure is running a little high . . . Can you do this?"

Lizette nodded, but wondered. Sandy usually did whatever she wanted. She felt like driftwood bumping around the sound, tossed here, dragged there, pulled by the tides. When she got off the ferry at Anacortes, she trudged to the bus stop, took the express to Seattle. She knew Rocket would help her batten things down, but felt awkward about calling on him, and, as she looked out the bus window at the blur of green forest and meadows, felt alone and threatened. She put those thoughts out of her mind and reminded herself to make an appointment with Dr. Finch.

# TWENTY

A FEW WEEKS LATER, Marian lugged her suitcase up Sandy's front steps, hoisted her black medical bag onto her hip, turned the door knob, let herself in, hollered: "Hello? Lizette? Sandy, I'm here!"

Lizette's voice tumbled down the stairs, "We're up here. Sandy's having contractions again. Hurry up!"

Marian's heart flipped as she charged up the stairs. Maybe she'd stayed too long at the ranch, missed something when she'd checked on them by phone or skipped over an important detail in the lab reports from Sandy's checks at the women's clinic. In the doorway, she paused and surveyed the situation. Propped up on red and pink pillows, Sandy beamed at her, belly round and high. *Baby hasn't dropped yet,* Marian thought. *Color's good. She's healthy, thank God. But, this could take a while.*

"Put your stuff in the baby's room," Sandy said, waving toward the hall. "We put a single bed in there and a crib. Liz fixed it up. She's using the bigger room as a studio. All her art shit's in there. The paint smells makes me want to erp. I have to remind her constantly to close the damn door."

Marian saw the women glare at each other and figured she'd arrived just in time to avoid a cat fight. She peeked into Lizette's room and saw an easel by the window, smiled at the thought of Lizette working there, and put her things in the newly arranged nursery. Lizette followed, closed the door, leaned her long body against the jamb.

"What do you think?" Lizette said.

"About what?" Marian sat on the bed, her black bag primly on her knees.

"Sandy!"

"I just got here. I think it's going to be a while and I'm going to need your help when it's time. She's not having labor contractions. Her body's just getting ready." Lizette looked at her skeptically. "Trust me. It's going to be a while."

For days after that, Marian sat in the nursery on the side of the slumping single bed while Sandy napped across the hall and Lizette hummed and chirped as she painted in her makeshift studio. Marian stared at the little white crib, unfolded and refolded the pink and blue baby blankets, stacked them neatly on the small white dresser. She studied the rosemaling—pink rose buds, white daisies and blue periwinkle set in fine swirling black lines, a Scandinavian folk art she knew Lizette had painted on the drawer fronts.

She lay on the bed and stared at the water stains on the ceiling, smelled the mold in the walls, yielded her body to the rot. She rubbed her abdomen knowing no baby would ever grow there. The doctors had confirmed that the gonorrhea had eaten away at her insides just like they said, damaging her fallopian tubes. The new round of antibiotics had made her sick and she'd stayed in bed for days, Abaya bringing her soup, while Lizette attended to Sandy in Seattle. She'd needed Lizette with her then, but couldn't abandon Sandy, couldn't call Lizette back.

She sat up now, pulled on her shoes, and went into Sandy's room, listened through her stethoscope for the flutter of the baby's heart. She moved the instrument slowly over Sandy's swollen belly until she caught the dual-toned whooshing, the beat synchronizing with her own pulse, her heart rate accelerating to keep up. This throbbing kept her going, this promise of new life, vulnerable in its dependence.

The date of conception couldn't be right, Marian knew that. Already this pregnancy was well beyond ten months, using Sandy's reckoning. The father couldn't be Big Al, either, no matter what she said. She pictured Albert Munoz, Hell's Angel wanna-be, playing pool at the tavern, skanky and mean, and was glad he was in jail. She watched suspiciously when Rocket came over and sniffed around Sandy like an old hound searching for a comfortable spot to curl up. She saw how he watched Sandy, stepped in to comfort her, how they shared whispered intimacies, and she saw how Lizette's face froze in a blank mask when the two of them were together, how she quickly disappeared.

"The heartbeat's strong," Marian said. To ease Sandy's frustration, she and Lizette fixed an early dinner, took Sandy for a walk. Lizette swiped spring flowers from neighbors' yards, gave them to Sandy to put in her hair. Lizette bent to pet a cat that came out from behind a hedge. They stopped to talk with a woman pushing a baby stroller. Lizette got down on her haunches, leaned in and adjusted the infant's knitted cap. Lizette held the baby's tiny hands, marveled at the petal points of its tissue-thin fingernails.

Then it was morning again and nothing—no miracles, no pains, no progress. In the afternoon there was a sign. Marian called it a "bloody show," a swipe of pink mucus when Sandy peed. "Finally," Marian said as she took the tissue to the toilet, the sound of the flush filling the house like the thunder. Huddled around the bowl, they watched the wad swirl and disappear.

The women went back to decoupaging magazine pictures on pieces of gray barn wood in the kitchen. Lizette sketched as the others worked. Marian looked over her shoulder to find the page filled with drawings of round, plump figures, torsos, thighs with bellies resting on them. Sandy got up and washed the dishes, swept the floor, wrapped a towel around the broom handle and went after cobwebs in the downstairs hall. She watered the plants, put fava beans on to soak.

Rocket came over after work and flipped on the TV in the living room and lounged on the sofa watching, "M*A*S*H". He periodically flew into the kitchen shouting "Incoming! Incoming!" and hit the refrigerator for a beer. It rained. The Dogs stopped by to sniff around. Lizette went for a walk around the block, studied the brambles and weathered cement foundations that reminded her of pictures she'd seen of the ruins at Pompeii. She tamped her anger down, walked back to the house and went up to her studio. That night Lizette slept on the couch in the living room, half listening to the women bumping around upstairs. Sometime in the dark the sound of running water woke her. Marian was at the kitchen sink, filling a big pot.

"Her water broke," Marian said, putting the pot on the stove and turning on the burner.

Lizette sat at the table, said nothing in her half sleep. She'd been to see Finch and got a prescription refill. The medication was piling up. Marian monitored how often she took her pills, pestered her everyday. Lizette craned her neck, closed her mouth to keep her tongue from thrusting, her body itched everywhere. Flushing, tingling. *Sometimes crazy feels better*, she thought, stretching her arms overhead to loosen her stiff back.

"It doesn't mean the baby will be born today," Marian said. "I've seen women go for days after their water broke. I want to give her a sponge bath. Go up and look. See how she's doing. Talk to her."

Lizette ignored her and went back to the couch, found sleep. In her dream, her own belly was big and she was crying, afraid. Her mother was standing there, dripping wet, laughing, telling her to swim. Lizette backstroked underwater, her body tight at first, then stretching out, feeling the pull of the current.

The sound of card shuffling woke her. Sunlight streamed through the windows, glanced off the crystals hung from the window frames in the dining room, casting rainbows everywhere. "My water broke," Sandy said as she watched Lizette cross to the kitchen sink for a glass of water.

"I know," Lizette said. "Marian told me."

"I made green Jell-O, did the dishes—again," Sandy said. "Right now I'm losing at solitaire. Story of my life."

"What day is it?"

"How the hell should I know?" Sandy shot a hot look at Lizette, who leaned against the sink, staring blankly. "Tuesday, maybe. You gotta date? I'm talking about the birth of my kid and you want to check your appointment book?"

Lizette poured hot water into a mug and swirled a silver tea ball, lifting the cup to smell the chamomile. "I can't remember when I have the next appointment with Dr. Finch. I don't want to miss it. That's all."

"Ask Marian. She always remembers that shit, writes it down. She made me some birth tea," Sandy went on, refocusing on herself. "She put in red raspberry leaves, blue cohosh, valerian and lobelia. I've already had three or four cups. Supposed to make you sleepy. Not me. I need tequila." She cackled like the comment was funny. The bells hanging on the front door handle jangled and Rocket barged in.

"Say mammas," he greeted them as he came into the kitchen. Lizette frowned and watched him take his jacket off and drape it over the back of the chair, stroke Sandy's hair. She stood up, clutched her stomach and gave out a gagging noise. Water splattered onto the floor. Rocket grabbed Sandy, made her sit down.

"Where's Marian," he said, looking scared.

He went to the bottom of the stairs and bellowed for Marian. Sandy doubled over in the chair, sat up, went rigid, stretched out her legs and watched her belly rise up under her nightgown. More water hit the floor. Marian appeared in the doorway, went to Sandy and took her hand, gently stroked her arm,

"Breathe," Marian said, blowing into her face to focus her attention. "We need to get you upstairs, sweetheart. Rocket, get her other side."

Marian called down, "Lizette! Bring up a pitcher of ice water." The phone rang and Rocket rushed down the stairs to answer. Lizette heard Marian upstairs saying, "Pant, pant. Don't push!" as she came up with the ice water. Sandy rolled side-to-side on the bed. Marian stroked her legs and tried to get her into a comfortable position.

"Set that down," Marian gestured toward the dresser. "Put a pillow behind her back. Where's Rocket? She wants to get to the bathroom. I need his help."

Rocket bounded up the stairs. "Need something?" he asked from the doorway, holding back, afraid to enter. His eyes seemed bigger, stretched by what he was taking in.

"Help me get her up," Marian said. "She has to go to the john. It's not a good idea, but getting her some bladder relief might help things along. Then you'll have to help me get her settled again." Rocket rushed over and started tugging on Sandy's arm.

"Who called?" Sandy said.

"Cadillac Carl, said you two had plans." He sounded annoyed, yanked Sandy up.

"Take it easy, Rocket," Marian said in a soothing tone. "Ease her forward. She's not a tug boat."

"I feel like one," Sandy said and giggled. "Did you tell Carl what's happening?"

The front door slammed. Sandy bent over and puffed loudly. Rocket held her around the middle. Lizette flattened against the wall by the dresser, trying to melt into the lath and plaster.

"No. Stop!" Sandy pushed Rocket away. "No. I don't want to pee. Get me back on the bed!"

"Hey, Rocket?" Someone yelled from below. "You up there?"

Rocket hollered back a big "Yo! Something's happening up here. I'm not sure what."

"OK, man," the voice answered back. "You just missed the opening pitch. Giant's game. Hurry it up." The man's voice lowered, took on a play-by-play tone. "Swing and a miss. Strike! Come on, man. You're missin' it. What the hell you doin' up there?"

Leaving Sandy and Marian at the side of the bed, Rocket thundered down the stairs, slipped on the water Lizette had dribbled on the risers, caught the handrail in time to stop his fall, muttered. The crowd roared from the TV as he dropped onto the sofa. The men laughed and cussed, made room for him. The front door tinkled again, then again, feet tromped from the living room to the refrigerator in the kitchen, beer bottles popped. Then *There's something about an Aqua Velva man*" jingled from the TV.

"Lizette, get over here," Marian said. Sandy sat naked in the middle of the bed. "Help me get her back against the headboard."

Lizette moved in behind Sandy on the bed, lifted under her armpits, Marian scooching her hips from the other side, spreading a sterile cloth across the bed and under Sandy's bottom.

"What're you doing?" Sandy said. "I can sit up by myself." Lizette let go. A contraction hit and Sandy's belly got hard, she fell sideways onto the pillows, moaned loudly. Marian kept reminding her not to push.

Lizette saw pinpoints of light in the periphery of her vision, felt dizzy. She got off the bed and looked at Sandy. She saw a yellowish egg and a messy nest balancing on slender branches and felt herself fall, landing on her knees beside the bed, cradling her head in her arms. Marian swabbed Sandy's thighs with orange antiseptic, put on surgical gloves.

"Get Rocket up here," Marian said.

Lizette stretched up from the floor and glided to the top of the stairs and started down. Rocket met her halfway up. They paused and mingled on the steps as Lizette changed direction and followed behind him.

"Get on the bed, behind Sandy." Marian commanded when he came in. She straightened Sandy's legs. "We need something for her to push against besides the headboard."

"I can push?" Sandy asked, sounding desperate. A contraction swept her. Lizette watched her puff through her blowhole like an orca, faster and faster, then stop and sink into the mattress, as if going under. Rocket, work boots and all, hopped onto the bed. He propped Sandy from behind and braced his back against the headboard, leaned forward as if sheltering her with his arms and shoulders.

Marian set Sandy's bare feet on top of his boots. She rubbed mineral oil on her gloved fingertips, sat on the side of the bed and waited out the next contraction. She cooed, told Sandy she was doing a great job, stroked her arms, said the baby was almost here, that everything was perfect, sponged away water and blood. Sandy sobbed. Lizette watched Marian gently massage the labial skin over the bulging red and black knob—rubbed and eased, swabbed, rubbed and eased—Sandy puffing.

Lizette knelt at the end of the bed and felt like they were girls again and she was helping with lambing, Marian calming the ewes, determining how many lamb's feet were in the birth canal, sorting them out, checking head position, pulling as the ewe strained, Lizette swabbing, untangling the umbilical cords. She felt calmer now, thinking back to those days. They'd done this before.

"The head's crowning," Marian said, looking up at Sandy, locking onto her eyes to guide her. "With the next contraction, push slow and steady. Get everything you can out of it." Sandy nodded and puffed hard.

"It's the third inning," someone yelled up the stairs.

The phone rang. Bomber bellowed up to them," It's the landlord. Wants to talk to Sandy. What should we tell him?"

"Tell him she's busy," Marian yelled. "If you guys want to see the birth, get up here!" Lizette hunkered down at the end of the bed, only her head bobbing above the edge of the mattress. The Dogs thundered in and were struck silent, as if someone had flipped the off-switch. Their mouths hung open, eyes wide, attention riveted on Sandy and Rocket, frozen.

A contraction hit. Sandy pushed, turning deep pink, sweat beads sparkling along her hairline. The baby's head emerged and lay limp in Marian's hands. They all gathered closer around the bed, leaned in, hardly breathing.

Another contraction and Marian said, "Push!" Sandy hunkered over her belly and pushed hard against Rocket's feet, stirruped under her own. She strained, turned red. The stitching on the side of Rocket's work boot ripped, exposing a dirty sock. Someone whispered "bummer," and they fell silent again, hypnotized.

Marian turned the baby's shoulders, unlocked them from behind the pubic bone, and it slithered out and gasped. Everyone gasped. The baby cried. Lizette burst into tears. Sandy fixed her eyes on the ceiling and chanted, "My God! My God!"

"It's a big, beautiful girl," Marian announced. The baby cried lustily, cutting the silence of the world that had gathered around the bed, then she shifted into a louder, messy squall. The Dogs laughed and slapped each other on the back. Rocket kissed Sandy on the top of her head, held her full breasts against her chest with his dirty hands, rocked her gently as she wept.

On TV the baseball crowd roared. The Dogs charged down the stairs to check the score. Someone beat on the front door and delivered Chinese food. Lizette recognized the sound of Cadillac Carl's measured, superior tone. The mailman rattled the door and the Dogs told him what happened. They gave him a beer and a seat on the sofa.

Upstairs, Lizette cleaned up the baby, Marian put a flowered gown on Sandy, folded the towels and sheets, stacked them. She bundled her tools into a clean towel to sterilize them later. Cadillac Carl stood in the bedroom doorway, surveying the scene with a bemused smile.

Marian pulled a piece of paper out of her bag and placed it on the dresser, signed it. "Here's the birth certificate." She glanced at the couple on the bed. "All you have to do is fill it out and take it to the county to register the birth. It might help when the baby grows up and needs a passport."

Marian went to Lizette, standing at the window holding the baby. She stepped back and watched as Lizette wondered into the tiny face. She leaned in to check the baby's color. *Good*, she thought, *eyes already tracking. Very good.* She went downstairs with Cadillac Carl to fix Sandy something to eat.

Lizette wrapped the baby more closely and crossed the room to the dresser, shielding the top with her back and the baby's blankets. She slipped the birth form into the blanket folds and took the baby to her nursery. She sat on the edge of bed, staring at the bundle in her arms. On the freeway above Franklin Street, she heard a big rig jam its jake brakes and blast a long-horned warning. Trains and tugs hooted and children threw tantrums, sounds burst out everywhere in a noisy crescendo and pressed the edges of the sky. Lizette looked deeply into the baby's eyes, into the pool of her soul, locking, swaying with her in the last gilded ripples of daylight. A fish leapt in Lake Union, spreading concentric circles that changed the shape of the world, but no one noticed.

# TWENTY–ONE

"OUCH! SON OF A BISCUIT!" Gizzard yanked his hand from the car's door frame, shook it, smeared blood along the cream-colored finish of Rocket's 88. He worked his Adam's apple, thrust his long neck side-to-side like a distressed turkey. "You mashed my fingers, man. How'm I gonna pitch? This is my throwing hand, dick face!"

"Why'd you stick your hand in the door?" Slick said and hoisted up his jeans, set his shoulders in case Gizzard took a swing on him. "You can see I'm loadin' gear." He put a canvas bag with bats and balls behind the front seat it. "Get the cooler, put it in the trunk, idiot. We'll get ice and a couple of cases of beer on the way to the game, that'll fix your fingers."

Inside the house, the Dogs crashed around, pushed each other out of the way, got down on all fours, dug through closets, cussed, reached under the couch, pulled out softballs and tennis shoes, broke dishes, turned over the garbage pail. The house had been in an uproar ever since Rocket called the game to honor Greg, challenging the dock workers who hung around the Rusty Tug to a match.

The Tuggers were more than happy to accept the challenge—losers paid for beer and pizza. There was unrest on the docks. Rocket knew money was tight. Their labor contract was up and the tug owners were telling the men mechanization would make them obsolete, that pretty soon they'd all be out of jobs, that they should take the paltry contract they'd been offered and start going to night classes to retrain, learn how to keep books or upholster furniture. Rocket figured the Tuggers were a tough team that needed to blow off steam, worthy opponents, especially with Little Dickie Armstrong playing on their side.

Under an old ship's wheel and faded sailing posters tacked to the smoke-stained walls, the Tuggers made their agreement with Rocket to play a game against the Dogs the next weekend. They put their elbows on the sticky table in the tavern's dim light after Rocket left and cooked up their game plan. They thought of the Dogs like they thought about bugs – little winged pests good for flicking, for pulling the wings off and smashing. But, winning is good, they thought, even if the opponent didn't matter.

As the Dogs prepared to play in the "Greg McLean Memorial Softball Game," they analyzed their opponents' weaknesses, which weren't many, they decided. It's not that they feared the Tuggers or missed the bandy-legged little Canuck and his stiff-necked ways, always talking big and acting small, it's that decency required some kind of response to Greg's death, if only because of his connection with Marian and the women. Actually, the Dogs were glad to be rid of the grasping little junkie, always looking for a fix, panhandling them for money, making a mess, nodding out, talking crazy and banging a woman way too good for him.

Just playing the Tuggers would secure the proper appearance of respect for a fallen player, Rocket explained. The Dogs couldn't lose no matter how the game turned out, he said. Not with Little Dickie Armstrong, the swingingest shit in Eastern Washington playing for the Tuggers. Losing a game to him would be such an honor, it would seem like the dogs actually won no matter how the game turned out. Everybody knew Dickie had played Triple-A ball for the Indians in Spokane with Tommy Lasorda at the helm, that the Indians had won the Pacific Coast League championship on his winning run. Dickie had been rehabbing on the Seattle docks for about three years after blowing out his knee in 1970. Some guys whispered Dickie was washed up, others counted on a comeback.

Now Rocket scanned the Dogs standing on the sidewalk, sizing up the talent. "Who's onboard?" he said, saw half of them were drunk or high, the other half probably would be in the same condition before the third inning. He got a few half-hearted barks in answer. He figured Rainman would be good for first base and Bomber was probably still sober enough to catch. He'd put gangly Fisher in left, maybe park Lucky in centerfield. The rest would have to spread out and cover the bases and the rest of the field. Greg had been pretty solid at shortstop. He'd give that job to Carl since they were a man short.

Next door, the women shuffled down Sandy's stairs, Lizette carrying the baby in a bundle of blankets, lugging the stroller, a diaper bag on her shoulder. Sandy bounced out in platform heels and tossed her long blonde hair, her legs looking tan and shapely in white cotton shorts.

Rocket went to Lizette and took the baby, pushed the ruffled edge of the blanket aside to see baby Violet's pink face. He nuzzled her, smelled the warm milk on her breath. Violet opened her eyes and cooed, startling him yet again with her lavender-colored eyes and long lashes.

"How's this little shit pants doing?" He spoke softly, to no one in particular, engrossed in the baby's sweetness.

Cadillac Carl pulled up, honked, arm hanging out the window of the yellow Caddie, diamond pinkie ring sparkling in the sunlight. Rocket handed Violet back to Lizette and went to Carl. "Whyn't you take the girls? Maybe one or two guys. Put Fisher in the back. I can get the rest in my car."

Carl threw him a thumbs-up. Marian, Sandy, and Lizette piled into the Cadillac, Sandy sitting in the front seat, next to Carl, fiddling with the radio knobs. Lizette got into the back with the baby. Fisher loaded the stroller and diaper bag into the trunk.

"Don't slam the goddamned door," Cadillac Carl barked over the backseat at Lizette after she closed the car door. Marian rode shotgun. Carl accelerated to the stop sign at the corner, Sandy fingering his crotch, playing her fingers lightly across the seams of his jeans, making him shift in his seat and grin, relax his shoulders. They'd been spending a lot of time together, Lizette thought, studying the back of their heads, sneaking glimpses of their faces reflected in the rearview mirror.

The Dogs piled into the Rocket 88 and they drove behind Carl down Eastlake Avenue, like the bereaved in a funeral procession. An unmarked cop car fell in behind Rocket along the way. Somebody in the backseat warned him to slow down. Rocket checked the speedometer, which stopped working in 1969, and said, "I am slowed down." They pulled up in front of Clown Liquors. Rocket and Carl went in, returned with supplies.

They pulled into Ravenna Park, clouds moving in from the west, breaking the July sunlight into puddles. Lizette got out with Violet and Marian took the stroller and diaper bag from the trunk. Sandy stayed melded to Carl in the front seat, whispering. The cops watched from their unmarked Ford. The Dogs pulled equipment from Rocket's trunk, carried it to the nearest battered green dugout and threw the bats and balls down in a jumble.

Stinky checked field conditions, tapped moist dirt with the toe of his boot, walked the baseline to first, scuffed the ground where the bag would go. He went into the dugout and changed his boots for Converse high tops, laced them tight, wiggled his toes inside, tucked his dirty "Dogs" T-shirt into his jeans then took the heavy gray bags out to the bases and squared them up against the imaginary baselines.

The Tuggers rolled up in trucks with gun racks and dented fenders. They tucked their matching blue jerseys into tight gray baseball pants, adjusted their jock straps, scanned the field, sized up the competition, snorted.

A powder blue Mustang three-speed cruised up. Dickie Armstrong, the Tugger's prize slugger, got out. Everyone turned to watch him standing there, preening in a sunburst, cleats thrown casually over his shoulder. One of the cops couldn't help himself and clapped. His partner elbowed him in the ribs and the cop stopped.

A flip of the coin and the Dogs won home field advantage. They spread out across the diamond, toed the dirt, pulled arms overhead to stretch, jogged in place, squatted. The first Tugger stepped into the box, tapped the depression that served as home plate, took a check swing, softened his knees, bat on shoulder. Gizzard's first pitch was high and outside, followed by a fat boy down the throat, swing and a miss. Two more strikes and one man down.

The cops settled on the bleachers, careful of splinters. Marian, Sandy and Lizette took seats near the Dogs's side. Violet let out a cry and Lizette pulled the stroller close.

"I hate the kid's crying," Sandy got up to pace on the grass. "Makes my tits tingle."

Lizette peered under the stroller's shade canopy. Violet wailed. She pushed the stroller away, through the parking lot and up a little rise beyond the outfield. She spread a blanket on the grass and lifted the baby out, laying her down on her back. She changed her diaper, adjusted her lime green sleeper so she could kick her legs, then picked Violet up, rocked her side to side, kissed her neck, intoxicated by the sweet smell of her body.

Sandy grabbed a beer from the cooler, popped the top, and leaned back on the bench, resting her elbows on the riser, offering smooth legs to the sun, flowing her long blonde hair behind her shoulders, sticking out her chest. She caught Carl's eye in the dugout, sent him a sly smile, took a gulp from the can, wiped her mouth with the back of her hand.

Toulouse showed up in the third inning, flourishing his cape. He walked to the pitcher's mound and took the ball from Gizzard's hand, turned it in the light as if studying the facets of a jewel. He faced the dugouts, gathered himself. The Tuggers complained about delay of game, but settled down when somebody said they were doing a tribute to a fallen player. Toulouse stepped forward, cleared his throat, addressed the crowd:

*"I think I could turn and live with animals, they are so placid and self-contain'd,*

*I stand and look at them long and long.*

*They do not sweat and whine about their condition,*

*They do not make me sick discussing their duty to God,*

*Not one is dissatisfied, not one is demented with the mania of owning things,*

*Not one kneels to another, nor do his kind that lived thousands of years ago,*

*Not one is respectable or unhappy of the whole earth."*

Toulouse grandly extended his hand from beneath his cape in benediction. "This is how we'll remember Greg."

Marian came onto the field then and stood beside Toulouse. The Dogs clapped. Spreading his cape, showing the flourish of its hot-pink lining, Toulouse stepped closer to home plate, hewing more to the Dogs dugout. Marian sprinkled ashes around the pitcher's mound from a simple wooden box.

*"I bequeath myself to the dirt to grow from the grass I love,*

*If you want me again look for me under your boot-soles."*

The poet wrapped himself in his cape with a flourish, bowed and escorted Marian from the field. Cheering and clapping broke out. "Fuckin' A, man!" "Far out." "Greg was a tough little dude, man." They pumped their fists and then the uproar settled. Somebody hollered, "Play ball!"

The Tuggers's next batter got up and the Dogs crouched in their playing stances, bent over, hands on knees. The batter sent the ball soaring into left field over Fisher's head, where it rolled into the bushes beyond the fence. The Tuggers got up from the bench and hit the dugout cooler, popping beer tops, slouching back into place, not even bothering to cheer. The Dogs frowned, threw each other hand signals, stood their ground.

Marian leaned over to Toulouse, sitting near her on the bleachers. "Your poem was perfect."

"Not mine. It's Uncle Walty's."

"Your uncle?"

"Walt Whitman, my good woman. *Leaves of Grass.*"

"Excuse me?"

Toulouse scowled at her ignorance and stalked off. He headed for the hill where he saw Lizette making a daisy chain in the grass. Violet slept beside her under the shelter of a blanket she'd rigged to the side of the stroller, protecting the baby from the sun.

"Elizabeth. May I speak to you?"

Lizette looked up, "What?"

"May I sit down?" She looked at the baby sleeping peacefully and back to the stilted, black-draped poet.

"No."

"I understand you may not care for me, but ... "

"You killed Greg," she said, looking down. "You almost killed Marian." She lifted her face to him and flared her delicate nostrils, the sun making her squint. "I know what you and Greg did. Because of it, Marian can't have kids. Because of you, you slimy bastard!"

"That's bullshit." Toulouse shifted, like he considered leaving. "Greg did what he wanted. Look, all I want to say is this. I want to help you. A dealer in New York looked at a couple of your paintings and . . . "

"How?" Lizette flew from the grass before he could answer and threw her body against him, knocking him down, grabbing him around the neck, choking, her thumbs cutting off his airway. "How could anyone see my stuff? You stole my shit! I know you did! I saw you!"

Rocket saw the attack from third base and charged up the hill. The cops got up from their seats in the bleachers, stumbled over some newly arrived hippies blowing soap bubbles, and hurried around the back of the dugout. They pulled her off and Toulouse rolled away, downhill a couple of yards. He rose breathlessly to his elbows, purple faced.

"You're crazy!" Toulouse shouted, crab-walking backward. Rocket had Lizette in a bear hug, pinning her arms. The cops hung back then and let the scene play out, the players stood by in suspense. Lizette spat at him. "I'm telling you, you've got some sales," he yelled at her. "They want you to do a show in New York. They think you've got something, you crazy bitch."

"Liar!" she shouted. Rocket held her tight as she strained for the poet.

"Listen to him, Liz," Rocket said in her ear.

"You had your chance," Toulouse said, getting up from the grass, wiping himself off. "Get your own agent then. I'll have the gallery send the check to the ranch, minus my ten percent. I'm done helping you." He stalked away and Rocket let Lizette go. She settled on the edge of the blanket where Violet slept, staring into the baby's placid face. Rocket limped back to the field, covered his base, played shallow off third. Lizette turned her back on the scene.

During the confrontation, the Dogs hit the dugout cooler and Carl slipped into the parking lot to fondle Sandy. They entwined, whispered, broke free when Rocket called him to get back to short-stop, but the cops blocked his path to the field. They hunched their shoulders around him and talked. Sandy stood to the side and everyone wondered what they were saying.

The Dogs arrayed themselves again. Cadillac Carl took his position. Lucky hobbled to centerfield, an oven mitt on his gimpy right hand, playing deep. The Tuggers were ahead by a run, with a man on. The teams exchanged at-bats, lousy pitches and bad fielding kept the score one-zero, Tugger's favor.

Bored with the game, disgusted with the level of play, at the top of the ninth inning the Tuggers had two outs, two men on, so they put Little Dickie up to finish it. They all agreed it was time to get back to the bar with the pizza money. Rocket signaled the Dogs to spread out, play deep. He looked at Lucky, leaning on his cane, near the centerfield fence, and scowled, signaled Slick to play over, trying to cover the gap.

Dickie stepped into the batter's box, rubbed his toe against the dip at home plate, wiggled his butt, joggled his knees and stared Gizzard down. Gizz gulped loud enough for the cops to hear in the top row of the bleachers. He jerked into motion, wound his arm twice and delivered low and inside, brushing Dickie back. Bomber fell on the ball for a catch and threw it back to the mound. Ball one. Gizzard turned and threw to second, almost picking off the lead runner.

He pivoted to address the batter, adjusted the brim of his cap, dangled his pitching arm and smoothed out his windup. The ball came sweeping toward the strike zone, a shoulder-high release with good movement. The ball dropped into the zone and Dickie was on it, eyes lit, hitting the ball about as hard as it could be hit without splitting the stitches and blowing the cover off.

The crack brought the bleacher crowd to attention. Lizette turned and shielded her eyes to watch the ball's white-lightning arc. The crowd noise rumbled behind the spinning orb, the sound fading like thunder after a hailstorm, gathering again, breaking in claps.

Rocket's eyes jumped from the ball to centerfield and there was Lucky, stumping hard on his cane, racing the ball to the fence, back turned, head down, plowing ahead. His heart sank. No way . . . but then he felt a flicker of hope. Maybe? Maybe?

Lucky's position was good. No time to think. Rocket fixed on the ball's speed, the pure beauty of its dizzying rotation. He ripped his mind from the ball, looked for an instant at Gizzard tracking it, shoulders slack, helpless. The runners advanced, confident the ball would easily top the fence and they could saunter home for the win.

Switching back to Lucky, maybe a split second had elapsed since the ball was struck, but time stood still. Lucky checked over his left shoulder again, lifted his oven mitt, scorch marks showing along the edges. Then Lucky changed his mind and kept digging with his stick, hobbling faster than the crowd could register, racing the ball with all his might, long, greasy hair flying behind him. His "A & S Towing" hat popped off and no one saw it hit the grass, so focused were they on the ball.

It was close to him now, hovering in the air, spinning on its path toward the fence, twenty feet from the ground, coming down fast. Rocket dared to think, only for an instant, for that fraction of time it takes an electron to pulse down a wire or an atom to split that . . . that . . .

Lucky slowed up so he wouldn't crash into the chain link and put both hands up, like he was tracking a well-thrown football pass in the end zone, using his good hand to lift his mitted one. He made a cup. Jumped. The ball sailed over his shoulder and dropped into the pocket like a well-struck billiard ball. Lucky went down, his good side collapsed on impact and he rolled in the deep grass. The crowd exhaled and waited.

The Tugger's base runners moved to and fro in confusion. Slick tripped the guy trying to get back to second base and he threw a punch. Lucky rolled over and held up the ball. Everyone surged onto the field, shoving and clapping.

Lizette cawed and clapped from the hillside. Little Dickie picked up his gear, got into his Mustang, gunned the engine, and was gone in a powder-blue cloud before the Dogs carried Lucky on their shoulders from the outfield to the dugout. Laughing and slapping, they crowded in and didn't notice the Tuggers trickling away, their tails tucked beneath their legs. In the heat of celebration, the Dogs forgot they'd lost the game, didn't take their last at-bat.

The cops stood at the top of the bleachers, surveying the hubbub in the dugout, chuckling at what had just happened, at the beauty of the moment, the improbable catch. Like everyone else, they didn't notice Cadillac Carl and Sandy Shore ease out of the parking lot and make for the entrance to Interstate 5, turning up the radio, picking up speed, not looking back, heading south.

# TWENTY-TWO

**THE WESTSIDE HOSPITAL ENTRANCE DOOR** inched closed behind Lizette as she climbed the speckled marble steps two at a time and stopped to catch her breath in front of Dr. Finch's office. She knocked softly on the door's wavy glass and ignored the faint, anguished sounds coming from the ward on the floor above. She tried the door handle but it was locked—like always, she thought. The hospital's false securities annoyed her, anyone could kick in the glass, but she didn't want to waste time obsessing about it, just settled herself and waited.

A weary voice from inside said, "Coming." The light shifted as Dr. Finch crossed behind the glass and opened the door. The room exhaled air thick with the smell of old carpets, dusty books and anxiety. "Elizabeth! You're on time for a change."

Dr. Finch stepped back, gestured for Lizette to come in, overlooked her smirk and guided her to the chair beside her desk. "So, how've you been?" Dr. Finch sat down on the opposite side of the desk and steepled her fingertips, brought them to her lips and looked over her glasses.

"Good."

"What have you been doing?"

"Painting. Hanging out with friends."

Dr. Finch got up, adjusted her Navy blue blazer, and went to the window bench. She bent over the potted plants and poked the dirt, nudged pieces of bark around an orchid plant. She stood and studied her nails for soil. Lizette noticed the leaves of the orchid were leathery and green, she wondered about replicating the effect with oils, how to capture the sense of dimension. The leaves looked healthy, she admitted to herself, but in all the times she'd met with her psychiatrist she had never seen anything bloom.

*A promise*, Lizette thought as she watched the doctor fuss, *but nothing to show for it.* When Dr. Finch sat down and looked directly at her, Lizette saw the problem, saw into Finch's twisted heart, saw it laboring to survive, felt the kinks in her vessels and the pooled blood eking through the constricted arteries of her core. *Nothing beautiful can flourish in such a twisted place*, she thought.

"Have you been taking your medication?" The practical question caught Lizette off guard, halted her silent musing.

"My friend Marian keeps track of it. She says you should adjust my dosage, that I'm getting too much."

"You're friend's a doctor?" She twitched her eyebrows, shifted as she waited for the answer.

"A nurse."

"With psychiatric training?"

"She's a midwife." The doctor sniffed and Lizette crossed her arms and scratched the back of her upper arms under her sweater sleeves. "I have ... I mean we have a baby. Her name is Violet. I need my meds adjusted so I can take better care of her. I itch and tweak. My skin crawls. I sleep too much."

Dr. Finch pursed her lips and studied Lizette. Silence mounted, piling up between them like cottony clouds. She opened the file folder on her desk and scanned the pages, holding a line with her finger, glancing up, she said, "That's impossible."

"What?"

"That you could have given birth. You had a pregnancy test when you were admitted as an inpatient last December. You were beaten and raped. We tested more than once, all negative. How old is this child?"

Lizette shrugged. She saw that she had made a mistake in letting the birth of Violet slip. She hunched her shoulders, swatted her wispy blonde hair going haywire in the humid office. Folding her long fingers into a fist in her lap, she waited, listened to the doctor breathe, looked squarely at her and would not glance away.

"Have you been having any other delusions? Are you experiencing breaks with reality? Disorientation? Hearing voices?"

"Well." Lizette paused and gathered herself, calculated her response. "Sometimes I see things before they happen, like when people get sick or hurt. Sometimes people turn into animals and fish or orca right before my eyes then turn back into themselves. It's freaky."

"Have you been using drugs?"

"Only what you've given me and that's probably too much, like I said."

Dr. Finch twirled around in her leather chair and looked out the window, at the dull light glinting like tin against the glass. "What about food? Are you eating? You're very thin."

"I forget sometimes. I get light-headed and have to lie down."

"Where are you sleeping? Your father says you haven't been staying with him, that he hasn't seen you in months. I checked with him, let me see." She turned to her desk and peered at a page in the file folder. "Oh, here it is . . . I spoke to your father two weeks ago. He said he didn't know where you were."

"That's a lie. He knows I've been staying with Marian out at the ranch. On Orcas Island."

"When you were released in February, I made it clear to you that you are coming close to involuntary commitment. Your behavior is becoming dangerous. You aren't giving us much choice."

"That's not true. Who told you that?"

"Your father."

"My father is a liar and you know it. He wants me to be crazy. He wants to cage me like a bird, like he did to my mother, feeding her seeds and watching her beat her wings against the bars. She killed herself. Doesn't that tell you something?"

Getting up and coming to perch on the edge of the desk above Lizette, Dr. Finch cocked her head and listened.

"He acts like he knows everything, but he's a snake." Lizette reached in her canvas bag and pulled out a bandana, wiped her eyes and nose. "He's old and feeds on dead carcasses, squeezes the life out of everything."

She stopped and caught her breath, started again. "He wants to watch me die too so he can gnaw my bones. That's what he did to my mother. I don't care how famous and well respected he is. He's sick."

"The agreement for release is that you stay with your father." Dr. Finch spoke with practiced calm, as if admonishing a naughty child while trying to avoid a tantrum.

Lizette got up and began to pace, noticing the small oriental carpet beneath her feet, the swirls and garnishes. She imagined looking past the colorful pile to the webbing that held the weave together, the sandy colored grid that fastened the yarns, the cross-hatch pattern as old as humanity. She thought about Violet in her crib, about the sweet smell of her neck, and pulled herself together.

"Look." Lizette placed her hands on the back of the chair and leaned toward Dr. Finch. "I'm living with a registered nurse. I'm painting again. I get good food and exercise. I work for friends at the farmer's market in East Sound. It's a regular gig. I'm surrounded by friends. My father is old and bitter. He wants to confine me and live in the past. He wants to pick over bones and steal the best things. He's a grave robber, for God's sake! I'm doing the right things to get better, to take care of myself."

"I agree that you're more aware of your feelings, and certainly this is the most open you've ever been about them. But you're still exhibiting some confusion."

The room suddenly seemed stuffy and Lizette felt herself sweating. "I'm better. OK? A lot better. I just want to check in with you and get my meds adjusted. That's all. I want to stay out of here and get back to work."

"A job?"

"I'm a painter for chrissake!" Lizette looked at the doctor and saw a plop, an inert wad, not a living breathing woman. She shook her head to dislodge the image. "That's my job. You know that."

"But you need to find steady employment, become self-sufficient, build a life. I know you don't exhibit or sell your work. It's nothing more than a hobby."

She flashed on her father, looking up from some thick book he was reading, puncturing her mother's plans to exhibit at a gallery downtown, or go to New York, or study in Paris, saying her painting was only a hobby, decorative he'd called it. Her mother would look crestfallen, deflated. She'd go into the kitchen and slam dishes while Lizette withdrew into the corner of the living room behind the couch.

"Do you want to spend the rest of your life on disability, pretending to be an artist, hanging around, never having anything permanent in your life?" Dr. Finch said. "Don't you want a family and a home?"

"I have to be honest here, Dr. Finch. I don't know what you're talking about. It's like you're the crazy one." What she'd said fell like a thud, startling her in its weighty truth.

"Do you think I'll be normal if I get a job as a bank teller or an insurance company clerk?" Lizette went on. "Will I meet your approval if I marry some mechanic and live in an apartment in Ballard, lugging greasy clothes to the laundromat?

"Lizette, please sit down." Dr. Finch got up and returned to her side of the desk.

Lizette realized she had raised her voice and felt like grabbing things off the desk and throwing them, bolting for the door. She looked at the scrawny plants on the window bench and felt an urge to dump them on the carpet. She sat down, took a cleansing yoga breath, clasped her hands, refocused.

"I want my meds adjusted. I want . . . "

Rapid knocking rattled the glass in the office door. "Doctor are you in there? We've got an emergency on the ward. You're needed on the floor!"

Dr. Finch moved across the office and yanked the door open. "What's wrong?"

"Melinda! She cut her wrists. It's bad. The other women are going off, too."

"Where?"

"Third floor bathroom. It happened during break. Most of the nurses were off, we just looked away for a minute. You need to come right now!"

Dr. Finch shoved a key ring into her pocket and told Lizette to stay put and not open the door. Lizette heard her running down the hall, up the stairs. Sharp wailing, far away, came to Lizette's ears. She moved around the desk and sat in Dr. Finch's chair, leafed through her own file and found the page listing the blood draws and the pregnancy test results. She tore the page out, pulled away the scraps of paper that still clung to the file fasteners and balled them up in her hand. She went to her bag and stuffed the papers into the bottom.

She was studying books on the shelves when Dr. Finch came back looking disheveled, her blouse untucked on one side, a run in her stocking, hands quivering.

"Sit down Elisabeth. Where were we?"

"We were talking about a new prescription. A lower dose."

"Oh. Yes. What dose are you on now?" Dr. Finch flipped through Lizette's file, paused and shook her hands as if to release tension. "Let's see . . . Seventy-five milligrams. That's already low. How about we try fifty and see how you do?"

"I just want to feel more alert," Lizette said. "I hate feeling groggy all the time."

"That's a usual complaint, but the alternative to not taking any medication carries grave consequences." Dr. Finch pulled a prescription tablet in front of her, wrote quickly. "I'll see you in a month? Is this time good for you?" The doctor wrote the appointment down in her book.

Lizette nodded, gathered the straps of her bag, stood. Dr. Finch came around the desk, took her hand, squeezed it.

"You are getting better, making progress. You don't want to continue being a prisoner of your illness, do you?"

Lizette shook her head and pulled her hand back. "No. I want to be OK."

"You need to be in a stable environment." Dr. Finch handed her the prescription. "You can't wander aimlessly for the rest of your life. It appears you're suffering from a psychosis of your own choosing. You'll make more progress, if you cooperate with us. Go home to your father."

Lizette bolted, doubled-timed it down the stairs, blew the front door open and jogged across the lawn toward the bus shelter. She looked up at Dr. Finch's office window over her shoulder and fumbled in the bottom of her bag. She settled on the bench in the narrow shelter, checked to see if a bus was coming. With no bus in sight, she pulled out the sheet of paper from her file and scrounged around in her bag again, feeling for a book of matches. They were damp, but she finally got one to flare and put the fire to the edge of the paper, turned her back to the street and watched the lazy yellow flames eat around the edges of the page. She held it with her fingertips and let it burn to and fro shifting when it came close to burning her. Bits of ash floated away from the shelter into the soft breeze, sticking on the nearby bushes. Long before the bus got there the paper was gone.

Marian's bags were by the front door when she got back to Sandy's. Lizette had been expecting her to leave, hearing the phone calls to Poland about problems at the ranch and the rescheduling she was doing with the clinic and the pregnant women she'd referred to other mid-wives. She could tell from hearing half the conversations that not all the women were happy about the shift. Marian seemed to love Violet and she'd been teaching Lizette a lot about infant care, but Lizette knew she was unhappy, heard her walk the floors at night, saw her tear up, snap at the Dogs. After six weeks, it was time for her to go. Lizette trembled at the thought of taking care of Violet alone until Sandy got back from wherever she'd disappeared to with Carl, how she'd react if Sandy got in the way with her and Violet. She also saw Marian's anguish, a sadness so deep she couldn't reach it.

Before Marian pulled away, she leaned out the window of her truck, "Don't forget to take your medication. Call me if you have a problem. Sandy'll probably be back soon." She honked when she turned the corner and disappeared from sight.

# TWENTY–THREE

LIZETTE TROWELED IN THE VEGETABLE patch she'd planted in the yard behind Sandy's house before Violet was born. The sun warmed her back now while she pulled weeds, loosened dirt around the bell peppers. At the tail end of summer, the peppers ripened into full-bellied shape. Brilliant-green, luminous in the sunlight, they were almost ready to pick, she thought. Scallions, cherry tomatoes, lettuce planted in short scraggly rows ripened, too. She wondered what Abaya's garden looked like now, missed her and Poland and her friends at the market in Eastsound, missed the way the water hugged the shores of Orcas Island, making it safe and separate, its own peaceful world.

The nursery curtains billowed in the breezes from Lake Union, waved the afternoon warmth into the room where three-month-old Violet napped. Traffic thrum from I-5 vibrated down to the garden where she dug. Fisher played Rocket's piano, striking the keys evenly, contentedly, the notes full of color as they escaped the open dining room window next door. She caught the melody and hummed it, picked small pebbles from the vegetable bed, tossed them onto the walkway where she sat musing, her legs folded under her.

"Hey!"

Lizette looked up at the sound. A man stood on the small back porch, staring down the dilapidated stairs at her, his hand cupped over his brow, shielding his eyes from the sun. She could see he was short-legged and dark-haired, familiar, but she couldn't quite place him. Not one of the regular Dogs.

"Sandy here?"

"Not now," Lizette said, getting to her feet and facing the man.

"Do I know you?" he said.

Lizette warbled softly in her throat, felt a surge of fear, thought about how to answer. "Who are you?" She wiped her hands on her jeans.

"Al . . . Al Munoz. Sandy's old man. Just got out of jail."

Lizette squinted at him, trying to recall what Al had looked like before he got busted for selling hot motorcycle parts to an under-cover cop behind Lenny's Tavern more than a year ago. She rummaged around in her head for what she remembered of this bandy-legged little guy she'd only seen a couple of times. She remembered long black hair, a cruel-slash smile, hard black eyes, the letters L-O-V-E crudely tattooed below his knuckles in black ink. She remembered Al throwing a platter of fried chicken at Sandy and bouncing her up against the wall, knocking the breadbox from the top of the refrigerator with the force. She remembered running next door to get Rocket to break it up.

Nothing about this man seemed familiar now as he stood there, clean cut in baggy jeans and a faded plaid shirt. A year was a long time, she thought, and she hadn't been paying much attention to details back then, at least not like now, since Violet was born. Everything seemed brighter now, more remarkable. The pitches of her crying, the colors of her clothes, her baby smells, the radiance of light itself.

"Where is she? When's she coming back?"

"Who?" Climbing the uneven stairs to the landing, clutching her heart at the thought of Violet, Lizette tried to decide what to tell him, how to get rid of him.

"Sandy!"

"Oh." She felt relieved.

"Where is she? Don't give me no shit. Is she with some other guy?"

"Sandy's away, visiting friends," Lizette said, towering over him. "On vacation. I'm house sitting."

"Who are you?"

"Lizette . . . A friend."

"Oh yeah. I remember you. Lizard. The tweeker chick. How you been and all that?"

Trying to distract him, get him off the back porch, she said, "Want something to eat?" She hoped food and a beer would help get rid of him. A quick meal, a swift goodbye.

"Maybe. After I get loaded. Man, jail's a bitch. I mean, they got dope inside, man, but it's not the same. You know? Too many *vatos*. Fuckin' with my business. Bunch a punk bitches."

Lizette brushed past him. In the kitchen she opened the refrigerator and pulled out a big pot of beans, put it on the stove, got some bread and cheese and set them on the table. She turned to the sink and washed her shaking hands.

"How long's Sandy gonna to be gone?"

"Didn't say." Lizette wiped her hands on a dish towel and leaned against the sink. "Just wanted me to stay here and take care of the place. She didn't say anything about you."

"Well, I didn't know exactly when the jerks were gonna turn me loose. Like they don't tell you, exactly, know what I mean? I got released a couple of weeks early because of overcrowding in their shit-hole jail." He laughed and turned, headed for the stairs to the bedrooms, Lizette on his heels, alarmed.

"I wrote her a letter a couple of weeks ago telling her I was getting out." Lizette flashed to the letter from King County jail that had come through the slot in the door, stamped INDIGENT in big red letters. She'd tossed it unopened.

"Man, I told her to pick me up, call the jail for my release date. This one cat, he gets out, man, and his ole lady picks him up in a limousine. They get in back and, like, she spreads her legs, you know, man, and she don't got nothin' on. So they drink champagne in those skinny glasses and . . . it was rich, man. I saw it, too. But, when I come through the gate, man, with these stupid shoes on," he looked at his feet . . . nothin'." He shook his hands like he'd been squeezing shit and couldn't get the stink off.

"I took the bus into town, man, had to walk over here." He stroked his black hair, smoothed it against his head with flat palms. He shouldered past Lizette, started up the stairs. She squeezed ahead of him, he ran his hand over her hip as she passed. "Give me some of that!" He laughed like he was coughing.

"Where're you going?" she asked, partially blocking his way.

"To get my shit. What's it to you?"

"What shit?"

"My stuff, man. My stuff was here when I got busted." He threw up his hands, clinched, splayed his fingers, bouncing L-O-V-E. Sweat beads had formed on his upper lip and he licked them, shifted his eyes like a cornered rat, smelled like oily piss. "I don't know what they did with my bike, my jacket and boots. Shit. I had my Angel's colors on when they got me. They took my jacket and gave me this lumberjack shit to wear before they let me go. They're pigs. Ridiculous, man. I look like a goddamn cholo farmer."

Lizette eased backward, inching up the stairs, Al stepping up along with her. When they reached the top, she went to the door of Violet's nursery, the room they shared, and closed the door. She rattled the door knob to her studio, making sure it was latched, too.

Al went into Sandy's bedroom and stood in the soft afternoon light. He filled the space, dark and square, a specter in the backlight from the windows. He went and looked out on the street, reflected light cast a bluish wash over his brown face, gave him a sickly pall. Lizette felt the suffused color, felt the need to sit immersed in this cool, subtle shade and capture it's tone in paint, put it on canvas as an ethereal background wash, but snapped back to face the threat.

"Looks the same," he said, moving toward the closet. "Get outta here, would ya. I need privacy, man. I just spent a year with people in my face. I gotta find my clothes. When did Sandy say she was coming back?"

"I told you, she didn't say," Lizette said, backing up.

"Yeah. Well, does the washer still work?" He went to Sandy's dresser and pulled drawers open, tossing clothes on the floor, feeling in the back and along the sides of the drawers. "I got laundry," Al said, running his fingers along the underside of the drawers, looking for dope, Lizette realized.

From downstairs, she heard the front door slam and Rocket holler, "Anybody here?"

Al scurried to the top of the stairs, hollered down, "Hey, man! Rocket! We're up here!"

Lizette followed, looked down and saw a shadow of irritation cross Rocket's face as he stared up at them. He climbed, pulled hard on the handrail, stood at the top with crossed arms.

"When'd you get out?" Lizette stepped mincingly back and forth between the men, a nervous crane in cold water.

"This morning, man." The men clasped hands, slapped each other on the back. "Feels good to get the *basura* stink outta my nose, man. I had to take the bus into town, riding like a welfare case. What's up with you?"

"Same old shit, man. Working the tugs, hangin' out."

"*Le vida loco*, eh?"

"Not too crazy. I'm under the radar."

"Like shit you are. Where's the crazy Canadian?"

"Greg?"

"Yeah, man. Thought you guys was buddies. What's he doin'?"

"He died the end of March."

"OD'd?"

Lizette began nudging Rocket toward the stairs. She glanced at the nursery door and Rocket caught her meaning.

"I got some beer downstairs, man. Let's crack a couple, catch up. I'll tell you what happened."

The men clomped down the stairs and Lizette went to Violet's door and looked in. The baby slept peacefully, making kissy mouse sounds. She could hear Rocket and Al slamming around in the kitchen, drawers squeaking, silverware rattling, and she paused, remarked on the golden tint the waning sun made on the magnolia wallpaper in the nursery, gilding the big white flowers. She swayed with the full feeling that cradled her heart when she looked at Violet. She left the door ajar so she could hear her when she woke.

The men had settled at the kitchen table, but Rocket got up when Lizette came in. They went to the living room. Al followed like a puppy, sat on the couch, Rocket facing him in Sandy's favorite chair. Rocket noticed the room's neatness, the baby's blankets folded in a stack at the end of the couch, toy rattle placed on top, furniture dusted. Al stretched out. Lizette slipped in and settled at the end of the couch, putting the pile of baby blankets on her lap.

"You on parole?"

"Yeah. Gotta see the man Monday morning. Gave them this address, if they want to find me."

"That's fucked," Rocket said, almost under his breath. "We don't need the cops."

"So what about my man Greg?"

"Got hurt out on Orcas Island," Rocket said, shooting Lizette a warning look. "Ruptured his spleen and he was in too bad a shape by the time they got him to the hospital. Couldn't save him."

Al shook his head, "Too bad, man." He looked at Rocket and Lizette. "I always thought he'd OD. Guy was a straight-up dope fiend. We got so loaded once . . ." He got up and went to the kitchen, returned with another beer.

Rocket started to get up and get another brew, but the front door blew open. Fisher stood in the front hall waving a bottle of whiskey in one hand, a can of baby formula in the other.

"Drinks're on me, gentlemen." He took in the glum faces and laughed. "Looks like a party," He grabbed glasses from the kitchen and put them and the bottle on the dining room table, looked at the men expectantly. "Who's going to join me?"

Fisher poured three fingers without looking at them and tipped his head toward Al. "Looks like you had a good vacation, all rested up and everything."

"Shit." Al got up for the whiskey, giving Fisher a one-armed embrace, reaching for a glass with the other. "You still playing piano?"

Lizette heard Violet's soft whimper and went upstairs. She scooped the baby up and settled on the bed, forming a protective pocket around the child with her body. She checked her diaper and looked into her still sleepy eyes, running her fingers around the edge of her chin. She poked the baby bottle she'd brought with her between Violet's eager lips and held her plump thigh while she sucked and got lost in the peace and satisfaction.

Lizette heard music blaring downstairs. Santana and the thump of *"Oye Como Va"* pulsing through the house. Violet started crying and Lizette felt tension—in her body, in the house. She changed the baby's diaper and put on a fresh pink crawler, noticed it was almost too small. *Maybe one or two more wearings,* she thought, *and it won't fit anymore.* She closed the snaps and lifted the baby, holding her close against her shoulder. At the top of the stairs she heard laughter and grumbling voices. She smelled smoke and hesitated before starting down. In the living room Al was grooving. *"Me ritmo!"* He thrust his pelvis, jerked his hips, coughed out a couple of dry hacks. *"Bueno pa' gozar!"*

He bopped some more and when the song ended, he collapsed on the couch, rocking side to side and kicking his legs in excitement. Lizette could see he was loaded, could smell the sulfur from the matches used to heat the white powder, saw the tubing and silver spoon on the kitchen table. She thought about how Cadillac Carl had loaded the cotton and took Fuzzy out, how she'd hunkered on the basement steps and watched the whole thing through the crack in the door, afraid to breathe or move. She hated Carl's callous indifference, but recognized the solution.

"Hey Lizard, give me that kid." Rocket reached out his arms for Violet and Lizette hesitated, glanced around at the Dogs, at the nearly empty whiskey bottle on the table and the beer cans littering the living room floor. She twittered and took the baby into the kitchen. Fisher came and stood in the doorway, watching her tidy the dishes, the baby peeping at him over Lizette's shoulder. He came forward and chucked Violet's chin.

"How's this little cutie doing?" Fisher asked, hovering around Lizette's shoulders.

"Good. She can barely fit into the crawler she has on. She needs some bigger stuff."

"You need money?" Fisher said.

"No. I picked up some county checks at my father's the other day when Rocket was watching Violet. They'd kind of piled up. I've got more than enough for the rent. I was just saying that to show how much she's grown. What were you playing this afternoon?"

"Schubert. An abandoned work." He curled Violet's fingers around his thumb and bounced her hand. "Schubert got bored so he didn't finish it."

"Sounded finished to me." Lizette rinsed dishes with her right hand and secured Violet with her left, wiping splatters on the counter as she worked.

"I saw you in the yard and played it for you," he said blushing, covering his horse teeth with his fingers. "Anyway, Schubert loved a woman, but they never got married, and he also never figured out the demands of the concerto. Wrote most of the one I played today on dinner napkins, then gave up."

"He wrote it in a restaurant?"

"How the hell should I know where he wrote it. Basically, the guy was a dog, probably wrote it in a bar, half swacked. The piece has a good melody though, what there is of it, don't you think?"

Lizette shrugged.

"Guy died of syphilis when he was 31," Fisher said. "That's two years younger than me, but he'd already written a ton of stuff by then. A genius."

"Who's a genius?" Rocket said, belching as he came into the kitchen and pulled another beer from the refrigerator.

"Schubert."

"Does he work the docks?"

"Yeah, with the rest of you music critics," Fisher said and headed for the front door, pulling it closed behind him.

"Give me this little shit pants." Rocket lifted the baby from Lizette's arms.

"Don't jiggle her. She just ate."

"No problem. I'll just sit her down in the living room so she can listen. Kids love sea shanties."

Lizette rolled her eyes and grabbed a chipped enamel bowl from the cupboard. "I'm going to pick some tomatoes and lettuce for salad. Don't let those animals touch her." She went out the back door and clomped down the steps.

Fisher appeared around the side of the house, pushing blackberry canes aside, and came to stand above her as she knelt beside the vegetable patch. Lizette said nothing, acting as if he were transparent. He gently held the tomato vines up so she could pick the ripest from underneath, dropping them like marbles into the bowl, layering tender lettuce leaves on top.

"What are you going to do if Sandy comes back?"

"What do you mean?"

"I mean are you just going to hand her Violet and go back to living on the streets?"

"What's it to you?"

"Look, I care about you," he said and let the vine drop. Several tomatoes fell to the ground. Lizette looked at him oddly. "I, ah . . . I mean we all do. And, we care about Violet, too. Are you going to let Al just come in and take her? Have you given this situation any thought?"

"Shut up." Lizette hiccupped. "Crap!" She walked pigeon-like up the narrow walkway, waddling as if she was carrying a heavy load that had squashed her normal long-legged gait.

Fisher caught her arm before she could go up the stairs. "All I'm saying is that you have to take the baby and get out of here."

"I'm not leaving. I live here."

"Are you crazy?" he said and instantly regretted it. Lizette glowered at him. "You don't know where the kid's mother is. You don't know who the father is."

"Are you two done picking shit?" Rocket stood at the back-door with a suspicious look on his face. "What's to eat?" Lizette shrugged. "Why don't you put some heat under those beans?"

"I forgot to turn the burner on," she said, irritated. "Where's Violet?"

"Chill out. Al's holding her."

Lizette charged in to retrieve the baby and halted. Al was say-ing to the Dogs, who'd packed into the living room now, "Your're shitting me? Right? This is my kid? With Sandy? She never . . . "

Rocket, Fisher, and Lizette stood together in the arch that divided the living room and dining room. Lizette held her breath and watched him touch the child.

"You know, my mother, man, she loves kids. That's how I grew up. Parties, my uncles gettin' drunk on Sundays, *tamales*. My mother would love another *nieta*. Why didn't you guys tell me this kid was mine?"

"Ah . . . We were saving it for a surprise," Rocket blurted. "I mean you just got out and all. Who spilled the beans?" The Dogs started laughing. "No offense, Al," Rocket said taking in the group. "Who?" All eyes looked down.

"When was she born?" Al looked at Lizette, who was chirping and subtly flapping her arms, craning her neck, agitation building.

"I don't know, April, end of May?" Rocket looked around for a more precise answer but the Dogs were silent. "Sandy said she's a Gemini."

"I got busted in April a year ago," Al said. "It don't add up. This kid's blonde. She's got some bitchin' eyes, though."

Lizette fixed her stare on Violet tucked in Al's arms and coiled, as if to pounce.

"Who's been doin' my stuff then?" He looked around at the Dogs, squinted. "Somebody here been plowin' my field?"

"You know how Sandy is," Stinky piped up from the corner. The room focused on him and he started rubbing his arms and licking his lips.

"Shut up," Rocket snapped and Stinky pulled his head in like a turtle.

"Let's look at her pussy," Al said, unwrapping Violet's blanket. "That'll solve it."

Everyone blinked. Lizette lunged forward, looking like a bob-cat, all fangs and claws, eyes bulging. The Dogs reared back in surprise and Fisher caught her around the waist.

"Chill out. I'm just talking like my mother," Al said. "Take it easy, man."

"Monster," Lizette hissed.

"No, no. You don't understand. My mother says if you want to see how brown a baby's gonna be when it grows up, you check the plumbing. The coloring is the sign. I'm not gonna hurt this kid. I just want to see if it's mine."

Al lay Violet down on the couch. She cried at being set down, at the angry voices, at the cold as Al unwrapped her and took off her diaper. The Dogs clustered around and leaned in to look.

Al put his knarly brown finger beside Violet's pink labia. "Somebody get a lamp over here." One of the Dogs on the outside of the cluster lifted a table lamp above the men's heads. Violet wailed. Lizette cried. Al leaned in, peered.

"I'm tellin' ya, this kid ain't mine," he finally said. "This is some white guy's baby." The Dogs exhaled. Lizette crawled between the cluster of legs and knelt beside Violet, who was crying, red-faced in the lamplight. She scooped the baby up and charged out of the room, sobbed up the stairs, slammed the nursery door, scraped a dresser across the floor and shoved it against the door. The Dogs could hear her screeching like a hawk as Violet's crying ratcheted down and faded away.

The house became silent, the air close. The Dogs drifted home, Rocket left looking solemn. Lucky stumped away toward his mother's place. Fisher, tall and boney, looked like the very image of death, his skeleton rattling as he walked to work downtown. At the Dog House, they switched on the TV.

CBS anchorman Bob Schieffer looked squarely at the camera. *"And now for the national news. President Nixon has declared war on drugs, announcing formation of the new Drug Enforcement Administration, saying that keeping heroin and all dangerous drugs off the streets of America is every bit as crucial as keeping out armed enemy invaders, noting that heroin use in the United States has more than doubled in the past two years."*

"That's a lie," Bomber said.

*"The Pentagon announced the U.S. bombing of Cambodia has ended, halting 12 years of U.S. combat activity in Southeast Asia that has cost the lives of more than 150,000 Americans.*

"Yeah, like who's counting?" Bomber asked the TV screen.

*"In Greece, members of the Black September movement opened fire at the Athens airport, here's footage from the scene. Authorities report three people dead and 55 injured. In Hong Kong, Golden Harvest studios has announced the death of actor and martial artist Bruce Lee."*

"Bummer!" Bomber stood up and flipped off the TV, went to the pallet in the basement, reached under the pillow for his bottle of Chevas, took a hit to chase away memories of the jungle, the thwap, thwap of helicopters, the flicker of tracer bullets in the night.

In the stillness at Sandy's house, Al Munoz found his duffle bag buried in the bottom of Sandy's closet and, from behind a framed picture of his mother, he pulled out what was left of his long-ago stash. After shooting up a pinch and neatly repacking his drug kit in the duffle, he lay back on Sandy's bed and tripped. He thought about the day's events and his family in San Jose, about his new tattoos, Our Lady of Guadalupe on his back, the other tats none of his brothers had ever seen. His mother's *tamales*. Sunday in the park. Piñatas.

He got up and plotted what he'd do tomorrow as he stood before Sandy's dressing mirror, pictures of her dancing with her snake tacked to the wall, her plump tits, the snake's tail winding between her legs. His mouth watered as he played with himself. Above him I-5 smoothed out and settled down. Once, in the blackest hour of the night he startled awake. A scraping sound. A siren screamed, but the noise faded quickly. He fell back into a deep sleep.

Lizette carefully pushed the dresser aside and opened her bedroom door. She crept from her room, listened to the regular breathing sounds coming from Sandy's room, pulled the nursery door closed, peed with a towel draped over her lap to muffle the splattering and walked spider-like down the stairs, stepping on the outsides of the risers to prevent them from squeaking, arms stretched to wall and railing for balance. She stepped around the rusted floor grate and tiptoed to the basement door. She slowly turned the handle, hearing the click as it unlatched, and headed down the stairs into the basement's deeper darkness.

Feeling her way to the big glass cage where Bella slept, she switched on the lamp that warmed the big snake. Bella was awake, her head weaving, tongue darting as if seeking prey, expanding and contracting her vivid cream-and-black reticulated girth. The wooden box by the washer where the live rabbits were kept was empty. Busy with the baby, Lizette hadn't found time to go down to Pike Place Market for a new supply, hadn't mentioned the need to Rocket or Fisher. She watched the snake watch her back, studied the intricate layering of her scales, the pearly pink of her mouth and the rows of backward raking teeth. They swayed together and Lizette wondered in amazement at how big she had gotten. She tried to guess her weight, but got lost in Bella's tongue flicking. The snake extended up and pushed at the grate covering the cage, her heavy body heaving, expanding, against the confinement.

Turning to the laundry baskets, Lizette sorted through the clothes, mostly Violet's little things, some clean, some soiled and smelling sour and ammoniated. Pulling out two pillow cases, she put clean clothes into one, dirty into the other, popped open the dryer and stuffed the things waiting to be folded into the clean sack. She leaned the bulging pillow cases on the bottom stair and looked around. She checked under the stairs where she'd laid a sleeping bag and hidden during the worst times of the past few years. She looked at the dusty bottles and cans forgotten on makeshift shelves, the bicycle frame wedged above her in the crisscrossed floor bracing.

Padding barefoot on the rough cement floor, she went to the narrow windows that looked out at ground level, the panes choked with spider webs and black in the blind night. She checked that the windows were locked. The pilot light flickered in the furnace, a soft hiss coming from the gas. She went to Bella's cage, turned the latches open on the cover grate, hoisted the pillow cases over her shoulders, quietly shut the basement door and went back upstairs to her bedroom. Violet slept undisturbed. Al snored loudly across the hall, whimpering once or twice, then resuming the sawing noises in the back of his throat. Lizette lay on her side facing the window, stretched cat-like and relaxed into the green neon shimmer of the downtown lights reflecting off Lake Union and waited for morning.

# TWENTY–FOUR

**TIDE DETERGENT,** with its big, orange bull's-eye box, sat on Sandy's kitchen table. Lizette put it where Al could find it later when he got around to washing clothes. Fresh coffee warmed in the electric pot on the counter. Bread and butter sat next to the toaster. Rinsed glasses dripped in the dish drainer. The streaming sunlight disturbed Lizette. It shouted, woke things best left alone. She heard a bumping sound from the basement and froze, listened, but the sound did not come again.

When she carried the baby downstairs to feed her, she heard Al snoring in Sandy's bed. At the bottom of the stairs now, she listened up, tried to sense if Al was stirring, perhaps preparing to come down or waiting for her to leave. She dressed Violet, shushed and kissed her cheeks to keep her from crying. She prepared three bottles of formula, popped her medication, then bundled the baby, full and cooing, into fluffy blankets. Banking sofa pillows around Violet so she wouldn't fall off, Lizette hurried outside.

She took the stroller from the front porch and unfolded it on the walkway in front of the house, clicked the safety latches into place, went back inside. Violet wiggled, trying to turn over. *Can't trust you anymore*, Lizette thought, smiling to herself, amazed at how fast Violet was growing.

A postcard from Sandy had come last week addressed to Marian, who'd gone back to Orcas a couple of months ago. Sandy said Mexico was a *gas* that they'd bought a boat and fished every day, drank margaritas by the hotel pool at night. Didn't know when she'd be back, she'd said. *"Off to Colombia on business. Stay dry. S.S".* The postcard had a picture of Acapulco Bay, lights from the hotels reflecting off the water. Lizette ripped it and threw it in the garbage.

The baby rested in the stroller's reclined seat and Lizette fixed the blankets around her to ward off the morning chill, fluffed the edges so the lace showed. *Egg in a nest*, she thought. She hooked her big canvas bag filled with diapers, ointments, changes of clothes, lotions and bottles, over the stroller handle. While packing, she'd added some crow feathers she'd collected and a yarn god's eye to the day's supplies. She rolled down hill, holding the stroller back so it wouldn't run away.

Garrulous blue jays flittered in the brambles under the freeway. Lizette twittered to them, feeling their spirit. She rounded a corner and came to a well-kept street with gardens overflowing in late summer—orange poppies with naughty black hearts bobbed in the breeze. Hot-pink fuchsias hung from baskets, the blooms shaped like billowing skirts, a profusion of immodesty. She picked lipstick-red roses and baby-pink buds, lavender pansies with black cow faces and fresh-cheeked daisies, placing them in the stroller, blanketing Violet, except for her pink nose and cupid's bow lips.

A dog barked. A man yelled, "What the hell're you doin'! Them flowers ain't yours!" Lizette couldn't see who hollered from behind a curtained window and hurried along, almost running. On the next block, she picked more flowers, quickly snapping the blooms from their stems with her thumbnail, glancing around, dropping them into the stroller. Pushing faster. The sky was gray with a hint of rain from the west. She adjusted the blue awning over Violet. A volley of robins took wing from a small lawn as they rushed past.

Along Eastlake Avenue, shopkeepers prepared to open. Sheets of oak veneer, lashed to a red pickup truck, waited to be unloaded beside the cabinet shop. Harbor Freight and Salvage, stuffed with surplus left over from the Vietnam War, displayed boat anchors, wool socks, screwdrivers, dummy hand grenades and a gas mask in its front window. Further along, an outboard motor repair shop, its metal door rolled up, blasted the morning news from a radio on a workbench.

*"One man died in a boating mishap in the Strait of Juan de Fuca after a Coast Guard rescue. His fishing companion reported the man fell overboard trying to save his catch from the jaws of an orca and drowned."* A guy in greasy overalls shuffled to the radio, sipping coffee in a paper cup, and turned up the volume. *"The new Marine Mammal Protection Act now makes it a crime to disturb orcas and seals. Officials said fishermen can expect maximum enforcement. On the entertainment front, Elvis Presley, King of Rock and Roll, will play the Seattle Center tonight. Promoters say tickets are sold out and concert goers should expect a heavy police presence."*

Hurrying on, the news chatter washed away on the wind coming from the lake. Lizette bent over the stroller handle and pushed for downtown, the dangling bag flapped against her shins. At the coffee house, she looked around at the Friday morning crowd to see if she recognized anyone and ordered a raisin snail with a cup of tea. It had been nearly a year since she'd been there and breathed the thick, rich smell of roasted coffee. Back then she'd been confused about the future. But now, even though the shop seemed the same, she felt new, alive with purpose.

Violet slept under her blanket of flowers and Lizette settled into her favorite chair by the window, pulled out her sketch book. The place was quiet in the gap between the morning rush and lunch hour. The stereo played a Haydn piano rondo. Fisher flashed through her mind, his interest in her and Violet feeling like a rubber band on her wrist. She dipped a flat brush in the glass of drinking water beside her and slopped water across the blank page of her sketch pad, wetted the brush again and charged it with blue from the color tray she'd pulled from her bag, deftly laid down a color gradient, then threw the scatter of robins from this morning's walk into the picture, the gardens jumbled with blooms. She worked quickly and set the sketch pad aside so the image could dry.

The harsh whir of the shop's coffee grinder made Violet stir. Lizette picked her up and the baby blinked, her eyes periwinkle blue in the mid-morning light. She drank half a bottle and fell back asleep. Lizette lounged content in the warm light streaming through the picture window. An image of Al crept to the edge of her consciousness and she shook her head quickly, dismissed the thought, hoping Bella had done her job and scared the bee-Jesus out of him. She prayed it would be enough to freak him out, that the beady-eyed little bastard would be halfway to Portland by the time they got back home. She laid Violet in the stroller and headed down the hill to Pike Place Market.

Produce vendors called to her. She waved. The fish monger came out to look at the baby. "I didn't know," he said, amazed, looking at her lean mid-section, bending down and pulling the baby's blanket away to look. "How old?" About four months, Lizette told him with pride. "Beautiful," the man said as Lizette moved on. Everyone had heard what happened to her, about the attack. They all felt sorry but agreed she shouldn't have been hanging around on the streets. Bound to happen, they said, shaking their heads. Such a pretty girl, so stupid.

*"Cara mia!"* The fruit seller tossed her an apple and she caught it one-handed as she hurried past, put it in her sack and turned onto the sidewalk.

At Pioneer Square she slowed, looked in store windows littered with clothes and cooking utensils. The galleries were just opening, yawning with their red-brick mouths open. She dawdled along Occidental Avenue, noticed a man in a long black raincoat at the end of the block sweeping the mottled brick sidewalk. She ducked into a gallery, its front decked with flower boxes, big hanging baskets, blue lobelia and white petunias cascading over the sides.

The interior was warm with wood tones, the lighting subdued and indirect, and she collected herself, stopped shaking. The colors drew Lizette first, then the framing and punch of unexpected shapes. Above her, mobile sculptures attached to the ceiling beams bobbed in the disturbed air. A big, white marble penguin commanded attention in the center of the burnished oak floor, the piece, rounded and graceful at the bottom, narrowed upward to its stylized head, beak tucked neatly under a sculpted wing, creating a feeling of repose. She looked for the artist's signature, found Bufano on the base. She sat on a hassock and took the sculpture in. She glanced over the framed sketches and to a mid-sized watercolor of birds and a garden, not more inspired in its execution than her own sketch had been this morning, and dismissed it.

"Welcome to Wentz Gallery," a flat voice said from behind a fussy carved desk in one of the dark corners. Lizette wasn't ready to interact with a stranger. She pulled inside herself and rocked the stroller back and forth with her foot.

"Are you looking for something in particular?" the voice said. "We exhibit contemporary work from local artists, some from outside the area that we think are imaginative. We specialize in out of the ordinary works."

Lizette turned her back to the voice and got up, walked to a painting illuminated by track lights from above. She'd noticed a line, a pattern from across the gallery and was pulled to stand in front of the big canvas. Her mind fuzzed electrically as she recognized the painting, *her painting*. Smells of the cabin came to her, the desolate sound of the sea folding in waves and hissing onto the beach in the cove below her windows, the spy-hopping seal, the ominous dorsal fin of Looney, flagging his hunt, the memories crackling through her like lightening. The aroma of cedar and mold, even how it felt to stand on the soft pine floor in front of a canvas, this canvas, light subdued, the cabin's corners murky. These sensory recollections overwhelmed her. Shocked, she couldn't hoist herself onto the raft of expressible feelings and stood before her own work, dumbstruck.

"This is one of my favorite pieces," the man said, standing close beside her. "We've only had it a couple of months, but it looks like we've already got a bidding war over it." The voice, a slight man it turned out, dressed impeccably in a moss-green tailored jacket and gray trousers, the corduroy wale so small Lizette thought at first glance the fabric was velvet, crowded her personal body space and she tipped away. His longish hair was swept from his forehead and he had a black silk scarf knotted at the side of his throat, cowboy style. *Calculated perfection*, she thought, becoming angry. *Pretentious fop!* But his translucent blue eyes were open to her, guileless and kind, sincerely helpful. Some of her internal tension relaxed.

"Curators from the Seattle Art Museum and the Museum of Modern Art in New York have been in to look at it, too." he said, proudly sweeping his arm toward her painting. "We may also have a collector interested in acquiring it." He walked to her painting. "We're quite pleased."

"How much?" Lizette said, moving closer to look at her signature in the bottom right corner.

"Well, this artist, she's some kind of recluse, we understand, lives on Orcas Island. She has an agent so the starting prices were negotiated. Initially we were talking about fifty thousand dollars, but it's probably going to be more than that." Lizette chirped, rubbed the muscles in her neck. "There are other paintings by this artist," the man continued, "if you're interested. We've already sold the few smaller pieces we had, sent the rest to our affiliate in New York, which is how the MOMA curator got wind of this artist."

Lizette stepped to within inches of the canvas, fascinated with her own work in the rich light. She saw where lines were too timid, where a clumping of chromium oxide missed the green she desired. She'd mixed it with pureed oatmeal and spit and saw that it was too full bodied for her purpose. The light did not pass through the layers as she'd intended. She'd used pure pigment, melted bees wax that she'd kept soft in a pot on the cabin stove, mixed in tree sap she'd gathered in the woods surrounding the ranch, fused the elements to create what she thought was the right viscosity, spread them sensuously on the canvas in the dark hours of her grief, adding charcoal from the fire, cranberry juice, clotted blood from her own menstrual period, scraps from decaying metal around the ranch. Then she'd shaped the undersea images with her mother's palette knife.

She'd distilled her visionary underworld on the canvas in the greens and blues and gloaming grays, creating a worldscape, expanses of ocean, kelp forests in the depths, the welkin submerged. Generally, she liked the work, once she got over the shock of unexpected confrontation. But, more importantly, she saw ways to better execute her vision, techniques that called for more refinement. She felt excited, butterflies fluttering in her chest, the urgency to work burned into a roaring blaze of desire. Her breath came in short gasps. She felt faint.

"The way the pigments fuse . . . " Lizette jumped, surprised again by the man's voice so near to her ear. "The effect adds to the ethereal quality of the encaustic medium. Some paintings have ten or more layers built up, but this work is extraordinary. There are easily two dozen levels, the coloration changing with the light source and time of day. This piece is quite seductive, tactile, sultry. It's like the canvas breathes life." A well-dressed couple came into the gallery and the man turned and went to greet them. "Welcome to Wentz Gallery," he said before his voice trailed out of Lizette's consciousness.

As she left, pushing the stroller toward the door, pausing, pulling it back and forth to soothe Violet's fussing, she asked, "Who's the agent?"

"Pardon me?" the man said, excusing himself from the couple and crossing to Lizette as she stood by the door. "The agent?"

"For the painter? The canvas we were looking at?" Lizette caught his eyes, searched for deception, found only honesty.

"Oh, yes," he said, figuring it out. "The agent is a local, Henri Toussaint. I think we have his number around here somewhere, if you want to contact him." He leaned toward her and added in a confidential tone, "He's a poet, although I hear not a very good one, but clearly he has an eye for art talent and he's well connected to the art scene. Do you want to wait while I find his contact information?"

"No," Lizette said as she rolled the stroller out the door, tipping it to maneuver the short step to the brick sidewalk. *Toulouse! You bastard! How did you get my stuff?* Then it hit her. He must have taken her paintings while she and Marian were away from the ranch at Sandy's, when Violet was born. She remembered finding him snooping around the cabin during the party, and wondered how Rocket figured in this.

She pumped up the street, jolting Violet on the uneven surface. The baby was wailing by the time she reached the corner. She pulled up beside the bus benches under the pergola at First and Yesler, sat down and lifted Violet out of the stroller. She carried her to the Tlingit totem pole, studied how the weather was wearing it away, aging it, and embraced the battered carving with both arms, squeezing Violet against the weather-beaten pole in a barrel hug. She cried along with the baby over the theft and loss. A middle-aged woman waiting for the bus put a hand on her shoulder.

"You all right here?" the woman asked. "Everything OK, honey?"

Lizette nodded, half turning. "Tired, I guess."

"Well, get some rest. I've had a few little ones of my own. My heart goes out to you." She peeked around Lizette's shoulder. "Such a pretty child."

"Thanks." Lizette held back a coo. When the bus came, the woman got on. She looked down on Lizette from the window with a worried expression, making Lizette fear the old bag might report her to the cops or something. She gathered herself, fuming, and struck off for Franklin Street, pushing the stroller hard, cackling under her breath. People stepped aside when they saw her coming. A man with a short gray beard hollered after her, "Slow down, girlie. You're gonna kill somebody."

# TWENTY–FIVE

SLOUCHED AT THE KITCHEN TABLE IN THE DOG HOUSE, Rocket sipped tea and held his ear toward the open window above the sink. He listened between the notes Fisher played on the piano. He'd asked Fisher who wrote the music, but couldn't catch the name he'd spat out the side of his mouth. Rocket stood over the keyboard briefly then went back to slump in the kitchen. *Some Commie Russian*, he thought, scraping dried egg stuck on the table with a fingernail.

It'd been a long week and he clutched the chipped mug for comfort and stewed over his mishaps. The hookup with the gravel barge from Vancouver hadn't gone smoothly. The Canadian tow boat had engine trouble and was late. It limped to the rendezvous under half power, its diesel engine straining into the swells that surged through the strait. Rocket thought he spotted Looney off to starboard, his black and white body splashing and rolling, dipping, breeching, but couldn't be sure. He slipped on the deck in the evening light, missed the cleat when he threw the tie-up lines, nearly went overboard. The first mate chewed his ass for the sloppy maneuvers, and later the old salt won a hundred bucks off him playing poker, but he suspected cheating. Then he'd had to deal with Al, and Lizette freaking out.

He listened now for the baby's cry from next door, amused at how her sounds were getting stronger, more like a human child than a kitten. *Spoiled*, he thought. He missed Sandy, sleeping late in her steamy upstairs bedroom, watching her waltz around the bed, completely comfortable in her nakedness. The curve of her hip, trim waist, the lush fall of blonde hair. He listened for the rattle of dishes in her kitchen, the front door banging, the wind chimes tinkling on the porch, Sandy's throaty laugh. He missed her and he missed Carl's convenient deliveries, hated hustling for drugs.

Big Al being over there with Lizette and Violet made him uneasy. He sensed nothing stirring and worried they'd gone out, that Al had taken them and was putting his filthy hands on Violet, changing her diapers, touching her privates, sending Lizette into orbit. His stomach turned and he checked the clock. *After two,* he thought and got up, put his mug in the sink, peered through the murky window at Sandy's house. *Better check.*

"Hey, Mama," he shouted from Sandy's front door. "Lizzie? Hey! Anybody here?" No sound came back. He went to the kitchen, tidy and cold. He could feel they were gone, but went and called up the stairs again anyway. The silence held. He turned to leave, hand on the door knob, but felt a bump, a heavy thud he sensed more than heard. Rocket scooted toward the basement door and listened again. Thump. "Aagh," faintly.

At the top of the basement stairs he called down into the darkness, "Lizette?" He flipped on the stairwell light and peered into the abyss. At the bottom was a throbbing coil of black and cream. Feet, human feet, protruded from the mangle. He started down the stairs, but pulled back when Bella turned her menacing head toward him, her jaw unhinged, displaying the full expanse of her gaping pink mouth, darting red tongue. She warned him back, the narrow tail of her body flicked like a whip. Rocket inched back up the stairs, slammed the door, ran.

"Help!" Rocket lurched head first through the front door of the Dog House, regained his footing. "God! Shit! Holy shit!"

He ran into the kitchen, yelling for help. Fisher jumped up from the keyboard when Rocket burst in, grabbed him by the shoulders. "What're you screaming about?"

"Call the cops!" Rocket yelled at him, pulling open kitchen drawers, rummaging like a madman, dumping the contents on the floor. He charged into the dining room waving a butcher knife. "Bella's got somebody!"

"Who?" Fisher asked, looking owlish behind his glasses, craning his long neck, dropping the piano's keyboard cover with a clap.

"All I could see is feet," Rocket gasped. "He's wrapped up!"

"No shit?" Fisher moved to the phone on the kitchen wall and pulled the dial around from zero. "Emergency! We need the police . . . a snake . . . In the basement . . . No. . . . This isn't a joke! . . . On Franklin Street. Off Eastlake . . . I don't know. I didn't see it . . . Because somebody else did . . . A boa constrictor . . . Yes. A big snake! A really big one!"

"Come on, man!" Rocket shouted, bouncing around the kitchen, waving the knife in Fisher's face as he spoke into the receiver.

"Franklin Street, 600 block. Above the boat works . . . Yeah. We'll be out front." Fisher hung up and picked up a long knife from the floor. "Let's go."

They charged down the front walk and ran next door. Stinky and Buzz bumped into them by Sandy's front gate, laughing at first, but looking worried as they realized the men held knives, that they were running into Sandy's with them. "What's up?" Stinky demanded, blocking their path on the sidewalk.

"Fuckin' snake!" Rocket pushed past them. "In the basement."

"Where's Liz," Stinky yelled, "and the baby?"

Rocket halted on the path, "Oh my God!" He broke for the front door and disappeared. A cop car cruised up. The officers rolled down the window and looked with bored faces at the men.

"What's up?"

"Snake in the basement!" the men blurted out. "Might be a baby down there, too!"

The officer on the passenger side got out, pulled the shotgun from the rack on the dashboard and swiped the gun butt side to side, pushing past the Dogs. Lucky stumped up the sidewalk on his cane, Gizzard arrived from the other end of the street. The cop on the driver's side rolled out with the car's radio mike in his hand, surveyed the ratty knot.

"Car 463, over. Responding, 612 Franklin, over. Claims there's a snake in the basement." The radio crackled back, something garbled. "Possible child involved, over. We're going in. Over."

The officer with the gun burst out the front door onto the walkway, "Call for back up! Thing is huge! A monster! Get animal control out here! Call an ambulance. We need a meat wagon."

"Where's Rocket?" Buzzard scanned the officer's frightened face.

"Who?"

"The guy with the knife!"

"He's got a knife?"

"For the snake, man," Buzzard shouted in his face. "Calm down. It's for the snake!"

"Jesus!" The cop nudged his partner. "Cover me. I'm going down."

Guns drawn, the officers inched down the basement steps, flattening their backs on the greasy wall. Sirens wailed in the distance, growing louder. They saw Rocket at the bottom of the flight, growling like a bear, plunging the knife into Bella's side, plunging and slicing, plunging, shaking blood from his hand, making grunting sounds.

"Halt!" the cop commanded. Rocket looked up the stairs, seeing the men for the first time. Bella snapped around and locked onto his free hand and Rocket yelped in pain, the snake's backward raking teeth shredded his skin. Her tail wrapped around his ankle, almost toppling him. "Stand aside," the cop ordered, gun pointed at Rocket's chest. Rocket swiped the knife at Bella's probing head, sliced her neck. She relaxed her body and he stepped back. She coiled tighter around her prey. One of Al's eyes popped out of his purple face and dangled on his cheek like yolk from a broken egg.

"Don't shoot, Jim!" the cop directed his partner as they studied the scene. They could see the victim was a man, his face slimed and bulging, Bella flicking blood that dripped from the eye socket. "You might hit the guy!"

# TWENTY–SIX

LIZETTE PUSHED THE STROLLER UP HILL, bending into the handle, pumping her long legs. The trudge home had leeched away most of her anger. She puffed and planned what she'd say to Rocket—about stealing her paintings, violating her space, his relationship with Sandy and Violet and Marian and Greg, and that idiot Poet . . . and . . . and. She planned to set him straight. The steam built again and she brushed the thoughts from her mind. A van whipped past, King County News pasted across the back doors. She turned the corner to find cop cars, flashing lights, the Dogs huddled on the sidewalk. Trucks, sirens, engines idling, then gun shots, muffled but distinct, hot reports.

She halted. Waited for the shots' echo to fade under the freeway bridge. In the collective inhale, the silent gap, the traffic on I-5 sounded jolly, rolling along overhead, honking and whirring, rhythmically pulsing into the void. In the pause, the Dogs looked around and saw Lizette. They thundered toward her in a pack. Newly arriving cops charged the front door and disappeared into Sandy's house.

"You OK?" The Dogs demanded, almost knocking her over.

She scanned their faces, smelled their fear and asked the huddle what was going on. They jockeyed for position around her, leaning across the stroller to touch her. Fisher ran up. She realized he had a big knife, his face white. She searched their faces. They offered garbled details: The basement. The baby. Thought she was down there, too. They heard shots!

"Rocket's still not out." Fisher wailed running up to them. "It's Al! Killed him! Ate his head." He ran back into Sandy's house.

Lizette felt her knees give like worn springs, sagging from too much weight. She pulled away from the gabbling, chirped nervously under her breath, tried to control her trembling. Violet started crying. The Dogs lifted the sun cover, leaned in. Bomber pulled the baby's blanket away and looked at her pink face. "She looks OK," he said. Everyone nodded, agreeing like puppets.

"She's hungry," Lizette said and tugged the stroller to the front of the Dog House. "Help me get the stroller inside." The men followed her up the cracked walkway, lifted the stroller across the broken boards on the porch and through the front door, Violet cried hard. In the kitchen, she picked the baby up, bounced her while digging in the diaper bag for a bottle. She popped the nipple in Violet's mouth and stood swaying in front of the kitchen sink where she could see a slice of the commotion going on outside Sandy's house. The baby quieted.

The Dogs circled around the picket fence. An ambulance rolled up and parked. A TV camera was screwed on a tall tripod, the operator scanning it across the front of Sandy's house. Another police cruiser rumbled up. People from down the street gathered by the curb, sniffing and leaning toward the house. One old woman finally talked to Gizzard, pulled him aside, but Lizette could see she wasn't satisfied with his answers. They rolled a stretcher up the walk and the sounds coming to her through the window became hushed.

When they wheeled the stretcher back out, the Dogs helped lower it down the front steps. All they could see was a long, black bag strapped securely on top. A young guy in a business suit talked into a microphone and looked earnestly into the TV camera while behind him they loaded the body into the back of the ambulance and slammed the door. The drivers paused, fawned for the camera, got in and pulled away. No siren. No need.

Everyone turned to stare at the house again, the front door wide open. A few people wandered away. The guy with the microphone approached the Dogs, tipping the mike toward their mouths and then away to his own lips. Lizette strained, but could not hear what they were saying.

A gasp from the crowd interrupted the interviews. An officer came through the door and onto the porch, Bella's big limp body suspended behind him, a pillowcase over her head. Then another officer, holding her further down, emerged, followed by Fisher at Bella's thick mid-section, then another officer, Rocket carrying her long tail. They coiled her like rope in the street, the TV camera moving in for a close-up, then, forming a scrum, the men lifted her into the animal control truck, pushing and squeezing to make her fit. The guy with the microphone tried to talk to Rocket, but he shooed him away. Two more cops came out of the house. They pulled Rocket aside, handed him a white towel for his bleeding hand, and the whole pack of men turned toward the Dog house. Lizette moved away from the window and into the living room.

"Liz?" Rocket hit the front door. "They want to talk to you."

"I'm changing Violet's diaper," she answered. The Dogs tromped in, flopped down around her, shoving aside food wrappers and empty beer bottles. "She pooped." Rocket stood over her as she sat on the torn couch and fixed the diaper pins, rolled up the dirty one, handed it to him. "What do they want?"

"They want to know what happened," he said, weighing the diaper like a brick.

"I went for a walk and came back to this scene." She stood up and placed the baby's head on her shoulder, patting Violet's back to soothe her. "I don't know anything. I wasn't here, didn't want to be alone with Al in the house."

"I'm hip," Rocket said, nodding his head. "I wasn't cool with the guy being there either. They just want to ask you some questions. Somebody said the baby was down there with Bella. They want to make sure she's OK."

They went next door. Rocket warned under his breath, "Don't say nothing about Carl." They sat in the living room, a cop in Sandy's favorite chair, notepad on his knee. "Do you live here?"

"We're house sitting while Sandy's gone," Lizette said.

"How about you?" he asked, turning toward Rocket.

"I live next door," Rocket said. "Came over to check on Lizette and the baby."

He spoke to Lizette. "What's your name?"

"Elizabeth Karlson."

"I know you," the cop standing in the doorway said, moving into the room to get a better look at her. "You were . . . ah, assaulted. At the Twisted Owl. Weren't you? In the alley. Last December?" Lizette felt the blood drain from her face, looked around at the men, held Violet closer. "I went over to the hospital," he said. "Went a couple of times. We tried to get a description of the guy, but you were . . . ah. We never caught him . . . How're you doing?"

"OK" Lizette said softly. Rocket looked away from her, she could feel him pull back, avoid touching her as they sat side-by-side on the couch, felt dirty.

"And the baby?" The cop looked searchingly at Violet, sleeping in Lizette's arms. "Is she?" He stepped forward, touched the edge of the baby blanket, looked up with sorrow clouding his eyes. "I mean." He stepped back, looked down, said softly, "Did you?"

"Yes," Lizette said flatly, her eyes focused on the floor.

"Sorry to hear that," he said. "I mean, maybe it's OK." He sounded flustered, looked around. "So, who lives here?"

"Sandy Shore," Rocket said. "She took a vacation."

"Isn't she that stripper?" the cop standing closest to Lizette asked.

"Yeah, but she doesn't dance anymore," Lizette offered. "She went on a trip with some friends who live on Queen Anne Hill. I don't know them. I'm just bringing in the mail."

"What's with the snake?"

Lizette looked at Rocket. "It was part of her act," he explained. "She danced with her—Sandy Shore and Bella the Beautiful Boa, that's how they billed it at Vixens. She kept Bella in a cage in the basement, fed her rabbits."

"Do you know the victim?"

"Al," Rocket said, frowning. "Al Munoz. Friend of Sandy's. Just got out of jail. Don't know him very well. She met him at work. He comes around off and on. None of my business."

The cop taking notes bobbed his head knowingly and scribbled. He reached over and turned on the lamp as dusk had crept into the room. The officers scuffed their heavy boots on the wood floor, shifted their weight from foot to foot like anxious horses, glanced around. Violet yawned in her sleep, wiggled.

"We found a duffle bag in the upstairs bedroom," the cop said. "Looks like Al was a drug user."

"Wouldn't know," Rocket said. "Like I said, he just got out of jail. Crashed here last night. Sandy's gone. That's all I know."

"We're taking his things for evidence," he said, hunching his shoulders, as if preparing for an argument. "What's the phone number here, in case we have more questions?"

"Evergreen six, 0543."

"How long will you be staying here?" the cop asked Lizette.

"Not too long," she said. "I'm taking the baby and going to live with my sister in San Francisco." Rocket looked at her sideways. "I'm house sitting as a favor."

After the cops left, Rocket got up and settled in Sandy's comfortable chair. "You don't have a sister in San Francisco." Lizette put Violet down on the couch and got up and went into the kitchen. "Why'd you lie?" he asked, following her. "I almost believed you. You could have said you were going back to Orcas."

"You should wash out those scratches," Lizette said, pulling hydrogen peroxide from the cupboard, handing it to him. "Serpent's teeth. Dirty mouths."

Rocket unwrapped the towel from his hand and ran it under the faucet until the water steamed. He lathered with dish soap, rinsed, and poured the peroxide over the scratches. "Not too deep," he said rotating his hands to check the scratches. "This one's pretty bad." He traced one gash down the back of his hand. "Wish Sandy was here," he said wistfully. "We'd get Chinese."

He went to the couch and pulled the blanket away from Violet's face, smiled down at her, turned and left. Lizette locked the door after him. Feeling the cold tendrils of fall sneaking in with the night, she flipped on the furnace and smelled the burning dust. Violet fussed and she scooped her off the couch.

In the kitchen, she held the baby to her chest and swished Rocket's blood spatters from the sink, gathered clean towels, and filled the sink with warm water. Laying Violet on the counter, she carefully undressed her, marveling at her plump thighs and round belly. She turned her over and examined her butt, looking for diaper rash, but found only dimples. She dipped Violet's toes in the water, smiled at her surprise. Violet smiled back, startled Lizette with her first laugh. She soaped the baby's neck, the folds between her legs and took her hands away to see if she could sit, catching her on either side when she tipped. Lizette leaned closer, swirled bubbles, and hummed in Violet's ear.

The front door rattled. "Open up!" Rocket banged on the door. "Who locked the goddamned door?" Lizette carried the dripping baby to the front door, wrapping her in a towel as she went and flipped the latch. Rocket burst in. "Turn on the TV!"

The image flickered on Sandy's TV. The news anchor, hair slicked into a pomp, looked at them directly . . . *"was bitten and squeezed to death by an 18-foot boa constrictor."*

"Burmese python," Lizette snapped and frowned at the TV screen.

*"Witnesses said the huge snake was kept as a pet in an Eastlake home. A friend of the victim, who gave his name as Buzzard, had this to say—"*

Buzzard's haggard face filled the screen. *"She was a good snake, always gentle, easy to handle. Don't know what got into her. He was just doing laundry. In the basement. We was worried about the baby. Kid's just a few months old. Real cute. Glad she's OK."*

The screen switched to pictures of the men carrying Bella's limp body to the sidewalk, then the young guy that had showed up at Sandy's with the microphone came on: *"In a heroic effort, officers tried to save the victim from the crushing strength of the giant snake, but were too late. Officers shot the animal in self-defense when it turned on them. Authorities say there are no laws prohibiting the keeping of exotic snakes, but the matter has been referred to child welfare officials for investigation because an infant was living in the home at the time of the fatal attack."*

"Idiots!" Lizette blurted, got up, paced. "Who told them about Violet?"

"You were here." Rocket looked defensive, picked at the fabric on the arm of Sandy's chair. "We were worried, we thought . . . "

"Shut up!" Lizette turned on him, machine-gunned questions. "Have you got any boxes at your place? Have you got gas in the car? How long does it take to get to Anacortes? What's the ferry schedule? When can you leave?"

# TWENTY–SEVEN

SHE LIFTED UP AND THROUGH THE CAR'S fogged windows and saw the veil of night dissolving in the sunrise. Mt. Baker stretched 11,000 feet into the sapphire-colored stratosphere, puffy clouds hung around its snow-capped peak. *Close enough to touch,* she thought, gazing at the mountain's ominous beauty. *Close enough to feel the heat.* Lizette knew the volcano had erupted long ago, ripped the sky, spewed hot ash, killed all the fish, set the forests on fire, but now the mountain preened in the dawn like a seductive, dangerous woman.

She glanced over the front seat at Rocket, asleep with his jacket balled up under his head, one of Violet's fluffy pink quilts covering him chest to knees. Turning to read the building sign, she located herself. "Long John Silver's. Fish and chips. Shrimp baskets." She scanned the parking lot behind the restaurant. Anacortes. They'd packed in a hurry, stuffed the trunk of Rocket's 88, tore up Interstate 5, missed the last ferry for Orcas Island, parked behind the restaurant to sleep until daylight.

She pulled the car's door handle down, pushed out, stood bleary eyed. She squatted behind the dumpster and peed, got back in and popped a bottle into Violet's mouth. Waited.

"You awake?" Rocket said through the seatback, wallowing himself into a more comfortable position.

"What time is it?" she asked in a dreamy voice, cradling Violet, and stretched her cramped legs against the passenger door.

"Looks like O-dark hundred, to me." He lifted up, settled back again.

"I don't want to miss the first ferry."

"Relax. First one leaves for Orcas at five thirty. There's another one at six ten."

"Rocket?"

"Yeah."

"Do you know what you want?"

"A raisin snail and a cup of coffee?"

"Funny." Lizette paused. She could hear him listening. She dug in her bag for a diaper and clean plastic pants, got on her knees in the backseat and changed Violet. The baby drew up her legs in protest, squeezed out a couple of crocodile tears from the edges of her squinched eyes. Lizette lifted her and suck-kissed under her jaw bone, forcing a giggle.

"Did that kid laugh?" He sat up.

"Isn't it cute?"

"I didn't know she could," Rocket said. "Hand her over, let's take a look." He joggled Violet, grinned into her little face. "I mean, I know she's smart, but I didn't think babies had a sense of humor." He lifted her back over the seat.

"Who do you think she looks like?" she said shyly.

"Who?"

"Well . . . Not Al, that's for sure." She laughed. "Or the land-lord . . . Or Carl." She saw Rocket's chest contract at the mention of Cadillac Carl, heard him breathing more rapidly. "Have you ever thought about fishing? Or buying a sailboat to live on? Moving out of Seattle?"

"I gotta job. Work a couple of days. Take a couple of days off. It's a good gig. Pays the rent."

"But, after they tear down the Dog House. You know they will. Someday. Where will you live then?"

"Shit. How should I know? Next door to my connection?" He twisted on the seat, chuckled, turned his back against her. "All I can deal with is today, man."

"I'm not a man and what about Violet?"

"What about her?"

"We could keep her. I mean, if Sandy doesn't come back."

Rocket was silent, lifted to stare out the window, glanced sideways at her.

"Yeah, we could drop her off, too." He turned away, irritation scribbled across his face. "At an orphanage or a fire station or on the doorstep of some big-ass mansion on Mercer Island, one with a swing set and a perfect fuckin' puppy in the backyard."

"Knock it off, Rocket. We could go to Europe. Take her to France."

"I can't talk French."

"I can. I could teach you. We could go to the Louvre. Check out Ingres, Delacrox, Fouquet, Poussin . . . ," the hope in her voice deflated as she searched his stony face.

"Yeah? What about a job? How do you say shit in French?"

"Mon dieu!" Lizette snapped and settled back, held Violet closer, pouted.

"OK, now I gotta piss." He got out of the car and went to the bushes at the edge of the parking lot. She watched his back, jacket hunched up around his waist. He shimmy shook his hips, zipped, walked back.

"Let's head down to the ferry," he said, sliding onto the front seat, tossing the blanket in the back. "We can get breakfast on the boat." The car's engine growled into action and he warmed it before shifting into gear. She got into the front seat. "What time is it?" he said.

"I already asked you that."

"Sorry." He looked straight ahead through the windshield.

They drove along the water, the town dark, silence hardening to granite between them. Violet lay bolstered by blankets and bags on the backseat, cooing, watching her hands in the brightening light. Lizette wanted to reach out, touch him, pierce his shield of annoyance, but she held back. They reached the ferry landing in time to watch the wide, flat-bottomed boat pull away, its horn blowing a warning as it sloshed into the sea toward the islands humped like pond turtles in the dawn.

"Crap!" Rocket smacked the steering wheel and looked around at the empty lanes used for loading. "It's gonna be another forty minutes." He got out of the car, slammed the door, popped the trunk, pulled his sea bag out, rifled around for a smoke and leaned on the rear fender, puffing. A Laura Scudders delivery truck pulled into line behind his car and Rocket glared at the driver, who checked his clipboard and acted like he didn't see Rocket standing there fuming.

Cars and pickups piled into line behind them. Lizette watched the sun's rosy glow strengthen, analyzed the shadows on the water and the play of light on the islands as they materialized from the mist. When the *Yakima* arrived, the deck crew lowered the steel ramp and signaled Rocket to board. He eased the big Olds onto the ferry and one of the crew shouted, "Nice car." Rocket grinned, gunned the 88, offered a finger salute. Pulling close to the ferry's super structure, he set the brake.

"Let's eat," he said, getting out.

Because the car was parked too tight against the wall to open the passenger door, Lizette lifted the dozing Violet from the back and slid across the seat. She followed him up the narrow gangway to the café, smelling of cheap coffee and sour dish rags, and took a table overlooking the water. She watched gulls make lazy circles around the pilings, water sloshed against the landing. Rocket came to her. "What do you want to eat?"

"Tea. Earl Gray, if they have it. Oatmeal." She settled the baby next to her on the bench seat. He returned in a few minutes with a tray and unloaded her mug and bowl. She got up and grabbed a glass sugar shaker from the cook's counter, looked disapprovingly at the two chili dogs, heaped with beans, onions and cheese, in front of Rocket.

"That's disgusting."

"Looks like work." He took a big bite, orange-colored juice running down the heel of his hand. "We eat like this on the tugs," he said with his mouth full. "It don't matter what time it is. Somebody's always coming off watch, looking for chow. Gets cold out there. Chili dogs warm your guts, keep you going."

The *Yakima* eased back from the landing. Rocket watched out the window as the crew untied the lines and coiled the ropes on deck.

"Missed a throw," he said, offhandedly. "Hey, look at that canoe!" He stood up and pressed against the glass. She leaned over and looked across the water. A big canoe, its tips shaped like orca fins, plowed through the Salish Sea. A dozen or so men pulled with long, decorated paddles, gaining on the lumbering ferry. A man stood at the back in a pointed hat, beating a round drum. The paddlers dug into the water, heads bowed, watch caps pulled over their ears. The rhythmic drumbeat carried across the water, overriding the ferry's engine noise as the canoe drew closer. Black and white Chinook designs were painted on the canoe's sides. *Lummi pattern, dancing salmon*, she thought. They caught up with the ferry and some of the men stowed their paddles, others dug into the sea in alternating intervals, maintaining an even speed, pacing the ferry.

"You could fish." She relaxed into her seat. "Buy a boat."

"What about my piano?" he answered, watching the canoe. "Those guys are really putting some muscle into it."

"You could sell the piano. Use the money for a boat. Violet could . . . "

"Look. I'm paying rent on two houses now. I have a job. Sandy'll be back. She's just taking a timeout. The kid's doing fine."

Lizette choked, oatmeal stuck in her craw. She slurped tea, wiped her eyes. "I'm just saying. What mother would . . . ?" Rocket got up, shoved the cardboard containers from the chili dogs in the garbage can, pushed through the door to the outside deck and leaned on the railing to watch the canoe. She studied him through the window, his sandy-colored hair riffling in the wind, golden stubble on his boyish cheeks bristling in the dawn. At Lopez Island, the canoe waited for the ferry, and again paced it through the strait to Shaw Island. At Shaw, the canoe pulled away while the ferry docked and the men paddled ahead, toward Orcas. Rocket came into the café and sat across from Lizette.

She leveled her eyes at him, put her fingers beside her cheek to stop her right eye from twitching. *Too much medication*, she thought and waded in. "You just have to sign it."

"Sign what?"

"What do you think?"

"I don't think," he snapped. "What're you talking about?"

"Violet's birth certificate." She pulled her bag from the floor and started rummaging. "It's right here."

"How the hell?" He spread his hands before her, shook his head in disbelief. "What're you saying? Where'd you get that?"

"I'm saying it's simple."

"What's simple?" He got up and paced beside the table, surveyed the empty café, sat down.

"Where it says father, put your name. Then I'll sign mine.
Simple. Done deal."

"But . . . She's not . . . "

"Look at her for chrissakes!" Lizette gestured toward the sleeping baby, her pink face folded in like a rosebud.

"We're almost to Orcas," he said and jumped up, pulled his
jacket around him for protection, eyed her suspiciously. "We need
to get back in the car." He got up and limped to the stairs leading
to the car deck, disappeared down the gangway. Lizette sat for a few
more minutes, lost in the muddle. Violet's fussing drew her back
and she lifted the baby, tucked her blankets, put the wiggling bundle on her shoulder and went down.

At Orcas Landing, Rocket pulled into the market's parking lot,
the potato chip truck right behind him. "Gonna get some beer and
smokes."

Lizette got out of the car, stretched her legs. Violet napped in
the back. A man burst from the group gathered by the lot's edge
where it overlooked the dock. "Lizette?" he called as he half jogged
to where she stood. "It's me. Raven."

"Oh my God!" she embraced him, they swayed. "It's so good to
see you. What're you doing here?"

"I'm home. Staying with my folks. Helping out at the ranch.
We were out canoeing this morning."

"I saw you, going really fast. It looked cool!"

"We're getting ready for a spirit journey, paddling up to Bella
Bella in B.C. We're gonna meet some other canoes on the way."

"I can't believe it's you. The last time . . . We, ah . . . " A black
shadow dropped over her heart. "You were on your way to Wounded
Knee. How'd it go?"

"We probably shouldn't talk about that, not now," he said, bowing his head, speaking softly. "Forget it. OK?" She looked away, took a deep breath. "What've you been up to?"

"I have a baby."

"No shit?"

Rocket came out of the store hugging a brown paper bag. Raven looked over her shoulder and she turned. "That's Rocket," she said. "I told you about him."

"The father? The tug boat guy?"

"You remember? Yes. Well no. Not exactly. It's complicated."

"Hey man," Rocket said as he got closer, suspicion on his face.

"This is Raven," Lizette said, grabbing Raven's arm. "We've been friends since we were kids. He's Poland and Abaya's son. The youngest one." Rocket extended his hand. The men shook. Lizette felt her anxiety settle.

"Good to meet you, man, but we gotta go." Rocket said, putting his hand on Lizette's elbow, nudging her toward the car.

"Headed to the ranch?" Raven said. Rocket nodded. "Tell my Dad I'll be out there in a while. We're finishing apple harvest. A lot to do, man. I think Marian's away right now on a birth. How long you staying?"

Rocket shrugged, put the bag on the front seat, got in, and slammed the door. Lizette waved to Raven and slipped in beside Rocket. When they got to the ranch, the barn door stood open and she knew Poland was already out working in the orchard.

"We can unpack later," she said. "I'll be down at the cabin. Tell me when Marian gets here."

"Will do. I'm gonna hit the sack."

She unlocked the cabin and stood inside, holding Violet and feeling weary, glad to be home, as if she'd been on a long, hard journey. She put her on the cot and got the wooden crate she'd used to nurse Tucker after the orca attack. She tapped it on the porch to clear the dust and bugs, wiped it out with a rag. She snapped fresh cedar boughs from low hanging limbs and layered them inside. She folded Violet's blankets and gently lifted the sleeping baby into the box.

She went to her canvases, tilted them away from the wall, counted, tried to remember how many there had been, couldn't recall. One of her favorite paintings, spring flowers in the bog near Olga was gone, and she despaired that it wasn't finished, that it was out there alone, unprotected. Mad as she was, she figured a complete inventory could be done tomorrow and shook out her sleeping bag, settled into the cot. Its familiar sag embraced her as she watched the water's light dance across the ceiling. A shadow made her sit up and hug her knees and look out the window. A long black fin cut the water's surface, then two more. They skimmed through the chop in formation, hunting. She shuddered and lay down, thought about wildflowers—yarrow, mayweed and wooly pussytoes—and fairies dancing.

# TWENTY–EIGHT

"ELIZABETH!" Poland stood over her, looking amused. "Wake up, sleepy bear. What you doing in bed? You sick?" She rolled out of the cot, checked Violet, offered a wan smile.

"We slept in the car last night. In Anacortes. Missed the ferry." She stretched, arms reaching overhead. Missed the first one this morning, too."

"Dreaming about snakes?" He had a miffed tone in his voice.

"Snakes?"

"Abaya saw it on the TV news. The guy that got squeezed to death. In the house where you were staying. Marian has been calling you every half hour, worried sick. She had a bad birth last night, almost lost the baby. Hippies from San Francisco. Living in a broke down school bus parked in the bushes at Massacre Bay. Finally, she took them to the hospital in Bellingham this morning. It's closer than Seattle and she wanted the baby checked right away. Just got back." He stepped to the box by the cot, peeked at Violet. "Marian wants to see you and this little butterfly. We're fixing lunch. Raven's here. Come on."

She heard excitement in his voice, but Violet was still sleeping and she felt like a mess. "I'll be up in a while. Is Marian back?"

"I already told you that. And, I picked fruit, just for you." She was surprised to hear begging in his voice and sensed the lunch gathering was important to him. "Abaya brought smoked salmon and sex cake."

"Sex cake?"

"Yeah. Her old cousin. Susie Two Deer. The shriveled one who lives at Doe Bay?" He checked her face to see if she remembered. Lizette said sure, but couldn't recall. "She made it. Calls it 'Better than Sex cake.'" He laughed. "Her memory never was too good, that girl."

"That's so sweet of you and Abaya. I'll get cleaned up." She stretched and looked longingly at her cot. "The baby's still sleeping. Where's Rocket?"

"Don't know." He shrugged, threw up his hands. "Didn't see him. Raven says he was drinking beer before breakfast."

"We saw Raven at Orcas Landing, by the village store. What's the canoe stuff about? They looked beautiful on the water. Smooth and fast. I loved that."

"Didn't start like that." He chuckled. "First time they went out, the canoe went in circles," he pointed his finger down and rotated his wrist. "All crazy, and a guy fell overboard, almost drowned. Bunch of lazy bones. Didn't know what they were doing. Then one of the old guys came over from the rez, gave 'em a few lessons. Raven don't drink now. Stopped. But, all he talks about is the American Indian Movement and dignity for his people, like he just found out who we are."

"He'll settle down," Lizette said and yawned.

"Yeah, I guess so. Vietnam's over. Time to go home, get to work."

"He said he's working with you."

"When he's not busy building what he calls *community*. Like we're not together or something. They built that hunting canoe. It's a big one. Raven says he's going back to his people's ways. I tell him he's going crazy . . . He gets these guys up in the dark and they go out and paddle around and don't catch any fish, waste time. Lift weights like that TV guy Jack LaLanne. I never knew no Indians who lifted weights. The ones I know work."

He pasted a look of disbelief on his face, but she felt his pride for Raven.

"When they come back from canoeing, they're too tired to get drunk. That's better, but it still don't get things done. I got a couple of 'em working out here with the sheep, don't know a ewe from a ram."

"Are they going to race or something?" She sat on the wobbly stool, its irregular balance familiar.

"Nah. Just paddle around like kids. Now they say they're going to paddle up to Bella Bella, meet Heiltsuk people in British Columbia, camp on the beaches. Have a ceremony with the tribes up there. Maybe Abaya and me'll drive up for that, if my old truck can make it."

"Sounds like fun," Lizette said, tired of his chatter.

"She has cousins up there. She has cousins everywhere, that girl." Lizette grinned at him, at his presence filling the cabin, puffing the air with enthusiasm. "Having Raven back makes her young again."

He sidestepped like a nervous horse, shifted foot to foot. "Always laughing now. But we're having the potlatch in about a month, beginning of October, before the storms come. Too much to do. Maybe we won't go. Raven can bring them back here for the gathering."

Finally, she stood and hugged him. "I need to do some things before I come up. OK?" She eased him out the door. "I'll hurry," shut it, rolled her eyes, the air still bubbling with his spirit. She brushed her tangled hair, laid out fresh clothes for the baby, tidied until she woke, checked out the window for the hunters.

Violet yowled as they headed to the house, empty baby bottles clanking at the bottom of her canvas bag. By the time Lizette burst into the kitchen, Violet's crying had become full blown. The baby pulled up her knees, stretched her body, demanded. Abaya leapt to Lizette's side, took Violet, pulled the blanket away from her face.

"Looks like a dove, cries like an eagle." Abaya whirled Violet around in the middle of the kitchen. She cried louder. Marian came in and crowded Abaya to get her hands on Violet.

Rocket stood bleary-eyed in the doorway by the hall. "What's going on? Somebody get killed? Kid's screeching like an owl."

"She's hungry," Lizette said. Poland took Violet and waltzed her into the living room, spoke secrets into the downy hair on top of her head. She quieted, but Lizette kept an eye on the two of them, rocking in front of the big window, ready to swoop in for a rescue. Rocket sat in the wing chair in the living room and watched.

"Got coffee?" Rocket said into the kitchen.

"Come and get it," Marian said. "Pot's ready."

Lizette took a mug from the cupboard, splashed milk into it, added two spoonfuls of sugar, poured coffee into it. Marian frowned as she took the mug to Rocket and set it on the side table, not caring what Marian thought about the new roles for women. Lizette pulled empty baby bottles from her bag. "Get that filthy bag off the table," Marian snapped. "Give me the bottles. They need to be sterilized or Violet will have thrush." She ripped the rubber nipples from their rings, ran hot water over them, filled a small pan and put it on the stove's back burner. "These need to be boiled, so do the bottles." She dried her hands on a dish towel.

"Grouchy?" Lizette said

"Long night, long morning." Marian took dishes down, jumbled them on the table. "Hippie kids. I never saw them before last night. The guy thought he was going to deliver the baby himself, cut the umbilical cord with his teeth, eat the placenta. Sheriff got me in the middle of the night. Somebody living nearby heard the girl screaming, called for help."

"Was it a boy or girl?" Lizette asked.

"Boy. On the small side. And it didn't look like she'd expelled the placenta completely. I recommended a D and C. Infection risk's too high. Just a couple of scared, stupid kids. They called the girl's mother. She's flying up from Los Angeles."

Raven burst in the back door, smelling of tractor grease and grass. "What's to eat?" Poland carried Violet in from the living room to greet him. Raven pulled the blanket aside, grinned into Violet's face. "Amazing eyes!" Abaya smiled, danced up to him.

"Good salmon for lunch," she said, pulling on Raven's sleeve so he'd lower his cheek for a kiss.

Marian ripped lettuce into a big bowl, chopped tomatoes and green onions, scraped them into the salad. She doused it with vinegar dressing, cracked pepper over it, dumped in some canned olives, slammed it on the table. Abaya sliced bread. Poland handed Violet back to Lizette and arranged chairs around the table. Lizette took the baby with a bottle to Rocket who was nodding out in the wing chair, stopped. *Dope,* Lizette thought, irritated, and deposited Violet on the couch, stuffed pillows around her, and she immediately started fussing. She retrieved Violet and sat in a corner chair at the table, the baby sucking hard on her bottle.

"How old is she?" Raven asked.

"Almost five months," Lizette said, looking wondrously into Violet's face.

"She needs immunizations." Marian sat beside her, visually examining Violet. "Has she had any well-baby checks?" Lizette shook her head, felt scolded, prepared for a lecture.

"You're putting this baby at risk," Marian said, her tone cutting. "I'm not going to stand by and watch you . . . "

"I'm taking good care of her," Lizette said, defiantly. "Look at her. You can see that. She's fine with me."

"You can't just take somebody else's baby!" Marian slammed her open hand on the table, startled Violet, got up, turned her back. Abaya came to Marian, tried to put an arm around her. She pushed it away. "I've made a lot of mistakes in the past few years, you know that. Not playing by the rules, ignoring problems, but you can't . . . "

"Can't what?" Lizette shot back.

"Let's eat," Abaya said and turned to get the platter with thin salmon slices fanned on it.

"Can I help?" Raven asked. Abaya shooed him away, opened the refrigerator, pulled out a pitcher of lemonade.

Poland called into the living room, "You coming, Rocket man?"

"Yo," Rocket answered in a sleepy voice. He shuffled in and slipped into a chair on the narrow side of the table, sitting with his back to the windows. Poland settled at the head of the table, Lizette already seated next to him, opposite Rocket. Abaya took the chair at the foot of the table. Marian and Raven filled out the other sides. Abaya reached out and covered Raven's hand with her own.

"Look, we have to figure out . . . " Marian said, glanced around the table. "What're we going to do about Violet?"

Lizette interrupted. "Can't this wait?"

"No." Marian snapped. "We've got somebody else's kid. We don't know where the mother is. Nobody's stepping up to claim they're the father." She looked at Rocket in disgust. "You can't just drag this baby around. People will ask questions. I have a license, a ranch to protect."

"Sandy's in Mexico, headed for South America. Colombia, I think," Lizette said, wiping Violet's mouth with the edge of her blanket. Rocket stiffened, paid attention.

"How do you know?" he said

"Sandy sent a postcard."

"What did she say?" Marian tore a bite out of a piece of bread, studied Lizette while she chewed.

"She said 'Stay dry.'" Lizette glared at her, thought, *take your shot.* "It doesn't matter where she is if she's not here. What do you think should happen? Put her in an orphanage? That is not going to happen. I won't stand for it. I don't care what you say. I don't care about your god dammed ranch and your nursing degree. You're no better than . . . "

"Please pass the salmon," Raven interrupted, reaching out his hand. "Did everybody get salad?" He put a couple of strips of salmon on a slice of bread smeared with cream cheese.

"We have cake for desert," Abaya added hopefully, looking around the table. "Lemonade?" She lifted the pitcher, poured herself a glass.

"I know how to fix this problem," Lizette said, looking squarely at Marian, defying her.

"OK. How? Are you and Violet heading for Bogotá?"

"No," Lizette said flatly and paused. She waited until everyone was looking at her. "Rocket's going to sign the birth certificate. I have it with me. You already signed when Violet was born," she said to Marian, whose eyes got big. "Sandy just left it lying around, never did anything about it. We'll register the birth with the county, use Rocket's and my name."

"The hell I am!" Rocket said and shoved the table. "I'm not moving to fuckin' France." Abaya's glass tipped over, spilling lemonade onto the floor. "You can't tell me what to do." He turned on Lizette. "You can't saddle me with this kid!"

He stood, looked down at her. "You can't even put one foot in front of the other—and you think you've got it all figured out? You're a head case, man."

He pushed past Abaya, swayed in the middle of the kitchen. "Sandy said Al's the father!" he yelled at them. "She should know. Now he's dead. And I'd like to know how Bella got out?" He turned to Lizette, who sat with her head down, shielding her eyes.

"Sandy said whatever she wanted," Lizette said into her lap. "She didn't want you. She played with you. Like a pet cocker spaniel and you lapped it up. Who's the crazy one?"

"Shut up," Rocket spat. "You don't know anything about it. You show up, freak out, disappear, sneak back in, parade around with your ass hanging out. Now, I call that nuts! Where do you get off talking about Sandy? At least she got paid for it."

Poland stood up, took Violet and went to the living room. The arguing continued, but he said nothing. He heard Rocket shout, "You've got big feet like a frog, bug eyes, too!"

Lizette fired back, "Worthless junkie. Think you're better than everyone because of that stupid piano. It's shit. You can't even play it! You don't know Mozart from Montovani!"

Poland rocked Violet, burped her, held her close and looked out the window at the sun on the grasses, at an eagle soaring above the trees, a black-tailed doe stepping gingerly in the forest's shadows. He chanted quietly into Violet's ear.

When the voices in the kitchen took on a dangerous edge, when he sensed Raven might jump in and square off against Rocket, he said, firmly, "Come in here. All of you. Sit down right now!"

Rocket glared at Lizette, spread his angry look around the room. Marian got up and put her arm around Abaya's shoulders, led her to the living room. Marian and Abaya fumed at either end of the couch. Lizette folded cross-legged onto the floor, making soft, intermittent tweets, holding the twitching muscle beside her eye. Rocket threw himself into the wing chair, cast a sly-eyed look at Raven who leaned against the wall with his arms folded. They waited. Silence filled the room. Bird songs came to them, soughing whispered from the trees and softened their hearts, the grasses swayed rhythmically in the field, a sheep baahed, a gate hinge creaked.

"In the time when people could still become animals, a beautiful girl of the Raven clan lived in these meadows." Poland spoke in a deep, even voice, gesturing out the window. "She was spoiled and headstrong, proud because her father was a chief."

He raised an eyebrow and looked around the room at each of them, settled on Lizette, who squirmed, re-crossed her legs. "In late summer, at berry-gathering time, she went with other girls into the forest to pick. Her friends teased her because she would not take a man. She turned away from everyone her parents offered. They told her she would turn into an old crow—sleek feathers, rough voice." He made a caw that startled Violet in his lap.

"The beautiful girl said she would know when the right man appeared. Along the trail, she tripped in muddy bear tracks and dropped her berry basket. She complained about clumsy bears as she got up, accused them of taking the best berries, making a mess of the forest. The girls shushed her, looked around, told her not to talk bad about the bears. She'd make them mad, they warned. The girl made an ugly face, said she didn't care."

Poland's voice coarsened and Abaya went to the kitchen, brought back a glass of lemonade. He slurped. Violet slept in his arms. Lizette stretched her legs.

"So the other girls kept picking, moving away from the beautiful girl. They sang songs to the bears to show respect. The beautiful girl did not praise the bears. She found a berry patch with the biggest berries she'd ever seen. She picked, ate some, picked more. It got dark and she couldn't hear her friends singing anymore. Then there was rustling in the bushes, a twig snapped. The girl was afraid. But before she could run, two men stepped from the trees, one was very handsome. The other one was short and limped."

Lizette eyed Rocket, but he didn't seem to be listening.

" 'It's getting dark,' the handsome one said. 'We'll help you find your way.' He took her berry basket and joked as they walked. She didn't see that they were moving up the mountain, away from her home. They came to a village, but she realized it was not her village. 'I want my father,' she said.

'No, you are ours,' the handsome one said. 'Wait while I talk to my uncle.'

"He headed toward a great longhouse and disappeared inside. 'I don't care how handsome he is,' she said to the short one. 'I don't like waiting. My father is a chief.'

"In a while, two men came from the lodge. She could see from their shaved heads they were slaves and she thought they'd come to serve her. Instead they grabbed her arms and dragged her to a small cave, shoved her inside and rolled a big boulder across the opening.'"

Violet cooed in Poland's lap, made a soft baby fart. Everyone giggled and he tucked her blankets tighter, made a serious face and looked out the window. He waited, regained his dreamy look, continued.

"The girl hollered to be let out. She cried and threw herself on the ground, but they didn't come back. Lying in the dark, she heard a small voice." He made a small squeaking in the back of his mouth. Lizette giggled.

"It was Mouse Woman. She told the girl she had been taken by the Bear People because her pride and rudeness offended them, but she said she had a plan. To get out of the cave, Mouse Woman told the girl to bite off small pieces of her copper earrings and bracelets, put the pieces under her tongue. Then, after they fed her each day, she should spit out a bit of copper and offer it as a gift to the chief. The Bear People liked copper, she said. The girl did this and in time the Bear People came to think she had magical powers."

"Hey, man. I need a beer," Rocket slurred.

"Don't interrupt," Lizette said, seeing him as she'd once seen Greg in the same chair.

"Fuck you, man." He lifted his droopy lids and looked defiantly at Lizette.

"I'm not a man." She folded her arms and gave him her shoulder.

Raven watched the exchange and lifted off the wall, flexed his biceps, took a step toward Rocket, looked at his father. Poland shook his head, tilted it toward the kitchen. Raven went to the refrigerator and got a beer, cracked it open and returned, handed the bottle to Rocket, who sheepishly responded, "Thanks, man."

"After the beautiful girl had coughed up copper for many days, they took her to the chief. His lodge was hung with many bearskins and he sat on a big bench carved with dancing Chinook. He called for mats and told the slaves to bring in his nephew. The couple kneeled before the chief. The old man got up and put a great skin over his head and shoulders, the room misted and he stood above them, half man, half bear. The girl was scared."

Poland waited, looked at each one's face, waited some more, until Rocket paid attention, then went on with the story. "The bear chief said, 'We have waited for a high-born girl like you, one with special powers. You will marry my nephew.'

"The girl wanted to run, but she knew the bears would catch her and she would be made a slave. That night they had a feast, a celebration like the ones the girl's clan had at home—salmon and halibut, crab and clams, wild onions, robin's eggs, honey and baskets of berries. All the while, the girl planned her escape, knew her father and brothers and cousins were out looking for her. She longed to be rescued.

"After the wedding, the girl joined in with the Bear People, did everything they wanted," Poland said. "But she still looked for signs and sounds that she would be rescued, even though her bear husband was kind and a good hunter, too. One day he gave her a bearskin of her own. He wanted her to put it on, to become a bear with him, but she resisted. Later, when he was out hunting, she tried it on. It felt good, warm and soft. She felt love for her husband and the Bear People and forgot about her other family.

"In time, she knew she was gonna have a baby, just like this little dragonfly." He kissed the top of Violet's head. She was awake now, looking around, taking in everything, cooing like a dove.

"That's one birth I wouldn't want to attend," Marian said. Everyone laughed.

"Well, when the baby was born, he looked like us." Poland moved his hand down his chest and gestured to Abaya. "But he tumbled and crawled just like a bear cub. When he wanted to, he put bearskins on and looked just like his father, but the girl wasn't afraid anymore. She loved her son and her husband and the Bear People, but sometimes she missed her own people, too. The loneliness for her father felt like a small pain in her side." Poland flattened his fingers and poked himself just below his ribs.

"In the fall, when the Chinook run," he said with new energy, "she was fishing with her husband and noticed he was quiet and looked sad. She asked him what was wrong and he told her about his dreams. He saw her brothers coming with spears. She felt her heart leap.

" 'They are near,' he said." Poland took a long drink of lemonade, held Violet out, offered her to Abaya, who got up from the couch and grabbed her like a hungry animal.

"When they returned from fishing, baskets full, they moved to a cave far up the mountain. The bear husband said he hoped they'd be safe there, but the dreams continued through the winter.

"When spring rains warmed the island, her husband said, 'Your brothers are very close now. My dreams tell me that they must kill me.'

"He put his bearskin on and went out into the sunshine. She sat with him, up on Turtle Mountain, and he told her 'Whenever one of your people kills a bear, the people must build a fire and decorate the bear's head. They must sing songs to honor the bear spirit and burn the bones. I will watch over you and protect you. I will always be here in spirit, if you do these things.' The girl cried and hung onto his bear leg. She went back to the cave and cuddled their son.

"In the quiet of the cave, she heard her husband singing his death song, and felt the spear when it struck his heart. The young woman's sobbing and wailing drew her brothers and they found her wrapped in bearskin. When she and her baby cub got home, she taught her family and the villagers all around the islands how to hunt like bears and respect and love them. The villagers got rich with good hunting. After that, they didn't need nothing."

Poland bowed his head and Lizette clapped, everyone else joined her.

"I don't get it," Rocket said. "All she did was go home and help her family? That's it?"

"What else is there?" Poland said, looking perplexed.

Abaya got up from the couch.

"Lunch is wasting," she said, heading for the kitchen with Violet. Lizette got up and stretched, twisted, bent at the waist and put her hands on the floor. She reached out to touch Rocket as she passed, but he paid no attention. He did not join them They ate lunch in silence, the humming of the refrigerator and ticking of the clock the only sounds. When they finished, Marian took Violet into her lap. Abaya cleared the table.

Rocket came in sounding refreshed, awake, "I gotta go," he said and sat down. "I work tomorrow, need to get home." Lizette dug in her bag, pulled a tattered paper from the bottom.

"Sign this." She slid the paper in front of him, handed him a pen. "Fill it out."

He looked at the paper, held it up, put it down, opened his mouth to speak, thought better of it, started writing: Raymond James Daniels. Where it said "Born" he wrote San Francisco. For "Date," he filled in May 19, 1950. He signed his name, looked the form over, stood up. He took Violet from Marian, rocked her, kissed her baby mouth.

"See ya, little shit pants."

He turned to Lizette, "Let's get the car unloaded." He handed the baby back to Marian.

They leaned into the car's yawning trunk, brushed shoulders as they pulled out boxes and bags, stacked them in the dirt. Rocket threw open the passenger doors and grabbed blankets, rolling them and setting them on the pile of things beside the car, mostly stuff for Violet. He hoisted the stroller out and set it up. Lizette pushed it into the barn. She came back and tapped his shoulder. He stopped arranging tools and flares and tire irons in the trunk, turned to her. She held him by his forearms, looked at his boy face, the freckles on his nose, his periwinkle blue eyes. She turned away, wiped her cheek, let him go.

"Listen." He looked down at his hands as if watching something slippery get away. "I . . . Ah . . . I didn't mean for things to . . . Look. I signed the birth certificate for Sandy's sake, for the baby. Everybody needs something more than a blank. But I'm not saying . . . you know? It's just that it's the right thing to do."

They stood before the open trunk, surveying the emptiness. "You can put that stuff in the living room for now," Marian called out the back door.

They gathered the boxes and bags and brought them inside. Rocket went out into the dooryard, looked back at the house. Lizette waved from the steps. He got into the Rocket 88, pulled it around and headed out. Inside, they all sat at the kitchen table, listened to the engine's throaty rumble, watched the car until it turned onto Horseshoe Highway and disappeared.

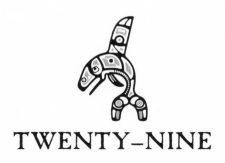

# TWENTY–NINE

ROCKET THREADED THROUGH TRAFFIC ON EASTLAKE, a flat pressure on his heart. He took a deep breath and turned onto narrow Franklin Street, sensing the void even before he got out of the car. The picket fence in front of Sandy's place had tipped over, the garden was weedy. Geraniums in the bedpan planter trailed over the porch railing, brown and shriveled. The commotion of Al's and Bella's deaths had evaporated into a sinking recollection. He looked at the blank windows of the Dog House, the missing boards on the porch. He got out of the car and stood in the mocking warmth of fall, sensed the season slipping toward winter.

He dropped his sea bag by the front door, listened, but heard only an empty silence. He hollered, "Yo! Knuckleheads! I'm home!" No greeting came back to him. The usual mess of dirty dishes clogged the kitchen sink, garbage spilled by the back door, the late afternoon light through the dining room windows rested on the piano. Rocket pulled out the bench and sat before the keyboard. He played a major ascending scale—C,G,D,A,E. Again C,G,D,A,E.

He leaned forward and rested his forehead on the piano's cool ebony finish, closed his eyes, surrendered to a splitting headache.

*Need to get loaded*, he thought, *shake this shit*. He went upstairs and got his stash, taped to the back of a water-stained print of Turner's *Shipwreck*—fishing boats trying to rescue the crew of a floundering sailing ship. Sometimes he thought the fishermen succeeded, other times he knew they all went down in the storm. He tied off, shot up and flopped back on his bed, the sheets smelling sour and greasy.

"Hey, Rocket!" He opened his eyes in the dark when he heard his name.

"Up here, man." He rolled out, stood. "Who's there?"

"It's me, man. Bomber!"

Coming down the stairs, Rocket saw Bomber was drunk, hanging onto the wall, asked him, "Where's everybody?"

Bomber lurched toward the kitchen "They split after the cops left." He yanked open the refrigerator door, stood in the puddle of cold water leaking from under the old Frigidaire. "They're lookin' for Lizette and Violet. County welfare people. They want to check that Violet's OK. You know, they found Al's stash and the snake thing. They got questions, man."

"What'd you tell 'em?"

"Whata ya think?" He pulled out empty mustard and pickle jars. "Nothin' . . . I left you a note, man, on the table." Bomber turned to the table and spread a wrinkled paper towel flat with his palms, pushed a business card to the side. "See?"

"What's this?"

"Landlord's givin' you seventy-two hours to get the hell out. Came in here with the cops, all puffed up and serious, like we're criminals. We were just sittin' around watchin' TV. I knew one of the cops, met him in a USO in Saigon. Pussy guy. Never thought he'd end up like that."

Rocket picked up the dirty paper towel, but the words didn't make sense. He looked at Bomber, waited for a better explanation.

"So." He thought for a minute. "OK. The landlord. Jerry, he, ah . . . " Rocket signaled for him to go on. "He shows up with the cops, like I said. They ask questions, nobody talks. The landlord hands me this business card." He picked the card up, handed it to Rocket, who scanned it. "Jerry says we got three days. We all leave. That's it."

"I need to sit down," Rocket said, heading for the living room. He settled into a chair by the window, cushion springs poking his behind. He shifted to one cheek to avoid being stabbed. "Then what happened."

"Nothing. Everybody split, like I said."

The front door rattled. Fisher stood there, craning into the gloom.

"What's up, man?" Rocket said.

"Hey, where you been?" Fisher nodded toward Rocket when he made him out in the dark.

"Took a run out to Wenatchee, cleared my head, watched 'em pick apples. Stayed in a fleabag motel, caught a game on TV."

"Which one?" Bomber asked and Rocket waved him off.

Fisher dumped himself on the couch next to Bomber, said, "Some bad shit came down here, man."

"I heard." Rocket frowned. "Looks like Al messed everything up. Did you see him? Eye popped fuckin' out. What a mess. You been back over to Sandy's?"

"Naw, creeps me out." Fisher said softly. "Heard the landlord's throwing you out."

"That's what Bomber says." Rocket turned to Bomber.

"Hey. It's not my fault." Bomber threw up his hands in surrender. "I was just sitting here. The cops and the landlord bust in, all big and bad. They said this place is a crash pad, that there's ordinances against it. They stood around like they were waiting for a hippie to pop up. Good thing nobody was smokin' a joint. We were just watching the news. That chick Billie Jean King said she'd play Bobby Riggs at tennis. Battle of the Sexes. She'll never win, unless they rig the match. Either way, Riggs is a lame-o to even play a chick. I'm not even gonna watch it."

"Shut up!" Rocket shifted in the chair and glared at Bomber, who looked hurt. "What'd they say about Sandy?"

"Just wanted to know where she was, that's all," Bomber said. "We told 'em she was on vacation, should be back any day now. That's true, ain't it?"

Rocket got up, walked to the piano, pulled the oil rag from the bench and wiped down its sides. "What am I gonna do with this beauty?" He rubbed the top lovingly, stood on his toes to wipe the whole surface, spit on a hardened food glob, rubbed it away.

Bomber and Fisher looked at each other, didn't answer. The air got heavy. Bomber turned on the TV, caught the baseball highlights. "Hey, get that? . . . Nolan Ryan just threw his second no-hitter of the season. Guy's throwin' smoke, man." Bomber stared at the screen as Ryan went into his windup, shook his head in amazement at the delivery. "The guy's on fire!"

Rocket went upstairs, dug in his sock drawer, pulled out some papers, went back downstairs. He sat across from Fisher. "I gotta go to work tomorrow morning. I need you to do two things. OK?" Fisher looked solemn, waited. "First, call the piano company and tell them to get the movers out here." He handed Fisher the papers.

"But, where do you want them to take it?" Fisher asked, alarmed. Then he thought a minute. "They could take it down to my old man's glass shop in Kent. Cover it up and put it in the back." Rocket looked thoughtful, got up and paced. "It would be safe there," Fisher added, "for a while at least. You know, they could wrap it up, in blankets or something, until you're ready to move it again. I mean, to your new place."

Rocket ignored the suggestion, walked around the house taking inventory.

"Where's Violet?" Fisher said, sounding worried. "She's just a baby."

"Yeah, well, she's gone now," Rocket said bitterly.

"Where the hell did Lizette take her?" Bomber asked.

"San Francisco," Rocket said. "Probably for the best. She'll fit right in with the head cases down there. Took Greyhound this morning."

"I thought you said she went to Wenatchee," Bomber said, scratching his head.

"Shut up," Rocket snapped.

Bomber looked hurt, turned back to the baseball highlights. "Looks like Oakland's going to the World Series, man. Reggie Jackson's on a tear."

"Listen, Rocket," Fisher paused, took a deep breath, waited for Rocket to focus on him. "I'll move the piano, but I want to talk about it."

The phone rang in the kitchen and Rocket answered. "Yeah, this is Rocket . . . How the hell should I know? I live next door. Yeah? Well it's mighty nice of the landlord to give my name and number . . . I don't know Al. He's a friend of a friend. Just got out of jail, I hear. Check with the cops, they know more about him than I do . . . Family? Heard they live in California. San Jose, I think. Look, check the San Jose phone book. I have no idea." He slammed down the receiver, stumped into the living room and faced Fisher's and Bomber's expectant faces.

"Coroner's office," he said and flounced into the chair, winced when the spring bit his butt. "Said they're trying to locate Al's family so they can get rid of the body. It's taking up space in their cooler. I don't know nothing about the guy."

"Sandy does," Bomber said in a helpful tone.

"Shut up, you idiot," Rocket snapped. "One more word and I'm gonna rearrange your fuckin' face." Bomber looked pained, sunk into his Army jacket.

"About the piano," Fisher started again. Rocket glared at him. "I'd, ah . . ." He swallowed. "I'd like to buy it. I'll give you five thousand."

"I'll bet," Rocket said sarcastically. "First of all, it's worth way more than that. If I was going to sell it, which I'm not, I'd ask for a whole lot more. The guy at the piano store already offered me fifty thousand cash. See, this is a special piano. It's not some church basement shit. It's for real."

"How about ten thousand?" Fisher waited. When Rocket said nothing, he broke the silence. "I'll sell it back to you when you get your new pad, man. I just need it to practice, that's all."

"You don't have ten thousand dollars and you don't have a place to put it either." Rocket let out a huge, frustrated sigh. "This is a valuable instrument." He gestured toward the piano that glowed from the dining room. "It needs a good home. It can't sit in the back of some glass shop, getting kicked to shit by knuckleheads. It's not the kind of thing you can just put anywhere."

"You're right, but for now it'll be safe there." Fisher remained calm, reasonable, sensing his advantage. "I'm trying to help, find a solution. That's all. Look, I don't want to be responsible for it, if it's not mine. It would be easier if I owned it. In case anyone came around asking questions, you know? I'll give it back when you need it."

Rocket shuffled through the papers on his lap. "Look, here's the number for the guy at the piano store. Tell him I'm out working on the tugs, can't get to a phone, have to move suddenly." He handed the papers to Fisher. "Get the movers over here tomorrow, tell 'em where to go with it. I'll be gone a few of days."

Rocket went upstairs, banged around. Bomber and Fisher sat quietly, listening. He came down with an armload of stuff, filled up the trunk of the Olds with clothes, went back up and came down with dresser drawers, odds and ends overflowing, pictures of his mother and grandmother fluttered to the floor and he bent to retrieve them. He lugged the drawers out to the car. Traffic buzzed overhead as he arranged his stuff in the trunk. An air horn blew and he heard the truck's breaks lock up, then a loud crumpling sound. He pictured the crash, the trailer crushed, lying on its side across three lanes, people getting out of their cars to check for injured, visualized the whole mess, went back inside. Bomber and Fisher sat glued to the idiot box. They'd offered to help him pack, but backed off when they sensed the offer just made him mad.

"I'm gonna catch some Zs," Rocket said and slammed the front door, hit the stairs. "Gotta get up at four in the morning."

"What about the rest of this stuff?" Bomber asked, gesturing around at the living room.

"Light a match." Rocket pulled up on the banister, stomped the stair treads.

"Can I have the TV?" Bomber hollered after him. Rocket slammed his bedroom door.

# THIRTY

"PRETTY BABY," the clerk said leaning over the counter. She smiled down at Violet nestled in her stroller. "How old is she?"

Lizette stepped between the girl's line of sight and the stroller. "About five months." She held back nervousness from her voice, willed herself to remain calm, hands steady. She forced herself to smile back, but it felt crooked on her mouth.

"Took you a while to get here," the girl said, pushing up heavy black glasses, staring at the torn birth certificate. Her stringy brown hair clung to the side of her face and she wore a stained blue cotton blouse with an orange-haired troll doll pinned on the collar. "She was born in June?" The clerk checked the form. "What does that make her? Gemini?"

"With Aries rising. My grandmother was sick in Portland." Lizette lied easily and focused on the scuffed counter. "Had to go down and take care of her. Broken hip."

"Sorry to hear that," the girl said, slipping a sheet of carbon between the pages before filling out a receipt. "Is she going to be OK?"

Lizette felt a twitter in the back of her throat and swallowed. Nodded yes. "How much does the birth certificate cost?"

"Ten dollars." The girl pressed down hard on the paper, checked the carbon impression on the page underneath. "Takes about three weeks for the embossed, certified copy to come in the mail. You want it sent to 4316 Greenlake Avenue? Right?" She looked up and Lizette gave her a confirming nod. "My grandmother used to live over by Greenlake, went to the big Methodist church right by the lake. Do you know that one?" Lizette allowed that she did to hurry the procedure along. "I can still remember Christmas service there, people dressed up like Mary and Joseph, the Three Wise Men. Did you ever rent paddle boats at the lake?"

"Do you need anything else?" Lizette put the money on the counter, grabbed the stroller handle, pushed it back and forth to comfort Violet, who fussed halfheartedly. "She's getting hungry."

"No, that's it. Except for the receipt." She passed the carbon copy across the counter to Lizette, who slipped it into her canvas bag. "Have a nice day."

"Thanks." Lizette pushed Violet through the double doors, the gilt "County Records" letters chipping off the glass, and rolled into the afternoon sunshine. She stood on the sidewalk shaking and put her face up to the warmth, smiled into the bright dome of the world with her eyes closed, heart yelling *"Yes!"*

Lizette pushed the stroller to the bus stop, kept herself from skipping and giggling. When the bus came, a passenger helped lift the stroller so she and Violet could get on. They bounced along, the city a happy buzz. She got off a few blocks from her father's house and dawdled along the familiar streets with the baby, enjoying the fall gardens, the colors fading into burnished yellows and russets, variegated greens. Shasta daisies and chrysanthemums reigned over grasses and ivy. "Bibbity, bibbity, boop!" She prattled into the stroller, surprising Violet into a giggle. Lizette laughed out loud, startled herself with the outburst, looked around to see if any neighbors were watching.

She found her father in the backyard, trimming shrubs across the back fence, a long pile of branches lay on the grass. He waved toward her with a gloved hand, holding the pruning shears aloft. She lifted Violet from the stroller and crossed the grass, stood in front of him, holding the baby out to him. "Meet your granddaughter, Violet Lena."

"My God!" he dropped the shears and grabbed the baby. "I didn't know . . . I had no idea. Why didn't you tell me? . . . I'm not prepared." He hunched over the bundle in his arms. "My God," he said looking up at Lizette with moist eyes. "She's beautiful." He twirled around with the bundle. Violet offered her little giggle and Einar roared, scaring the baby, making her cry.

Lizette stepped forward and took her, put Violet on her shoulder and soothed her with quick pats on the back. Her father sat down on the grass, knees spread, head lowered, offering his bald spot to the sun. "I'm not prepared for this. Never expected . . . Didn't think . . . I need some water." He got up and went to the house. Lizette settled on the grass, spread Violet's blankets. The baby gathered herself, rolled, couldn't quite turn onto her belly, let out a cry, tried again. Lizette watched, but didn't help.

Einar came back with two glasses of ice water and a plate of crackers and cheese. Lizette took them and he sat down. "When did this happen?" he said in wonderment.

"About five months ago," Lizette said. "Everything went pretty well. Marian was there."

"She's a good girl, Marian. But what about the baby's father? Where's he? Are you married?"

"His name is Rocket." She saw the confused look on his face. "Raymond. Raymond Daniels. He's from San Francisco. He works on the tugboats in the Sound. He's a seaman, an inland boatman, actually. Everybody calls him Rocket because of the car he drives."

"My father was a seaman," Einar said, trying to reconcile the situation. "Worked out of Seattle and Tacoma in the 30s and 40s."

"So does Rocket," Lizette said.

"It's a hard job," Einar said knowingly. "Keeps you away from your family. I feel like I hardly knew my dad. He was always working. Paid for my college, though. I'll always be grateful." He picked up a cracker and layered slices of cheddar cheese on it. "Where are you living?" he said, cracker crumbs dribbling from his mouth.

"Out on Orcas. With Marian. Rocket's gone a lot."

"Well, at least you won't be alone." He picked Violet up, studied her face. "Her eyes are breathtaking." He set her down on her back. "Just amazing."

"Everyone says that. I wish Mom could see her," Lizette said sadly.

"I can't even imagine how excited she'd be," he said. "She would've run around, planning the nursery, painting little pictures, matching paint, driving everybody crazy." He coughed on a chuckle. "She'd have been in her glory. It's times like this when I really miss her." Lizette reached out to him, covered his hand, rubbed the ropey veins.

They sat silently, watching Violet struggle to roll over. As the afternoon slipped away and a breeze rustled the trees, they got up and went inside. Lizette prepared a baby bottle. "You're staying for dinner," her father said and she didn't argue.

"I can catch the bus back to Anacortes in the morning," she said as he moved around the kitchen, opening cans and putting pots on the stove. She took Violet into the living room, settled on the couch and looked out the window on houses and streets already etched in her memory, but new to her somehow, with Violet safe in her arms. She banked pillows around the baby after she fell asleep and went to the kitchen to help with dinner. He handed her plates and glasses, napkins and silverware. They ate in comfortable silence then washed the dishes and cleaned up. It was still light outside and the house felt warm and full. They tiptoed into the living room and settled quietly into chairs.

"Do you have a crib for the baby?" Einar asked softly.

"Hadn't thought about it," Lizette whispered. "She's been sleeping in an old apple box." He frowned. "It works fine. I mean, she'll outgrow it eventually, but not yet. Don't worry."

"I don't want my granddaughter sleeping in an apple lug like some fruit tramp's kid," he said roughly and saw Lizette flinch, felt her willfulness dig in. "Sorry. I didn't mean . . . It's just that your old crib and dresser are up in the attic. You could use them for Violet." He got up from his chair and stood above the sleeping baby. "Do you think she's safe here? We could go up now and take a look."

"Not now, Dad." Lizette signaled him to sit down. "It's OK. I can get her whatever she needs. I don't have a way to get the stuff to Orcas anyhow. Don't bother."

"No bother. Your mother would've wanted it. She put all your baby things away. Said maybe you'd want them for your own baby, someday. So, it looks like this is the day." He chuckled and bent for a closer look at Violet.

He headed down the hall to the stairway and she followed. She hadn't been in the front hall in years, hardly able to stand going further than the kitchen. She paused to look at the paintings on the walls, mostly her mother's landscapes done *plein air* on Orcas Island, places she knew well, the play of light at different times, the angles for composition. She could see her mother's self-centeredness in the canvases, her failure to meld with the scene and render truthfully. Her own work was framed there, too, and she looked closely at the structure of her paintings, leaned in to study her own brush strokes. She realized how much her work had evolved from these early efforts. It had grown into something that excited her, that tugged at her, demanded her urgent attention. She hurried upstairs, saw her father had been watching her from the landing. His intent look caused her to pause beside him, feel as if he'd been reading her mind.

"What?" She searched his face, but it went blank. She slipped past and took the second flight of stairs two at a time.

At the end of the upstairs hall, she opened the narrow door to the attic and went up again into the dimness. The air was close, the heat of the afternoon trapped in the steepled rafters. Cobwebs dangled from the bare wood, translucent in the light from the small, knee-high window that overlooked the front garden and the street. Her father flipped the light switch at the bottom of the stairs before climbing up and the bare bulb cast a decayed glow over dusty boxes and sheet-draped furniture.

"This place is like a tomb," she said when his head reached the top of the narrow stairway and he paused, squinting like a gopher at the boxes, lamps, and chairs piled there. "Where do you think the crib is?"

"I haven't been up here in years," he said. "I can't quite remember where I put it. We'll have to move some things around. Do you think we'll hear Violet if she cries?"

"What's this?" She pulled an old rocking chair from under a sheet, dragged it to the middle of the floor and sat down.

"My mother rocked me in that chair," he said. "I always thought it had a good sway. The runners are long and balanced. I loved the claw feet when I was a kid, the glass balls gripped in the talons looked Medieval, made me think of knights and castles. I used to crack walnuts while she rocked." He stood behind her as she pumped her ankles and smoothed his hands along the edge of the chair back. "Your grandmother was a good woman."

"Can I have it?" She turned to look up at him, but his gaze seemed far away. "It would be good to rock Violet in. I could put it in the cabin."

"You can't keep that child in an old shepherd's cabin," he said. "You can't stay at Marian's forever. You've got a baby now. You have to make plans. I've still got that piece of land on Orcas, out on the point."

"We're moving into Rocket's," she said firmly. "He has a house in Eastlake, by Lake Union. It's big. He just has to get rid of his roommates and that might take a while, but then we can fix things up. He has a grand piano."

"Does he play?" Einar asked, more interested.

"Yes. Well, no, not very well. Fisher plays it. He's a concert pianist, used to play with the Seattle Symphony."

"Rocket, Fisher?" he said. "I don't know these people." Lizette got up and went to a stack of boxes by the window.

"My drawings from high school are still here!" She leafed through the top box, knelt by the large box beside the stack of smaller ones. "Wow! I'd forgotten about this stuff." She pulled canvases out, held one to the light to examine it, laid it on the floor. "Not bad for a teenager," she said, embarrassed by her self-praise.

"Lizette." She looked up at his serious tone. "Please sit down. I have some things I need to tell you."

"OK," she said, going to the rocker and sitting, working her feet rhythmically, watching him warily as he paced in front of her.

"Your mother . . . " He paused, turned to her. "She . . . ah." Lizette leaned forward, searched his face. "She loved you very much." She gripped the arms of her grandmother's rocking chair, waited for him to continue. "She was very proud of you, from the time you were a small child, from the moment you were born." Lizette bobbed her head in understanding and he continued. "She saw your talent. She had dreams. She . . . ah, she knew you had something special." He pulled an old dining chair from under a sheet and sat, balancing on the seat's edge, like he was sitting on a tightrope and might topple over. "She thought the world of you."

"I understand," Lizette said, trying to put her father at ease. "I really do. We don't need to talk about it."

"We do need to," he said sharply. Lizette blinked at the shift. "You need to know."

"Can't we just find the crib and get it downstairs? Violet might wake up. She can turn over now. She's getting really big."

"Listen." He swallowed, took a deep breath. "I got a letter, maybe three or four months ago. From an art dealer in New York. He'd heard your mother died."

"But that happened six or seven years ago," Lizette said. "What took him so long? I mean, New York's far away, but not that far, even if he got the news by Pony Express."

"He offered condolences, of course," Einar continued. "But, he wanted to ask about the signature on your mother's paintings." He focused on her face, connected with her eyes.

"Signature?" Lizette blinked, looked confused. "What about the signature?"

"Well, she always signed her work L. Karlson."

"Dad, I know that," she said impatiently. "We have the same initials. So what?"

"He had a couple of new paintings at his gallery."

"Jesus, Dad, get to the point." She flashed back to the guy at the gallery downtown, remembered his talk about New York and museums and collectors. She felt trapped and the heat was making her sweat. "Violet will wake up any minute. We have to go downstairs."

"The paintings he was selling were signed Lizette Karlson," he said.

"Lizette?"

"Yes, but the ones that sold ten years ago and the new ones appeared to be by the same artist. He called the new ones more evolved, that's what he said in the letter. In both cases, the artists last name is Karlson from Seattle." He clamped his mouth shut and settled back in the chair. "The buyer of your mother's paintings, a collector, had asked for authentication before buying any of the new ones. These people. They're investors. They spend a lot of money. They want answers."

"What did you tell them?"

"I don't know what to tell them. I didn't answer. You were in the hospital, again. I just couldn't. . . couldn't bring myself to explain. I can't."

"Can't what, Dad?" He twisted sideways in the chair.

"You know what happened." He started again, turned to her, eyes watery. "What happened when your mother died."

"Do we need to go through that now? I know what she did. Everyone was shocked. I ended up in the hospital, lost it. We all did for a while. We still haven't gotten over it. Why bring it up now? We just came up here to get some stuff for the baby."

"Even without the body, I knew it was her," he said, very quietly. "The water badly damaged the canvas, but I knew it was her. I saw what she did."

"Did what? You're freaking me out. What're you trying to say?"

"Remember the painting you did that won the grand prize at the state fair?"

Lizette glanced at the big box of her old canvases tucked under the eaves. She got up, started to go to the box to look for the painting.

"Wait." Einar ordered. "Sit down. Listen." Surprised by his adamant tone, Lizette dropped back into the rocking chair. "The painting they found under the bridge. The one the bus driver saw her tuck under her coat before she went over?" Lizette stared, more interested. "It was your painting from the fair."

"No!" The heat in the attic turned stifling, the dusty air filled her lungs. She choked, coughed into her fist, scraped her scalp, looked at the ruins around her.

"I recognized the colors and some of the underlying pen strokes that guided the piece even with all the water damage. In the lower, right hand corner of the canvass, it said L. Karlson, it was faint, but I knew the signature had been altered." Then, in a rush, he said. "I think she'd been forging her name to your work for years, at the same time undermining you, pushing you to work harder, always finding fault, interfering, picking apart whatever you did, trivializing your efforts, making you crazy." He stood up, sat down, looked like soft wax melting into the wobbly chair.

"My God, Lizette," he blurted. "I'm so sorry. I love you so much! I'm sick about this, that I didn't protect you, didn't see how twisted and desperate she'd become. I don't know how long the deception had been going on, maybe not that long. I don't know, can't imagine." He coughed deep phlegm from his throat, tears rolled down his cheeks. She knelt beside him, put her arm around his shoulders, laid her cheek on his, rocked him like a baby as he sobbed.

"Dad, please don't cry," she begged. "We can figure this out. I think I know how my paintings got to New York this time, how they showed up in galleries in Pioneer Square."

"How?"

"It's a long story," She patted him and wiped his face with her fingertips, looked into his watery blue eyes. "I've been busy with the baby, but I'll straighten it out once we get settled. Don't worry, really."

She began lifting sheets, sneezed from the dust. Deflated, her father sat watching.

"Lizette?" She turned to him. "Please understand. I think she just couldn't live with herself, with the lie. I mean, with what she'd done. She so much wanted to be a success."

"Really, Dad. That's enough. Stop. Don't say anymore. Please." She looked around at the draped jumble. "Help me find the crib."

Violet's wailing rolled up the attic stairs, gaining strength.

She bolted from the attic and down the stairs. She scooped the baby up, walked in the living room, holding Violet against her chest. When her father came down, she avoided him by taking the baby to her old bedroom, unchanged since she was a teenager, the edges of her Beatles posters faded and curling. She took a pill from the bottle in her bag, lay down on her old bed with Violet and played with her, waited for the drug's calming effect. Later she took a bath with her, poofing bubbles on her head, wiping them away with a washcloth. After they played some more on the floor, Violet drank a bottle and fell into a sweet sleep.

In the morning, Lizette found her old nursery furniture in the front hall, the crib parts leaning against the wall by the front door, the dresser, changing table and little wooden footstool beside it. The rocking chair blocked the door to her father's study. She had a deep memory of the antique white furniture with pink, blue and red flowers painted on the headboard and drawer fronts, vines encircling the legs, scrolls and curlicues. She saw her mother's hands, sure and graceful, stenciling and freehanding the ancient rosemaling design, Swedish froth and lace, hearts and flourishes. The shapes and colors were familiar. She'd done the same thing on the furniture at Sandy's, but nothing like the beauty of her mother's shaded work. It astonished her and she had a twinge of guilt about taking it to the ranch, setting it up in the cabin, realized that not only was it too beautiful for such a place, it also was way too big to fit into the small cabin and still allow enough room for her to work.

She went to the kitchen and put water on for tea. Waiting for the water to boil, she tried to envision the furniture in Marian's house, in Mr. Cutler's old bedroom, but the idea felt wrong. She poured the steaming water into a mug and decided to thank her father for offering the crib, but it wouldn't work. A wave of sadness washed over her as she sat in the memory-filled kitchen, the cuckoo clock's ticking, her mother fluttering around the stove, the canaries singing in their gilded cages, lingonberry jam sitting on the table, waiting for the toaster to pop up. Gathering her homework, taking her sack lunch, always with celery sticks that she threw away before she got to school.

She got up with her mug and pushed out the back door, went to her mother's studio, tiptoed in, set her mug on the cluttered workbench under the window, pulled up a tall stool. Northeasterly light pressed against the dusty panes. She mentally searched herself, but found only stiff regret, frozen anger, hardened compassion, indifference. She heard Violet's complaining cry and looked up to see her father coming across the lawn with a wiggling bundle in his arms.

"It won't do any good to brood," he said, handing her the baby, looking around. "I heard her crying in your bedroom and looked in to see what you were doing, but you were gone. I thought I'd find you here."

She looked around the studio and saw that time and moisture were dissolving her mother's workspace, that her sketches and paintings were breaking down like duff in the rain forest, moldering into the earth. "We've got to pack this stuff up," she said to her father. "You've waited too long, everything is ruined."

"I couldn't bring myself . . . didn't want to see."

"Or feel," Lizette said bitterly.

"I don't know what to tell the people in New York. About the artist, whether she's dead or alive. It makes a difference in the value of the paintings, you know? What do you want me to say?"

"Dad," she looked at him carefully, saw his innocence, paused and tempered her words. "Listen," she said gently. "I understand what happened with Mom, not completely, but generally. I'm still sorting through things in my mind. I thought about it all night and

I understand about the paintings. I know there'll need to be some answers. I have an agent here in Seattle who can help with that." She flashed on Toulouse and swallowed hard, started again. "But I want to get back home and get Violet settled so I can straighten things out, continue to work on my canvases. I can't stop living."

"How will you get home?" Worry etched his face. He pulled Violet from her arms, put the baby's head on his shoulder and rubbed her back, swayed. "Will Violet's father take you to Orcas?"

"We can take the bus and the ferry," she said. "That's how we got here."

"But, the crib and dresser, the rocking chair?"

She really wanted the rocking chair, already sensed Violet's comforting weight in her arms, rocking together in the night by the cabin windows, waiting for dawn, for the orcas to come hunting, the stove crackling beside them with sweet red cedar logs. But, she couldn't take the rest of it. She watched a fat black bumblebee drink from the flowering vine that dangled from the studio's eave, bumping from bloom to fading bloom, unconcerned about stealthy winter creeping in on the breeze.

"You can take us to Rocket's," she finally said. "He's only over in the Eastlake District. If he isn't there, maybe Fisher can borrow one of his father's trucks or one of the other guys will take us. I have to get back to Orcas, for the potlatch. Poland and Abaya have worked on it for a couple of years. I promised to help." As an afterthought, she said, "Why don't you come?"

"That'd be nice. I haven't . . . " She felt a gush of regret for even asking, for the disappointment in Rocket, for the emptiness in her heart, for the lies, for the frozen loneliness and picked up a rusty knife, ran her finger over the still sharp edge, tuned her father out and imagined feeling—welcomed the wince from a deep, clean slice. She laid her forearm out on the workbench, looked at the smooth, white skin, pictured hot red blood running around her wrist and through her fingers and an image of the man, stabbed and leaning against the tavern window, welled up. She felt overwhelmed by the memory of the rich, throat-clutching color on his hands, the shock, the black overcoat engulfing her. Violet belched, loud and long, giggled.

"You little dog," Einar said, nuzzling her.

Lizette flinched and grabbed the baby from her father's arms and ran, flapping her big feet across the dewy lawn, hitting the back stairs, bursting into the cold kitchen, looking for a baby bottle. The phone's ringing sent her to the receiver. "Hello? Oh, Marian. Thank God it's you!" She shuffled Violet from one hip to the other.

"Everything's messed up. I'm getting out of here . . . I don't know. I feel like killing myself . . . I don't know why. My father . . ." She saw Einar standing by the refrigerator, shifting from foot to foot.

"Who is it?" he said softly.

She put her hand over the mouth piece. "Marian," turning her back on him. He lifted Violet from her. "What do you mean? Did it burn down completely? Sandy's place too! I can't believe it! Has anybody talked to Rocket?"

She slumped to the floor, leaned against the side of the cabinet, the curly phone cord wrapped around her neck. "Yeah. I'm still here. It's just, well. It's a shock. He said he was working this weekend. I don't know where he is. I can't think right now."

She slid further down, stretched her legs akimbo across the threshold to the dining room, wiped her wet cheeks, made quick chirps, listened. "Bomber? No. Jesus, please no! He was harmless. How do they know it's him? . . . True, he slept under the basement stairs and he always wore that filthy Army jacket."

"What's going on?" Einar loomed over her slouched body, reached for the receiver. Lizette pulled away, flapped her arm at him, rolled onto her hip to get away.

"Dad!" She glared at him from her rumpled position on the floor. "Nothing. Sorry. He just wants to know what's going on."

She listened into the receiver. "But, how do they know it's Bomber? That's where they found him? . . . I feel really bad about that. But what about the piano? Oh! Thank God! At least they got it out. Who called you? But was Fisher there when the fire started? . . . Well, at least the piano's safe. Rocket's gonna totally freak!"

Lizette got up and twisted around the wall to stand in the dining room, out of her father's view, the phone cord straining at its connection. "What'd the cops say? I was going over there this morning. No, I don't have to. My father offered us a ride to Orcas. Don't worry. I won't go. What did the cops want? No, I promise. I won't go. Yeah, I love you, too. Probably in three or four hours, depends on the ferry schedule. We still have to pack the car and feed Violet. It gets crowded on weekends. Sometimes you have to wait for the next ferry. I'll be careful. Promise. Stop worrying. Yeah, bye."

# THIRTY–ONE

**SLOWING FOR THE GRAVEL DRIVEWAY** to Cutler Ranch, Einar took a deep breath and drove through the gate toward the familiar house and barn. The ranch looked the same, except for a subtle slumping, less erect now with Henry gone. *The peace and beauty remains*, he thought with relief, scanning the meadows and orchards, aching to get out and walk. He glanced at Lizette, frozen beside him on the old Volvo's front seat and felt calm. He knew she and Violet would be safe here at the ranch, at least for now. Maybe he could figure out something later for the little piece of land he and Lena bought years ago, but not now.

He glanced at the back of the station wagon. They'd packed in a hurry. He'd put together an overnight bag and carried his boxes of artifacts from the study's closet to the station wagon, set them gently to the side, loaded the nursery furniture and the stroller, tied his mother's rocking chair on top.

"What day is it?" Lizette asked in a trance.

"Saturday," he said, startled to hear her voice, pulling up beside the barn.

She hadn't spoken since she'd hung up the phone with Marian and asked him to drive her to Orcas. He'd watched her closely on the ferry, marveled at her ability to withdraw and shut out the world. Even her response to the baby's crying was distant, reserved. He realized he'd gone too far in telling her about Lena, that he'd selfishly unburdened himself, had miscalculated the impact of revealing her mother's betrayal. He'd gotten out of the car on the ferry and gone up to the passenger deck, stood outside in the wind, gulped the fresh air. Alone in the Sound, seduced by the jade green water, he contemplated joining Lena.

"Put the stuff in the barn," she said, snatching Violet from the backseat. "I need to be alone, please, take some meds. Tell Marian and Abaya I'll be over after while." She headed for the worn trail behind the house. Tucker appeared out of nowhere to nip at her heels. *Leg's better*, she thought. *He's going to make it.*

Einar watched them disappear down the slope toward the trees and felt like he was standing in a desert, the gravel biting through the soles of his boots, the world sucked dry, empty without them. He unloaded and drove out, followed Horseshoe Highway toward Poland and Abaya's place, the road familiar and yet brand new in the dazzling sunlight.

Turtle Mountain, shaped like the rim of a protective bowl, sheltered everything he had left to love. The forest blanketed the mountain's graceful hump and against the variegated green backdrop, eagles lofted on gentle winds, soared, wing tips riffling in the shifting breezes, the air heavy with sea salt. Along the road, Canadian black-tail deer browsed, indifferent to the Volvo's humming approach. Dandelion dotted the fields and, here and there, the yellow blooms had gone to fluffy white seed. He felt a sudden urge to stop and walk in the tall grass, wade into the verdancy.

The road was strangely empty of cars, as if he alone traveled the world. He pulled over and slipped under a barbed wire fence, stepped into a lush pasture, stood knee-deep in grass and gazed down Crow Valley to the orderly rows of fruit trees in a far orchard. The leaves rustling in the breeze showed green and silver, a few fluttered in the air ahead of leaf drop. He fell face down in the grass, pressed his heart to the earth, let the grass enfold him, took strength, then rolled over and over. He roared with laughter and flopped an arm over his eyes to deflect the sunlight and relaxed into the flood of emotions he'd been swimming against for years, let the feelings freewheel, overtake him. He picked up a warbler's song and clinched his vocal cords to call a return. After a long while, he gathered his bones and stood, unsteady, went to the car and fired it up.

Rounding a bend, he saw cars and pickups lining the road's shoulders on both sides, parked tight, nose to tail. He hesitated, thought about backing up, parking at the end of the line, walking the distance to Poland's place, but remembered the boxes in the back of the station wagon, too big and cumbersome to carry a long distance. He turned off the highway and threaded his way between cars on the long dirt road that led to Poland and Abaya's farm, admired the split rail fences Poland built with his sons so many years ago, still stout, zigzagging to the ranch's dooryard. Before he reached the broad opening between the white barn and the house, a young man stepped out and put up his hands to signal a halt. Einar braked, rolled down the window.

"No parking," he said. "Every space is taken. We have to keep the road clear for emergencies. Park out on the road." Einar protested about the boxes, declined to leave them unattended in the yard.

"So, dirty old man. You've come!" Poland boomed as he moved from the barn to the side of the car, embracing Einar through the window. He waved the young man away. "You're just in time. We're putting out food for an early supper. Then, when it's dark, we'll build up the fire and do spirit dances." Poland glanced in the back of the car. "Where's Elizabeth?"

"Resting. At the cabin. With the baby."

A worried shadow darkened Poland's face. "She's my best ranch hand. This is no time to rest. How's that little poop pants of hers?"

"You mean my granddaughter?" Einar faked a solemn face. Both men burst into grins. "She's a little brat, of course."

"Park over there." Poland directed Einar to the far side of the house, to a spot near the propane tank. He followed the car, knocked on the back panel when the car was safely in place. Einar got out and lifted the station wagon's hatch, pulled the boxes to the edge.

"What you got here?" Poland said trying to snoop over Einar's shoulder.

"We better take this stuff inside." Einar loaded him with boxes. "I'll show you."

The two men sat on the old, saggy couch in the living room, the boxes on the floor in front of them. Einar pulled the flaps open, lifted out an object wrapped in newspaper and tore the paper away.

Poland fell back on the sofa cushions. "Raven." He exhaled the word like a prayer and took the carved mask from Einar's hands, turned it slowly, looked inside and found a second mask, put that one to his face, turned to Einar, and in that moment he became the bear spirit, alert and ominous.

Recognizing the mask's spirit power, Einar gasped, saw the fullness of its authority, understood how keeping the mask and all these things, had been wrong, how it had robbed not only his friends, but also the spirits. He put his hands to his eyes to feel his blindness and understood his need for forgiveness.

Rifling through the box, Poland pulled out another object and unwrapped it, lifted the two-headed dance rattle from its wrapping, and the green and red wolf mask, with its tufts of human hair fringing the edges, the black and orange dance wand with orca fin. The doeskin spirit drum with painted Chinook and orca chasing around the edge. Then he dug deeper into the big box and unwrapped the painted cedar warrior mask with inset abalone shells, then the goose-feathered frog mask. Watches Underwater came out too, her wary eyes alert, red lips pursed for supping air, and he thought about Lizette, how she floated on the edges of life, moving beyond his grasp. The pile of ceremonial masks grew too large to arrange on the couch between them. Poland got up and cleared the boat-hatch cover that served as a coffee table. He ordered the masks on the table and turned to dig deeper in the open boxes.

Einar fell back, drained by the emotion of the homecoming and the events of the past few days. He looked around the living room, surprised at its unchanged modesty—noticed a red-and-black print of salmon dancing, photos of the boys when they were small, a picture of Poland standing in a canoe, preparing to throw a fish net, the cheap frames listing crookedly on the walls, the smell of cedar smoke and fish flavoring the air.

"Will you dance tonight?" Einar asked.

Poland stopped digging, looked thoughtful.

"No. Tonight beginners dance. Then the people will send them away, coax them back, scold them and praise them. The new dancers don't know how to make spirit power, not yet. But these masks will help them. My great uncle always liked this one best." He held up a red and black sea monster mask, its fierce mouth holding a fish, its eyes glaring. "He always chose this one when he danced, said it helped his fishing. He was the best fisherman I ever saw, lost an eye to a hook."

"You silly men." Abaya blew through the back door like a whirlwind, apron flapping, abalone earrings clacking, on her head a crown of curled bear claws attached to a deerskin headband, tied in a bow in the back. Her long gray hair trailed to her waist.

"Einar! Einar!" She rushed into the living room, grabbed him as he stood up to greet her, toppled him back onto the couch, erupting into apologies and laughter. "You honor us!" She paused and surveyed the collection of masks, rattles, wands and drums on the coffee table and couch, laid her hand on her throat. "Our treasure. It's home. . . . The spirits have come to us!" She burst into tears. The men jumped up and reached for her, embraced her tiny body, each gathering a part of her to him, shoulder, elbow, waist, swaying with her, speechless in response to her emotion.

"Hey. What's going on?" Raven stood in the doorway, hands on hips. They turned to him, embarrassed by the intrusion. The men pulled away from Abaya, who stood sniffling, trying to smile toward her son. "I thought you came to get mayonnaise for the venison burgers," Raven said to his mother and went to the refrigerator and bent to search for the jar.

"You don't need that junk on good deer meat," Poland groused, mostly to himself.

Raven came into the living room, surveyed the mask collection. "What's all this?" He made a dismissive gesture toward Einar, picked up Watches Underwater and thought about Lizette, about the night they'd talked in the coffee shop, about what he'd said to her, calling her father a grave robber, how she'd seemed so lost and wounded. He turned the mask in his hands, admired the vivid colors, the supping mouth, alert eyes, and silently resented Einar.

"Our spirits have come home," Abaya said softly and found a chair with the back of her legs, collapsed into the seat, adjusted her crown, looked delicate and queenly. The men nearly bowed in the gray-green gauze of afternoon light.

Raven turned to Einar, put the mask down. "What the hell are you doing here?" His voice boomed, indignation crackling around the edge. He threw a scorching look at Einar, who retreated to avoid the heat. "You stole our spirits, disrespected our history, now you come here with cardboard boxes to share what's already ours? Man, you've got a lot of nerve, acting all holy, while you hoard our stuff."

"That's enough!" Poland was on his feet, moving toward his son, who pivoted to show his chest, defiant, presenting his full body as a taunt to his father. Poland coiled like a metal spring, vapor escaped his nostrils.

In a whisper, Abaya began: "Long ago the world was only a great sheet of water. There was no land. There were no people. Only Thunderbird lived. His wing beats made booms across the world." Poland turned from his son and sat beside Einar on the couch, leaving Raven to shift like a stiff, unsteady pole.

"Then Thunderbird flew down and touched the water. The earth popped up. Then he flew down again and touched the earth. Animals jumped up and scampered around. Thunderbird created all living things except people, who are descended from the animals. Dog was the ancestor of the Lummi."

Raven settled into a chair across from his mother, glowered, put the mayonnaise jar by his feet. "I never heard this story," he said, accusingly. "We're Salish. Lummi people come from Salmon and Orca."

Ignoring him, Abaya continued. "Thunderbird gave a sacred arrow to the Lummi. He warned them, said this arrow was never to be used or lost, so they buried it like a dog does a bone. It was safe there and because of that the people never died. The people wore out their throats with eating. They lived so long their feet wore out from walking." She cleared her throat and searched her son's face, but saw only sullen resentment. "They were happy."

"What does this story have to do with grave robbing?" Raven sat still, but balled his fists.

"While the sacred was safe, the people were too," Poland growled. "But people, white people, began to dig up our bones.

Our spirit masks and dance things were in danger, but they've been safe with Einar. Our people live. You have returned to us."

"More important," Abaya cut in, "Einar paid us for them, used them for teaching about our people at the university, never let them get away. We used the money from Einar and Lena to buy this farm. How do you think we got this place? Picking apples?" She glanced around, as if taking in the whole island. "Our cousins sold things to him, too. You've lived a good life here because of it." She settled her gaze on her son, who sat with his head down, and she said in a chastising tone, "Einar guarded our sacred things. Now they're here again. And he can take them back when we are done. They're safe with him. Nothing is stolen."

She set her mouth and crossed her ankles. The sound of children whooping in excitement tumbled into the room. They heard one of them yell, "Tag! Another shout, "You're it!" Then a shriek and a fountain of laughter overflowed. Inside, the four of them sat stone-faced.

Abaya smoothed her skirt under her apron, recrossed her ankles primly. "The people disobeyed Thunderbird. They used the sacred arrow, let it fly away, sold our spirit history for pennies to thieves who didn't care about us—not like Einar. That's why the Lummi die now like other people." Raven got up and turned from them, resignation showing through the shirt on his back.

"You'll dance the beginner's dance tonight," Poland said to the insolence glowing from the back of his son's head. "In a mask of your own making."

Raven slammed the door on his way out.

Einar sighed and dug in a box. Abaya came to the floor on her knees, pulled out the wrapped objects, stripped away the paper, marveled, went on digging. Leaning way over, Einar rummaged with her to a box bottom and paused, head in the paper. Slowly, he straightened, lifted a cloth-wrapped object, handed it to Poland.

Abaya gasped. The pure white ermine pelts dangled, luminous, the soft black-tipped tails still inky-colored after all these years. She took the circular reed frame of the headdress from Poland, shook it carefully to free the feathers and tails, straightened the reeds on top of the Thunderbird mask that formed the headdress's crown. She set it on Poland's head, handed him the two-headed wand carved from bear femur.

Einar watched them from the kitchen door as they walked hand-in-hand across the dooryard to the meadow, children falling in with them, gamboling and whooping in the golden fall. He felt a catch in his heart and remembered Violet. He needed to get her and Lizette. He put his hand in his pocket to check for the car keys.

# THIRTY-TWO

**VIOLET TIPPED**, first toward one side, then the other. Lizette knelt over the baby, packed a pillow and rolled baby blankets around her, kneeled and pressed her palms against her tiny sides, let go. She flailed her little fists and toppled. "You can almost do it," Lizette said to the gurgling baby. "Won't be long before you can sit up by yourself." She kept working with Violet, grabbing her hands, coaxing her, letting her fall back on the pillows.

Tucker crawled to the window on his belly, growled deep in his throat, alert. He jumped up and paced, went to the door, scratched. Lizette got up and let him out, resettled on the floor, played with Violet, blocking all thoughts, just feeling the warmth and quiet, waiting for her meds to kick in, welcoming the calming feeling. *Rocket,* she thought. *Please come. How can you not love this.* She bent to kiss Violet's cheeks, wiped teething drool from her perfect, pink lips.

She went to her work table, moved paint rags and a broken metal Slinky aside. She picked the broken toy up, mused over its possibilities for dipping in paint and making the spiral patterns she'd been envisioning for a new canvas. Under a rumpled sheet of paper, she found the box of teething biscuits and crossed to the baby. She paused to scan the western horizon, saw dark clouds piling up. *First storm*, she thought, smelling wet dust in the air. She extended the biscuit. Violet wrapped her fingers around it, put it to her mouth, smacked her lips, pulled it away, considered it, went after it again with eager lips. Lizette leaned back on her heels, watched with pleasure.

A rap on the cabin door startled both of them. She heard Tucker's nervous barking from the beach. "Come in," Lizette said. She'd expected Marian, braced herself for the gush of efficiency, Marian's instant assessment of Violet's development, the directions on infant care and treating her own condition. Instead, Toulouse stood there, pirate hat under his arm, the long, white ostrich plume pressed against his black cape, his thin dark hair failing to cover his white skull. His skin looked reptilian. He blinked at the sparkling light reflected into the room from the water.

"May I come in?"

Lizette glared then waved him toward the wobbly stool by the table. She pulled up from the floor, through her ankles to her knees, and stood pole straight, imperious and frowning. "Just wanted to see how you're doing," he said, his voice showing a hint of nervousness. "I mean about the fire and everything. Too bad about the Dogs." She folded her arms across her chest, listened. "I guess they'll all just drift away now. Except Bomber. Too bad. He was a sweet guy. He survived Vietnam, but not this." He glanced at her, quickly looked away. "Have you heard from Rocket?"

"I've been wanting to talk to you." She pulled a wooden apple box from under the work table, set it on end, sat down, looked at him without flinching.

"And I you," he said, sounding falsely superior.

"Cut the crap, Toulouse. I was at Wentz Gallery a few days ago. You've got some explaining to do."

"Ah." He exhaled loudly, shook his head, reached under his cape, pulled out a white envelope. "I'm sure you were pleased," he said bravely. Lizette rolled her eyes, shook her head in disbelief. "This is for you." He pushed the envelope across the rough table to her.

"What is it?"

"Open it."

She pulled out several sheets of paper, folded to letter size. A check fluttered to the table. She picked it up, saw it was made out to her for three thousand four hundred and fifty dollars. "What's this for? Hush money? You're a thieving bastard and you know it."

"It's not like that Lizette. This money is for the small canvases that have already sold. I'm working on some bigger deals right now. At prices I'm sure would surprise you. You don't understand."

"I know about the prices and understand that you came in here and took my paintings without permission." She slapped the table with the flat of her hand. "I understand that you put them in places where people would see them and start asking questions. Some of them weren't even finished."

"Rocket helped me," he said, lamely trying to deflect responsibility.

"You've created a huge mess, you idiot!"

"I . . . ah." Then, as if a light bulb had switched on, he realized there was something more going on, asked, "Mess? What do you mean?"

"What would you call art fraud?"

"Well, I know I didn't have permission to represent you, but . . ."

"Forget your hairy butt," Lizette spat. "I'm not talking about you taking my stuff and exhibiting it without me knowing. That's bad enough."

"Look, there's the check for the sales," he pointed to the check laying on the work table. "The details on who bought the paintings and for how much. It's all listed there on the page. I just took the usual fifteen percent commission. It's all there . . . and a back-dated contract saying you agree to have me represent you. All you have to do is sign it."

"Go to hell! All I have to do is call the cops and have you thrown in jail! You're a lying bastard." She got up and paced, scanned the table looking for something sharp, felt like scratching his black lizard eyes out, fingered a paint spattered coffee can, considered throwing turpentine in his face.

"You don't understand," she finally said. "My mother . . . she struggled."

"All artists are tortured in one way or another," he said, consolingly. "Look at me, for example."

She looked at him, a scrawny beanpole in dusty drapery, and sniffed. He got up, walked to her canvases. "May I see?" She said nothing. He turned the top canvas around, gasped, stepped back, whistled softly, exhaled "Magnificent." She fluttered her long, tapered fingers at him dismissively.

"I'm wet," he said and turned to face her. "This seascape takes me into the depths, to the water's secret places. I'm stunned, really. I don't know what else to say."

She saw his guileless truth, his mask of condescension stripped away, and felt triumphant, felt her canvas had achieved her vision and intent, had pierced to the heart. Toulouse had understood all along what she'd been aiming at with her painting, recognized its power, but she'd resisted his intrusion, withdrew. Now she was finally ready to share her work, that it was good enough and that Toulouse would stand behind her while she shared it.

"Sit down," she said quietly and explained the situation with the sales of her earlier canvases, signed by her mother, the questions from the New York art dealer, the investor's concerns. When she'd finished, he jumped up.

"Nothing the art world likes better than a good scandal," he said. "There's a way out of this. It's a good story." He went to the small window by the door that looked up the trail to the forest and the ranch's main house. "I have a friend, in New York," he said with his back to her. "He writes for *Art Forum* magazine. We could tell him what happened, take pictures of you, here on the island, put an article together. Time a solo show to when the article comes out. There'd be a storm, probably just a squall, you're not famous . . . yet, but it would jack up the prices for your paintings, people would feel sorry for you. At least until they saw your new work. Then they'd know what's really going on with you, that you've transcended. What a narrative!"

"But I don't want to tell people about my mother or about me," Lizette said. "It's embarrassing and scary. I just want them to see the work. I'm not Andy Warhol or Peter Max. I'm not gonna paint portraits of Chairman Mao or do graphics for record albums. I'm not going to parties with strangers and show off on TV."

"That's not what I'm talking about." He turned to her, looked at her slumped over her work table in a faded sweatshirt. "I'm talking about calling attention to your work, straightening out any misunderstandings about the authenticity, enhancing its commercial value, bringing it to wider audiences. I'm not talking pop culture rip-off. My fear, however, is that you're not stable enough to pull this off. There's more to making it as an artist than putting paint on canvas."

"You should've thought of that before *you* ripped me off," she said. "It's too late." She flipped through the pages he'd put on the table, found the agent's agreement, reached for a splattered ball-point pen and signed it, looked up at him defiantly.

"It's done, then," he said, folding the paper and putting it into his pocket. "If I hadn't taken action, brought some attention to your work," he pointed at Violet, lolling on the floor, "how'd you plan to feed that kid?"

"Leave her out of this. I've adopted her. She's mine." Lizette got up, turned to Violet, heard Tucker's angry barking, realized it had been going on for a while, and went to the window. The dog circled a black lump on the beach, dug in his hind quarters, stretched toward the mound, barking with his head close to the sand, signaling alarm. At first she thought it was a big rock, but knew nothing like that had been there before, protruding from the sand. She scooped Violet up. "Come on," she said to Toulouse and bolted for the door. "Something's down there."

When they got to the beach Lizette handed Violet to Toulouse, who moved back from the water line. She pulled Tucker away, held him by the shoulders as he lunged and barked himself hoarse. She gave him stay commands and the dog sat twitching. The orca's mouth lay open, slack-jawed, conical ivory teeth exposed. Its pink tongue lay flaccid in its mouth. "Looney!" She yelled. "It's Rocket's orca!" She saw Toulouse didn't understand. "He's dead!"

"Rocket?"

She took off her sandals and waded to the orca's side, looked into the abyss of its filmy black eye, the spirit gone. She put a hand over Looney's sunken blow hole, confirmed that he wasn't breathing. His long dorsal fin that once had moved through the water like a victory pennant, lapped in the surge. She moved around the animal, surveyed its body. A fishing net was tangled in his tail flukes, parts of the torn strands floated on the water's surface, blood pooled at the water line beside his head. There was a smell, sweet and fetid, coming from his body. *Looney has been dead a while* she thought and watched flies feed on his blank eye. She turned to Toulouse, who'd moved further up the sand from the water, felt anguish clog her throat, realized he was no help.

"We've got to get Marian," she croaked. "Carry the dog."

"The dog? I don't want wet dog hair on me," he said, holding Violet closer to his chest.

"Oh, for chrissakes!" She scooped up Tucker from the surf and stormed up the beach, Toulouse wobbling behind her in his pointy-toed Beatle boots and silly hat.

She cleared the trees and the house came into view. Her father's Volvo and a big truck with a metal rack on the side were parked by the barn. The sign on the truck's door read: Fisher's Glass and Sash, Kent, WA, with a phone number. She hurried faster, relieved that she wasn't alone, burst into the kitchen, dropped the wet, sandy dog to the floor.

"Rocket's orca! On the beach! In the surf! Oh, my god!" She paced in front of the sink, bent and poured her anguish into the bowl shaped by her hands. "Just lying there! I don't know for how long!"

Marian came out from her bedroom, her father stood up in the living room where he'd been drinking a beer with Fisher, concern drawn on his face.

"What's up?" Marian said, rushing into the kitchen. "Slow down. Stop babbling. Rocket's here?"

"No, Looney! Rocket's orca!" she shouted, mince-stepping in a circle, hunching her shoulders, shaking her hands.

Einar entered the kitchen, gripped Lizette's arm reassuringly, snatched Violet from Toulouse, who stood there blinking. "Who's this?" Einar said, jerking a thumb toward Toulouse. "We haven't met."

Fisher stepped forward. "He's OK. We know him." Einar looked at the hat and cape and seemed unconvinced, held Violet closer, rocked side to side with her, patted her back.

Lizette wheeled on her father, caught his wary eye, lifted the baby from him. "He's my agent," she said haughtily. "The one who's going to get us out of the little mess we're in with the New York art gallery." She raised knowing eyebrows at her father and turned back to Toulouse. "Meet my father, Einar Karlson." Toulouse stepped forward, tried to smile, extended his hand. Einar shook it limply, stepped back.

"Lizette, please sit down," Marian said. "I don't understand what you're saying."

She took a deep breath. "Looney, the orca that hunts in the cove. The one that attacked Tucker? The one with the scars on his back?" Marian made a big "Oh" with her lips. "He's the orca that waits for Rocket, follows his tug when he's working in the Sound. It's Rocket's orca, his spirit guide."

"I don't know about that," Marian said. "Just tell me what happened. Did he go after Tucker again?" The dog wiggled between the two women, begged for attention. Marian patted the dog's head, shooed him away with her leg, glanced down. "He looks OK."

"Looney's washed up on the beach below the cabin," Lizette said, pulling out a chair and lowering herself. "He's dead." She put her forearms on her knees, leaned forward, head in her hands.

Marian went to the drawer under the counter by the phone. She pulled out a battered notebook, leafed through the smudged pages of numbers compiled through the years for ranch business. Her finger stopped. She studied an entry, turned and dialed a number.

"Jim? This is Marian Cutler, out in Crow Valley . . . Yeah. It *has* been a while. How's the game warden business? . . . Poachers deserve to be caught. Everything's fine here. We didn't have too much trouble with predators this lambing season. We've got good dogs. But there's a problem thought you should know about. We've got an orca washed up at our place."

She listened into the receiver, looked impatient. "Down at the cove . . . No, there's just a foot path. Too steep to get a truck down there . . . Cutting it up will take too long, make a big mess." She wrapped the phone cord around her finger, turned to look at them clustered there, rolled her eyes. "Poland's not here . . . On vacation. Probably couldn't get to the carcass for a week. It's too much for him to handle, anyway. How about getting those guys at the Marine Research Station? Can't they haul it off the beach? . . . I have no idea how much it weighs . . . I thought they're supposed to respond under the new Marine Mammals Act . . . OK, thanks for checking. Tomorrow will be fine."

She hung up and faced Lizette, shrugged, as if to say: That's all I can do.

"It can't stay there." Marian said and paused, saw the orca meant more to Lizette than just another washed up marine animal, that her emotional balance remained delicate. "Look, sweetheart. I'm sorry about Rocket, really, I am. I understand . . . " Her voice trailed off as she realized the men were watching her and Lizette, who looked crumpled. "These things happen," she said scanning their faces, looking helpless. "Usually not a full-grown male, but still, we find seals and gray whale calves washed up all over the islands. It's nature." She focused on Lizette. "You can't let this upset you, Lizette. Please?"

Silence settled into the room, movement suspended, breathing went shallow. The clock ticked. The refrigerator hummed. The faint washing sound of the sea flowed into their midst. They waited, watched Lizette.

"OK," Lizette said finally, stood up, clicked her tongue softly. "Poland and Abaya are expecting me."

"That's right," Marian said quickly. "Did you take your meds?" Lizette gave her a mind-your-own-business look. "Are you guys ready?" she said to the men.

"I've got to get clean clothes for Violet, diapers, bottles, comb my hair," Lizette said. Marian went to the refrigerator, handed Toulouse a beer. The men went to the living room and sat, Einar holding Violet. Tucker settled at his feet. Lizette ducked out the back door, Fisher right behind her.

"Wait," he said. "Listen."

She stopped in the dooryard, looked impatient. "What?"

"About the fire," he said, looking down, nudging at the gravel. "No one knew Bomber was down there, in the basement, I mean. We just got out when we smelled the smoke. Didn't know."

"Somebody should have checked," she said accusingly.

"It was the middle of the night," he said.

"What about the piano?"

"I'd gotten it out that morning. Took it to my old man's glass shop. Just like I told Rocket."

"Have you talked to him?" She looked at Fisher closely, watched his reply.

"I offered to buy the piano from him," Fisher said.

"What'd he say?"

"He was OK with that, sort of. Offered him $10,000 and said he could buy it back later. That's the deal. Now it's here, in the barn."

"Here?" She looked over, the barn doors were shut. "I thought you said it was at your father's glass shop."

"I couldn't leave it there," he said. "It's so beautiful. Rocket's right. It would get beat to shit at my old man's place. I didn't know what else to do. They want me to start an orchestra here. In the islands. We need the piano. I put it to the side, in the barn, next to some baby furniture. But, I can't leave it here. It has to be played. Honestly. It's the most beautiful thing I've ever touched. It needs a home. I need one too." He raked his thin hair and shoved his glasses up on his nose, shook his head. "I don't know what to do."

"Me either," she said, and turned, heading down the path to the cabin.

# THIRTY–THREE

DRUMBEATS PULSED ACROSS the meadow as they headed for the stand of trees at the edge of Poland and Abaya's farm. Beyond the trees, the trail dropped steeply to a U-shaped cove with a sweeping beach and gentle waves hissing on the sand. Switchbacks through pink heather and huckleberry made climbing down easier. Lizette clutched Violet to her chest and took care with her footing. Her father took the lead. Fisher followed her, Marian on his heels, Toulouse lagging behind.

Men's voices, chanting rhythmically, rolled up the cliff. Einar stopped to listen, the drone folded into the sea's cadenced lapping, carried up on strengthening winds that soughed in the cedar and fir boughs. Bonfires smoked on the beach, gathering power from the wind. Men in red-and-black "Chilikat" dancing cloaks with Thunderbird, Salmon, and Orca designs outlined with mother-of-pearl buttons milled around the fires, beat drums and sang ancient songs. A cluster of painted canoes were hauled out at the far end of the beach.

Lizette smelled meat cooking and her stomach cramped with hunger. Her father moved ahead on the trail, glanced over his shoulder, turned to hold her arm as she stepped over a knotty tree root. Violet gurgled against her chest. She had a sense of entering a different world, a sacred place.

Set against the cliff, the big pitched-roof shelter held a mismatched assortment of tables—folding, garden, even a couple of battered kitchen tables—all covered with bowels and platters, heaped with food. The boxes Lizette recognized from Abaya's barn were stacked in the back. Striped Hudson Bay blankets were laid end to end on the sand floor. Wicker laundry baskets, filled with colorful gifts, sat on them. Abaya's lavender boxes with satin bows poked out of the jumbles. Children scampered everywhere. Finally, she located Abaya in the back, waving a wooden spoon, her hair flowing, bear claw crown lopsided as she prepared food with a group of women.

Hay bales stacked in rows in front of the potlatch house formed an amphitheater on the beach. A jumble of camp chairs and benches sat off to the side. Further down the sand, a collection of tents, some canvas and sagging, others green and yellow, flapped in the breeze. Blue tarps staked to driftwood poles leaned this way and that. Pup tents were scattered among the larger tents. Lawn umbrellas with beach towels clothes-pinned to the edges formed makeshift enclosures. On a raised dune, a magnificent teepee overshadowed the encampment.

Children and dogs played by the water, splashing and throwing balls. Little girls blew soap bubbles. At the far end of the cove, she saw teenagers and heard guitars and coquettish squeals. A boy lifted a girl and twirled her, black hair flying, dumped her in a heap on the sand. Laughter erupted.

A late canoe arrived and a very old woman stood in the bow, proud in a red-and-black cloak. She balanced triumphantly with a metal walker as the canoe bit into the sand. Raven jumped from the canoe into the water and carried her gently to the shore like a child. A paddler brought her walker. The old woman surveyed the teeming scene, a wistful look on her face. Several children danced up, calling "Auntie! Auntie!" The old woman raised her hand and greeted them with a dignified wave. An older couple came up, kissed her and took her elbows, helped her up the beach.

The drumming intensified as men gravitated to the fires. Wrestling broke out and they made a scrum around the grapplers, shouting and beating circular drums overhead. Her father fell away and joined Poland and the other men by the fire. Fisher watched fascinated as the men struggled.

Lizette walked toward Abaya to join the women. Marian had waited at the bottom of the cliff for Toulouse, who wobbled down in his pointy, high-heeled boots. She caught up with Lizette and they surveyed the huge buffet of salads and casseroles, platters mounded with meat. At a campfire in the back of the shelter women roasted salmon on long skewers, slowly turning the pink flesh over banked coals.

In front of the potlatch house, Poland came and stood beside a short, colorful totem pole and called out in Salish, words Lizette did not know but understood. People moved slowly across the sand toward the shelter, elders going first, families in single file—men wearing funnel-shaped hats, women jingling silver and shell jewelry, toddlers hiding in their mother's skirts. Abaya stood back, at the edge of the shelter, clasped her hands to her heart, looked exultant.

As they feasted, winds swept the sea into sparkling riffles. Puffs of moist air blew more life into the smoldering bonfires on the beach, orange flames licked the piles of driftwood. They crackled and sparked as they burned. There was laughing and scolding, a whoop from a child who dropped a full plate of food in the sand. A woman scurried to soothe the child and clean up the mess. A dog got to the meat first and slinked off.

Lizette sat with her father on the edge of the crowd, holding Violet, eating salmon and macaroni salad with her free hand. A man came up to Einar, clapped him on the back. They shook hands, smiled and her father pointed at Violet. Einar took the baby, got up and showed her around, compared her with other babies in arms. Lizette relaxed into the feeling of fullness, went to the dessert table, got a big piece of chocolate cake, took a bite, sucked fudge frosting from a plastic spoon, wandered onto the beach.

She sat cross-legged by the water's edge, scanned the surface in the growing darkness for signs of seals or fish, watched brown pelicans sweep the channel beyond the still waters of the cove. Raven sat down next to her. "Elizabeth, I want to apologize. I'm sorry about what I said." She gave him a questioning glance. "About your father. When we had dinner downtown, last winter. I mean, what I said about him stealing our things."

She shrugged. He reached out, took her hand from her lap. "Really, I'm sorry." He looked into her eyes. "I didn't know my parents sold him that stuff, that he kept it safe all these years."

"I knew he wouldn't steal," she said softly. "He loves you too much."

He dropped her hand and Lizette sensed his shame.

"I'm going to dance tonight, made my own mask," he said boyishly. "Are you gonna watch?"

"What are you going to dance?"

"Raven. What else."

She giggled and elbowed him. "There are different raven stories," she said with mock gravity. "The good one who brings the sun and the selfish, jealous one," she said, scanning his face in the growing darkness. "Which one will it be?"

"I made my own mask," he said again, pulling back from her gaze. "First we'll have the Cry Ceremony, then . . . "

"What's the Cry Ceremony?"

"It's not really Lummi, but my mother has Tlingit aunts and cousins. They came down from British Columbia. Probably be here a month. They're going to send the sadness away."

"But what is it?"

"What is what?"

"A Cry Ceremony?"

"It's sort of like a funeral," he said. "The dancers paint their faces black and cry out loud. They don't dance exactly, just walk back and forth. They have special movements and they'll put on masks for my brothers."

"Your mother never talks about them, about what happened, I mean. I've been with her a lot. It's like a blank."

"Making a big deal out of death is wrong," he said defensively. "It hurts the living, puts things out of balance. My people believe too much sadness about those who've passed puts living relatives in danger, breaks down their spirit protection. You've seen a husband or wife get sick when one or the other dies?" An image of her father flitted before her eyes and she nodded in understanding. "My people don't want that to happen. That's why my mother never talks about it. I think it's a way she tries to protect me and my father. She stays strong so our spirits will stay strong."

He stood and extended a hand to her, pulled her up. Walking back to the potlatch, she studied the dancing shadows cast on the cliff from camp lanterns glowing on the tables. The feast was breaking up, people spilled onto the beach. She looked for her father and found him in a far corner with the men, playing with gambling bones, money stacked along the edge of a card table. A paper bag with a bottle moved from hand to hand, mouths taking quick sips lest the women see. She tapped her father's shoulder and threw him a question with upturned hands when he looked up. He jerked his thumb over his shoulder and turned back to the game, a wreath of pipe smoke ringing his head, huddling with the men over the game.

Violet saw her first as she searched through the guests and gave a cry, reached out for Lizette with baby hands. She saw Violet was gathered in Marian's arms, in a circle of young mothers holding infants on their laps, laughing, dangling their babies, encouraging them to stand and bounce. *Marian probably birthed most of them*, Lizette thought and reached over her shoulder and snatched Violet, checked her diaper. She searched for her canvas bag, bent and scanned under the empty tables.

"When you're done changing her, let's get a seat on the hay bales," Marian said. "I want to be close." Lizette agreed and moved away, found a quiet spot and spread a blanket on the sand. She pulled out a diaper, dug down for the ointment tube, quickly changed Violet, and stood up. She looked for Marian, who'd moved toward the hay bales.

They settled in the front row, on the side, in case Violet fussed. A drumbeat began, growing in power as more spirit drums joined in. She saw Fisher was on the opposite side of the group, beating a drum with the rest, his expression rapt. Firelight glinted off his glasses. Lizette felt the throbbing rhythm take over her body, tapped her feet and rolled her shoulders, bobbled Violet.

On the makeshift platform, three hay bales were covered with red-and-black button cloaks. Owl, Eagle and Frog symbols decorated the cloth. Black-faced dancers stepped onto the platform and paced slowly. The crowd quieted. Poland, Abaya, and Raven came to stand beside the platform, in front of Lizette and Marian. The drumbeats slowed and the dancers stopped and let out plaintive "oo's," then more drumming, more pacing, more "oo's." Lizette saw her go down first, Abaya crumpled in a heap on the sand.

Marian bolted from her seat, went to her knees, laid Abaya flat, loosened the cape's tie around her neck, threw her head back. She put her fingers on Abaya's pulse point on the side of her neck. The guests stood and gawked, the shaman came out, wearing a green and black mask, carrying a storytelling stick. "The spirits have come," he said to the crowd. Children watched him wide-eyed, sheltered close to their parents. "Sit down. Listen." He told stories of Owl, Eagle and Frog, the totems of Poland and Abaya's lost sons. Marian helped Abaya stand. Raven studied his mother, held her around her waist. Poland stood outside the circle of light, grief and worry wrinkled his face.

"Hasn't eaten anything in about two days," Marian said, shaking her head in annoyance when she returned to her seat beside Lizette. "I should have been watching her, but she had me so busy getting ready for tonight, I was running in circles and didn't notice."

When the stories ended and the black-faced mourners exited with the shaman, Abaya walked onto the platform, Poland and Raven followed, stood back from her. She walked to the edge, surveyed the crowd. The water sloshed ashore, the bonfires crackled and someone threw a big piece of driftwood on the nearest fire, sending sparks flying high into the air. The faces, orange in the fire's glow, waited for her to speak.

"My children danced like salmon going to the spawning grounds," she said, moving her arms in wave shapes. "Not all salmon spawn. Some get eaten, others aren't strong enough to make the journey all the way to the end. Spirits take them and they slip away unfinished." She put up her arms as if reaching for the moon. "Children are like salmon, they fill the streams of our lives, feed our spirits, then slip away." She wiped her cheeks, swallowed hard, said softly, "Sometimes, when the seasons change, they return." She glanced in Raven's direction.

She paused and let out a throaty "oo." The black-faced chorus responded from the edge of the platform like an long echo. Abaya waited for the grief sound to die away. "We cannot cry about this, tears weaken us, take our breath away. The spirits of my sons are gathered here." She swept her arm across the cloak-covered hay bales. "Cry with me once more and I will stop my tears and my sons will join the spirits."

The families began "oo's," the sound fading with breath, others picking up the sound, more voices joining in, until there was a great wail that lifted from the sand and carried up into the trees, the stars. A bald eagle swooped from a snag on the cliff above the cove and in the darkness glided down to the water, skimmed the surface in the firelight. The majesty of its flight silenced everyone. Abaya turned and watched in amazement with the others until the eagle disappeared into the thick, black night.

Child dancers pranced onto the stage whooping and clowning in their homemade hats and masks, tugging on Abaya's skirt and cloak. She ran to the side, laughing, the children chasing her like demons. Raven stepped into their midst in a crudely shaped mask with a fat, hooked beak and sharp, slitted eyes. The children shook rattles at him and waved him away with sticks. The people hooted and booed, they shouted, "Get Out!" "Go Away!" "Get lost!" The children looked hurt and confused. Raven led them away, around the shelter, back into the dark beneath the cliffs where they could watch.

More dancers, with beautiful masks and costumes, came forward. Some masks, Raven realized from a distance, he'd seen earlier in the afternoon in his parent's house and felt another pang of shame, scanned the audience for Lizette, found her smiling on the side. Some dancers wore robes embroidered with animal symbols, and reed hats. The Tlingit danced, then the Haida, finally the Lummi. Then everyone joined the dancing, the tribes intermixing, children holding hands with the elders, dogs wagging their bodies in between legs. Old Auntie gripped her walker and bounced.

When the dancing slowed, parents led their children off toward the tents. Lizette found her father, standing apart, studying. *Always the anthropologist,* she thought. *Needs to lighten up.* She had her bag over her shoulder, Violet bundled against the cold wind that had grown stronger, sending smoke low across the sand, making her eyes water. "We need to go," she told him. "I'm tired and it's cold."

Poland came to her father's side. "Lizette needs to get the baby back to the cabin," Einar said.

"I thought you guys were going to sleep in the teepee with me and my old girl friend." Poland sounded disappointed. "It's a gift from the Spokane people for the potlatch."

"It's beautiful," Einar said. "I'm staying, but Lizette has to get back to the ranch with the baby."

Poland waved toward a group of men to get their attention. Raven stuck his head out of the huddle. Poland raised his arm and gestured "come here." Raven jogged over and Poland asked him to take Lizette and the baby back to Cutler's.

"Do you need help getting up the trail to the car?" Einar asked, leaned over Violet's blankets and kissed her on the head, squeezed Lizette's arm. "Want me to go up to the meadow with you?"

"Naw, I got it," Raven said, taking Lizette's bag and putting the straps over his shoulder. "This thing's heavy," he said to Lizette, grinned.

"Everything I own is in it." She laughed at the truth, pivoted on the sand, wondered when she'd stop living like a turtle with everything she owned on her back, stumbled. Raven caught her before she could fall. "I'm so tired, I'm staggering."

"Better go," her father said. He watched as they started up the switchbacks to the meadow above, waited until he saw they'd made it to the top.

"Go this way," Raven pulled her to the trail that followed the rim edge of the forest, instead of taking the path toward the house.

318 | Kate Campbell

"I parked my truck in the back so I could get in and out when I need to." They walked slowly in the dark, thick clouds had piled up in the night sky, no moonglow to light the way. An owl hooted and Lizette jumped. "Take it easy." He chuckled. "He won't hurt you. Hunts the meadow every night." Around a bend in the trail, they saw his white truck, the color standing out from the trees like a beacon. He opened the passenger door and settled Lizette and Violet on the seat. They rode in relaxed silence to the ranch.

"I'll walk you down to the cabin," he said as he got out and took Violet from her. Lizette went to the main house, got a flashlight from the back porch, shined the beam on the trail as they picked their way down to the cabin. The light startled a big frog licking the grasses beside the trail. They paused to watch its gray-green lump of a body. It turned beady eyes to the flashlight beam, flicked its forked tongue and hopped away.

"Do you want to come in and sit down?" She pushed the door open and went to the table, lit a couple of candles.

"I can't." He handed Violet over, stepped back toward the door. "I'd like to, but we got a canoe race tomorrow morning, over to Friday Harbor and back. I'm meeting the guys at first light. Gotta get back, make sure they don't get too drunk. We're racing some good boats. Maybe you could come back over tomorrow? We're having food and a war canoe ceremony. I figure we'll get back by two."

"Sure," she said, then looked toward the windows and the little cove. "Depends on what happens with Looney."

"Looney?"

"There's a dead orca on the beach," she said. "It's Rocket's orca. He calls him that. They're supposed to come over with boats from the research station, haul him off." She looked downcast, hated to think about sleeping while the orca lay there, didn't want to say so. It wasn't that she was afraid, it was the emptiness of his eyes that haunted her. "Depends on when they get done, I guess."

She settled the sleeping baby into her apple box and put an extra blanket over her. Raven reached out and gathered her in a hug. He leaned in to kiss her cheek just as she turned to look at him and he accidentally brushed her lips. He pulled back as if he'd touched a hot coal, closed the door soundly as he went out. Lizette felt the urge to chase him, let the sensation go.

# THIRTY-FOUR

THE THROATY DRONE OF A HEAVY ENGINE WOKE HER. Morning light cut through the moisture-glazed windows. Lizette settled back on her pillow, closed her eyes and the dream came back, vivid and bright. Rocket lay among tousled sheets, his flat hand resting on the bed. She crawled gently, hovered above his peaceful body, lowered herself, kissed the back of his hand. He roused in the sun-warmed bed, rolled over, smiled. "I'm going to take a bath and shave," he said.

"Can I come?"

"Sure." He held out his hand. He slipped into the steamy tub, filled with bubbles that crackled softly as he washed, his foot lifted gracefully above the frothy bubble cloud. She sat on the cool tile floor, back against the wall.

He laughed, the sound transferred into a contented rumble in her chest. They talked about anything, nothing. In her dream they were intimate and comfortable, melded like the soap bubbles on Rocket's back. There was no friction or hardness now, just acceptance melting warmly between them, completely relaxed. She looked up from where she sat and watched him shave, pulling the razor smoothly across his throat, lifting his innocent chin to the light.

The rumble of engines reversing jerked her from her reverie. She got up and walked to the window. Through the raindrops spattering the glass she saw men standing on the beach around Looney. She watched them huddle and move down the orca's sides, as if planning what to do. She pulled on jeans and sweatshirt, zipped up a yellow rain parka. Violet slept soundly. She closed the door softly on the way out.

At the waterline, she greeted the men, stood aside. One nodded at her as he took measurements. Another wrote in a pocket notebook. "About twenty-five feet long, maybe ten tons," the one with the measuring tape said. "We can wrap lines around the flukes and try winching it off. Pretty heavy for the outboard motor, but it should get lighter if we can refloat him." Lizette looked at the small boat bobbing in the waves rolling to shore on the incoming tide. "Don't want to burn out the motor. Then we'd really be stuck."

They wore waders and moved to thigh depth in the water, stretched lines around Looney's tail flukes. One guy got into a rubber dinghy with a small outboard motor. He pulled the starter rope, gray-blue smoke belched from the engine and the acrid smell of burnt gas filled the air.

Lizette felt a tap on her shoulder, turned to find Toulouse, rumpled and bleary-eyed, the white ostrich plume on his hat limp in the rain. Tucker danced around his legs. Lizette bent and cuffed the dog, he re-approached and she scratched him behind the ears before he scampered off to sniff Looney.

"This won't take long," Toulouse reassured her. "A few tugs and it will be gone."

She turned from him and walked to the yoga platform, leaned against the edge and looked out to sea. White caps peaked in the channel between Orcas and Shaw islands, rainwater ran down her cheeks. A big research vessel hovered offshore in the strait. She figured the ship was waiting for the smaller boat to haul Looney off the beach and then drag the carcass to it. She knew when they got it aboard they'd perform the necropsy, find out why Looney died. She let out a soft "oo" and kept the sound going.

The men wrestled with the ropes, the dinghy came around and they threw the lines to the tender, who gathered them in gloved hands, straightened out the lines. He eased back from the shore, careful not to tangle the ropes. Looney's limp body shifted with the tugging, lifted on the rising tide.

One of the men stood by the puddle of dark blood in the sand. His voice carried to Lizette on the wind. "Shot." He fingered the round wound behind Looney's eye. "Looks like a heavy caliber rifle from the size of the hole." He pushed Looney's body and it seemed to come right, the big orca resting on its belly, dorsal fin flapping to one side, deflated. "If I had to guess, I'd say he got shot for stealing, probably from a commercial catch by the look of the net. We'll need to report it to the Coast Guard once we get him on board and confirm it. And, he's got some nasty propeller scars." He ran his hand down Looney's sleek back. "They look old. From the description, this must be the rogue that's been screwing around in the shipping channels, chasing tugs. Looks like that problem's solved."

He yanked at the fish net tangled around Looney's flukes. "Wonder where the rest of the net is?"

"Probably wrapped around a half a dozen harbor seals by now," the man standing next to him securing lines answered. They grunted to each other in disgust and kept working.

Toulouse paced above the waterline in the soft sand. His black-and-fuchsia-lined cape flapped foolishly in the wind and rain. He held up a sheet of paper, "Wordsworth," he shouted to her over the wind and the whine of the outboard motor. He went on pacing, reading poetry in deep, sonorous tones that carried to her on wind gusts.

She caught some of his words, "The tide rises, the tide falls." He raised his arm in grandiloquence and turned to face her, stopped his pacing for a moment. "But the sea, the sea in the darkness calls, the little waves, with their soft, white hands, efface the footprints from the sand." She looked at him gravely, he offered her a theatrical head bow and continued. "The tide rises, the tide falls, but nevermore returns the traveler to the shore."

When he finished, he wiped away tears, but it might have been the wind that watered his eyes. Standing alone at the water's edge, looking like a drowned Three Musketeer in his wilted three-corner hat, she saw his honest sympathy, his sincere desire to help. He fluttered the page into the wind. It lofted into the air. She watched it go and knew then, truly knew it was done. She knew she'd never see Rocket again, that those days were gone. She accepted the loss, let his spirit go, listened to the wind, breathed a long "oo."

At first it sounded like a kitten mewling. The sound came again, changed pitch. A lusty cry! She flew across the beach, kicked up sand, took the slope in a gallop, charged toward Violet, to all that matters. The baby was kicking and flailing when she burst into the cabin. Lizette picked her up, patted her back, kissed her head, and shushed her, then walked to the rain-veiled windows, sat cross-legged on the floor with Violet in her lap, puckered her lips, supped air and watched, as if floating under water.

# NOTABLE EVENTS*

1973

**January**
- The Marine Mammal Protection Act, passed in October 1972, begins protection for all marine mammals in U.S. waters, including orcas and seals.
- U.S. President Richard Nixon inaugurated for second term.
- *Roe v. Wade*: The U.S. Supreme Court overturns state bans on abortion, legalizing the procedure nationwide.
- U.S. involvement in the Vietnam War officially ends with the signing of the Paris Peace Accords on January 27.

**February**
- The U.S. dollar devalued by 10%.
- The American Indian Movement occupies Wounded Knee, South Dakota.

**March**
- The last U.S. soldier leaves Vietnam.

**April**

- The World Trade Center officially opens with a ribbon cutting in New York City.
- Watergate Scandal: President Nixon announces that top White House aides and others have resigned.

**May**

- The 71-day standoff at Wounded Knee, South Dakota, ends between federal authorities and American Indian Movement activists.
- *Skylab*, the United States' first space station, is launched.
- Watergate Scandal: Televised hearings begin in the U.S. Senate.

**June**

- The U.S. Drug Enforcement Administration is founded and the War on Drugs launched.
- The U.S. Congress passes the Education of the Handicapped Act (EHA), ushering in rights for the disabled.
- Martial artist and actor Bruce Lee dies and is buried in Seattle.

**August**

- Top-grossing movie "American Graffiti" released.
- The U.S. bombing of Cambodia ends, halting 12 years of U.S. combat activity in Southeast Asia.

**September**

- *The Battle of the Sexes*: Tennis professional Billie Jean King defeats male tennis pro Bobby Riggs, making a statement about women's equality.

- United Farm Workers union opposes sanctions on employers who hire undocumented immigrants.

## October
- U.S. Vice President Spiro T. Agnew resigns and then, in federal court pleads no contest to income tax evasion.
- The Arab Oil Embargo against several countries that support Israel triggers the 1973 U.S. and global energy crisis.
- Watergate Scandal: "Saturday Night Massacre" leads to dismissal of Watergate Special Prosecutor Archibald Cox, raising calls for President Nixon's impeachment.
- The Oakland Athletics win baseball's World Series, defeating the New York Mets 4 games to 3.

## November
- Congress overrides President Nixon's veto of the War Powers Resolution, which limits presidential power to wage war without congressional approval.
- President Nixon signs the Trans-Alaska Pipeline Authorization Act into law, authorizing construction of the Alaska Pipeline.
- Watergate Scandal: In Orlando, Florida, U.S. President Nixon tells 400 Associated Press managing editors "I am not a crook."
- The U.S. Senate votes 92–3 to confirm Gerald Ford as Vice President of the United States.

## December
- The American Psychiatric Association removes homosexuality from its list of mental disorders.
- OPEC doubles the price of crude oil.
- Congress passes the Endangered Species Act.

**January 1970-1976:**

In the late 1960s, millions of American teenagers left home and headed out on a grand hippie adventure. By the early 1970s, many of these young people—now in their early- to mid-20s— were beyond the reach of social programs for children. Many were strung out on alcohol and drugs, living on the streets, working as prostitutes, physically maimed, and/or suffering from mental illness. An untold number of them, including young women and, in some cases the children they bore, did not survive.

Karen M. Staller, author of *Runaways: How the Sixties Counterculture Shaped Today's Practices and Policies* (2006, Columbia University Press) writes that passage of the Twenty-sixth Amendment to the U.S. Constitution in 1971 lowered the voting age from 21 to 18. One result was that rules governing runaways, dropped to below age 18.

The severe U.S. economic recession of the era, followed by soaring inflation, halted new U.S. initiatives to expand medical care and other social programs, which likely could have helped the walking casualties of the late1960s. Midwives were not licensed to practice in Washington State until 1976.

Due to the winding down of the Vietnam War and the ongoing recession, the Seattle-based Boeing aerospace company cut its workforce from 80,400 to 37,200 between early 1970 and October 1971. By1973, unemployment in the Puget Sound area topped 17 percent (*Seattle Times*). Seattle suffered massive home foreclosures and severe urban blight. During the economic bust, a famous Seattle billboard asked: "Would the last person leaving SEATTLE — turn out the lights?"

Sources: *Seattle Times*, University of Washington Library, Worldwide Web

*\*Adrift in the Sound* is a work of fiction and, while the social-political events mentioned in the novel took place in 1973, the occurrence of events in the story is not historically precise as to month and day.

# DISCUSSION GROUP QUESTIONS

1. How are national events used to frame the novel?

2. What role do spiritual values play in the characters' lives?

3. How does the environment shape the story?

4. Compared to 1973, where are we now as a people and a nation? What has changed and what has remained the same?

5. What do the Native American characters and the other characters in the story have in common and what makes them different?

6. What role do the various civil rights struggles—women, Native Americans, Chicano, gay—play in the novel?

7. Discuss Lizette's relationship with Marian.

8. Discuss Lizette's relationship with Rocket and with her father.

9. What is important to Lizette's journey toward a greater sense of well-being?

10. What does baby Violet represent in the novel, actually and symbolically?

# ABOUT THE AUTHOR

A native Californian, Kate Campbell grew up in San Francisco and on family ranches in Marin and Lake counties. She holds a journalism degree from San Francisco State University and has worked as a reporter and freelance writer for newspapers and magazines throughout the West and beyond. She writes frequently about natural resources and the environment and publishes The Word Garden, a weekly blog that focuses on the arts, gardens and the environment at www.kate-campbell.blogspot.com. The mother of two grown sons, she lives at the confluence of the American and Sacramento rivers.

## About the Mercer Street Books Fiction Prize

*Adrift in the Sound* is a 2011 finalist for the Mercer Street Books Fiction Prize. This literary award recognizes emerging writers who have a completed a novel, but have not yet published it. The prize is sponsored by Mercer Street Books & Records in New York City's Greenwich Village.